# NYMPHOMATION

www.**books**at**transworld**.co.uk/jeffnoon

# NYMPHOMATION

## Jeff Noon

**BLACK SWAN**

**NYMPHOMATION**
**A BLACK SWAN BOOK : 0 552 99906 7**

Originally published in Great Britain by Doubleday,
a division of Transworld Publishers

PRINTING HISTORY
Doubleday edition published 1997
Corgi edition published 1998
Black Swan edition published 2000

1 3 5 7 9 10 8 6 4 2

Copyright © Jeff Noon 1997

Extracts taken from 'A Narrow Fellow in the Grass' by Emily Dickinson.

Designed and typeset in England by Fresh Produce.

Black Swan Books are published by Transworld Publishers,
61-63 Uxbridge Road, London W5 5SA,
a division of The Random House Group Ltd,
in Australia by Random House Australia (Pty) Ltd,
20 Alfred Street, Milsons Point, Sydney, NSW 2061, Australia,
in New Zealand by Random House New Zealand Ltd,
18 Poland Road, Glenfield, Auckland 10, New Zealand
and in South Africa by Random House (Pty) Ltd,
Endulini, 5a Jubilee Road, Parktown 2193, South Africa.

Printed and bound in Great Britain by
Mackays of Chatham plc, Chatham, Kent.

for Cheryl

and the Deansgate Survivors

But never met this Fellow
Attended, or alone
Without a tighter breathing
And Zero at the Bone—
*Emily Dickinson*

In the summer of 1949, as England began its long recovery from the war, a government inspector was sent to a junior school in one of the outlying districts of Manchester. The inspector's name was Benjamin Marlow. A second-year class at the school had produced some rather interesting results in the recent exams, and it was Marlow's appointment to investigate for any fraudulent behaviour in the schoolchildren. Cheating, in other words.

The class was known as 2c. There were twenty-eight children in the class: sixteen boys and twelve girls, average age, eight years old. Their teacher's name was Miss Geraldine Sayer. In the recent exams the class had performed normally in all subjects but one. The more than interesting anomaly was mathematics. In this subject, all but one of the children had scored marks above 78 per cent. Such excellence was deemed unacceptable.

When interviewed, the children could only point to Miss Sayer. The way they said the name, to Marlow's ears, sounded very much like 'Messiah'. When interviewed, Miss Sayer broke down in tears and started to roll around the classroom floor. She was covered in chalk dust. Marlow reports that she was speaking gibberish; 'speaking in tongues' is how he describes it, referring to old pagan rituals. He could make out only one phrase – 'Play to win!' – which she repeated, over and over. 'Play to win, my children! Play to win!'

Two weeks later she was removed from her post, and the following week Benjamin Marlow took early retirement.

**PLAY TO WIN**

# Game 40

It was Domino Day in lucky old Manchester, and the natives were making love to the television, all glazen-eyed and drunken as the opening credits came into view. A tumbling ballet of dominoes, forever changing their spots. Dig that tumbling! Even the air was excited, loaded with messages, buzzing out loud. Blurbflies, singing the streets alive with adverts. Play to win! Play to win! And all over the city that wet Friday evening, three hours from midnight and surrounded by the rain, hordes of punters were clacking their little bones on coffee tables and bar tops, computer desks and kitchen counters, watching the dots pulsate in tune as the theme song started up.

It's domino time! Domino time!
Dom, dom, dom, dom, domino time!

**Blurbflies**

In offices and hospitals, bedsits and penthouses; all-night shopping malls and non-stop garages; in restaurants, cinemas and whorehouses; in cars and taxis, and even on the trains and buses; anywhere there was a private TV or a radio or a public screen, all the gamblers were stroking their hard-earned domino bones, hoping that Lady Luck would come up dancing, just for them.

**Blurbflies**

Why not chance a throw?
You might as well have a go!
With your lucky little domino!

Chaos fever 1999 style, running high. Bringing the city to stillness that night, and every Friday night, as the players steeled their hearts, took a collective breath, honed their bones, rubbed their lucky charms, chanted prayers to the gods of circumstance, sold their souls to the joker. As the blurbflies glittered through the rain, dive-bombing the people with sweet whispers.

Play to win

Somewhere in all this stilled commotion, in each of their chosen locations, the various people who would later form the Dark Fractal Society were preparing their dominoes for the outcome. Maverick gamblers who would one day try to kill the game. One such player; a tousled, ragged blonde called Daisy Love.

Sure, an embarrassing name, and how she hated her parents for the privilege, but take a look. A sparkle-eyed eighteen-year-old. A first-year student of mathematics at the University of Manchester, studying Game Theory under the esteemed Professor Max Hackle. With a first-term report full of Hackle's wonder at her grasp of the probabilities of losing, you would expect Daisy to be among that tiny bunch of killjoys who preferred not to play.

But no; here she was, glued to the black-and-white portable in her bedsit in Rusholme Village, clinging tightly to a single domino. Trying her best to ignore the scents of Lamb Rogan Josh and Chicken Tandoori, drifting up from the curry house downstairs. The Golden Samosa's neon sign painted her window with an afterglow of colour, rippled by rain and the wing-flap of blurbs.

Daisy could ration herself to a single onion bhaji or a lonely poppadom, or even a foolhardy golden samosa, but a raging, full-on Rogan Josh with Pilau Technicoloured Rice? Leave it out. Way beyond her means. A Chef's Special Chicken Tikka? Forget it. Daisy was on a scholarship; a small chunk of money from the university itself, because she was so good at the numbers. Just because Professor Hackle rated her. This weekly treat of an only bone was Daisy's one wicked pleasure. A tiny handful of luck. Listen:

A little fun is hardly a sin,
    You might as well play to win.
Dom, dom, dom, dom, domino time!
Domino time! Domino time!

**Blurbflies**

Who could resist such urgings? And even as the theme song played out, there came a knock upon Daisy's door. Inevitably, it was Jazir Malik, first-born son of the Golden Samosa, from way down below in the curry pit. Trilby-hatted and sunglassy, he brought with him a stolen take-out of a one-meatball Beef Madras, a greasy piece of naan bread, some few sticky grains of plain boiled rice. Daisy knew that Jaz had the hot and spicies for her, but she was keeping him at bay, while gorging herself on his stolen curries. It wasn't that she found him unattractive: in fact, Jaz Malik was heavenly gorgeous, once the hat and glasses came off. Skin the colour of twilight, a smile shining like a garlic slice of the moon. It wasn't that he was too young, because Daisy felt herself younger than him, in many ways. And it wasn't even that Daisy knew that Mr Saeed, Jaz's head chef of a father, would not be too pleased with his first-born consorting with a lily-white girl.

'Here's your dinner, love,' said Jaz, his voice a complex mix of northern drawl and Asian lilt.

'Cheers, Jaz.' Daisy dug, straight off into the food.

'Sorry I'm late. My father was grilling me about school. And he wants me waiting-on tonight. Hope I haven't missed anything, love. Cookie hasn't come on yet?'

'No, it's just beginning. Sit down. And stop calling me love.'

'Why? It's your name, isn't it?'

'You want some of this?' Daisy shoved a forkful of beef under Jaz's nose.

'I'm stuffed. Had me a Jeezburger at the Whoomphy bar, earlier. Now shut up, please. Let's watch.'

It was a ritual between them, this Friday-night viewing of the AnnoDomino show. Daisy and Jaz, watching the monitor. A sweep of the camera playing over the faces in the studio crowd; a sea of greed, screaming loud.

Play to win! Play to win!

Bumptious Tommy Tumbler came dancing into view, beaming his polished smile and in a vibrant suit of purple dots on orange. 'Hello punters!' he chanted. 'All the way from the House of Chances!' And the studio audience, and most of the city too, chanted back to him, 'Hello, Tommy Tumbler! Good chances!'

'Hello, Tommy Tumbler!' shouted Jaz at the screen. 'Oh please won't you let Cookie Luck deliver me a winning bone this week? Oh pretty please!'

Daisy Love kept her chanting to herself, as usual. 'So your dad's playing up again, Jaz, about you going on to university?'

Jaz was almost seventeen, just a crazy kid really, in his final year at the well-heeled Didsbury High. Studying Maths and Physics, and good with it – tender meat for higher education.

'My dad's too damn proud,' he replied, eyes stuck tight to the glitz of Tommy Tumbler. 'You're lucky not having one.'

Daisy looked at him, shocked. Jazir knew full well that she was an orphan, that her mum and dad were dead. That was the reason she was so poor; none of the usual luxuries: no loan from the parents, no birthday car, no carting of the laundry home.

'But you know I think learning sucks,' he continued, regard-less. 'I just want to be in business, that's all. Away from my father's clutches. I just want to sell some bad-arse gadgets on the filthy streets. It's all about chance, isn't it? Life and death; how we live and how we die, it's all about chance. Shit, Daisy! You try your best at playing to win, only to find yourself playing to lose.'

'Maybe I could help you, Jaz. With your exams—'

'Will you leave off, love. The game's about to start.'

'OK punters!' cried Tommy Tumbler. 'Clack those bones together! Here she comes, the Queen of All Fortune! Lady Cookie Luck!'

# Play to win

The whole city went wild with the gambling fever, as the screen fluttered into darkness. Pulses of music. Circles of light, starting to shine. An undulating darkness, littered with stars. Revealing the dancing queen of randomness. Cookie Luck's skintight and black catsuit was snug-fit to the country's dreams, an Emma Peel of forever and a long shot. Skintight black, constellated with an ever-changing fractal of white dots, like deep, deep stars, where all the good life lay waiting.

This is what the punters were playing for; the good life above the dour grime of Manchester. Lady Cookie Luck was a walking, talking, dancing, stalking, living, loving domino. A doll of numbers. And every Friday night, at precisely nine o'clock, after a whole week of changing, the dominatrix would dance herself into a climax. The dots on her body would settle, at last, into a winning pattern.

This is how it worked.

Each Lucky Domino cost a single puny unit. Any number of the bones could be bought during a week. In that time, your chosen bones would be forever rearranging their silvery pips, due to some deep, hidden, random mechanism. And all the punters would spend the week watching the bones dance, their eyes chock-full of dots. The I Ching, the rosary beads, the tarot cards, the horoscopes; all in the trash can. The AnnoDominoes replaced them all. And as Cookie's costume at long last became Friday-night stilled, at the very same time, your lucky bones would solidify into a tight pattern. If any one of your dominoes even halfway coincided with the dancer's fractal, then you were the winner of that week's bumper collection: 100 punies for a half-cast; 10 million lovelies for a complete matching.

An undisclosed number of people won the 100; only one person won the 10 million. Just as long as Lady Luck favoured your chances.

Millions of lovelies, all for the cost of a single puny.

## PLAY THE RULES

1a. The makers of the game will be the AnnoDomino Company of Manchester, England. Mr Million will be the Manager of Chances.

1b. The players of the game will be the populace of Manchester, England.

2a. AnnoDomino will implement the game in Manchester for a trial period of twelve months, fifty-one games all told; after which, if the Government so deems, the company will be allowed to introduce the dominoes to the whole of the United Kingdom.

2b. The populace of Manchester will be allowed to play the game for twelve months, during which time

AnnoDomino will be allowed to measure the response.
3a. The game is sacrosanct.

## Play to Win

Game forty, eleven to go. Almost nine o'clock, Manchester. Amid the swirl of rain on a road called Claremont, in a district called Moss Side, just south of Rusholme, three men were sitting in a parked car, keyed into the radio. The AnnoDomino channel, of course, where the sweet and sexy Cookie Luck was doing her dance of numbers, calling out the numbers. Visions of loveliness inside the head.

Three men in the car, another three students at the university. Two of them were studying Maths, the other studying Physics. One of them was much older than the other two. Two of them were white, the other one black. One of them was straight, another one gay, the third balanced evenly between the two. One of them was a virgin. One of them had a diamond through his nose. One was studying Pure Maths, another studying Computermatics, the third Genetic Calculus. Their names were Joe Crocus, DJ Dopejack and Sweet Benny Fenton. Not in any order. One of them had green hair. And no, not the gay one. Although the gay one did have the nose stud, twinkling in a fractal display. Three men; all of them gazing deep into their dominoes and listening up as Cookie's invisible dance played over the waves, the last waltz of the world.

'Lick my numbers, sweet Lady!' one of them cried.

'I'm starving!' cried another. 'Can we get a curry after this?'

'Shut the fuck up, I'm concentrating!' cried the last.

'Dot shit!' cried the first. 'I just got a Joker Bone come up!'

'You're OK then,' replied the second. 'Look, it's changed already.'

'Sorted,' said the third. 'You never get a double-blank more than once a week. Everybody knows that.'

A blurbfly bounced off the windscreen, buzzing out loud its slogan.

'Play to win!' echoed the three men. 'Play to fucking win!'

Somewhere else in Manchester, that very same moment, a young girl calling herself Little Miss Celia was standing amid a sodden crowd of cheap, down-market chancers, outside an all-night luxury store. There were seventeen and a half televisions for sale in the window, and all of them tuned into AnnoDomino. Even the homeless made sure a puny was put aside for each Friday night.

The homeless with their secret homes.

Here they are, the ragged brethren of society, the vagabonds, praying to whatever gods would still care to listen, clutching at their miserable puny bones like a last chance of escape, even as the blurbs fluttered around their heads in a halo of messages. 'Get off me, you nasty flies!' the youngest amongst them muttered at the troublesome cloud.

Play to win! Play to win!

Celia Hobart was only eight years old, and she had to stand on tiptoes to catch even the occasional glimpse of Cookie Luck's dance through the pack of beggars and the haze of flies. She had long, straight, metallic-blond hair, in which a green-and-yellow bird's feather was knotted. Celia had run away from home only a couple of months ago, during which time she had scraped together a meagre living. Celia hated begging for life, but she'd chosen to be a runaway. The first few days had been the worst, moving alone through the city, so young. Terrified, until discovering the brethren. The other vagabonds had taken her under their cover, united against normality, especially a big, old guy calling himself Eddie Irwell.

Eddie had found Celia one morning, queering his official begging hole in St Anne's Square. 'What the fuck is that shit in your hair?' were his first words to her.

Celia, touching the feather, like a faraway magic wand.

'This is Big Eddie Irwell speaking,' the man continued, 'and this is his fully paid for hole. Now get your half-arse out of my life.'

Eddie was the alpha beggar, with his real home hidden so deep.

Celia ran away, fearful of the big man, even as he settled his bulk into the tiniest of begging holes. But the very next day, there she was, back again, sitting in his hole long before the big guy was even awake, and a whole nano puny in her begging hat already. Eddie had chased her away once again, but ever after, and for the next six days, this little kid had beaten him to the hole. In the end, he gave up, more or less adopted the girl and street-christened her Little Miss Celia. He found her a personal hole on Deansgate Boulevard, right outside a bookshop – prime pitch – just to keep the girl out of his dreadlocks. Which turned into a kind of love.

Nine o'clock, almost striking.

The brethren of the streets were close and warm, despite the rain that almost always poured upon them, and now Irwell was gathering Celia up into his arms, and from there to his shoulders, from which mighty position she could finally see Cookie Luck dancing in all her changing glory. Celia kept glancing at her single domino and back at the screen, wafting away the blurbs, touching her feather. Wishing all the time, and with all of her heart, for Lady Luck to be kind upon this day, this special day.

Eddie always bought her a bone every week, a bone of her own. Four weeks ago Celia's bone had come up half-cast, winning her 100 punies, but Eddie had claimed it all for himself, the cheat, only to spend it on ultrabooze and metaburgers. But this was Celia's very first bone, bought with her own money, so she was wishing harder than ever. Special wishing.

Never before had she begged enough to spare, but last Saturday just gone, the kindest woman in the whole world (or else the richest, or else the poorest) had thrown a whole glistening *pair* of punies into Celia's hole. The woman had then tried to step inside the bookshop, but Celia had stopped her dead. A clutch to the ankle from deep within the earth.

'Thank you, kind miss,' said Celia to the deliverer. 'What's your name, please?'

'My name?' The deliverer looked puzzled.

'Just for the records, you understand. I have to declare all my earnings. To the town hall, you understand?'

'Daisy,' replied the deliverer.

'Daisy? Nice name. You buying some books today?'

'Selling them.'

'Wow! You've got employment! Daisy what?'

'Love.'

'Daisy Love. How embarrassing!'

'Tell me about it.'

'Your mum and dad were neo-hippies, right?'

'Please. I have a job to do.'

'Daisy Love, be proud. You have saved a beggar's

soul this Saturday's morn.'

'Just go spend it. On something wise, please.'

You bet your life! Celia spent one of the punies on a full English breakfast and banana milkquake at the local Whoomphy's burger bar, and the other on a domino. Of course, Eddie Irwell still had to buy the bone for her, Celia being far too young to gamble. But surely this week was different . . .

'Just make my numbers come up, sweet and lovely Cookie Luck!'

Celia was calling out to the dancing stars, her small voice lost amongst the screams and urges and the rabid desires of the begging crew. 'Just deliver me away! Somewhere good, please. Somewhere ever so beautiful.' As the blurbs flew in convoy round her head, twinkling like all the forever lost chances, all the forever yet-to-come chances.

Dancing, dancing, number fallout.

**PLAY THE RULES**

3a. The game is sacrosanct.

3b. AnnoDomino may not coerce any of the populace into playing the game.

3c. The populace may play, or not play, according to their wishes.

3d. 0.01% of the purchase price of every domino will go to charity. All parties will adhere to this ruling.

And still the dance continued, playing the punters like a city of lovers. Daisy Love had her only bone tight in her fingers; Jaz had his five spicy chances arranged in a circle on Daisy's Formica coffee table; both of them watching in awe, as the dots on their bones slowly settled down in tune with Cookie Luck's body.

'Play to win!' shouted Tommy Tumbler from the TV screen.

'Yes! Come on, my beauty!' shouted Jaz to the faraway TV dancer. 'Even a measly half-cast would do! Just don't let the Joker Bone come calling!'

'Cookie can't hear you from here,' said Daisy.

'You want a slice of hot root?' Jaz cut some shreds from a pungent garlic bulb.

'Ultragarlic? No thanks. I'm clean.'

'Clean as a blank bone, sure. Virgin-style.'

'I've got my assignments to do. I need a clear head.'

Jaz Malik laughed and then swallowed two whole slices of the ultragarlic. His breath went sordid, his mind rainbow. Sunglassed eyes back to the dancing screen. 'Come on and dance for me, you fucking bitch of all bones!'

Nine o'clock chimes, and at last . . .

'Game on!' chants Tommy Tumbler. 'Play to win!'

'Game fucking on!' chants back Jaz.

And at a long last . . .

**Blurbflies**

> That's the way! That's the way!
> That's the way the cookie crumbles!

Mr Million has deemed it so.

A five. A three. A five and a three. The stars of Lady Luck fall into the shape of a five-and-a-three bone: one dot on each nipple, another on her navel, two more on each of her kidneys; and, below the dividing-line belt of her domino costume, a single on her left hip, another on her crotch, a final on her right thigh. Eight pips of chaos, finally found on a field of sexy black. And all over the city, that exact moment of surrender, countless punters banged down their losing bones in frustration. And Daisy Love was just another loser, her single lonely domino coming up with only a measly two-and-a-four configuration. Jazir Malik, the same loser; his big fistful of chances delivering nothing but mismatches.

'Fuck it!' said Jaz.

Game over. Manchester sighs.

Two more losers; another few ounces of money lost to the beast. Another cityful of losers. Daisy and Jaz could only gaze through neon tears of rain as their dominoes went totally cream, used-up and invalid.

Dead bones.

'Somebody, somewhere,' called out Tommy Tumbler from the city's screens, 'just won themselves ten million lovelies! Remember, my friends, my losers, next week is another game. Another chance to win. Purchase in advance.'

Purchase in advance! sang the blurbs on the street. Play to win!

Jaz switched off the TV in disgust. 'Fuck that winning shit! Would you like to kiss me now, Daisy, please?' he asked. 'Just for some comfort in losing?'

'With that stink on your breath? I think not.'

'OK. Fine. What you doing tomorrow night, for instance?'

'Tomorrow night? Nothing much. Why?'

'You want to do nothing much with me? I'm going down the Snake Lounge club. DJ Dopejack's spinning the decks. You know Dopejack? He's in the second year at your college? Some silly guy on the computers. You up for it?'

'Jaz, you're too young to go to a club.'

'I can get in there. Got contacts.'

'Next week, maybe.'

'Next week it is. Definite.'

'I'm not saying definite. I'm backed up with assignments.'

'Assignments, shit! Jaz is gone.'

## Play to win

Fifty-seven separate punters were now raising a small cheer at having won a half-cast, the five or the three, still pulsing on their dominoes and 100 punies to collect before tomorrow's midnight. One of these punters was killed for having won so much; it was his second win in the last few weeks, and some loser was too jealous of him. Whilst some more innocent stranger, somewhere else, held tightly on to a living bone; the full and magical five-and-a-three combination.

Chosen combination! Winning hand! Golden hand! Play to win!

Because when you won the big one, you didn't have to collect the prize; the prize came to collect you. The 10 million lovelies of a domino's kiss, delivered by Cookie Luck herself. The curvaceous ghost of numbers, coming out of nowhere, coming out of television, to drag you down, screaming with pleasure.

As the blurbflies fluttered through the darkness, singing out loud.

**PLAY TO WIN**

**PLAY TO WIN**

# Game 41

**D**omino Day, lucky old Manchester. The next Friday, game forty-one. Native gamblers, stuck superlove crazy to the televiz, goggle-eyed and numberholic as the credits came in colours. Tango the dominoes, forever changing. Pipsville, dig those chances! Bulging air, message heavy. Blurbflies in a swarm, singing streets alive. Madverts. Dream to play! Play to win! Win to dream! All over the city, that wet and slippy evening, surrounded by biscuits and crumble, herds of punters were banging their bones on café tables and dashboards, mouse pads and park benches, watching tiny dots pulsate in crooked rhythm.

It's domino time! Domino time!
Dom, dom, dom, dom, domino time!

**Blurbflies**

Mr Million has made it happen, the secret boss of bones.

In monasteries, nunneries, football stadiums, birdcages, all-night shopping churches, non-stop brothels, restaurants, cinemas, telephone boxes, bicycles, Rolls-Royces, Pullman carriages and double-decker omnibuses; anywhere there was a switch-on, all the natives were stroking their bones, hoping for a winning kiss.

Why not chance a throw?
You might as well have a go!
With your lucky little domino!

**Blurbflies**

As little kids ran through the downpour, clutching their domino dolls, pulling strings to activate voice boxes, and learning how to play. Learn to win! Learn to win! The city brought to stillness and desperation.

The tousled, ragged blonde called Daisy Love. Take a look at her this time, once again stuck tight to the black-and-white portable in her bedsit, clinging fast to a treasured domino. Trying her best to ignore the scents of Chicken Tikka Masala and Lamb and Spinach Balti, drifting upwards from the curry house.

A loneliness of spice and air. A tiny handful of luck.

A little sin is hardly much fun,
You might as well play conundrum.
Dom, dom, dom, dom, domino time!
Domino time! Domino time!

**Blurbflies**

How could a young girl possibly resist such urgings?

Learn to win

Daisy was born in Droylsden, Manchester, in 1980. Changing schools at the age of five, she missed some important lessons. By the time she settled, the other kids could already add up, never mind subtracting. Daisy could only guess at the answers, not knowing the underlying structure. The new teacher had no time for such inaccuracies. Punishment was in hand.

Daisy asked her father to help her, knowing he was good at numbers. He said no, that she could learn for herself, or not at all. She went to her mother, who knew nothing at all about numbers. Her mother was good at cooking and she placed two jam pies on the kitchen table, asking Daisy to count them.

'One . . . two . . .'

'That's correct. Well done!' She added another two. 'How many pies now?'

Daisy counted them, out loud. 'One . . . two . . . three . . . four

. . . Four pies?' she answered.

'That's right. Two pies add two pies, makes four pies.'

'This is all that adding up is?' asked Daisy. Nobody had ever explained it to her before.

'Isn't it easy,' said her father, disgusted.

Daisy's journey began.

## Play to win

Domino time! And even as the theme song played away, there came the usual knock upon Daisy's door. Jazir Malik. Daisy's only friend. He brought with him another stolen take-out. 'Here's your dinner,' he said.

A meagre offering. Mostly rice, no naan, a few particles of meat.

'Cheers, Jaz.' Daisy dug deep, looking for flavour.

'Hope I haven't missed anything, love. Cookie hasn't come on yet?'

'It's just beginning. You want some of this?' Daisy shoved a forkful of rice under Jaz's nose.

'Fuck off, Daze. I'm concentrating.'

Play to win! Play to win! As bumptious Tommy Tumbler came, lover-dancing, all the way from the House of Chances.

'Hello, Tommy Tumbler!' shouted Jaz at the screen. 'Oh please won't you let Cookie Luck deliver me a winner this week? Oh pretty, pretty please!'

Daisy Love kept her chanting to herself, as usual. 'Why do we have to do the exact same thing every week?' she asked. 'You know we're only going to lose.'

'Will you leave off, girl! The game's about to start.'

'OK punters!' cried Tommy Tumbler. 'Clack those bones together. Here she comes, the Queen of All Fortune. Lady Cookie Luck!'

Cookie Luck! Good Lady Cookie Luck! Almost nine o'clock, Manchester. Once again, in a swirl of rain on a road called Claremont, in the rundown district called Moss Side; three men sitting in a parked car, keyed into the radio.

'Lick my dotties, sweet Lady!' DJ Dopejack cried.

'I'm starving!' cried Sweet Benny Fenton. 'Can we get a curry after this?'

'Shut the fuck up, I'm trying to win!' cried Joe Crocus.

'Dot shit!' cried Benny. 'I just got a Joker Bone come up! That's the second time in two weeks.'

'You're OK then,' replied Dopejack. 'It's gone already.'

'Sorted,' said Joe. 'You never get a double-blank more than once a week, Benny. I told you that already, didn't I?'

'You think that makes it easy?' Sweet Benny's voice, fading into doubt, as a blurbfly bounced off the windscreen, buzzing out loud.

'Play to win!' echoed Dopejack. 'Play to fucking win!'

'I hope so,' murmured Benny, losing himself.

'I am just a fractal,' cried Joe, 'split for action and a million chances. Let the bones come down!'

There are dots and lines and squares and circles and cubes and spheres and fourth-dimensional hyperglobes and from these things the world and its players are made and there are stranger shapes yet scarcely imagined such as the fractal curves which exist between the dimensions for instance the coastline of Britain gets longer the closer you look at it forever hovering between a curve and a surface and the closer you look the more information it contains so that an infinitely branching pathway has an infinite potential for capturing knowledge and a game of fractal dominoes would have more permutations than the spots can show which tells us that meaning falls in the cracks and that everyday life is an infinite branching mazeway set in the multiverse where every choice leads to another life another game won another lost highway.

Wish to win

A young girl calling herself Little Miss Celia, amid a sodden crowd of cheap down-market gamblers, outside yet another all-night luxury store. Moved on by the cops since last week, their latest window had a measly nine and a quarter televisions for sale. All of them tuned into AnnoDomino, of course. Lady Luck, forever dancing.

It was Celia's second personal bone, only. Thanks again to the generous girl who worked on Saturdays in the bookshop. Once again, enough to spare for a flutter. Allowing Celia, perched on Big Eddie's shoulders, once again to call out to the dancing dots, 'Just deliver me away, Cookie! Somewhere beautiful, please.'

As the blurbs flew in orbit around her head.

**PLAY THE RULES**

4a. AnnoDomino will allow every player an equal
    chance at winning.

4b. Every player will have an equal chance at winning,
    if they correctly follow the rules of the game.

4c. The game being sacrosanct, there shall be no
    favourites.

4d. Mr Million's identity will remain secret, in
    perpetuity.

The city of chances, domino dancing. Daisy Love, with her latest
only bone tight in her fingers; Jazir Malik, with his five new spicy
chances. Both of them watching in awe, as the dots on their
bones were slowly settling down with synchronicity.

Game on. Cookie Luck's body, falling and folding.

'Come on, my beauty!' shouted Jaz to the faraway dancer.
'Make me a happy man.'

'The lady really can't hear you, Jaz,' said Daisy.

'You wanna bet? You know there's some more-than-lucky
bleeders out there, who just can't stop off from winning. They are
the chosen ones, and I wanna be one of them bleeders. Come
on, my Lady Fortuna! Come tumbling towards me!'

'Nobody's chosen in the bones, Jaz. It's all down to chance,
remember.'

'So that's why you only choose a single bone?'

'Five is no more lucky than one, Jaz, with such desperate
odds. It's the gambler's fallacy. Surely you've learned that?'

'For the likes of us, maybe. But wouldn't it be nice to be more than lucky? You ready for a slice of the good garlic yet?' Jaz was cutting some wickedness from his latest Friday-night special.

'No thanks.'

Jaz Malik swallowed at least four slices. 'Wow! That's juicy! Really, Daze, you've gotta give in someday.'

'I've got assignments.'

'Bloody students!'

Nine o'clock chimes, and at last . . .

'Game on!' chants Tommy Tumbler. 'Play to win.'

'Game on!' chants a bleary Jaz.

And at a long last . . .

**Blurbflies**

> That's the way! That's the way!
>     That's the way the cookie crumbles!

A four! A blank! A four and a blank. The stars of Cookie fall into the shape of a four-and-a-blank bone: one dot on each nipple, two more on her kidneys, nothing below the belt. Four pips of chaos, finally found on a field of sexy black. And all over the city, that exact moment of surrender, countless punters banged down their losing bones in frustration. And Daisy Love and Jaz Malik, both of them also losers. Nothing but mismatches.

Dead bones.

'Fuck it!' said Jaz. 'Fuck that losing.'

Game over. Manchester sighs, a spectral breath.

'Somebody, somewhere,' called out Tommy Tumbler from the city's screens, 'just won themselves ten million lovelies! Remember, my friends, my losers, next week is another game. Another chance to win. Purchase in advance.'

Jaz switched off the TV in disgust. 'Can I have that kiss you promised me now?' he asked. 'Just for some comfort?'

'I didn't promise.'

'You did. Last week. You said maybe next week.'

'I meant going to the club, maybe next week. Not a kiss.'

'OK. This is next week. I'll meet you tomorrow night, ten o'clock. We'll go down the Snake Lounge. Frank Scenario will be singing.' Jazir tipped his trilby.

'You're still into that neo-cool thing?' asked Daisy. 'Isn't he a little old to be a pop star?'

'He's not a pop star. He's lived, has our Francis. The living comes out in the songs. Anyway, he's singing tomorrow. You up for it?'

'Assignments. Sorry.'

'Assignments, sorry! That's all it is with you, Daze. One of these days . . .'

'What?'

'Nothing. Look, I'm sorry for going on about your dead dad last week. I know how much it means, to be unappreciated. I wasn't thinking.'

'That's OK.'

'Fuck off.'

'What? What's wrong now?'

'Nothing much.' He was already leaving.

'Jaz, please—'

'Never say it's OK that your dad has died. That's all.'

'I never did. You said—'

'I'm gone.'

**PLAY TO WIN**

**PLAY TO WIN**

**PLAY TO WIN**

**PLAY TO WIN**

**J**azir left Daisy alone and descended into the curry pit. He snatched his plum-coloured velvet waiter's jacket from his locker and wrapped it around himself, even as his father was calling from the kitchen, where in the world had he been all that evening! Jaz ignored the call, ignored also the stupid smiles of his younger brothers. He burst through the swing doors, into the Golden Samosa's floor show and circus. The place was Friday-night jammed. Jaz spotted a group of trash-white students on table five, waiting aggressively for somebody brown to take their order. He hurried over, digging his notepad from the jacket's pocket. Shit! How he hated wearing this plum-velvet Sixties gear, but it was his dad's idea of smart. 'Have you been making your choosing, kind sirs?' Jaz asked the table, in his best put-upon English–Asian.

'We made it ten thousand years ago, gunga,' one of the guys stated. 'Where the fuck were you? Back in the jungle?'

'Very sorry, kind sir, for the delaying.'

Medical students, thought Jazir to himself. And even worse, University Rugby Team. Blue and cream shirts stretched tight over muscle. One of them had a personal blurbfly resting on his padded mountain of a shoulder. The fly was singing the team's praises: 'English schools for English tools! No foreign muck. Vote for Purity!' Jazir recognized the blurb owner, the dreaded Nigel Zuze, self-proclaimed leader of the League of Zero. Fascist bastards . . .

'If you please, sir,' said Jazir, 'but we cannot be allowing the blurbflies in the restaurant, because of the health regulations.'

'So throw him out, garlic-breath!' Nigel shouted, and the party laughed along.

Best keep the feelings tight, thought Jaz. Best make with the soft voice, or else they'll grow even uglier, if that's at all possible. 'Very good, kind sir. If the pet keeps under control. Please you tell me now your choosings.'

'Prawn Rogans all round!' cried the Zuze. 'And make it double quick!'

Jaz calculated the table, found a whole half-dozen of the sad-fuck players dribbling there, each with their creamed-out dominoes lying idle. Jaz pulled back his bile, and said, 'Oh yes, kind sir, that's six King Prawn Rogan Josh, very good choice. Did you have bad luck in the lottery? My bones, also, were much to be desiring.'

'Do we have to put up with this foreign shit just to get a cheap meal these days?' answered Nigel. 'I knew we should've gone down Whoomphy's for a burger! And fuck these numbers to hell and back!' There was a TV in the Golden Samosa, upon which Cookie Luck was frozen for a day in the week's winning numbers. The leader threw his losing bones at the screen, crying out, 'Fuck you, Cookie Luck!' And all the forks in the Golden Samosa were poised around the moment, some of them even banging down in agreement.

## PLAY THE RULES

5a. AnnoDomino will not permit the players to become addicted to the game.

5b. The players of the game will not give themselves up to addiction.

6a. We cannot allow society to be threatened by addiction.

6b. We must always be searching for profit.

6c. Rules 6a and 6b must never come into conflict with each other.

PLay to win

Jazir swung back through the kitchen door, calling out for six King Prawn Rogan Josh, and at this very second. The underling chefs took up his order, made it good, made it spicy. 'Make it extra good and spicy,' said Jaz, 'you know what I'm saying? These are medical students we're dealing with.'

'Where were you previous, my first son?' Jazir's father was working the biggest karahi pan, deftly, swirling a batch of Chicken Dhansak like the master-of-spices that he was. A cloud of dreamy smoke and spices from the homeland cookbook . . .

### CHICKEN DHANSAK

*Take one breast of chicken, sweetly cubed, slowly cooked, karahi-bound. Plenty of grease for the English. Add sugar and turmeric and the secret curry paste. Sweet and hot, simmered with lentils and chosen vegetables, and then mated with tender pineapple chunks. From a tin, of course. Add a sprinkle of garam masala, and stir lightly. Traditionally served with brown rice. Although, for the English, only pilau fried rice will do.*
*Maybe throw in a naan bread or two, for the juices.*
*Heat Rating: medium*

'I was studying, Father,' Jazir replied to the deep recipe.

'Studying the nasty dominoes, maybe?'

'Father, you know that gambling is against all the teachings.'

'Good. So you were studying that lodger woman upstairs? Meanwhile, myself and your diligent brothers were suffering a Friday-night onslaught. Isn't that more than correct?'

Jaz looked over to where his underage twin brothers were smirking at him for being so troublesome. Rogan Josh! thought Jazir to himself. All the karahi paths that I have to burn myself out in before my freedom comes calling, away from the rulings, away from the spices. If only I could win even a half-cast of lovelies on the dominoes! If only to turn Rogan Josh into roguish dosh. Then I would be really travelling! Anything to get away from this stench of burning flesh.

'Her name's Daisy, by the way,' Jazir answered to Saeed, 'and she's not a woman, she's just a girl. And she's paying you rent.'

'She's a white girl.'

'Oh, you noticed, Father?'

'I don't want you messing with her, and certainly not bringing her dishes. Oh yes, I've been seeing you sneaking up the outside stairs with the takeaways.'

'So reduce her rent, Father. She's only a poor student. An orphan.'

'And how's your studying coming on, Jazir?'

'It's coming on fine, Father.'

'I hear it's coming on dreadful. According to your lastest report.'

'I'm trying my best, Father, but all I want to do is sell my wares; just like the family has always done.'

'You know I want you to go to the university next year. What have you learned yet?'

'I've learned that maths is poetry, and that in the calculus, as $y$ approaches 1, $x$ approaches infinity.'

An old and very well-known equation. Because Jaz hadn't being paying attention to his latest lessons; after all, he already knew everything he needed to know. But it was enough to get his father going.

'Good! Now you keep quiet! You shut up! And take that hat off!'

'But Father, aren't you understanding this equation?'

'No, I'm not understanding, and that's very good. I'm wanting my sons to know more than I do.'

Jazir took off his hat, revealing the glossy hair.

'Now take those glasses off, please. It's not sunny in here.'

Jazir took off his sunglasses, revealing the dark, mischievous eyes.

'Now you go and serve table nine, right this second!'

'Yes, Father. Table nine.'

Jazir stored his hat and glasses in his locker, slicked some more coconut oil through his dark-night hair. Back to the kitchen. He picked up a Dhansak, and also a Korma from the hotplate, and then carried them deftly through the swing doors. He deposited them in front of a loving couple, and then took an order from another table: three Chicken Baltis and a Lamb Madras. Meanwhile, the medical students were braying for their food, goaded on by the leader. 'Where the fuck are our curries?' cried Nigel Zuze.

'Very next thing, your meals are delivered. We're making them very special, sir. Very spicy! Are you sure that sir can take it, sir?'

'I can take the devil's arsehole! Now bring it quick!'

'Coming up super quick, kindest sir.'

Meanwhile, the restaurant was buzzing, chock-a-block with losing students and the various other spicehounds, causing Jaz to rush between the tables, taking the orders and delivering, keeping all the punters happy. Whilst also keeping a small place free in his mind for some delicious thoughts about the young girl upstairs. Oh my dearest Daisy Love, how upon this earth can I get to your caresses?

Into these secret desires came the latest hit song by Frank Scenario:

> *I've got that woman's taste in my mouth,*
> *Making me play the dominatee.*
> *Playing my bones along with Lady Luck,*
> *Wherever she may take me.*

At first Jaz thought a stray pop blurb had flown in, and he was all set to swat the pest, until he saw that it was only Joe Crocus gliding into the Golden Samosa, singing the song alive and aloud for all the curry punters to hear, and harmonized by his acolytes, DJ Dopejack and Sweet Benny Fenton. Jaz welcomed them all with a trayful of complementary poppadoms and chutneys.

Regular customers. Jaz was thrilled that such a great student had chosen to adorn his father's restaurant. Jaz had friends at the university, and it was well known that Joe Crocus could make the numbers dance like crazy. 'Did you have any luck tonight, sir,' asked Jazir of Joe, 'on the dominoes?'

'The good Cookie Luck was sleeping, alas.'

'Alas and alack, myself the same. And a very good evening to you, Sweet Benny.'

Benny gave him a wink. Jazir gave it back. Whilst the Dopejack just threw a smile into his menu. Even Jaz had to admit that Dopejack was a most excellent DJ, cooking the latest neo-cool tunes like a top chef, but apart from that . . . Jaz hated the man. Jazir fucking hated him! Simply because the DJ was the university's supposed best student of Applied Physics, which was Jaz's natural subject, the making of strangeness. They were both working at the same equation: how to make a computer give up its inner secrets. Info-jealousy, for sure, but did the student have to be so ugly, and did he have to dye his hair that hideous green colour, just to prove a point? Trying to prove what? Some kind of ugly weirdness? Dopejack was closer to Joe Crocus than Jaz could ever be, unless he joined the learning race.

'An interesting result, nonetheless,' said Joe, 'on the game tonight.'

'In what way, sir?'

'Call me Joe, please. Well, it's the first time a blank's come up. We all know that the double-blank is a nasty.'

'Joker Bone!' Benny shivered even just saying the words.

'But I'm wondering about the consequences of winning a half-blank.'

'Right,' said Dopejack, 'like what does half a joker do to you?'

'Thankfully, we shall not find out. Enough! What shall we partake of?'

'May I recommend the Chef's Special?' enquired Jazir.

'Good thinking, my man. Open all channels; connect to everything. Surprise us! Only not too greasy, mind. I don't want that English crap. Nice and dry and full of marination.'

'Of course, Mr Joe! Just like my mother makes it at home.'

Nobody knew exactly how old Joe Crocus was, although the campus connection placed him at forty-five orbits of the sun. All the punters were looking over to the table, the men and the women both, because Crocus was finely carved for both male and female desire. Loverman supreme. With his braided, long, ebony hair; his frockcoat of many colours; his cut of Byronic swath.

Jaz took their orders. 'Three Chef's Specials for Crocus and Dopejack and Sweet Benny Fenton!' Cried in earnest, as he banged through the kitchen door. 'And easy on the grease this time.'

'What's that?' gasped the underlings and the brothers. 'Easy on the grease?' Like it was some kind of sacrilege.

'Just fucking cook it!' shouted Jaz. At which sound, his father howled down the kitchen, 'How dare you be cursing on my premises?' And Jaz had to run for cover, back to the feeding floor.

Five minutes later, a drunken party of five ladies, slumming it from leafy Poshtown, came falling through the Golden Samosa's door, letting a rogue blurbfly in with them, singing about how the next domino game was the best-ever bet. 'Buy your numbers early! Make a wish on the future. Play to win!' The other diners protested at the disturbance, and it was Jaz's job to swat at the blurb, to urge it back outside with the fanning of an extra-large naan bread. All that wafting in vain, because the blurb refused to leave the premises. It was going crazy with its own messages, obviously thinking it was a lone hunter. And that's when the rugby blurb launched itself.

'English schools for English tools! No foreign muck. Vote for Purity!'

Advert war!

The two blurbs fought it out, slogan against slogan above the diners, sparking the air as their messages clashed. Horrible message flies, trying to bite each other. Blue and cream flashed the stripes of one beauty, rugby-shirt style; whilst white dots on black pulsed along the domino fly. Poor Malik could only apologize dearly to the ducking-down customers, as the rugby-fly twisted and turned like a purist bastard with medical knowledge, until the domino fly retreated through the doorway.

Jazir made some more deliveries, and pretty soon the medical students were sweating under the extra spices included in their King Prawn Rogans. 'What the fuck is this?' Nigel Zuze cried. 'We're burning our guts out on this shit!'

'Is it too hot for the mightiest, sir?' Jazir asked with concern.

'This isn't a Rogan. This is a Thunderloo! Take it away. I can hardly breathe!' The big medical student threw his plate on to the floor, then stood up to grab Jazir by the collar. 'You're playing some fucking Paki joke on me!' And with a vicious head-butt Jaz was laid out on the Golden Samosa's shagpile carpet.

Joe Crocus strode over from his table. 'Fellow learner,' he

said to the Zero captain, 'you have imparted damage to an innocent chap. A friend of mine. For this mishap you must surely be punished.'

'Eh? What fucker's saying so, fuckface?'

'The loverman is saying so,' said Benny Fenton, quietly, from his seat.

'And what are you? Some kind of a black queer? Ought to be a law against it.' One of his compatriots informed Zuze that there was already a law against it and was told to 'shut the fuck up' for his trouble. The rest of the crew laughed along, standing tall in defence of their leader. Meanwhile, the rugby-fly hovered aloft, ready for battle time.

Six medical rugby players and a blurbfly against two mathematicians and a physicist, and made up to a paltry quartet when Jaz Malik finally managed to raise himself from the restaurant's floor, bleeding from his eyebrow.

No contest. The rugby fuckers were primed to kill.

But then Saeed, the boss, and his two younger sons came out of the kitchen, followed by all the underlings, all the waiters, and suddenly the rugby players were surrounded. 'Fuck the lot of you and get back to the jungle!' Nigel Zuze shouted to the circle, before pushing his way through them, towards the door. 'Compatriots, retreat!' With a last notice that he'd be back 'in vengeance one fucking day'. Out onto the pavement. The curry crew followed them.

Showdown in Spicetown, showered by the rain.

Somebody else, somewhere, must have called up the burgercops, because now the beefy sirens were singing harmony to the night, mashing it up with their big scarlet 'W' sign, flashing like a neon menu.

And all the glittering blurbflies were swarming, buzzing the fighting mob with messages: 'Breathe Our Air! Play Dominoes! Eat Whoomphy MegaBurgers! Suck Chocolate! Pseudosoup! Bank accounts! The latest sex star! The latest song by Frank Scenario! The latest burger-image from the cops! The dance of Cookie Luck! The Virtues of For Ever! Downfall of Hope! Tinsel Time! Burgerball and Domidome!'

Can you guess who won?

**PLAY TO WIN**

**PLAY TO WIN**

**PLAY TO WIN**

**PLAY TO WIN**

**WIN PLAY TO WIN**

**PLAY TO WIN**     **PLAY TO WIN**

Daisy Love heard the commotion from her room above the curry house, tried her best to ignore the usual Friday-night trouble and the sirens and the screams and the pitches of the blurbflies, and then spent the rest of the night working on her latest chaotic equations. The chances of this, and the chances of that; the chances of living and loving.

And when the telephone rang, well, she was torn awake from numberland. 'Who's that?' she asked.

'It's me,' answered the phone. 'Your father.'

'Who?'

'Jimmy Love, you remember? So nice to hear your voice.'

'Who is this, please, some kind of joker?'

'Guess so.'

Daisy banged down the phone, back to work. Really, she should've been asleep by now. On Saturdays she worked in a bookshop, and it wouldn't do to turn up docile. But her father had called to her from far away. Shit! he'd actually called her! Had he really called her? After so many years.

And after she'd told everybody that her father was dead.

This was the only reason she had gained the sponsorship from Max Hackle, because both her mother and father were dead. Orphan money pay-off.

Her mother really was dead, but her father wasn't. Not yet. He was just ignored, lied about. Too many memories, too many dreams, unappreciated.

Her father had been a great mathematician, if only an amateur, the muse kept hidden. In reality, Jimmy Love was a plumber, but every night he would come home dirty, to work on his numbers alone. Never letting the Daisy in.

Horrible thought, but Daisy was drawn backwards, towards the memories. Back to when she was a young kid, aged seven and a half, playing the dominoes with her father. Her mother already dead.

A child who would hardly speak, her father forced to take up her education. Utilizing the old-style dominoes, a cheap and black plastic set of numbers.

## PLAY THE RULES (HISTORY)

7a. There are twenty-eight pieces in a standard domino set, ranging from the double-blank to the double-six, containing all permutations of the numbers between, paired across a centre line. In total, 168 dots in play.

7b. In the old game, each player chose five dominoes to begin. The player with the highest double played first. Each player played in turn to match an exposed number, until they could play no more. They would then knock on the table and choose from the draw-pile, which was the pile of dominoes still waiting. They would draw until they found a playable piece. The winner was the first player to get rid of all his pieces.

7c. Some believe that the ancient Egyptians played a similar game of numbers, carved on human bone. Others believe it a medieval invention, an offshoot of the *memento mori* fashion accessory, fragments of a portable skull. The game, as described in rule 7b, came to light in the eighteenth century, in Italy. The dominoes were carved from ivory, from which comes the vulgar name.

7d. The Company may take its imagery and devices from the historical game. The new rules, however, shall be of its own devising, and are herein contained.

7e. The proper name of the game comes from the Latin: God the father, Christ the son: *Dominus*. Anno Domini, the year of our Lord. So the game has always had a religious attitude. Or else it refers to the Italian word for master: *domino*. Which word was shouted aloud by the winner: *domino!* Meaning, 'I have won! I am the master!'

7f. No such outburst by present-day winners shall be permitted, except during the first ten minutes after the result.

Play to win

Backwards, in time. 'Domino! I've won! Daisy, I'm the master!' Her father takes a winning swig from his whisky, and Daisy throws her remaining bones onto the living-room floor in a sudden tantrum.

The numbers, the beautiful numbers, a rain of losing dots.

'Daisy, my love,' her father says, 'you are such a bad loser.'

'Nah, nah, nah!' cries Daisy.

'You've got to learn how to play to win, my child. Just because you've only got half of a brain, that doesn't mean you—'

'Nah, nah!'

'Stop that noise!'

And then her father hits her, right across the face. The young Daisy goes all silent for a frozen moment, until the voice in her head comes calling, 'Fuck you, Father!'

But all that comes out is, 'Nah, nah, nah.'

'That's OK. That's fine, my child,' says her father, stooping down to pick up the fallen bones. 'I'm sorry for hitting you. Please forgive me. Let's play again.'

Another swig of whisky. 'Let's play to win this time.'

The words came back to Daisy, as she rested, half asleep over her latest assignment. What had she been back then? A brain-dead child with no hope of ever winning anything. Really? The words in her head were superfine, but by the time they got to her lips . . .

'Nah, nah, nah.'

The younger Daisy Love was a mental nightmare, a self-absorbed child, living only within her own head. How her father must have hated her feeble mutterings . . .

'Nah, nah.'

'Fucking choose!'

Daisy chooses, rubbing her smarting cheek. She takes her five bones from the pile and then lets her father choose his army. Memories . . . Her father viciously bangs down his final bone to her weak-brained double-five, with another shout of 'Domino!' The master. 'Do you really think it's only a game of chance, Daisy? Did your mother die in vain?' Her father's words, full of a distant longing, a love of some kind, an urging. 'You see this, Daisy?' He's showing her his necklace again, on the end of which swings an old, old domino, the five-and-the-four, with the centre spot of the five pierced for the leather thong. 'I won this when I was a kid. Look, this time I'll play to lose, OK? I'll play my worst domino every time. There are no winners without losers. Do you follow me?'

Nah fucking nah! An easy game, but still Daisy loses.

'Won't you ever shout out "Domino", my daughter! What's wrong with you?'

'Nah, nah, nah!' Meaning the game isn't proper.

'OK, now we play again,' says her father. 'But to win, this time. OK? Have you learned your lessons?'

'Nah, nah.'

But Daisy doesn't want to play any more. She sulks her way into her bedroom, there to cry into her pillow, and then, suddenly, never to cry again. She opens her tatty exercise book, jots down a row of numbers, corresponding to the dots on all twenty-eight of the dominoes. Daisy works through all the possibilities of playing. Of playing to win. She can't speak properly, she can't communicate her problems to the world, but she can count, can't she? She can count way beyond all the other children, and all the problems. Daisy lives within her own darkness, since her mother's death, no words to comfort her, only the secret numbers making any kind of sense. Idiot savant, the doctors have called her. A mathematical, crazy genius, but totally unschoolable.

How the dumbness came.

## Play to Lose

Daisy had done some research, when she was old enough, into the exact circumstances of her mother's death.

First, a faulty traffic signal on the road into Manchester. The chances of that, Daisy had worked out, were approximately 1 million to one. Bad chances, causing a free-for-all jam at the junction with Grey Mare Lane, lodged with cars too eager to get somewhere, throwing away the rules.

Secondly, the family Love was going into town to buy a puppy, thinking it would help five-year-old Daisy to make some friends. Average chances, the kind of thing concerned parents did for difficult children.

Thirdly, a lorry driver called Bob Tyler was late for a delivery of the marmalade he was carrying. Bob's overseer had already called him to task twice that week for tardiness, so he was extra keen to make this appointment. He was speeding. Average chances, two to one, given the job prospects.

Fourthly, some roadworks at the junction had been left undone. More bad chances, according to Daisy's calculations, but not too high given the council's lack of funds: approximately fifty to one.

Fifthly, Daisy's father had been drinking all morning. Odds-on favourite, because he always drank.

Sixthly, now he was drinking and driving. Chances: five to one.

Seventhly, he was swearing at his wife for wanting the puppy, turning his eyes from the road, just as he attempted to cross the obstruction, the roadworks, the traffic jam, against the dead lights. Chances: inevitable, given the drink and the anger and the hopeless love.

Eighthly, Bob Tyler decided he couldn't wait any longer for his deliverance. Ten to one, maybe less, maybe more.

The chances of this, the chances of that. The chances of all these crazy circumstances coming together, according to Daisy's constant calculations: ten billion bad chances to one lonely good one. Approximately astronomical. Hopeless chances you would never bet a puny on, never mind a lovely, never mind the old money, but happen they did.

Daisy was in the backseat. 'Jimmy!' Hearing her mother calling out, suddenly. Last words.

'Shit!' Her father calling . . .

The world exploding. The words going wrong, all so very wrong.

Mummy had gone through the windscreen, taken away by the god of bad chances. A big, bad truck banging into their world, banging their heads. A shower of glass falling over baby Daisy and her father. The Daisy and the father that had survived and the pain hidden behind the numbers.

Falling . . . falling . . . still falling . . .

Her father, reluctantly, took over her education. A learning curve of fire. By the age of six, that surviving baby could fully iterate a global function. Couldn't speak a single word of English, of course; totally dumbfounded by the crash. Her mind filled with glass and blood and the truck in front. But Daisy was a goddess, a goddess of equations. The bang on the head must have released something fine, a continuous unravelling of the world into its probable causes and the numbers thereof. Something fine, something stilted, something cursed and cold. No friends, but top of her class and always the winner in the various games of chance: ludo, snakes and ladders, dominoes. Except against her father.

She wanted to win; more than anything, Daisy wanted to win, for once, against her father. Those stupid fucking bones . . .

Remembering . . .

The young Daisy works out the new chances and challenges her father to a domino match the next day. Her father grins to see her tight smile, sober for a while. 'That's my girl. Choose your bones. Choose wisely.' Daisy chooses her pieces, and her father the same, and then they play. Daisy leads with the double-six; her father answers with the six-and-a-five. Daisy slots in a five-and-blank, her father comes back with the dangerous double-blank. Daisy replies with a blank-and-a-one.

And so the game continues, until most of the bones are extinguished. But all the time Daisy is working out the new mathematics of the game, playing to win this time. Play to fucking win! Until she has only a lonely pair of bones left, and her father a full four.

She bangs down her second-to-last domino, a five-and-a-four, knowing her father can't possibly have a matching bone. She cries out in delight.

'Domino!'

Her first word ever spoken, since her mother had died. Domino, meaning master. Meaning she has finally mastered her father.

Except . . . 'Well spoken, my child,' says her father. 'But it's not over yet.' He plays a four-and-a-blank bone, causing Daisy to knock the table and make a gasp. She hadn't worked out that possibility. The chances against him having that confounded lucky number, too much to bear. And having to watch her father play all of his bones out, only watch in despair, and bang her knocking hand on the table, again and again.

'Daddy Domino!' screams her father, laughing out loud.

But Daisy had found her voice again.

## Play to win

A building called the House of Chances. A hologram sculpture floating above the forecourt, a tumbling domino, suspended in air, forever changing its spots, dancing, dancing . . .

This is where they make the bones.

You want to pay a visit? You want to talk to Mr Million?

Go ahead. Make a wish. Why not try?

Security blurbs orbit the building, beaming on you for acceptance. Play to win! Play to win!

OK. Flash your passport, pray the blurbs acknowledge it.

Accepted. Through the satellites.

A pair of big dominoes for a door, forever changing. Show the door your invitation, if you have one. The door might just give you the nod.

Let the door swing open.

Into a vast, empty hall, lined with flowers, wafted with perfume and muzak. Find the desk, if you can, amid all the hidden lights that shine down in dots of roving colours. With the lobby-blurbs that fly in a bombing squad . . .

'Play to win!'

Give your name to the receptionist, the one with the gun strapped to her waist. Tell her you've got an appointment with Mr Million. Show her your pass, let her check it against the computer's diary. Tremble as she does so.

OK. Ascend the elevator to the top floor. But first, the lift attendant asks for your day's credit. Do you have one?

You do! Excellent! Give it to him.

Ascend and play to win.

Step out. Face the guard, the one with the electroknife. Allow him to take a nick out of your forearm. He checks your blood against a DNA database. Your very own double helix, spiralling on a screen.

Genetically cleared, walk towards the operations room. Another guard at the door. There's a password. It changes every five seconds. If you hesitate or guess, the guards take you away.

Only by doing all of this will you get to see Mr Million. The bones, the bones, forever changing. They say he has 168 faces.

Good luck.

## Play to win

Friday's midnight turned into Saturday's first breath, and Jaz Malik spent the time in the Golden Samosa's kitchen, letting his father hold a raw garlic bulb to the wound on his forehead. The two younger sons were all smug smiles, as their brother suffered, immensely.

'Father, it's killing me!' Jazir cried out.

'Nonsense, my first son,' Saeed the father replied, 'the heat will draw out the poison. You did good this night, my child. Didn't we show those purity ninnies the door? If only the burgercops hadn't turned up to save them! I would've fried that Zuzeman to cinders, believe me. Now stop you this crying, please.'

'Sorry, Father. Dreadfully sorry.'

Meanwhile . . .

Joe Crocus and Sweet Benny lived in the attic flat of Professor Hackle's house in West Didsbury. They had argued for a while, because Benny wasn't too keen on Joe getting into fights, especially with roughneck medical students who might dent his masterly good looks. Joe told him to go fuck himself. Benny said he had other ideas.

The two of them made it up in the usual way, bedwards, joined at the hips with love and wounds and blood, all of them spilt in the war against *purity and rugby players and bladder-brained medical students and the death of the nation's soul*. This kind of speech was Joe's idea of foreplay, covered with a condom. Good enough to bring some deep sleep to the partaker, and a restless mind to Benny the sweet receiver. He couldn't stop thinking about how things were between them, this constant knife-edge. Exciting, sure, but . . .

Meanwhile, DJ Dopejack was working in his flat in Fallowfield, studying his collection for what he would play that Saturday night at the Snake Lounge club, alongside and behind the great and coolish Frank Scenario. Such an honour it was, to have the sacred Frank come visit. He chose Ella Fitzgerald singing Cole Porter's 'Night and Day', and also Lady Day singing 'Loverman'. Lady Night and Lady Day, Dopejack mixed them both to a wild drum and bass, and then into his twin-decked memory.

Dopejack's room was a small lab of home-made equipment, gadgets stolen from the computer rooms at the university, all mixed together into new ways of being. Flickerings of the beat, in numbers dancing upon his computers. Stealing samples as he may, feeding them direct to the groove, his green hair sticking up in fever.

Nobody knew his first name (Donald) or his last (Jacoby) and nobody ever would. Nobody would ever know that the green hair was completely *au naturel*, a crazy outcome of the genes, the Mama Dope and the Papa Jack of stupid genes. Too much of the drugs in his mummy's belly, too much of the games from his father's brain, making the lonely Dopejack what he was.

Ugly as a bad dream. Too lonely. Lost in music.

The mix brought home.

The rain stopped at two in the morning. As Daisy Love lay awake in her bed, unable to sleep now that the constant downpour had turned into mist upon her window. Oh Father, oh Father . . .

Daisy got up from her bed, put on her clothes and went down the outside stairs. The Wilmslow Road. All along the curryfare the neon signs were dimmed, and the spicy smells were just a wisp of forgotten adverts. A few sad and wet blurbflies still fluttered here and there, singing their messages of desire and loss to only the lonely. Daisy kicked her way through all the discarded dominoes that were littering the streets, all creamy and still and frozen in their losingness.

Dead bones.

Why had her father called? And after all these years?

As Little Miss Celia lay within her abandoned shop on Swan Street. A former hardware store that had closed down years ago; Celia had made this place her secret own, finding it and breaking in. It was the ruling you see, that no vagabond could claim a legit begging hole unless they were 'officially homeless'. Celia's dead bone lay on the pillow beside her head. Another losing session, after all that she had wished for. Pretty soon, Celia was sure that Big Eddie would grow tired of supporting her illegal play.

So she really did have to win, one of these days.

As Jazir Malik, back in his parents' house, worked late into the morning. Locked tight in his bedroom, he had a half-dozen orders to fill before next Friday. The room was lined with feedbeds and workbenches; feedbeds in which his crop of ultragarlic sprouted; workbenches on which his pseudoblurbs lay scattered in pieces, awaiting his flight path.

Because Jazir was so good at making things happen, he had built a replica out of bits and pieces, stolen from here and there; cellophane for the wings, wire for the structure, papier-mâché for the thorax, a small electric motor to move the wings and make it fly, a disembowelled Walkman to play the message, a couple of batteries, a little chip and motherboard to work the streets.

Trash fly. He sold that first specimen to a drug dealer down in Moss Side. Homie Winston was his name. 'Homie Winston! He sure do make the trip! Smoke to win!' Jazir got a full five punies for the sale, all of which he used to fuel another two fly specimens.

In business!

Because Jazir's bedroom was now an Asian computer, the Spicelab, wired to the world and crazy. Even as he chewed on another slice of the good garlic, even as he glided down the imagined streets of Manchester. The fractal map he had stolen from the council's motherbase. Jazir loved the fractals, those twisting shapes between the normal dimensions, where an infinitude of knowledge made play. Naanchester, along the burgernet.

Jaz hated the fact that the Whoomphies owned the space inside his computer. Information should be free. He had his own special devices to carve out a secret plot. A ghost in the machine, fighting the enemy, and teaching his latest copyblurb the knowledge of the streets. Jazir made it through in flying colours, only to find Miss Sayer waiting for him.

Play to win

Jazir Malik first shook the joystick back in 1994, at a kids' arcade on Oxford Street, Central Manchester. He was only twelve years old. In those days, playing games was a clumsy affair, moving your image slowly through the mechanisms. So frustrating. But by the age of thirteen he was the Number One All-Asian Champion of Ganga Jal: Space Trooper, a dream of a game in which the participant battled against the white imperialists on the planet Bhangra. The whites had colonized the planet in order to mine for ultragarlic, a bulbous drug that could easily control the universe in the wrong hands, making the dream too real. What else could the Roganites do, after 100 years of servitude, but finally fight back? It was all an illusion, of course, but Jazir found himself hooked to a winning dream, in which he could always regain his independence. Hooked enough to win the championship.

Two years later he found an intruder in one game, a little inserted face that kept puzzling him. Eventually he pressed on the insert to let it come large.

The intruder's name was Miss Sayer; she called to Jazir from far away, in typescript, 'Grab the Wings', and then disappeared.

Jazir answered, as only he could, because he had heard rumours of these mystical intruders – Game Cat being the most famous – that popped up to bring the player to the next stage.

It took him a whole week and a whole other load of game-won nanopunies to find the games mistress again. All the time and expenses in the world were just a feather in the wind when Jazir finally bowed down at the great teacher's inset. 'Most revered Miss Sayer,' he stated, 'if it pleases you, I have travelled many games in order to prostrate myself thus. I am your most pitiful subject.'

The great teacher was seventy-seven years old, made young by the computer. 'My child,' she type-whispered, 'I understand your journey, for I myself once made the same sacrifice. Is it the knowledge that you seek?'

'I am too pitiful for such a gift,' said Jazir.

'But only the most pitiful shall interest the wise, and I am growing old. Soon I shall die, and my knowledge with me, unless I take on a pupil. I believe you have an inkling of the numbers involved.'

'The tiniest of inklings, great mistress. I am most unworthy.'

'Your journey has only just begun. You must grab the dream by the wings.'

Jazir heard the message.

# Play to win

Present days, Miss Sayer was waiting for him on the computer screen. 'Time is nearly,' she whispered from nowhere. 'Come grab. Find a wing.'

This virus had been visiting him ever since way back. Turning up at random, like some unwanted hippy-death *Game Cat* mag cheatmode. And at every appearance her voice becoming more limited, more painful.

Whatever, Jazir closed down the inset, undocked the new blurb's flight path from the computer's mouth. The pseudoblurb itself was still lying on his workbench, its belly wide open. Jaz slotted the new flight-path disk into the blurb's stomach. Now it was complete. He slid the completed creature into one of the Golden Samosa's takeaway trays and crimped down the soft aluminium holdings. Jazaways he called them, these nice little earners. Enough work for one night. Deliver this one tomorrow morning. Of course, it would crash in a few days or so, being only a pseudofly. But that was money in the bank, five lonely punies a fly. More bones, more bones! If he could only find a way to make a real fly! How much would he earn? How many bones could he buy? And always, in these moments of rest, Jazir's mind went back to Daisy, the sweet and innocent Miss Daisy Love. Her sweet voice calling to him, dismissing him. If he could only persuade her of his faithful intentions.

Three o'clock found Sweet Benny climbing out of Joe's bed, carefully. He went outside and climbed the wall opposite into the Southern Cemetery, his favourite place. It wasn't so peaceful these days, since the AnnoDomino had opened their headquarters near by. Couldn't he ever escape the twin demands? Hackle's sweet home and the bone pavilion, both of them calling. The House of Chances dominated everything, of course: with the giant domilith flashing its mutant dots in the forecourt, the securiblurbs patrolling the ground, singing go-away songs; the swarms of adverts flying over the cemetery, either heading hivewards with old messages, or outwards with new. Flashes of wing-beat, a whispering million. Sweet Benny shuddered.

As Daisy Love, cold at heart, headed back to her flat. To sleep a thousand miles, unconscious. As the city dozed in its losing bones.

Manchester sleeping. Daisy and Jaz and Benny, finally, and Celia and Joe and Dopejack. Even the winners of the half-blank were asleep; no harm came to them, by the way, except that they all dreamed the same dream, of a skeleton chasing them through some misty landscape, all rattling bones and clattering teeth. They all woke up at precisely four in the morning, covered in sweat.

Somewhere else, somebody else was still dancing. The very final person awake that night, holding tight to a living chance, the magical four-and-a-blank combination. His name has no importance, only the winning bone that he couldn't quite believe. Domino! The master! The 10 million lovelies of a domino's kiss, delivered by the good Cookie Luck herself. The queen of numbers, coming out of television.

Somewhere else, maybe somebody was taking a hammer to a dead bone, swinging it again and again to break the domino. Believe me, the hammer would break first.

Somewhere else, another person lay dead in a car park, killed by petty human jealousy. That's the way it is with the game, winners and losers.

As the blurbflies circled in the air. Singing, so singing.

PLAY TO WIN

PLAY TO WIN                    PLAY TO WIN

PLAY TO WIN
PLAY TO WIN      PLAY TO WIN

WIN PLAY TO WIN

WIN PLAY TO WIN

PLAY TO WIN        PLAY TO WIN

PLAY TO WIN

# Game 42

**D**omination Day, lucky old Bonechester. The naked populace, making foreplay to the domiviz, bone-eyed and numberfucked as the opening credits came in a shower of pips. Tumbling jig of dominoes, watch them dance now, forever chancing zero. Jig that sexy jumble! Even the air had a hard-on, bulging with mathematics. Turning the blurbflies into a nympho-swarm, liquid streets alive with perverts. Play to win! Play to love! And all over the city that hot and juicy evening, three hours from midnight and shrouded, gangs of punters were plaguing the city, stroking their bones on napkins and trousers, blouses and dresses, breasts and groins. Voyeurs of probability. Gazing, full-on, as some fractal dots pulsated to the theme song.

> It's domino time! Domino time!
> Dom, dom, dom, dom, domino time!

**Blurbflies**

Game 42. The year dot. Mr Million, the King Bone had deemed it so.

In factories and bathrooms, abattoirs and dog kennels; all-night shopping toilets, non-stop cemeteries; swimming pools and sauna pits; anywhere there was a private TV or a radio or a public screen, all the Mancunians were lubeing their wishes with winning-juice, hoping for a Cookie Luck kiss.

**Blurbflies**

> Why not chance a throw?
> You might as well have a go!
> With your lucky little domino!

Go on, go on! Chance a puny. Chance a fucking puny! Why not have a go! Go on, roll them bones! Look at the kids even, running through their dreams, playing with their Dominic

Domino dolls. See them squeeze that bone! Singing aloud and learning how to play. Learn to win! Learn to win!

Play, play, play! Make yourself 10 million lovelies!

Play to win

Ignore Daisy Love and Jazir Malik for the moment. Let them go through the usual rigmarole ritual. They're only going to lose again, anyway. And then Jazir's gonna ask Daisy to the Snake Lounge, Saturday night. He's gonna tell her that the ultracool Frank Scenario is singing again tomorrow night at the club, but she's still going to refuse. Assignments, assignments.

Also, try your best to ignore the scents of Aloo Josh and Tandoori Murghi, drifting ever upwards from the curry house.

Forget Dopejack and Sweet Benny and Old Joe Crocus, all in a car somewhere. Let them all lose. Because when Cookie Luck dances to a standstill that Friday night at nine, her costume is a map of sad chances. A pip on each breast. Pips on each hip, a pip on each thigh, another in the groin. The way the cookie crumbles, sadly.

A two. A five. A two-and-a-five, the lonely winning bone. A seven combination and an extra prize for the winner, another million lovelies.

Instead, focus on the kid, Little Miss Celia . . .

Look at that girl fly! Running through the dark streets of the city, her little domino in her little hand, with a tribe of big old dirty beggars chasing after her. The once proud and faithful family of tramps, chasing Celia along Market Street where the bombed-out Monstermarket lay dark for renovation. Along Tib

Street where the nocturnal joke shops sold their 'pink and steamy adult toys', a left turn on to Swan Street, where the Snake Lounge club lay waiting with its posters about Saturday's gig by Frank Scenario and DJ Dopejack. Also upon this street, Celia's chosen and secret homeless house, out of bounds with the pack of tramps sniffing for her winnings. And where in the hell was Big Eddie Irwell when Little Miss Celia needed him the most?

Without his protection and so scared.

From Swan Street, another left on to Shudehill, where the pornomarts did the dirties, selling filthiness to the all-night self-abusers. Along streets where discarded loser bones lay in piles of cream, this young girl with a feather in her hair. See how she runs. In her tightly clenched fist a desperate bone; one of the few still half alive that night. Dotted with a one-and-a-five combination; the one gone to cream, but the five alive and black and lovely and pulsing . . .

Celia had won a second half-match! Yes! A glorious five for a fistful of punies, just waiting to be clenched. She had wished and wished to be a winner and now her strong wishes had come up half true. If she could just outrun this drunken mob of loser tramps; if she could only find Eddie in time for the prize-giving.

Way past midnight, and Celia has to present her half-bone at the winners' enclosure before the following midnight. That was the ruling. Piccadilly Gardens, the deadline for collection. Only the purchaser could collect the winnings, so she would have to find Eddie Irwell, whilst still dodging the tramps that wanted to steal her prize. What was happening to the brethren? Blame it on the bones.

But 100 punies! A way out of the begging, at last, if she could only find Big Eddie and then stop him from claiming the prize as his own. So much work to do. Running loose on street knowledge.

Little Miss Celia, escaping, finally sleeping, in a chosen doorway, next to an air vent, of course, but still shivering cold, her newsprint overcoat wrapped tight around her. Only the half-winning bone in her fingers. The pulsing five-spot. Dreaming of home. Where the hell was home? Celia had woken up one day with nowhere else to go, that was the truth.

Home was where you laid your bone, and another three people died that night; half-casters, killed out of jealousy, winnings stolen.

## Play to win

Jazir woke at eight the next morning. Skipped breakfast, skipped dressing. Fallen asleep in yesterday's clothes, he walked along Oxford Road to the university.

Early morning blurbs, all around his head. All the companies of Manchester, playing out their messages. Blurbs for the burgercops: Arrest to win! Blurbs for the whoomphies: Eat to win! Blurbs for the dominoes: Play to win! Blurbs for the tinker: Sell to win! Blurbs for the tailor: Stitch to win! Blurbs for the soldier: Fight to win! Blurbs for the sailor: Float to win! Blurbs for the rich man: Steal to win! Blurbs for the poor man: Steal to win! Blurbs for the beggar man: Plead to win! Blurbs for the thief: Steal to win!

Every company had a corporate message to fly, as long as they paid the subscription to AnnoDomino.

Steal to win, steal to win, steal to win!

But Jazir offered an alternative route.

His first client was waiting at the gate, as prearranged. 'What's happening, Jaz?' Benny Fenton asked. 'Did you get what I asked for?'

'It's done.'

'I need that message.'

'Here's your take-off, Benjamin.'

Benny looked deep into the polythene bag, eyed the crimped-up silver box within, heavy with the stench of something hot. The bag was faintly pulsing in his hands. 'Thank you, very much,' he said. 'Is it programmed?'

'It's done.'

'What's the cost?'

'No cost, Benny. Just a future favour.'

'Already granted, whatever it takes. Cheers, Jaz.'

Benny went off happy, and Jazir entered the university. Just outside the library doors he met his second customer: a fellow Asian boy, a first-year Chemistry student called Baljit Pandit. Jaz handed over a takeaway tray with a nice fresh pseudoblurb inside. 'That should get you laid.' Jazir accepted the payment in return, a card of infinite depth.

The university's library was open between half-eight and twelve on a Saturday, in order for the diligent students to partake of the knowledge in peace. Only one librarian was on duty, because hardly any students were ever that keen to get up so early after the Friday-night revels.

The lone librarian was a Miss Denise Crimson, spinster of the parish.

At 8.35 precisely a certain student presented himself at Miss Crimson's desk, asking to be allowed access to the computers. 'My, you're eager this morning,' the librarian said. 'Your name, please?' She made it her duty to know the faces of all the keenest students, but this was a stranger to her books, a dusky stranger . . .

'Pandit, Baljit,' answered Jaz Malik, knowing the librarian would appreciate this reversal of the names. He then pulled his payment from his shoulder bag: a student's ID card. Gold dust!

Jaz kept it moving as he flashed his best smile at the spinster.

Miss Crimson saw a lovely Asian boy, plus a lovely Asian photograph on the card. The man and his card, eager to learn. 'Study hard, Student Pandit,' said with lonely love.

The one good thing about being an Asian boy in Britain was that the white girls thought you all looked the same.

Jazir walked through the bookshelves, freely.

On the way he had to bat a blurbfly out of his vision. Not just any old blurbfly, mind; a University of Manchester blurbfly. A blurb full of educational messages: 'Study hard, my students,' it sang. 'Stack your knowing bones for a good life. Learn to win! Win to learn!' The blurb was a Saturday-morning loner, supplied by AnnoDomino, as all the legit madverts were. Working overtime for the chance of being upgraded.

Fat chance.

Jazir sat himself down at one of the ugly but powerful computers the university had bought a few months ago with a sponsorship grant. He pushed the borrowed card into a hungry slot and had to wait a whole two minutes whilst an animated Whoomphy burger floated around the screen, proclaiming the health-giving benefits of a regular intake of special beef. All the boundless joys of corporate logos to sit through, until, finally, the burger actually asked for the diner's name. Jazir tapped in Pandit's name, to make a general enquiry menu appear. Punched on an item called Motherlode, got back a 'Password please?' message. This was expected. Jazir then reached into his shoulder bag, pulled out a disk of his own making. He looked all around as he fed the disk into the computer's mouth. Nobody was there, nobody watching. Jaz's disk caused a wave of animated curry sauce to form on the screen, and a rogue window to open up, called 'Chef's Special Recipe'. A box within the recipe demanded ingredients, so Jaz dragged the 'Password please?' icon across the screen, dropped it into the chef's karahi pan. A whir and a click, and then a 'Currently Cooking' message came along, to apologize.

Minutes going by . . .

### INFO JOSH

*Ginger, garlic and water. Put them all into a karahi. Add chunks of information to brown. Cardamom, bay leaves, cloves. Peppercorns and cinnamon. Sliced onions. Stir and fry. Add the secret curry paste. Coriander and cumin, paprika and cayenne. Mix some yoghurt with the dish. Stir and fry. Add some more water. Bring to the boil. Cover and cook for an hour or so. Boil away the liquid. Sprinkle with garam masala. Stir and serve. The wanted knowledge will be revealed. Heat Rating: red hot*

The library's blurb landed on the screen, as though trying to eat the image of curry sauce. Jazir knocked it aside, angrily.

Jazir tried to be patient, he really did. The Chef's Special had never failed him before. It could surely give up the university's password. 'Come on, Father,' Jaz whispered to the screen, 'cook me a hot one, please.' That's right, he called the intruder program after his father. Well, wasn't his father the best chef in all of Rusholme's curry corridor? Wasn't his father the guardian of the secret spice mixtures? You bet your last dancing domino he was! Father Saeed Malik cooked up the spices; Jaz, the son, cooked up the info. Mutual engineering. That was the way of the world, if only his father would one day see it.

Five whole minutes of cooking it took, until the father finally delivered the goods to the son: 'Kind sir, the recipe you have ordered is called "Maximus". Enjoy your meal'. Excellent service! Give my compliments to the chef.

Jazir tapped 'Maximus' into the 'Password please?' box. The screen went dark for half a second, and then came back to life with a new menu:

**ADMINISTRATION**

**SPONSORS**

**SUBJECTS**

**STUDENTS**

**BURGERNET**

Jaz pressed on STUDENTS, got the next window . . .

**OLD**

**CURRENT**

Pressed on CURRENT, got the name? enquiry. Jaz tapped the words 'Love, Daisy' into the name box, waited for the file to download . . .

**Love, Daisy Marigold**

**First year, Mathematics**

**Date of birth: 13/2/80**

Marigold? Daisy *Marigold* Love? Jaz could only think her parents must have been raving, fucking neo-hippies-a-gogo! And it was Daisy's nineteenth birthday today! The chances of chances, most very excellent!

**Mother: Love, Marigold (née Green). Deceased.**

**Father: Love, James. Deceased.**

## Personal tutor and guardian: Hackle, Maximus.

OK, so Daisy got the middle name from her mother. Both her mother and father dead, as expected. But Maximus Hackle? That was more interesting. Jazir knew, from his contacts, that Max Hackle was the big guy at the university. Max Hackle was Daisy's personal tutor, OK, but also her guardian? Jaz had often heard Daisy talking about the professor, but never for a moment had he considered what the Max stood for. But Maximus? Which, of course, was the password into the Motherlode. So Max Hackle must have programmed the university's defence system. It made sense: Max Hackle was the best mathematician for miles around. And Jaz was suddenly smiling, because his own invention, his Chef's Special Recipe, had managed to break through the defences of the greatest mathematician. Back to the screen, pressing the mouse. A new menu, unfolding on the Love, Daisy . . .

### EXAM RESULTS
### PERSONAL HISTORY
### WORK TO DATE
### WHOOMPHY'S

Whoomphy's? thought Jaz. Why should there be a Whoomphy's listing in a student's file? Jaz pressed on it, only to find out that student Love, Daisy had consumed a grand total of only nine Whoomphy burgers since she had joined the university last September. Sad total. What was wrong with her? The burgers were listed, with dates of consumption and the type of burger consumed. Jaz was astounded to find this knowledge; it meant that part of the Whoomphy's sponsorship deal was to collect marketing data from all of the university's students. Like, the burgers were getting everywhere these days!

Jaz went back to the main menu. He wasn't exactly sure what he was looking for. Just some info on the love of his life maybe. Something, anything, everything. Whatever it took to make Daisy come out to play. He pressed on her personal history file, only to get back yet another 'Password please?' message. Sighing, Jaz typed in the Maximus code and got back another message, saying this time, 'Password unacceptable'.

Jaz couldn't see why a second level of security was necessary for a student's personal history. What was so very bad about Daisy's history that the authorities were keeping it hidden? Jaz dragged the password message over into his Chef's Special window and pressed on enter.

It took fifteen minutes to cook it out; fifteen minutes in which Jaz sent off the library fly another seventeen times. Finally, the chef came back to him: 'Kind sir, the recipe you have ordered is called Labyrinth'.

'About fucking time, Father!' Jazir typed the new password into the personal history file. He got a whole load of stuff unrolling, from the mighty Max Hackle himself; stuff about Daisy's first term, her genetic love of numbers, her worrying addiction to the bone game, stuff about how she had already been punished for late-arriving assignments. Boring stuff, not good enough. What's to hide? Jazir pressed on – into a private note from Hackle, for nobody else's eyes. 'Miss Daisy Love is a most excellent student,' it began. 'She has an acute grasp of mathematics. However, her family history leaves something to desire. I have gone along with Daisy's wishes, only because of her rare talents, but her denial of her father only brings me pain. How can I persuade her otherwise? To call your father dead, when he's very much alive, is a crime against humanity.'

'What?' Jazir moved closer to the screen.

'It's nice, isn't it?'

'What?'

Another student had sat himself down at an adjacent computer. 'A nice day for it, don't you agree?' this fellow chirped. 'A nice day for working early.'

'Fuck you, sucker.' Jazir raised his glasses for a tiny second, long enough to give the bad eye to the intruder student. 'Like, get the fuck out of here.'

The student slipped away, like a hurt lamb. Jazir turned back to the screen, only to find that the blurb had landed to feed upon pixel juice. 'Tikkashit! What do I have to do these days?' 'Play to learn, my student,' sang the fly. 'Learn to play. Study hard for the University of Manchester. Courtesy of AnnoDomino Co. Play to win!' Jazir was just about to swipe the creature away when Miss Sayer's little face appeared in an inset, smiling. Intrigued, Jazir pressed on the icon, letting the teacher's face fill the screen. The blurb was disturbed for a second, brittle wings all fluttering, but then landed again to crawl all over Miss Sayer's image as she spoke. 'Time to move. Grab the wings.' Before disappearing as simply as she had come. The vital data on Daisy also vanished with the virus. The screen went blank. The blurbfly, meanwhile, was still crawling over the dead computer, obviously confused, all whispering drowsy and user-friendly.

**RULES TO FLY**

8a. The blurbs are the property of the AnnoDomino
     Co., invented to perpetuate their messages of
     luck and hope beyond the normal channels.

8b. Blurbflies are allowed to travel the streets, buzzing
     their adverts alive and direct to the punters.

8c. Blurbs shall stand for Bio-Logical-Ultra-Robotic-Broadcasting-System.

8d. Only the Company may manufacture the blurbs. Other businesses or individuals may purchase blurbs from the Company, pre-loaded with messages and armed to the teeth, for the appropriate price.

8e. None but the Company shall know the insides of a blurb.

8f. None but the Company shall capture a blurb.

8g. If captured, a blurb may take the necessary steps to escape.

A sudden idea came to Jazir. Well, yes, a new specimen . . . how

Play to win

about that? A domino-sponsored fly; what dreams it could reveal. A million messages, flying around the city. You didn't have to pay for them, no more cheap replacements. All you had to do was reach up, just like this, grab the blurb, spicy-hot and drunk.

He squeezed the advert into a slow submission, smuggled it into his shoulder bag, wings flapping weakly now to make an escape. Game over, my buzzing beauty! Jazir turned off the computer, quite calmly, retrieved his Chef's Special from the input slot, and then left the library.

A bag of winnings.

**PLAY TO WIN**

    **PLAY TO WIN**        **PLAY TO WIN**

      **PLAY TO WIN**
      **PLAY TO WIN**    **PLAY TO WIN**

           **WIN PLAY TO WIN**

           **WIN PLAY TO WIN**

      **PLAY TO WIN**      **PLAY TO WIN**

                **PLAY TO WIN**

**E**very Saturday daytime Daisy worked part time in a bookshop. There was no one in the begging hole this morning. Most puzzling. Daisy almost always threw a little something to the young girl. The young girl with the feather in her hair. These last few Saturdays Daisy had thrown a whole *pair* of punies down into the hole, ill afforded. But so guilty about her own wasting of good money on the bones, what else could she do?

And every week the kid was waiting, eager in the hole, clutching her little card, 'Hungry and dreamless, please help'. But this week she wasn't, she wasn't there to ask for help. Strange. A begging hole was never empty.

Daisy didn't even know the girl's name, but felt an affinity with her; another young runaway, no doubt. Because Daisy had made the same escape.

Never mind, time to toil. A gruelling nine-hour shift in the Games and Puzzles Department, which had taken over more than half the shop since Manchester had won the right to test the dominoes. Daisy was tired from lack of sleep, her mind flickering with random images. Last night's assignments had been more than difficult, as though Professor Hackle was trying to defeat her with probabilities.

And then so many hours in the bookshop, in which she sold over fifty copies of *How to Win the Domino Game*, and nearly 100 copies of *Making Love to Lady Luck*. Even a kiddie's disk called *Dominic Domino, Numbernaut*. An animated bestseller.

Bone manuals. Books about the chancing at life.

Daisy was kept busy, working on empty, earning just enough for herself to pay for a week's worth of poppadoms and chutney. Maybe just enough to throw some punies away to the beggars? Sure. And maybe just enough for another domino? Sure, just a little one, maybe.

# eat to win

A big scarlet W, fluttering over a doorway, imagine. Daisy spent her Saturday's well-earned lunch hour at the local Whoomphy bar, where she shared a meal of jeezburger and econofries with another student employee at the bookshop, the young black boy who called himself Sweet Benny Fenton. Plus two enola colas. Daisy felt quite safe in Benny's company, even though he was a second-yearer. Maybe this had something to do with Benny's gay abandon and the diamond in his nose; maybe something more to do with how the boy had quite willingly bought her the meal and the juice.

'How's your love life?' he asked of her, by way of conversation.

'Oh . . . well . . .'

'Oh well? That's all?'

'Oh well, I'm too busy for love, maybe.'

'I like that maybe on the end. Look, Daisy, maybe I should do your Genetic Calculus? Maybe I'll pinpoint the little fucker who keeps you so lonely? Go on, Daze. Just a little slice is all it takes. One sliver of pain.'

'Maybe next week, OK?'

'Please yourself.' Benny shovelled another mouthful. 'What about that two-and-a-five winning last night? Fucking bastard, eh? Somebody's won an extra million.'

An in-house blurb, passed as pure by the health authorities, fluttered above the heads of the diners, singing the menu. 'The Big Whoomph! It certainly packs one! Eat to win!' Street gossip had it that the big scarlet W actually contained a pheromone message, making the viewer feel hungry.

Eat and eat and eat!

Benny gave the fly the V sign, and then washed down a chunk of meat with a gulp of cola. 'You coming to see Dopejack play tonight, Daze?' he asked. 'Frank Scenario's on the lyrics. His last gig in town. Should be a honey.'

'Not tonight, Benny. Can't afford it.'

'I can get you on the guest list, no problem. Joe Crocus will be there.'

Daisy Love had heard a thousand rumours about the third-yearer who called himself Joe Crocus: how he was the new surfer of the latest numbers, the self-proclaimed wizard of the Black Math ritual.

'Tonight I'm busy, studying. Professor Hackle is really testing me, lately. Sorry. Maybe next week.'

Maybe next week. Maybe next Saturday. Maybe all the next days of Daisy's life will be filled up with wanting; lonely wanting and patient numbers and for ever the dominoes . . .

'Maybe next week the world ends,' said Benny. 'You know, Joe Crocus let me unravel his DNA for him. That man has got no qualms, I swear to God. And you know what came up in the numbers? A fucking cancer gene, that's what.'

'Jesus. You told him?'

'Of course I told him. That's what he wanted. "Joe," I said, "Joe, you've got six years at top, before the bastard comes calling. The old Joker Bone, deep down in the marrow." You know what the man said back to me? He said, "Good." Good! Just like that. "Good, because my father died of the same. Now I know what I've got to do." Can you believe the man, Daisy? "To do what, Joe?" I asked. "To squeeze all the juice from life," he answered. All the life, all the juice. Shit! I'm sorry . . .'

'That's OK,' said Daisy. 'No apologies. Here, take my

handkerchief.'

'Thank you. I don't know why I'm crying, really I don't. I've done hundreds of unravellings. I've found goodness in there, inside the DNA; long lives, sweet innings, good dreams. Like I know I'm gonna live for ever; it's in my genes. Unless the chance-god comes calling, early. OK, the gay gene is in there, but I knew that from the age of seven, when I went behind the garages with Alan Bradshaw. But every so often, a really bad gene turns up in a reading. Usually I keep quiet about it. Usually I do. But how could I keep such deep knowledge from Joe Crocus? How could I? He means too much to me. Too fucking much. And the man accepts it, like he's won a fucking double-six domino! The man's a saint, I tell you. A fucking saint.'

Benny blew his nose then.

'Here's your handkerchief back,' he said, 'slightly stained, I'm afraid.'

'It's all right. You keep it.'

'Don't worry, Daze. I haven't got any nasty diseases. I've tested myself.'

'I wasn't—'

'Cheers. It's nice. You sure you don't want a reading done?'

'Thanks for the offer. It's just that I don't feel ready yet, to know my future.'

'The whole of life is a game of dominoes,' said Benny, chewing on a piece of meat, 'and the winning numbers are hidden in your genes, alongside the losers. Some can improve their lives by knowing the ending, others just go all weak. It's your choice, babe. Really it is.'

Daisy chewed on her own meat for a moment. 'So you don't mind having the gay gene?'

'Mind? Why in the hell should I mind about it? Oh, I know it's against the law, but it's my love destiny, OK? Straights are straight, and gays are gay. And the gays have more fun. Ain't that the truth? Why do you think I got this?' Benny was touching the diamond in his nose.

'How would I know?'

'Because it matches the one in my tongue. Good for secret stuff. You know a diamond is a fractal surface?'

'So?'

'So they vibrate with energy. Yum yum. Like feathers, leaves, wounds and coastlines. It's a mystical vibration. Good for licking.' He stuck his tongue out to prove it.

'This is Joe Crocus talking, right?' said Daisy. 'The Black Math stuff?'

'OK, so he's weird. Why do you think I love him so much?'

Benny produced a small package from his gentleman's shoulder bag. It was an aluminium box, tightly crimped. A takeaway curry box that Benny opened up to show Daisy.

'Shit, Benny. You bought a blurb?'

'That I did, only this morning. Isn't he a beauty?'

Certainly, a beauty; folded there on a bed of silver, with wings all a tremble, even whilst sleeping . . .

'How do you know it's a he?' asked Daisy.

'Well I've checked, haven't I? Males are more aggressive, don't you know?'

'Yes. But they're expensive.'

'I got it cheap. From your lovely Jazir himself.'

'It's a bootleg! Surely you're not trusting Jaz to deliver you? Don't you know his blurbs go crazy? Nothing like the real thing. Just cheap copies. They crash.'

'Nah. It's been programmed. No troubles. Scooter's a beauty.'

'Scooter? You've given your advert a name?'

'Of course I have. Aren't you a little beauty, my lovely Scooter?' Benny was actually talking to the folded-up specimen in its box, tickling its throbbing thorax. 'He's going to sing my praises from now on, Daisy, and also protect me from the slur wars. Isn't that right, Scooter?' Benny took a chunk out of his burger, pushed a half of it into his sticky mouth, and then fed the rest of it to his blurb.

'Benny . . . put the lid back on,' said Daisy, 'the waiter's looking over.'

'This fly is gonna travel wide! He's gonna send my message of gay love all over Manchester.' Benny's lips were smeared with wild ketchup.

'Put the fucking lid back on!' It wasn't often that Daisy swore.

'Homo almighty!' spat out Benny, suddenly. 'This big beef tastes like shit. I'm sure they shovel cow dung into the vats. Why do we keep on eating this crap? Can you tell me, please?'

'Because there's nothing else, except for curries?'

'Right. Chicken spicy, or beef processed. That's our lot, until the good bones come up.' He said this around a piece of gristle, which he then spat out in a rain of spittle. 'Urghhh! What the fuck is this I'm eating?' Benny's voice was a snarl of disgust as he watched the ejected chunk of meat scuttle across the table. 'Jesus Burger! I've been eating something still alive!' He raised his fork to catch the miscreant, nudging aside the blurb box, even as Daisy made a move to escape the monster meat. And that's how Sweet Benny managed to stab his fork into Daisy Love's forearm.

'Ouch!' squealed Daisy.

'Oh fuck, I'm sorry,' said Benny, jerking the fork free of her flesh. He wiped her arm with the borrowed handkerchief.

'That's OK,' apologized Daisy in the English manner.

Meanwhile, the lump of meat slid down the table's leg to the floor. A waiter came running with a net to catch the wild gristle, by which time Benny's blurb had risen from its bed of aluminium. Now the fly was hovering and buzzing, and starting to flutter its message to the world. 'Sweet Benny Fenton, he's the gayest gypsy of your genes. Let Sweet Benny unravel your destiny for a single puny. Gay to win! Gay to win!'

The diners were screaming and climbing onto the tables, as the lump of Whoomphy fat slithered away from the net. Legal additive No. 27459 making a dash for freedom. Benny's blurb dive-bombing all the customers with its advert for camp pride, which caused the Whoomphy's burgerfly to go into battle.

At which point the burgercops came storming the pavement outside in their battle-scarred meatwagon, emblazoned with the scarlet W of their sponsor, writ large. Some tight-hearted diner must've given them the tip-off on the walkie-phone, all about the gay blurb's presence. Maybe it was one of Zuze's crew, taking a small revenge for a beating. 'Time to make an exit, my dear,' whispered Sweet Benny Fenton, coming close, holding up the bloodstained handkerchief. 'Something to remember you by.' And then he was away, calling the blurb home to his shoulder, slipping out through the back door of the café.

Daisy was left alone to face the cops as they burst into the place. They had their instruments with them, their probing instruments, and they were demanding the whereabouts of the rampant gay blurb, which had violated all the regulations of health and vitality. Some nanonerd raised up his piping voice: 'The homo black boy, he went that-a-way . . .'

The burgercops followed the direction of the thinnest of all fingers.

A small aside for social historians. Burgercops are the warriors of orthodoxy. They had given in to the tightening of state budgets and allowed themselves to be sponsored. Whoomphy Burgers won the franchise on the law, ordering the cops to wear, at all times, the logo of the company. Which made the cops one easy target for assassins; all the killers had to do was focus the crosshairs on the illuminated scarlet W.

Easy game. The real cops protested, of course, but the forces of the market held true. It was laser-etched into the contract: 'No police officer shall fight the war against crime without proudly carrying the corporate symbol.'

The game goes on.

Daisy left her burger half uneaten and walked back to the bookshop on Deansgate. The begging hole was still empty. But now a dozen scowling vagabonds were clustered around the pit, as though expecting a dotfall. 'Celia, Celia!' they were chanting, each to each. Daisy pushed through them to get inside the shop, rubbing at the wound on her arm.

Whilst Jaz Malik, upon that same afternoon, was upstairs in his parents' home. Hat and shades off, computer on, dissecting the squishy body of a blurbfly. A stolen blurb full of university education: 'Learn to win! This message brought to you courtesy of AnnoDomino Co'.

At last, a real-life blurbfly!

Of course, he could've purchased such a creature from AnnoDomino itself, sure thing, if he had 1,000 lovelies to spare. But this little bugger had cost him nothing. He had it clamped in the vice on his desk. The thing was struggling for flight, but Jazir was gonna tame the monster. He had a range of copyblurb disks lying on his desk, just waiting for a personal message.

'Jazir Malik! Gadgets of love! Order to win!'

He stabbed a knife into the real blurb's thorax, some evil-smelling gunk spurted out of the wound, purple it was . . .

(Fuck! It burns!)

. . . and now the fly had twisted around in the vice, somehow constricting its body. Its little teeth had sunk into Jazir's hand.

Thunderloo!

Jazir felt the pain, clutched his hand, and went dizzy for a second. The blurb was almost free of the vice. The knife dug deep until Jazir breathed again, wiped the gunk off his face and looked at the wound in his hand, then at the blurb. Wasn't there supposed to be some coding that stopped them from biting humans? Play to win, play to win . . . an insect dying into a gasp of air.

He spliced the thing open. Inside he found only more of the evil-smelling gloop, some wires, but no mechanism of any kind. No clues as to how it flew or where it kept its message, or even how it broadcast the message. Jazir was shocked to discover himself in awe; the thing was totally organic. That's when he started to fall in love with the AnnoDomino Co. Because how the hell did they make such a wonder?

Jaz cut deeper. Muscle and wire and message-juice. Such rich meat. Maybe Jaz should introduce it into a curry one night?

Maybe make a Rogan Blurb curry out of the fly? Fried with special sauce, a new meal for his father's limited curryverse? How would the punters love that?

### ROGAN BLURB

*Ginger, garlic and ghee; put them all into a karahi. Add chunks of blurbfly, until they brown. Cardamom, bay leaves, seven cloves and a peppercorn. Cinnamon and sinnerman. Add the slogans, the secret curry paste, coriander and cumin. Add water. Bring to a boil. Cover and publicize for an hour or so. Boil away the liquid. Sprinkle with garam masala. Sprinkle with logo. Stir and serve to the public.*
*Heat Rating: media hot*

Psychedelia Smith! The punters would love it dearly. And his father the same, maybe at last admitting Jazir to his world. Jaz poured some of the gloop into a test tube and put a cork in place. He had it now, the real inner workings of a domino fly. All he needed was good analysis. Some of the gunk had splashed over a pile of computer disks. He tried to wipe off most of it, but the stuff was actually sinking into the casing. Out of curiosity, just to see if the disks could cope, he slipped one of them into his computer. It went in nice and cool, even easier than usual, like a Frank Scenario ballad number.

Meanwhile, waiting for love, a young, homeless girl was trawling St Anne's Square, hoping to make contact with a certain Eddie

Irwell, in order to cash in her domino. But the big Eddie was nowhere to be seen. His begging hole was filled up tightly instead with a rather bulbous secondary specimen.

'Is Eddie not here today?' the girl asked of the fat tramp.

'Eddie can go fuck himself,' the tramp replied. 'This is my hole now.'

'What do you call yourself, fellow traveller?'

'I'm calling myself Fats Domino.'

'Ain't that a shame.'

'What you calling yourself, smart-arse girl?'

'Can you tell me where Eddie is, please?'

'Eddie didn't turn up today. Hard cheese. This is my hole now.'

'I think you should get out of there, fatty.'

'Aren't you that famous winner of a half-bone I've heard about? Please, let me relieve you of the burden.'

'You can't claim my winnings without Eddie. No way!'

'Little Miss Celia . . .'

Another voice this time, and when Celia looked round the square, she saw that all the beggars had come over from Deansgate to surround her. 'Little Celia . . . we've got your Eddie safe and tight in bondage.'

A crusty old woman speaks up, glistening with road-juice for all to see. 'Now all we want is the half-cast bone. Surely you're not going to disappoint us? Play to win, baby. Isn't that the ruling?'

And as the tramps close in . . .

**PLAY THE RULES**

9a. The Company must always ensure that the game is played according to the rules.

9b. No purchase price will be refunded, unless rule 9a is broken.

9c. The penalty for breaking rule 9a is a private
    matter between the Company and its ruling bodies.
9d. No player may use artificial means to win the game.
9e. The penalty for breaking rule 9d is public
    humiliation, a hefty fine and a lifetime ban
    from playing this or any other game.

Play to win

Daisy Love found herself battling against a customer who wanted
a loser's discount. Every Saturday it was the same: some sad-
hearted failure would arrive with the latest guide to winning the
bones under their sweaty elbow. He or she would bang the manual
down hard on the counter, declaim, 'I've lost!' and, 'This book,
right, this book's a pile of shit! I followed all the advice, didn't win
a fucking bean!' or even, 'It shouldn't be allowed, selling such
rubbish!' Then they would invariably demand their money back,
in the loudest tones possible, so that all the other customers
could hear. The complainer, this time, was a leopard-skinned posh
woman, of passing years, complete with matching handbag and
hairdo. 'Well, young lady,' she howled at Daisy, 'are you, or are
you not, going to refund my purchase price? Because if you're
not, well . . . I shall have to have words with your manager.'

The customer was not to know, of course, that she had chosen
the wrong girl to shout at, at the wrong time of the month, on
the wrong day of the year, and with the worst kind of cut on her
arm. Luckily, the manager himself then came drawling over the
checkout desk. 'Can I be of assistance, madam?' he slurred.

'Are you the manager of this establishment?'

'The very same. Is there a problem?'

'Most certainly there is! This book . . . this pathetic tome!'
The woman nudged the book into the manager's pink and
startled face.

'It is the policy of the company . . .'

'Company policy! Don't talk to me about company policy! I
demand my consumer rights.'

'. . . never to give refunds, except for faulty goods. Is the
book faulty in any way? Are the pages printed backwards, for
instance?'

'Oh, they're printed forwards, all right! It's the advice that's
backwards. I was guaranteed a winning by this book. I staked a
whole twelve punies on this book's advice. Lost every single
specimen! Every single one! Is there no recompense for that
kind of loss? Well, is there?'

'What is the book in question, madam?' asked the manager.
'Oh yes, In for a Puny, In for a Lovely. I see it now. As written
down by the noble Sir Godfrey Arrow. I do seem to recall that
this particular writer did, once upon a few months ago, win the
first prize in the domino game. Surely that entitles him to write a
gambling manual?'

'He ought to be locked up for fraud. Now then, are you
going to give me a refund, or am I going to complain to the
Standards Committee?'

A gaggle of consumers was gathered around the checkout,
so the manager decided it was time to cut his losses. 'Very well,
under the circumstances, madam . . . would twelve punies be a
suitable recompense?'

'Plus the cost of the book, of course,' said the lady.

'Very well . . . let's call it sixteen punies. No, let's say a round and comfortable twenty. Daisy . . . would you please make this refund?'

'You're not really going to do this, boss?' asked Daisy Love.

'Certainly I am.'

'But the woman's a fucking nightmare!'

'Well I never!' said the woman.

'Daisy . . . language, please,' said the boss, 'on the shop floor.'

'She's a con-artist! Too posh even to care a jot about money.'

'Daisy!'

'Just because she lost yesterday, she's blaming us. I lost yesterday, *you* lost yesterday, the whole of Manchester lost yesterday! What makes this bitch so different that she has to claim back her purchasing price? Domino shit! Maybe *I* should start some reclaiming?'

'Daisy! Will you please make this refund!'

'No! She can go fuck herself to death in Poshtown!'

Like it was said: the wrong girl, the wrong time.

'How dare you speak to me like that?' cried the customer.

'Because you deserve it.'

'Outrageous! I shall be calling my lawyers!'

The other customers had now reached riot point and it was the manager himself who jumped into the till, scooped out the cash and presented it to the woman. 'My apologies are fulsome,' he spluttered. 'I can only hope that the kind madam will revisit our establishment at another date? Yes?' And how his tongue lolled, outwards and upwards, to lick his greasy forelock.

'May your books rot in hell!' The woman turned to leave, only to be suddenly sent flying by a small explosion of wild hair and screaming oaths. It was a young kid, a girl, running into the bookshop, out of breath and luck, in equal measures. The kid pushed the posh woman aside, bounded up to the counter, grabbed at Daisy's jacket. 'Please! Please save me!'

And with her came her companions: filthy, evil-smelling tramps, like a nightmare in germs and tatters and matted hair. A whole troop of beggars, hustlers, whores and vagabonds; they pushed aside the consumers, to form a furry circle around the checkout desk.

Daisy recognized the feather in the hair, the young beggar girl from the Deansgate pit. 'What's wrong, girl?' she asked the child.

'They want to kill me!'

'Is this true?' asked Daisy of the tramps.

'Nonsense,' one of them replied. 'It's only a game. We just want a little bone she's carrying.'

'Daisy,' asked the manager, 'are these people friends of yours?' He had already pressed the discreet cop-button.

'We're friends with everybody,' the tramp said.

'Save me from them!' shouted Little Celia. 'Please, save me!' She had now clutched herself tightly around Daisy's waist.

'Come on, Little Celia,' another of the tramps said. 'We only want the half-cast bone. Nobody need get hurt . . .'

'Keep away from me!' screamed the girl. 'You killed Eddie Irwell! He was my champion.'

'Irwell's not dead. He's just resting.'

'Get out of here,' shouted the manager to the tramps. 'And that includes you!' to the girl. 'The burgercops are on their way.' His words prompted a response from the homeless; more than anything, even more than going hungry, the homeless hated the cops. Begging could only be done from an officially paid-for hole; this was a strict law, the breaking of which delivered a full nineteen weeks in prison.

Five seconds later the cop sirens could be heard, a raucous calling from the street. The tramps scattered, fleeing by the exits.

Some of them got away, and some others got arrested, but the girl calling herself Little Celia was still clinging tight to Daisy. Daisy that didn't know what to do, how to move, how to love. 'What's your name, girl?' she asked of the last vagabond.

'Hobart, Celia, Miss,' the girl replied, backwards like an ID card. And then slipped out of Daisy's grasp, even as the manager turned on Daisy. 'Given your swearing at a most prized consumer,' he sneered, 'and given your most obvious celebration of the beggar's culture, I can only dismiss you.'

Daisy had no words, no snappy rebuttal. Her eyes were lost on the runaway.

And then, finally, Daisy said to the manager, 'Go stuff your job.'

Can you guess who won?

Well, can you?

## Play to win

Old Joe Crocus and Sweet Benny Fenton were performing their latest Black Math ritual. Joe Crocus was the focus, Sweet Benny the bait for a demon. The lights were out, curtains drawn. They had the seven candles arranged and smoking, the deep red wine poured, Schoenberg's *Verklärte Nacht, Opus 4* on the stereo system. The carpet was pulled back to reveal the floor-boards. Benny was chalking out the mathemagical diagram on the floor, large scale: the circle, the triangle, the pentagram, following Crocus's whispered instructions. Benny's newly personal blurbfly asleep on his shoulder, talon-deep and dreaming like a vulture.

Around and around, the geometry of luck.

Benny was nervous, as always; not that it might go wrong, rather that mad old Joe would get it right for once, that he might just summon up some rabid number he couldn't fully control. Black Math was a dangerous undertaking, a dark secret merely hinted at in the official histories of numberlore.

'Stop shaking, Benny!' hissed Joe. 'You're spoiling the equations.'

'Sorry, master.'

'And must we put up with that fucking fly?'

'Sorry, master. His name is Scooter, by the way.'

'Scooter? Well fuck me! Such a lovely creature.'

'Scooter's my new image, master.'

'Is it Scooter's fault that you didn't turn up for work, this afternoon?'

'No . . .'

'No? Exactly no! Can't you show me anything else but surrender?'

The truth was that Sweet Benny Fenton thought this whole ritual a waste of time, a joke, an embarrassment to a brother's soul, especially with these long, tacky black cloaks they both had to wear. Sweet Benny only joined in the game because he wanted to keep Joe Crocus sweet on his love, and now . . .

Finally the geometry was complete: all the vectors correctly aligned to their proper angles, all the shapes containing each other, all the numbers cascading inwards to the infinity symbol that lay at the centre of the diagram. Two teardrops kissing. Benny stepped into the right-hand loop of the symbol. In the other loop he carefully placed a pile of new dominoes. Seven bones in number, bought that same evening. Six bones for Joe, a lonely single one for Benny.

Joe Crocus was outside the diagram, studying his sacred

tome, the leather-bound *Mathematica Magica*. From within its rich pages he chanted a number spell. 'Oh my Lord of Infinite Numbers, come down to us now. Grace us, your pitiful calculators, with your generous presence. Oh my master, oh my Dominus of Chaos. Come down to bless these, my simple bones of offering, my humblest of chances. Oh my Darkest Fractal, may these my pitiful tokens be forever graced with your winning spirit. Open all channels. Connect to everything . . .'

Benny's blurbfly decided then to hover aloft from the shoulder, the naughty little pet, broadcasting its message to the bedroom. 'Sweet Benny Fenton, he's the gypsy of your genes. Gay to win!'

'Will you please control that advert of yours,' cried Joe. 'The ritual!'

'I'm trying my best,' replied Benny. 'I've haven't quite got the hang of the user's manual yet. Sorry, master.'

'Stop apologizing!' Joe Crocus shot out a hand, caught the blurb in mid-flight, squeezed at it until the exoskeleton cracked and the insides ran free. But there was nothing in there, no gloop, only some papier mâché and a few bits and pieces; a disk and a toy engine and a motherboard.

'Master! What have you done? You have killed my Scooter . . .'

'You bought a fake! Wait! Where are you going?'

'Out.'

'Benny! The ritual . . .'

Out. Southern Cemetery, the refuge. He always came here to escape the master's wrath. One of these days, for sure . . .

No matter. He wandered for a time or so, just enjoying the marbled names, the birthdays and deathdays, and the intense glow of the domino factory in the distance. Why was everything always in the distance?

He took out Daisy's handkerchief, looked at the stain of

blood on it, sniffed at it. He smiled. Did he really want to go dancing that night? Sure he did.

Play to win

Saturday evening, Platt Fields. Amid these bare trees and along this boating lake, surrounded by screaming kids, Daisy wandered. And as the sky grew darker with the threat of renewed rain, she found herself thinking about the beggar girl. Celia? Was that her name? And the rain fell, at last, in thin dregs.

A pair of blurbs were fighting in mid-flight in the chilly air. It was a vicious mating ritual, the crunch of mandibles, because Daisy knew that blurbs passed on their messages by biting the lover. A domino fly with a curry fly; what mutated advert would these two produce? Chicken Tikka Bones? Domino Madras?

No job. No punies for leisure. Only the shrivelled-up student sponsorship. Only mathematics. An assignment to complete for Monday morning, but no desire to finish it. The numbers suddenly went cold, too difficult. The cut on her arm. And it was her birthday, for crying out loud, with not a single present – the downfall of being hooked on loneliness. Some ducks quacked, a flap of owl dusted the air, the trees shivered their wet branches. Daisy reached into her pocket for her handkerchief, to wipe away the tears, you understand, but found no welcoming cloth. She had bequeathed it to Sweet Benny. It had her blood on it. 'Something to remember you by.' Shit! He could do a DNA analysis from that. And digging deeper, just for comfort, her fingers knocked against something hard and warm. Puzzled to pieces, she pulled out the intruder. It was a domino bone, one half of which was a dead and creamy one-spot; the other half a still black and vibrant five-pip. Pulsing with a winning half-life.

Daisy knew where she had to go.

One hour later found her banging on a door in Droylsden, North-west Manchester. 'Oh, it's you,' says her father. 'What you after?'

'You called me.'

'Did I? You'd better come in, I suppose.'

A dark-lit house, fuelled by only an anorexic gas fire. No bulbs aglowing, no cheery pictures, no rainbows. Only the single element. A couch in the living room, covered with dusty blankets. Father's bed. A saucepan beside the couch, filled with urine. His toilet. Vomit stains on the floor, amid the fallen wine bottles, the dregs and the numerous creamy bones.

Dead bones. Dead father.

'So, you're still a gambler?' asked Daisy.

'I want escape, just as much as any old sod.'

'How old are you now?'

'You don't know, Daughter?'

'Late fifties, I suppose. No. I've forgotten.'

'That's funny, so have I.'

'This place stinks!'

'That's life, Daisy.'

'No, it's not.'

'You were brought up here.'

'Brought down, more like. How did you get my number?'

'Through the regular channels, of course.'

'You called the university? They don't give out personal details.'

'Not even to a lonely father?'

'Now they'll know you're not dead.'

'And how that hurts. I couldn't believe it when the secretary told me I was officially deceased. I told her I was half alive, at the very least. I had to go higher. I had a nice little chat with your Professor Hackle.'

'He wouldn't talk to you.'

'Oh, we go way back, Maximus and I. We went to school together.'

This was news to Daisy, and she had no reply to it.

'I want another match,' her father continued. 'That's why I rang. I want you to win. That's all I live for. Let us play.' He tipped a set of twenty-eight dominoes onto a dirty table, clattering. 'Choose your bones.'

'Play to win?' said Daisy.

'You bet your life. And happy birthday, by the way.'

So, he'd remembered. But no presents.

**PLAY TO WIN**

**PLAY TO WIN**          **PLAY TO WIN**

**PLAY TO WIN**

**PLAY TO WIN**

**WIN PLAY TO WIN  PLAY**

**WIN PLAY TO WIN P**

**PLAY TO W**

**WIN PLAY TO WIN**

**PLAY TO WIN**

**PLAY TO WIN**          **PLAY TO WIN**

**PLAY TO WIN**          **PLAY TO WIN**

**D**J Dopejack worked the crowd down the Snake Lounge into a slow frenzy of cool dancing. Ten o'clock, late Saturday night.

Watch that DJ. He was using his heavy knowledge on the turntables, travelling the vinyl, turning the crowd into the most perfect equation. Movement and pleasure, making rhythm.

Joe and Benny were there, reunited to witness the frenzy from the comfort of their upper-level private alcove, fully paid for by Joe's season ticket. Newly joined together as always, watching the dance on closed-circuit television. Listening to the music over a loudspeaker system with its own volume and tone controls.

Sweet Benny turned up the volume, revelling in the beat. 'Dopejack's good tonight. Listen to that deep, cool bass, Joe.'

'I'm listening.'

Jazir Malik was down on the floor, surrounded by the noise and the crowd and the music, shot up to the ears with ultragarlic. It sure gets you hot and colourful! But where's the juice?

OK, here comes the juice, like the sky was bursting.

Frank Scenario comes on stage to a bossa nova fanfare, wearing a powder-blue demob suit, tinted glasses and a sun-coloured trilby hat. He does his famous dance, one two, one two, slide. And even Old Joe Crocus, up in his box, deigns to move his head slightly towards the booth screen, in order to hear better the coolest man still alive . . .

> *I've got the numbers in my brain*
> *That dance like shadow bright.*
> *Playing my cares along with Lady Luck,*
> *Wherever she land tonight.*

DJ Dopejack worked the samples behind the song; mixtures of Billie Holiday and Ella Fitzgerald, heavy bass stolen from a

Curtis Mayfield record. A song about giving yourself up to the circumstances, subsuming them:

> I'm just a pawn in your game, my love,
>     Just a simple man of flesh alone.
> And all the games that you play, my love,
>     Lead me only to a losing bone.

Sweet Benny was wide-eyed at the message of the lyrics. Joe Crocus, a carefully measured cool. Whilst Jaz Malik was twisting down in the clutch of dance. He had his favourite suit on, feeling good, complete with trilby hat and matching glasses. Copying Frank alive, just for the occasion, the same dance.

One two, one two, slide . . .

Whilst Daisy Love took it all in from her place on the edges; the singer and the mob and the song, and the DJ who delivered the sexy beats. Yeah, Daisy was there; she'd turned up despite her excuses, fuelled by the bad day, the ache in her forearm, the memories of her father, the losses, and the half-bone in her pocket. She'd taken a chance on Sweet Benny still keeping true about the guest-list promise. Her name had been included. The bouncer had hustled her inside, whispering, 'Free passage. Good music. Loving touch. Make a wish.'

Loving touch and a good wish? Well, she could do with some. She'd come here straight from her father's house, having lost every single game. Sad to see her once irrepressible father now shivering and sunken. She had received no love, no explanations as to why he had called her. Except that he wanted her to win, for once. Something she could never do.

Lonely girl.

So Daisy watched the whole shebang from the sidelines. And

after Frank had left the stage to loving applause, and after DJ Dopejack had slipped a fevered coupling of 'Let's Get it On' with 'My Funny Valentine' on the twin decks, she pushed her way over to the bar, where she ordered an orange juice.

That's right, an orange juice. Keeping her cool.

'Daisy, you turned up.' A voice behind her, a hand on her shoulder. Jaz Malik, smiling his silver moon against twilight. 'You're drinking orange juice, love. Can I get you some additives for that? A little vodka maybe? Vodka and orange is what Joe Crocus drinks. So I hear.'

'I'm fine. What's wrong with you?' Daisy had to come close up and cheeky in order to be heard over the music.

'Pardon?'

'You keep scratching your hand . . .'

'Just a tiny wound. No worries.'

'Snap.' They compared wounds. 'Well, whatever,' shouted Jaz in Daisy's ear. 'It's great to see you.'

'I've had a terrible day.'

'Tell me about it.'

'Is Benny here?'

'What?' Closer . . .

'Is Benny Fenton here tonight?' Daisy repeated.

'Upstairs. Private booth. You want to meet him?'

'He stole my handkerchief.'

'So?'

'It has my blood on it.'

'Big deal. Oh, I see. And he's threatening to . . .'

'Yes.'

'And you don't want him to?'

'No. But that's just the start of it. I got fired today.'

'What?' Closer, closer . . .

'I got *fired*. From the bookshop.'

'Shit, Daisy. Bad news.'

'And I got handed this.' Daisy pulled the half-bone from her pocket.

'Wow! There's your rate of exchange then.'

'You reckon?'

'I reckon you're in need of a good dance. And also some of this, maybe?'

'What?' Daisy had to move so close in order to catch Jaz's dropped-down voice; so close, it was almost like kissing. Then she saw the powder he was offering to dissolve into her orange juice. 'Ultragarlic!'

'Keep your fucking voice down, girl!' This was whispered as he poured the bounty into her drink. 'I made it special for you. A present. Beginner's mix.'

'You reckon?'

'Most definitely. It's your birthday, isn't it?'

'I never told you that.'

'Did a little research, didn't I? On the university's computer.'

'They have passwords.'

'And Jazir has the key. You really shouldn't have lied about your father being dead. That was cruel.'

'Oh.'

Daisy had never taken drugs before, but now here she was, downing her powder cocktail in one. Seeking a release from the day.

Seeking . . .

So, they danced. Jazir and Daisy. They danced the neo-cool step to Dopejack's mashed-together beats, the music of forgetfulness. The crowd went loopy, dancing like Frank, and Daisy couldn't help but mellow, especially when the ultragarlic finally kicked in. The world was so full of hazy fire, so spicy and hot, that Daisy Love truly forgot herself for a moment.

Somewhere in the darkness, Daisy kissed Jaz.

## Play to win

Outside the club, that very moment, Little Celia was staking out her abandoned shop of a home, knowing all too well that some greedy tramps might be waiting for her inside. A faint light glinted through a gap in the wooden battens covering the window. Somebody was in there.

Celia could hear the Snake Loungers' music, muffled by the walls, and over this, surely she heard a noise from within her carefully chosen home. Somebody laughing? Was some vagabond tramp laughing at her, waiting for her return, hoping to steal the prize she no longer had. After finding her naked of the bone, wouldn't they just kill her?

You bastard tramps! That's my secret house you're messing with! We're supposed to look after each other.

She didn't shout this out loud, she just thought it to herself, but the pain was real, the sense of loss, abandonment. As she walked over the road. This is my house. This is my fucking house! Celia could see that her usual hidden way had been savagely torn aside. The door was splintered, flapping wide like a mouth. Somebody coughed from inside. Celia called out, 'Who's there?' No answer, and the light within wavered and then died. 'I'm coming in now. You'd best be ready.' Why was she being so brave? Because it was her home, that's why. And the homes of the homeless are the deepest homes of all.

# Play to win

Jazir Malik banged his fist on the door of the private booth, upstairs at the Snake Lounge club. A slatted peephole slitted open, and a voice called out, 'What the fuck do you want?'

'We've come to see Joe Crocus.'

'Joe doesn't want no visitors. Bye.'

Jazir recognized the voice. 'Sweet Benny,' he replied, quickly. 'It's Jazir Malik here. I just want to shoot the breeze.'

'Go fuck the breeze.'

'I've got Daisy Love with me. She wants to talk to Joe.'

'No visitors.'

'Sweet Benny, all I'm asking is a little audience. Daisy has something good she wants to show Joe. It's about the dominoes.'

'No.'

'Benny, Sweet Benny. Have you forgotten already the favour you owe me?'

The door was finally, reluctantly, swung open. 'Come in then, you two. Be quick about it.'

Jaz and Daisy were super quick about it and, within a second's breath, the door was shut and locked and bolted behind them.

The private booth was small, mainly filled with a table, and a TV screen, a music system, both turned to low. Along one side of the table was Old Joe Crocus, his face stony like a blank bone. Benny Fenton muttered something like, 'Hutch up, Joe. Make room for the girl.' He got a scowl for his cheek.

'I'll stand,' said Daisy. 'I'm fine just standing.'

'Please yourself.'

Daisy was well out of it, to be honest; the garlic was frying her brain; the drugs, the reported music, the slight delay on the closed-circuit screen, the coldness of the company, the stupidity of that stupid kiss, the stupidity of showing the half-cast bone to Jaz.

'The professor thinks highly of your work, quiet girl.'

It took Daisy a few seconds to realize that she was being spoken to, and a few more to realize that the speaker was Joe Crocus. 'Max Hackle has told all about your probabilities.'

'Benny Fenton's got something of mine,' Daisy said.

'That's right, girl,' answered Joe. 'Benny's shown me your handkerchief. He hasn't put it through the mangle yet, so don't worry. But how come you're so worried about your precious DNA? I've had the spoonful done. I know exactly when I'm going to die. Of natural diseases. It's actually kind of peaceful, knowing it. Makes you want to exhaust your little life. So what's so special about your destiny?'

'I just want it back, that's all.'

'So then, what can you offer?'

'OK, Daisy,' said Jaz, smiling. 'Show them the gift.'

Daisy Love took the half-winning bone out of her pocket.

Little Celia pulled aside the last of the wooden battens and then stepped inside. Amidst the shadows of her former comfort, hearing a cough from faraway, over the splinters of dust.

'Who's there?' she whispered, fearful of her own voice, echoing.

'Who's there?' Her own voice, echoing, whispering . . .

Through the motes of dust and the darkness. 'Who's there?' whispering, another echo.

'Is that my little charmer?'

Daisy placed it full-square on the table. Where it pulsed and flashed. Where the half-winning five-spot winked and seduced. And where Joe and Benny and even Jazir were all drawn to the dance of all dots.

'Cookie Luck!' squirmed Benny. 'That's worth a hundred.'

'Told you so,' answered Jaz.

'What time is it?' asked Joe.

'A quarter to midnight,' answered Benny, and then to Daisy, 'You've got fifteen minutes to cash it. We can just make it to Piccadilly, if we run.'

'It's not my bone,' said Daisy.

'Whose is it then?' asked Benny.

'A young kid,' answered Daisy. 'She's called Little Celia. She's a tramp.'

'We've got to find her,' said Benny. 'Especially with all these killings of half-casters. What do yer reckon, Joe?'

Joe said nothing.

Little Celia was sitting at a battle-scarred workbench. Eddie Irwell was sitting opposite her, drinking a mug of chicken pseudo. They could hear the distant music from the Snake Lounge club. It meant nothing to them; cool music means nothing to the street merchants. Music is the tinkling of puny coins in a cup.

'You're not captured, then?' asked Celia.

'Unless I'm a ghost,' answered Eddie.

'I thought the others had caught you.'

'They let me go, a half-hour ago. I think they gave up on finding yourself and the bone. They're basically moral.'

'They didn't hurt you?'

'I said basically, didn't I? I'm not excusing them. To more important matters; we can still make the winning post, Celia. Let's see the good bone.'

'I haven't got it.'

'What's that?'

'I gave it away.'

'Away? Who to?'

'A stranger.'

'What? Why so?'

'I thought you were dead, Eddie. Or something . . .'

'There is no something other than death. Now where's the bone? Where the fuck is it? And stop twiddling with that feather!'

'How could I dare to let the others take our winnings?' Celia said. 'So I slipped the bone into the pocket of this woman.'

'Woman. What woman? Where is she?'

'I don't know. I don't know where she is.'

Daisy Love, where she was, only a few yards away. All eyes around the Snake Lounge table were glued to the barely alive dots of the domino. As the clock drained away in seconds towards midnight.

'I told you the Daisy had something to show,' said Jazir. 'Didn't I, Joe?'

Joe said to Daisy, 'You said the real winner was a young girl?'

'About eight years old,' replied Daisy. 'Something like that.'

'Eight years old!' said Benny. 'That mean's she's . . .'

'That means she's too young to buy the bone herself,' carried on Joe. 'Which means that somebody else bought the bone for her. We're not even looking for the winner. Sweet Benny, what time is it?'

'Five minutes to shutdown.'

'Shit. OK. We lost. Give Daisy what she wants.'

'But Joe? Hackle said . . .'

'Never mind that. Give it up.'

Reluctantly, a blood-stained handkerchief was handed over a table.

At the Piccadilly winner's enclosure, a gang of hopefuls were gathered. Some of them were of the rightful fifty-nine winners of a half-prize, but most of the tribe were just voyeurs of the prizegiving, hoping to make a mugging. That's why the burgercops were standing guard, fully loaded, on the pay-out orifice.

Even as Eddie Irwell berated Celia for giving away the winning bone. 'How the fuck could you?' he cried. 'That was our ticket out of the mess.'

'I was scared, Eddie. Anyway, you'd only spend it on burgers and booze.'

'That is most unfair.'

'We can buy another bone, can't we?'

'There she blows,' said Eddie. 'Game over.'

The siren sounded all over the city as midnight struck. Daisy's half-a-bone on the table, faded from a ripe five to a cold and heartless cream for the uncollected.

'Game over,' said Benny.

'Can I go now, please?' asked Daisy.

Benny opened the booth door, Daisy slipped away.

'Fucking bastard dominoes,' said Joe. 'One of these days . . .'

'One of these days, what?' dared Benny.

'I'm gonna break these bones in two!'

'Will you let me join now, Joe?' asked Jaz. 'The Black Math club? Haven't I earned it yet? Bringing you a half-bone? I can help.'

'Fuck off! OK!'

'Yes, Joe. Right away, Joe. OK, Joe. So you won't be wanting this, then?' He was waving a test tube around, inside which some kind of purple, sluggish grease moved slowly.

'What the fuck's that?' asked Benny.

'Let me explain.' Jazir smiled.

PLAY TO WIN

PLAY TO WIN                    PLAY TO WIN

PLAY TO WIN
                    PLAY TO WIN

WIN PLAY TO WIN  PLAY

WIN PLAY TO WIN P

PLAY TO W

WIN PLAY TO WIN

PLAY TO WIN

PLAY TO WIN          PLAY TO WIN

PLAY TO WIN                    PLAY TO WIN

# Game 43

**B**one Day. Pippy old Dotchester, game 43. Rabid natives, making wild honey to the televert, with slippy brains as the chimes came floating, a fog of numbers. A smoke of dominoes, forever changing their leopardness. On wings of breath, the blurbflies, dreaming in download. Singing the streets, alive with libido.

Mating on the wing, biting to propagate.

Play to win! Play to win!

And all over the city that sticky, wet Friday, three hours from clampdown, surrounded by burgerwrap and porno-stain, there was only one big, happy horde of punter-bone. One big mass of gamble, creeping towards nine o'clock, clacking its tiny chance. Garage slab, gravestone, wedding bed. Watching the dots pulsate.

> It's domino time! Dribbling domino time! **Blurbflies**
> Dom, dom, dom, dom, domino time!

As the players sacrificed some dumb animals to the pagan gods of chance. And so many adverts now clogged up the streets, it was like living in blurb soup.

Mr Million had deemed it so. Play to win! Play to win!

A pair of flies, banging against a window in Rusholme. The Golden Samosa, upstairs flat. Focus. Inside . . .

Daisy with her tiny handful of no luck. Yeah, *no* luck. She hadn't bought this week. Her first time ever of not playing. Her assignments were suffering, leaving much to be desired. '*Much to be desired*,' Max Hackle had written.

> Pitch your chances, make a wish,
> Dream a dream and make for bliss.
> Lady Luck, come kissy kiss kiss!

**Blurbflies**

No thanks, said Daisy. She returned to her work. This was her real life; numbers, probabilities and why life was a game with no winners. If the other players would only realize this, there would be no more money wasted, no more killings. Just to satisfy herself, she did a quick calculation of exactly how much money could be saved, if nobody played at all.

OK, fine words, fine numbers, but why then did she have the television on, and why couldn't she stop turning to see the outcome?

To gloat, her answer would be, if Jazir was there.

And that was another reason for her going bone-free; she hadn't seen her friend since last Saturday's dance. That Joe Crocus and his pathetic hangers-on, that Black Math crowd; they were all madmen, obsessed with trifles. Daisy wasn't obsessed, she wasn't. Just another little look at the television, that's all.

Tommy Tumbler was stirring the city into a frenzy and Jazir still wasn't here. She was missing him. Despite his stupid hat and glasses, and his garlic and his stolen kiss, she was missing him.

For Jazir, take another blurbflight down from Rusholme, along the Wilmslow Road for a mile or two, until reaching West Didsbury. Float over the cemetery. You're very near home, little blurbfly, but don't get excited; it's not the Hive of Chances you're aiming for, your shift isn't over yet. Instead, turn right. Barlow Moor Road, that's the one. See the house, the third one along, with the upstairs light, the faint flickering light. OK, that's your target. Fly to the window. Focus. Inside . . .

Candlelight and cathode glow. Four various men, playing their various games around a television set. The set is in the middle of the room, at the centre of a series of geometrical shapes on the floor. One man is cross-legged in front of it, his black skin dancing with dots of chance. Is that a domibone he holds against the screen? A second man, taller, older, is pacing around the television carrying a large black book. He appears to be mumbling. Could he be chanting, maybe? The third man is sitting at a computer screen, on which Cookie Luck is also dancing, along the Burgernet. His fingers move like a swarm over the keyboard. Does he have green hair? He does. The last man is working at another computer. He has a hat (a trilby?) and a pair of glasses (cKs?) This guy isn't working the keyboard, he's just gazing at the screen. Is he dancing, slowly, gently, in tune with Miss Cookie Luck?

There's your Jazir, and Daisy was still missing him.

She gave up her work, gave in to the television, the dance to see which numbers won. Sure, just for research you understand, to see if one of the more unusual combinations came up. But that just made her think about that girl, that lucky/unlucky girl who had given her the half-bone last weekend. Daisy hadn't seen her since then, and she couldn't stop thinking . . .

Another blurb! Quickly! Take us to a district called Gorton, West Manchester. Once thriving, then dead, now a half-alive wasteland studded with all-night burgerbars catering to the all-night cinema complexes. A few old-style public houses here and there, buttressed, and a dingy row of shops, catering to the drunks. Find the last TV shop in that row, zoom in . . .

A young kid sitting on the shoulders of a big bear of a man, both of them staring at a lonely, barely alive TV screen. Beggars, therefore. Both of them fixated upon the bones in their hands. There are no other beggars around, so the child must actually be happier on the giant's shoulders. The blurb descends to buzz around the young girl's head. 'Get off me, you nasty fly!' she mutters at the bug and bats it away, not daring for a second to miss the last seconds of Cookie Luck's dance.

There's your Celia, and Daisy was still thinking about her as nine o'clock chimed . . .

A two! Another two!

. . . to a standstill.

The double-two. The way the cookie lovingly crumbles, once in a million games. Game over. Manchester cries. Shock and despair. 'Somebody, somewhere,' called out Tommy Tumbler from the city's screens, 'just won themselves a day in the House of Chances!'

But none of our chosen players, alas.

Daisy smiled and congratulated herself on not having played that week. Of course, there was always the feeling of 'dominoid': what the punters called the feeling that you might well have won, if only you'd played. Especially when a double comes up . . .

**PLAY THE RULES**

10a. Not all of the dominoes are equal. Some bring greater prizes than others.

10b. Any winning domino whose pips add up to a lucky seven — the one-and-six, the two-and-five, the three-and-four — allow the winner to claim an extra million lovelies on top of the normal prize.

10c. The double-one domino allows the winner a pair of seats at the next live staging of the domino game.

10d. The double-two allows the winner a day within the domino's headquarters, where they might witness the fair and scrupulous preparation of the next week's game.

10e. The double-three allows the winner to wear with pride a genuine Lady Luck costume, fully functioning with dancing dots, custom-tailored to fit, whether male or female.

10f. The double-four allows the winner to appear on television during the next domino game, close enough to stare at Cookie Luck even as she dances the numbers wild.

10g. The double-five allows the winner actually to dance with Cookie Luck, live on television and all over the city.

10h. The double-six of dominoes is the ultimate prize; like a court card and an ace in the game of pontoon, it allows the winner to become the new Mr Million.

10i. The double-six is a prize beyond all reckoning. The chances of winning it should be meaner than any other combination.

10j. The double-zero of dominoes brings the winner a prize of mystery, which shall be deemed a bad prize, the so-called Joker Bone. The nature and the exact detrimental effect of this prize shall remain secret until the actual winning.

Play to win

The following Monday, Daisy reached college early. Grabbing a coffee from the refectory, she carried it carefully to the library, where she handed her student's ID to the librarian, a certain Miss Crimson. Daisy got clearance and walked through to where a bank of computers were lying idle, only waiting for a student's button-touch. As the Whoomphy Burger graphic played itself out, she looked over her assignment notes: 'What are the chances of winning first prize in the AnnoDominoes, when only 75 per cent of the gamblers are playing to win? Solution to be delivered by

Monday, at the very latest. (That includes you, Ms Love!)'

Monday already, and Daisy was panicking. She'd spent all Saturday night and the whole of Sunday working on it, getting nowhere, because the question raised so many further problems. It was the first time the professor had directly referred to the dominoes. But more than that, what did he mean when he said that only 75 per cent of the gamblers were playing to win? Surely all the gamblers were playing to win? And how could the actual number of players affect the outcome? Weren't the dominoes a game of chance alone? Wasn't 'Play to win' just a blurbfly's mating slogan, designed to increase the takings?

So many questions. Like, what exactly did Professor Hackle know?

OK, only the university's computer could find it out, maybe.

Daisy opened up a window, into which she pulled the library's database and asked for the 'Mathematics Dept: Documents'. On a keyword searcher she typed in 'play to win'. Pressed on the button.

Bingo! Results . . .

Fifty-two papers had been published containing the 'play to win' words. She scanned the titles, and decided that 'The No-Win Labyrinth: A Solution to Any Such Hackle Maze' sounded the most interesting, mainly because of the words 'Hackle Maze' in there. The paper was first published in 1968, in a mathematical journal called *Number Gumbo: A Mathemagical Grimoire*, and written by a certain Hackle, Maximus. Wasn't that what her father had called Hackle? Maximus? So he did go to school with him. And magical mathematics? What was going on here, with her fabled professor; was he a student of the Black Math ritual? Number Gumbo? OK, so this was way back in '68, and no doubt the prof had been a raving hippy, but still . . .

Out of curiosity, she studied the titles and authors of some of the other papers the search had found. Sure enough, all fifty-two of them were written by Hackle, all of them published in the Sixties and Seventies. All of them called things like 'Twisted Hackle Paths and Other Such Wanderings'; 'The Trickster Virus, its Effect upon Play'; 'Maze Dynamics and DNA Codings, a Special Theory of Nymphomation'; 'Sealing the Maze, the Theseus Equation'; 'Lost in the Love Labyrinth'; 'Becoming the Maze, a Topology of Virgin Curves'; and even 'Fourth-Dimensional Orgasms and the Casanova Effect'.

Daisy just had to try that last one.

But no matter how hard Daisy pressed to open up the file, all she got back was a 'no access' message. She tried at least another twenty papers, the same no-go coding each time. What? The professor was keeping his secrets tight?

Only one paper opened to her touch. It was called 'The Bifurcation Less Travelled', published in 1979. As the screen filled with words and numbers, Daisy felt that the paper was choosing her, rather than the other way round, especially when she read the opening lines: 'The Hackle Maze may be navigated successfully only by choosing to be lost. The best wanderers will subsume themselves to the maze, thereby becoming the pathways.'

Digging deeper in the text she saw this: 'To play to win a Hackle Maze, all the various wanderers must actively fall in love with the puzzle. Every player is dependent on every other.' And then this: 'In the lover's labyrinth, there are no winners without losers, this is the ruling.' Again and again she saw the strange word nymphomation, used to denote a complex mathematical procedure where numbers, rather than being added together or multiplied or whatever, were actually allowed to *breed* with each other, to produce new numbers, which had something to do with 'breeding ever more pathways towards the goal'. Daisy had never

heard of this procedure, never mind 'having the courage sometimes to take the bifurcation less travelled'.

What was the professor on, way back then? Some crazy,
mind-altering drugs, no doubt. He never mentioned any of this
stuff in his lectures. Lost in the love labyrinth, indeed! Mind you,
from a quick scan of the equations, it looked like real high-level
mathematics. Beyond her horizon. The professor cultivated a
shadowy figure in the university, and these lost pages hinted at
further depths to the shadows.

She wanted to study this further, but the computer refused to
save the file to floppy. It wouldn't even let her print a hard copy;
apparently she could only read the file on screen. Again, that
feeling of being dragged in by the text. The screen seemed to
be scrolling without her help, unless her hand had slipped . . .

A blur of numbers travelling downwards, faster than the eye,
becoming one long equation, without beginning or end . . . to
stop. Dead! On the following line: 'Exactly 22 per cent of the
wanderers must play to lose themselves, in order for the real
winner to flourish. The relevant equations follow . . .'

Daisy Love kept her chanting to herself, as per usual, even as
the new equations fell like complex rain. She didn't want to
question what had happened, not yet, just to go with it, while
she could. OK, work on this; let's say the professor isn't just mad,
let's say he really believes in this nonsense. All we need do is
reverse the ratio: 78 per cent of players had to play to win for one
of them to claim first prize. But the professor's question stated
that only 75 per cent of the punters had been playing to win.

Which means that *nobody at all* should have won. Surely the
professor was wrong.

The professor could never be wrong.

Daisy opened a new window to type up her answer. This was
surely the easiest assignment in the world. 'The chances of

winning first prize in the AnnoDominoes, when only 75 per cent of the punters are playing to win, are *zero*.'

She printed out a copy and then wired the textfile to max@uniman.burger., and spent the rest of the morning attending a boring lecture about Random Topology, during which her mind drifted. She already knew most of the knotted stuff anyway, instinctively, and deep inside she couldn't stop thinking about the paper she had just delivered. She was nervous, elated, thrilled, and rather too anxious that no other student should find the correct answer.

Daisy knew that Max Hackle would take the assignments home with him that evening, that it would take him at least until Wednesday to mark them. But Daisy couldn't wait that long. She had to know if she'd got the answer right.

Lunch, finally. Daisy had brought sandwiches with her, astrocheese, because no way was she touching a Whoomphy after Benny's had come alive, right in front of her. She ate alone, as usual, working in an exercise book. A few tables across, a crowd of students were gathered around as Joe Crocus and Benny and Dopejack held court. Further away, another crowd gathered around Nigel Zuze's table. They all need something to believe in. Daisy ignored them. She ignored everybody. Only Max was interesting enough. Oh God, maybe she was falling in love with the old man.

Sure enough, when she checked her pigeon-hole after lunch, there was a note waiting for her.

'Ms Love. My office, straight away. Skip lectures. Max H.'

It was almost like a love letter.

Play to win

'Now then, about this paper of yours.'

'You've marked it already, sir?'

'Well, it's not difficult to mark, is it? What . . . two lines long. It's certainly the shortest answer I've ever received. Apart from 'Please sir, the dog ate my homework', but that was ages ago. Tell me about your workings, please?'

'Well, I . . .'

'Go on.'

This was the first time Daisy had been inside this office; this large brown office of brown carpets and brown furniture. Max's hair, still thick and brown, his jacket of brown tweed. All the books, along every brown wall, were lined in brown leather, and the titles were dizzying.

'I'm waiting, Ms Love.'

'I . . .'

'Yes?'

'Well I was curious, Professor.'

'Good. I like that.'

'About your mention of playing to win?'

'Oh yes?'

'Because I'd always thought the dominoes were a random game?'

'You have decided otherwise?'

'It was at your urging, sir.'

'More.'

'Well, I was curious. So I looked inside the database. I found your paper about choosing the bifurcations in Hackle Mazes. It mentioned a play-to-lose equation. I reversed it out and obtained a play-to-win.'

'I see.'

'It was very interesting.'

'Hm hmm.'

'Especially the equations about something called nymphomation.'

'Ah yes.'

'It was the only paper I could access. Why did you hide all your other works? Wait! I get it. This week's assignment could only be answered with access to your papers on nymphomation and love labyrinths. To make it even harder, you hid all but one of the references. Crafty!'

'Very good. Except it's the other way round; my work on nymphomation is always out of bounds. It is dangerous knowledge.'

'OK, so you let one file loose, just so your students could possibly find it.'

'Not just any old student, Ms Love.'

'You chose me! The computer—'

'I mean that only you received the play-to-win question. The rest of them were given a rather simple task involving Chaotic Economics.'

'But we could've compared notes?'

'Ah, but you never do. Isn't that right? Too jealous.'

'But . . . but why? Why me?'

Professor Hackle got up slowly from his desk, walked over to the window of his office. When he finally spoke, without even looking at Daisy, his voice was quiet, almost to himself. 'Look at them all, down there, making their way to lectures, carrying their assignments. Students! Glorious students! The city would be quite dead without the September intake.' Finally he turned around to look directly into Daisy's eyes. 'Youth, Daisy! Young people! How keen they are, how eager to learn!'

It was the first time he had ever called her Daisy.

'Hundreds of new students, every year, every one of them with a dream, a hope; a dream of learning. Oh, I know, most of them are deadbeats, but perhaps a small percentage will go on to discover something new. A new shape, a new map. A new way of counting the universe. That's my job in life, Daisy, to nurture the best. I believe you could be such a student. Would you like to be?'

Daisy nodded; it was all she could manage.

'Good. I'm initiating a new project: I intend to break into the AnnoDomino game system. And I'd like you to be part of my team.'

'But nobody's ever—'

'I trust you've noticed the similarities between my work and the game?'

'You think somebody's stolen your work? Mr Million, perhaps.' Daisy was keeping her voice steady, just about.

'Perhaps,' Hackle said. 'Or else we're both coming from the same place.'

'So you'd like to win, to get your own back? And you're prepared to cheat. I'm not sure I can—'

'It has nothing to do with winning. I have all I need. Nor with pride.'

'So, what then?'

'I want to find this Mr Million and destroy the dominoes. It is my duty.'

'It's just a game. I don't understand.'

'Come round here.'

Daisy walked around the desk, where Hackle was punching keys on his computer. Daisy's paper vanished under a list of names. 'These are all the half-winners so far,' he pointed out, 'listed with the number of times they have won.'

'Isn't that classified information?' Daisy asked. 'You can learn who has won, but not how many times.'

'It is quite easy to break in at such a low level. Now, as you can see, the vast majority have won only once, which we would expect from the laws of chance. However, here, and here, you see? Some of them have won twice on the half-casts.' A key-press separated a few names from the hundreds that were scrolling downwards. 'Ten of them, to be precise. This is straining the probability envelope, don't you agree, given the short—'

'I know one of those names,' said Daisy.

'You do?'

'Yes. Edward Irwell . . .'

'You know him?'

'No. I just know the name. Don't ask me where from. It rings a bell, you know?'

'Try to remember, please. It could be important.'

'It is strange that so many have won twice,' said Daisy. 'From a rough guess, I'd say one or two, at the very most, should be the score.'

'Of course. Let's call it a freak blip. But could we claim the same for this result?' Hackle had dragged another two names from the winners' list. 'Janice Albright. Gerald Henson. These two players have both won three half-casts.'

'No. That's impossible.'

'Is it? You saw from this week's assignment that the dominoes don't always follow the rules. Somehow, the play-to-win factor has been increased.'

'Only if it's true that the game is based on your own work.'

'Very well. Let's say I'm mistaken. Here's another list for you.' Another key-press opened a new window. 'These are the people who have been murdered because of the game, the so-called jealousy killings. Fifteen players, all found clutching a half-winning domino. Study them, if you will.'

Daisy did so. The two names jumped out at her.

'I don't understand.'

'It's very simple. The two people who have won three half-casts, Albright and Henson, have both been killed. What are the chances of that? Another freak blip?' Hackle turned off the computer. 'This week's assignment was merely to focus your attention on the fate of the half-winners. What do you think?'

Daisy went back to her seat. 'OK,' she said. 'The very fact they have half-won three times is what drove the killers into action. Jealousy, magnified.'

'Maybe. In the meantime I shall be trying to locate the ten who have won twice already. If one of them wins again, and is subsequently killed, would you still be so sure?'

'What are you saying? That the AnnoDomino is killing them?'

'Yes, I think so. Under the cover of jealousy killings. The police are no use, of course, being in the pocket of the game.'

'Isn't this bad for Mr Million's image? What does he gain?'

'You have heard of the lucky bleeders, I presume?'

'The natural-born winners? Sure. You think they really exist?'

'How else do you explain people winning three times? If you were Mr Million, what would you do? Let them go on winning? No. Of course not. AnnoDomino would rather breed out the good luck. And that means killing the carriers. You see now, the urgency of the matter. Should I stand aside and let more innocent people die? Well, should I?'

Daisy thought about this for a moment, trying to accept it, but always running away from the outcome. It wasn't her kind of world being described. Where were the laws of mathematics in this? She had nothing to fall back on, nothing to guide her. Numbers, for sure, but just a total of the dead. Hackle was talking about murder!

'I'm not sure about this, Professor.'

'Of course. I understand. It is only the beginning . . .'

'But nobody knows who Mr Million is. The security is a government-level system. It's unbreakable.'

'There are ways. And regarding Mr Million . . . I already know who it is.'

'You do?'

'I think so.'

'Do I get to find out?'

Hackle stared at Daisy for a few seconds, as though working her out, a tangled equation, and then spoke.

## Play to win

I was a terrible child, keen to do the worst of all things, never the best. Blame it on my upbringing, if you will, or else my place of birth. Or else the time of birth, 1941, conceived by the war. I make no such excuses. I was a self-made brat, only interested in myself. Fuck the world, that was my most complex statement, and believe me, I knew such words at the age of four. Primary school was a disaster zone with me around. If I couldn't learn, why should anybody else. Not that the teachers cared, they were the bottom of the pile themselves, working in this God-awful dump of a school in Droylsden. Nobody cared about us, you see? That's the key to what happened later. Nobody cared if we all failed and beat each other up in the process. I can honestly say that by the time I was seven and ready to go to junior school, my knowledge of the world was limited to the end of my nose. I could barely write my own name, never mind add up a series of simple numbers. The funny thing is, I wasn't anywhere near the worst pupil in class, but more of that later.

Junior school didn't help. The teachers there probably cared less about us than the primary teachers. I guess, having reached that age without an ounce of knowledge, we were already marked down as factory fodder, or potential beggars. I honestly can't remember much of the first year, only the intense pleasure of escaping into the summer holidays. I was in two minds about going back, I can remember that. The whole thing seemed so pointless. Only my dad's threat of the strap persuaded me to turn up on the first day of second year. I was put in this class called 2c, and the first thing we knew, the headmaster came in and told us we had a new teacher starting today, and that she was going to look after us. We were going to make her life hell, more like. After all, that's why our last teacher left. Anyway, the head introduced us to this Miss Sayer, who was fairly young for a teacher. She must have been in her late twenties, I suppose. Nobody knew where she came from, or why she'd chosen this particular job. Punishment, most probably, for some earlier crime. The headmaster leaves us to it.

Miss Sayer just stared at us for a while, and then smiled at us, and some girl started giggling. She didn't even say hello, or ask us to call out our names. Her first words were these, and I shall never forget them: 'Who can tell me how many children there are in this classroom?' This must have confused us a little because some of us even tried to look round to work it out. I was one of them, even though the highest number I could count to was thirteen. 'Has anybody got an answer for me?' Nobody had. 'Very well, I shall tell you myself. There are twenty-eight children in this classroom. Now, has anybody ever played a game called dominoes?' That was easier. Most of us put up our hands. 'Good.

Because I've brought a set of dominoes with me.'

I think we were all a bit puzzled by now, or else expecting an easy ride. Games were what you played in primary school, surely. Then she started to count the dominoes out loud as she lay each one, face-down, on her desk. 'One . . . two . . . three . . . four . . . five . . . six . . .' and so on, all the way up to twenty-eight. 'Now isn't that interesting? If anybody ever asks you how many children there are in your class, you can tell them there's the same number as there are pieces in a domino set. Won't they be impressed? They will be, because *they* won't know how many pieces there are in a domino set. So you'll have told them the right answer, without telling them the answer.'

By this time some of us were getting pretty excited. But the next thing she did was even stranger. She had all twenty-eight of the dominoes face-down on her desk, and she shuffled them all around, like this, so we couldn't know which was which. Then she asked us to come up and choose a piece at random, any piece we liked. 'But choose carefully,' she said, 'because this will be your number from now on until you leave me. OK, who wants to choose first?'

There was a slight pause and then one of the girls came forward, Susan Prentice, if I remember correctly. She chose a domino and Miss Sayer asked her to say its numbers out loud to the class. 'It's a five and a blank,' said Susan. 'Good, but we shall call the blank a zero from now on.' 'Five-zero,' said Susan. And so it went on, some of the more eager kids getting up for their dominoes and calling the numbers out loud: Four-one. Six-two. Three-one. Four-three. Two-two. Miss Sayer stopped us for a moment here, to explain that the double dominoes were special, and she gave the kid who had chosen it a chocolate bar. Well, after that we were all keen to get up there and find those other doubles.

A few more kids got to choose, until Miss Sayer stopped one singing boy in his tracks. 'Can anybody tell me', she asked, 'which domino this boy will choose?' That was a question without an answer, because how could we possibly know. But somebody shouted out anyway, 'Six-six!' just guessing. It was Paul Malthorpe who shouted it. Remember, I told you earlier there were kids worse than me in the class, well I meant Paul Malthorpe. This was the first time I had ever heard him respond to a teacher's question. We were friends and enemies, at the same time, in that special way that can only happen at that age. But Paul was tougher than I was, and more popular with the other kids, especially that Susan Prentice I mentioned. She was the beauty of the class. I was more of a loner, I suppose. Anyway, Miss Sayer then asked what the chances were that the next boy would choose the double-six domino. None of us had a clue what she was going on about.

'OK, how many dominoes are there in a set?'

'Twenty-eight, miss,' someone shouted.

'Good. So how many chances are there of choosing any single domino?'

There was silence for a while, and then a quiet voice from the back whispered, 'Twenty-eight, miss.'

'Excellent. We call this twenty-eight to one, and we write it like this.' She wrote the ratio on the board.

'It's just like me dad, miss,' said Paul, 'with his horses. Twenty-eight to one, the rank outsider.'

There was some laughter at this, as there always was for Paul. But what really struck me was his sudden enthusiasm. And he'd called her *miss*, for crying out loud. That never happened! Of course, Miss Sayer was full of praise at this connection, and she played upon it, asking Paul what the chances were, therefore, of the next boy choosing the double-six? 'Twenty-eight to one,' Paul immediately answered, proud as anything.

'Can anybody tell me why this is wrong?'

Nobody could, not for a while anyway, until somebody dared to answer. 'Because there aren't twenty-eight dominoes left?'

'That's right. Those with dominoes already, please hold them up. How many is that?'

'Twelve.' An answer.

'Subtract twelve from twenty-eight . . .'

'Fourteen.'

'Nearly.'

'Sixteen.'

'That's right. There are sixteen dominoes left to choose from. So what are the chances, Paul, of the next one being six-six?'

You could almost hear Paul's mind working away as he struggled with the concepts, until: 'Sixteen to one!' he shouted.

'Good. The odds are shortening, as your father might say.'

'He does! He does say that!'

'OK. Carry on choosing. Play to win.'

The poor boy we were talking about didn't get the six-six, of course, and you could see from his face that he felt cheated. I think he was crying, believe it or not. But as more and more of us chose, every so often, Miss Sayer would ask us to call out the current chances: twelve to one, nine to one, six, five, four, three to one, until there were only two dominoes left. It was Paul and I, of course, who had waited so long to choose, still vying against each other, even in the game. Both of us knew the double-six was up for grabs, alongside some measly normal domino.

The class went quiet, that special quiet just before a fight was about to break out. This was another thing Miss Sayer managed, releasing the violence through the game. We didn't know that at the time, of course, too hung up on competition. 'Who wants to go first?' she asked. I thought, let's get this over with, so I stood up, but Paul jumped in and made his claim. He knew by now that it didn't matter who went first, but the idea of not choosing, i.e. just *picking up* the last domino, I think it would have been too weak for him. He sauntered up to the desk, putting his best walk on, picked up his choice, looked at it, smiled, looked at me, just the once, then whispered the numbers to the class. It was an anti-climax, obviously, for me to do that long walk to my designated numbers. I never got to choose you see. I had the leftovers of Paul Malthorpe, but just as I was reaching for the last domino, Miss Sayer stopped my hand.

She wrote a long word on the board, and told us that we had started to learn about it. Probability. The mathematics of chance. Then she told us she was going to ask a question, and the first person to get it right could go on their break early. We were all excited by now, and I could see Paul grinning at me from his desk, that evil grin he used just before a killer punch. He was sharpening his pencil, dusting a new page down for the question, but Miss Sayer told him to close the book. 'There will be no pen and paper used in this lesson,' she said. 'You must use your heads. Is everybody concentrating? Very well. Who can tell me what this last domino is? Children . . . play to win!'

Immediately panic set in.

I was still standing at the front of the class. From that position I could see the look of fear creep over every kid's face. Someone on the front row stood up then, and that started a stampede. They were all up and running around in circles, banging into each other, trying their best to find a pair of numbers that none of them had. It was chaos. Paul was actually going round stealing dominoes off the weaker kids, hoping to stockpile his own little abacus, with one missing piece. 'We've got to work together,' he shouted, by way of justification. He was only helping himself to the answer. Cheating, in other words. The strange thing was, Miss Sayer didn't seem to mind this behaviour. She was smiling at the chaos she had created.

She was smiling at me. It was as though she was inside my head, guiding me to the answer. Maybe that was only my brain hurting with this sudden onslaught of numbers, but something definitely happened that day, something I still can't explain, even after all these years.

'Two-zero.' It just came to me. I whispered it first. And then louder, and then louder still. 'I think it's the two-zero domino, miss.'

Maybe I'd been subconsciously counting the dominoes as they were chosen. Maybe. I don't know.

'OK everybody!' The teacher clapped her hands for quiet. 'This child thinks he has the answer. Tell us, please.'

'It's the two-zero domino,' I repeated.

'Bollocks!' That was from Paul, of course.

I lifted up the last domino and turned it over in my hand . . .

'He peeked! He peeked at it, miss!' Paul again, coming forward to see for himself.

'No. I was here. I kept my eye on him. Not everybody needs to cheat, double-six. Well done, two-zero. You may go to break now.'

I gave a whoop of delight, right in Paul's face, and ran out of the door. There were only fifteen minutes left till official break anyway, but I didn't care. I'd won! Domino! At last I'd won over Paul..I was the master, and I couldn't stop laughing all the way down the corridor.

Play to win

'You know what happened then, don't you, Daisy?'

'You went back?'

'Yes. I did. I stopped at the doors to the playground. I couldn't stop thinking about what I might be missing. What was Miss Sayer teaching the other kids without me being there. What were the dominoes doing now? I'd won, but I'd lost. So I went back, and that was the start of it. The start of my career.'

'And you think this Paul, what was it . . .?'

'Malthorpe.'

'You think he's the Mr Million?'

'The thing is, we all became rather good at mathematics that year. Miss Sayer was very special. She taught us to play a mean game of dominoes, and during the play we'd be fed the principles of higher maths. She didn't treat us like imbeciles, you see. She didn't teach us adding up and subtraction; she started off with probability and combination theory, disciplines like that, and left the basics to seep down from the top.'

'It could have been any one of you.'

'Possibly. I have here a printout of all twenty-eight pupils. Myself; Two-Zero. Prentice, Susan; Five-Blank. Malthorpe, Paul; Six-Six. The team will need to check on them all, but my money's on Paul. You know the prize for winning the double-six AnnoBone?'

'You get to become Mr Million.'

'That's typical of Malthorpe. He loves the dangerous bet. And consider this . . .' Hackle pointed out another name on the list. 'Horn, George; Zero-Zero. He was the runt of the class, Georgie Horn. A skinny little thing, all buck teeth and inane giggles. Slightly subnormal. Looking back, I guess we were very cruel to him, the names we called him and the things we did. Malthorpe was the worst, of course, but I stand guilty as well. So when

Georgie chose the double-zero domino, it raised a terrible laugh from the whole classroom. Miss Sayer tried to tell us that the double-zero was one of the most important numbers, but we were having none of that. The strange thing is, as soon as he won that number, Malthorpe took Georgie under his wing. They became a partnership, the double-six and the double-blank. It was perfect, and another example of what was going on in that classroom. It couldn't just be chance, considering the Joker Bone.'

'Let me see that list,' said Daisy.

Hackle handed the paper over to her. She looked down the names for a few seconds: Jagger, Adam; Six-Five. Kelly, Caroline; Four-One. Latchkey, William; Three-Two . . .

'You're looking for your father, I presume?'

'Here he is. Love, James; Five-Four. He's still got that bloody domino.'

Hackle smiled. He pulled open a drawer, placed an old, battle-scarred bone rectangle on the table. It was the two-zero domino.

'A year we shall never forget,' he whispered.

'No wonder I can never beat him,' said Daisy.

'He was a quiet kid, sat at the back, staring out of the window. Miss Sayer really turned him around. Your father became the best mathematician in the year. I'm sorry to find him so destitute these days. A fine talent. To have to pretend he's dead, in order to get you a scholarship. Really, it is a great waste.'

Daisy looked over the list of pupils for a few seconds more.

She was trying to connect with the past. Her father's childhood with her own. The connections between them. What he had become. What she was becoming. The mathematics . . .

'OK. What's the plan?'

'Excellent news! Report at my house this Friday, six o'clock. Last Friday we did some preliminary research, but this will be the first proper meeting. Meanwhile . . .' Hackle reached into his drawer once again, this time pulling out a green cardboard folder. It had Daisy's name on the cover.

'You knew I'd say yes, then?'

'I was hoping you would, that's all. Inside are some of my papers for your perusal. They will explain the connections.'

'Do I get to know who I'm working with? Joe Crocus, I presume?'

'Of course. Joe will be the leader of the group. I won't be directly involved, but Joe will report to me. Under him will be student Dopejack, on computers and the Burgernet, and Benny Fenton on analysis. Yourself, of course, as the probability expert.'

'That's it? Just the four of us, against the dominoes?'

'Well, I'd like to find a natural, of course. We're looking at that. And then there's Jazir, on the—'

'Jaz! You've got Jazir? Where is he?'

'Right outside.'

'He is? I was worried . . . I mean, I haven't seen him since—'

'He's the key, Daisy. The way in.'

PLAY TO WIN                    PLAY TO WIN

PLAY TO WIN              PLAY TO WIN
PLAY TO WIN

PLAY TO WIN

PLAY TO WIN

WIN PLAY TO WIN  PLAY

WIN PLAY TO WIN P

PLAY TO W

WIN PLAY TO WIN

PLAY TO WIN

PLAY TO WIN          PLAY TO WIN

PLAY TO WIN
PLAY TO WIN                  PLAY TO WIN

**J**azir and Daisy, walking along the Oxford Road, away from the university. The time was approaching five o'clock, filled with rush-hour traffic. Daisy wasn't in the mood for talking. Not yet. Still in shock from Max's request and her acquiescence. Outside that office, outside the university's cloisters, the whole mad scheme started to feel like paranoia, and she was already working out the chances broken by her acceptance.

'You got the package off Max, right?' asked Jazir.

'What? Oh, yeah.'

'That list of pupils. What do you reckon? You reckon that Paul Malthorpe's the one we're after? Do you?'

'I suppose so.'

'Your dad's on that list, isn't he?'

'So? So is Max Hackle.'

'Come off it. No way is Max Hackle Mr Million.'

'So no way is my father, OK?'

'OK. Fine.'

It was fair weather, which brought the blurbflies out in swarms of whispers.

'Watch this, Daisy.' Jazir held out his arms on both sides, hands palm upwards. Immediately a blurbfly landed on his left hand, another on his right.

'Jaz? What are you doing?'

'Just a little trick I learned. Watch. Keep watching.'

More and more of the blurbs were attracted to Jazir. The flies started circling his body, filling his shape with song. A personal message about how he was the best ever player of the game and deserved to win untold riches.

Play to win! Purchase a thousand bones! Play to win! Adverts in orbit. Daisy had never seen anything like it.

'Jaz, people are looking at us.'

'Jealous, more like.' He turned on the onlookers. 'I'm the fucking pied piper, me. Go on, get your own fucking blurbs!'

'Jaz!' A few stray blurbs had landed on Daisy's head. 'Urgh! Get them off me!' She was scrabbling at her hair.

Jazir laughed at her. 'Oh dear. They must think you're my partner, you know, my lover, my mate.'

'This isn't funny.' Daisy was still struggling.

'You're right.' A clap of his hands. 'Blurbs be gone!'

Immediately they flew off and dispersed, to plague the city, normal style, blurb style.

'What's wrong with you, Jaz?'

'I don't care. It's bloody exciting, whatever is it. Come on, let's walk.'

Jazir had refused a bus ride, to make sure he got home after his father had left for the restaurant. His mother would be in, also his sister, but they wouldn't mind him bringing Daisy home. It was only his father who had the purity streak. Still, he was nervous as they approached the doorway.

Daisy, for her part, was even more nervous. She'd never been to Jazir's house before, never been invited or even told the address. It was all Hackle's doing. Jazir had been waiting outside the office for her, chatting up the secretaries. He was full of himself, the knowledge that Hackle had responded to his work, and that he had a secret to impart.

The first thing was the smell. Daisy could catch the scent as Jazir led her upstairs to his bedroom; the high, thick stench of ultragarlic.

'How does your family put up with it?' she asked.

The door was labelled with a SPICELAB sign: RESTRICTED ACCESS! 'They know I'd leave home without it.' Jazir unlocked the door.

The second thing was the light. The curtains were drawn, the room was dark, except for a strip of ultraviolet that glowed over the garlic's seedbed. Daisy went straight over to it as Jazir locked the door behind him.

'Jaz, there must be a law against this. What if the cops find out?'

'Who's gonna tell 'em?' He turned on the main lights. 'You're not gonna tell 'em, are you, Daisy?'

'Bloody hell!'

Daisy had turned round to see the rest of the room. The floor was covered with burgerwraps, computer disks, *Game Cat* arcade mags ('This Month: Sure-fire Unintendo Cheatmodes!'), discarded dominoes (cream), empty packets of individual-portion cornflakes, half-eaten curries, books on winning the game, losing the game, ignoring the game, cheating the game, loving the game, underpants and the odd sock (quickly stuffed behind a pillow), Frank Scenario recordings (including a rare vinyl edition of 'How Cool Can You Go?'), hefty programming manuals, a map of Manchester (overdrawn by felt-tip markings, alternative routes), tubes of toothpaste, a box of chocolates, a green folder with his name on, spewing papers and diagrams.

'It's a tip!'

'Yeah, you like it?'

'Don't you ever clean up?'

'Me? That's me mum's job.'

'So why doesn't she do it?'

'She can't get in, can she? I keep the Spicelab locked. In fact . . .'

'What?'

'You're the first . . . I mean, the first to come in here since . . . well, since years ago.'

'Oh.'

For furniture, there was only a single unmade bed and an

office chair that nestled under Jazir's computer station. Along one wall, another table served as a workbench. This was the only tidy area. A rack of tools was fixed to the wall under a large poster of 'Our Frank of the Cool'.

'Nice computer,' said Daisy.

'Yeah. Me dad bought it me. You know, keen? Erm, would you like to sit down, erm, on the bed, like, or something?'

'I'll go for something.'

'The chair then?' He pulled the office chair from under the desk.

'I'll stand, OK.'

'OK. I'll sit on the bed, anyway.'

Daisy couldn't believe she was doing this. OK, Jazir's mother had been happy enough for her to 'help Jazir with his schoolwork', but did she really have to be locked in this bedroom with him.

'Maybe you should open the door,' she said.

'Why?'

'It's a bit stuffy.'

'I can open the window.' He did so. 'That better?'

'Look, Jazir . . .'

'Yes?'

'Hackle said you were the key to the dominoes.' Trying to break the mood.

'Right.'

Jazir jumped up and took her over to the workbench, and Daisy saw for the first time that he was as nervous as she was. His hands were shaking, so very uncool.

'You remember your birthday, right? At the club?'

'Of course.'

'After you left, I showed some of this to Joe.' Jazir had taken a test tube out of a rack. Inside it the purple gunge slopped around.

'Urgh! What is it? A new curry sauce?'

'Almost. It's from the insides of a blurbfly.'

'How did you manage that?'

'Simple. I caught a fly. I cut it in two. The juice poured out.'

'Nobody catches a blurb. Aren't they dangerous when cornered?'

'Nah, it was a pussy cat. I drugged it, didn't I? I mean, does this look dangerous?' Jazir lifted up a dirty tea towel from his bench. Underneath was the splayed body of a blurb, dissected down the middle, each side of flesh pinned back. Bits of wire poked here and there from inside the opened gut, where drops of gunge were coagulating.

Daisy stepped back instinctively. 'Cover it up!'

Jazir laughed at her distress. 'There you go. Horror show over.'

'You're a head case, Jaz. You really are.'

'It gets better. Here, hold out your hand.' He had the test tube poised over her hand. 'Palm up, stupid.'

'Is it safe?'

'It's better than safe.'

Jazir opened the tube and poured out a large globule.

'It's horrible.'

'A slight burning sensation. It soon passes.'

'No. I mean it's greasy. And . . . oh . . .'

'Yes?'

'It tickles!'

'Good. It's still alive.'

'What?'

'It's still alive. Where it came from is quite dead, but it lives on. Don't you see what that means? Everyone thinks the AnnoDomino created some kind of robot. Sure, there's wires in there, but mostly the blurbs are organic. I think most of the workings are in the gunge. It's a biotech creature. That Mr Million is one cool bastard.'

'Can I get rid of this?'

'Allow me.' Jazir picked up a syringe, which he filled with the blurb juice off Daisy's palm. 'Now, watch . . .' He dragged Daisy over to his bedroom door. 'You wanted me to open the door, right? OK, try the door.'

'It's locked. You locked it.'

'Try it anyway, just to make sure.'

Daisy tried it. 'It's locked.'

'Good.' Jazir shoved the syringe into the keyhole. He pressed the plunger. 'Give it ten seconds . . .'

'And?'

'Try it. Go on.'

Daisy looked at Jazir like he'd gone mad, a clear possibility. Then she turned the doorknob. It swung open, nice and easy.

'This is a trick?'

'Well, it's magic. Come here . . .'

He dragged her over to the bed, where he picked up a traveller's alarm clock. 'Take the batteries out.' Daisy did so. 'The clock has stopped?'

'Of course it's stopped.'

Jazir squeezed a little blurb grease into the empty battery well. Immediately the clock started again. The room was quiet with Daisy's frozen breath and the ticking of the clock, like a countdown broadcast.

'Don't worry.' Jazir took Daisy's hand. 'I was the same when I found out. Can you imagine what I could do with this? I could make a killing. All I need is a name for it. The stuff that opens anything! The universal lubricant. The oil of the world! Can't you see the sales pitch, the marketing campaign. Puts Vaseline and KY in their place, don't you think? Jaz vaz! Yes. I can see it! Lovelies galore!'

'It's not your invention. Anyway . . .'

'Ah, but we're gonna take the AnnoDomino Co. out, aren't we? Us two, together. Me and you, Daisy, and Joe Crocus at the wheel.'

'It's evil stuff. Can I have my hand back, please.'

'One more demonstration, then we go to bed.'

'Now look . . .' Daisy was backing away.

'You kissed me last week.'

'I was under the influence.'

'You want some garlic now? You liked it, right?'

'Let's work, that's all.'

'The door's open, Daze. It's all vazzed up. You can leave any time.'

'Just show me what I need to know. What Hackle wants me to know. Then I'm leaving.'

'Fine. The computer.' He hit the space bar to vanish his official dancing Frank Scenario screensaver. He picked up a new box of disks, still sealed. 'I want this to be foolproof.' He ripped off the wrapping, took out a disk and slotted it in. A 'disk not formatted' message came up. 'It's empty, right?' Daisy nodded, Jaz hit the button. The computer went to work. 'It'll take a few seconds.'

'I'm very confused by all this,' Daisy admitted.

'It just shows the magnificence of Mr Million, whoever the fuck he is.'

'You sound like you're in love with him.'

'I admire him. The man has got vision. Come on, don't underestimate the enemy, you know that ruling. OK, here we go.'

The disk was ready. Jaz pressed on it to open an empty window. He didn't ask this time, just looked at her. Daisy nodded. He took the disk out of the slot. All that was left in the syringe was then applied to the casing. He held open the sprung protector to allow the grease to seep inside, onto the floppy.

Back in the slot it went. The disk icon was pressed again, opening the window. This time an icon floated in the space: a tiny
domino, the double-six.

'Hutch up.' Excited, Daisy sat on one half of the chair. She
took the mouse out of Jazir's hand, steered the pointer to the
domino, did the double-click thing. Nothing happened.

'Needs a little help from the Chef's Special,' said Jazir, loading a new disk.

'What's that?'

'My own recipe. Hacker mix. Watch this. It's good, this bit.'
The curry sauce started to fill the screen, and the domicon went
straight for it. More or less dived right in. 'You see? You don't
have to drag it anywhere. The domino's attracted to the sauce.
This is how I caught the blurb in the first place. It kept flying into
the screen and becoming drowsy.'

'What's in the chef's program?'

'Just the usual algorithms. Codebreakers, splicehounds,
infobots. You know much about hacking?'

'Nothing.'

'No matter. I mixed it all with the latest fractal paths. This is a
curry with a thousand spices. Infinite knowledge, right?'

'If you say so.'

'I can only guess that Mr Million feeds these blurbs on some
kind of fractal sugar base. It's attracted, you see. Look, it's opening.'

The domicon split in two right along the divider, a six and a
six, separate now, hinging apart . . .

'How many people would like to do that?' asked Jazir.

. . . out of which poured a swarm of tiny blurb icons, a few
pixels to each of them, with tiny wings. Too many to count, they
started to feed off the curry. Pretty soon two of them were fighting
over a juicy morsel, while another two were actually working

together to fight off a third. Some more were staking out territory.

'There's one hundred and sixty-eight of these flies to start with,' Jazir said. 'You know that number?'

'Sure,' answered Daisy. 'The total number of dots on a set of dominoes.'

'And what does the screen remind you of dominoes?'

'The Game of Life.'

'Right. One of the first artificial life systems. Cellular automata. You set up a map, an environment inside a hard drive, design some creatures to live in it, give them some basic rules, randomize the pattern and start the program. Evolution inside a computer. When you read Hackle's papers you'll see he was involved in this work, only he called his system nymphomation: sexy knowledge. Look! Two of them are at it already.'

Indeed, two of the minute blurbs were merging together on the screen.

'That's enough, you guys. Time for bed.' Jazir clicked down the window. It dwindled to a domicon on his hard disk, aligned with another seven. Jazir clicked on the first of these. 'Here's one I made earlier.'

The screen was pitch black with a throbbing mass of information.

'What's happened?' asked Daisy.

'They've reproduced. This is only five days old. Very fast permutations. I'll scroll down to find an edge.'

He did so. It was ragged, like shadows of itself, smoky tendrils. Occasionally a tiny shape would escape from the mass, to float away into space.

'It's a fractal!'

'A new one. And it's just given birth. Believe me, Daze. This is big. It's like AnnoDomino have taken Max's work and pushed it to the limits. I've found another three of these masses floating around. Sometimes they fight each other, like galleons. They steal supplies off each other. They eat each other. They fuck each other. They give birth. The cycle goes on. This is only a representation of the process. Imagine what it's like in real life. There's no end to it.'

'How does it help with breaking the dominoes?'

'Right. I gave a disk of this to Joe, and a tube of vaz to Benny.'

'You're really calling it vaz?'

'For now. Benny did the DNA analysis on it.'

'And?'

'He didn't have a clue. Said it was an unknown genetic structure. We showed the results to Hackle. He went crazy, saying it was a Hackle Maze made flesh. Apparently the genes don't just split in two, like in men and women. They split into many different strands. A more random way of reproducing. More chance for evolution to make play. Benny couldn't keep track of it. Hackle said he never would.'

'What about the disk? What did Joe do?'

'He only gave it to Dopejack, didn't he? I mean, all my own work, going to waste.'

'And I bet Dopejack did good.'

'Sure, he did good. Used my findings, didn't he, to find a deeper way into the bones. But I could've done good as well. I could have.'

'You could have done better, Jaz.'

'Dopejack's got better equipment than me, that's all.'

Daisy smiled.

'What you smiling at?'

'Nothing.'

'You are. You're laughing at me.'

'I'm not.'

'You are.'

'I'm not!'

'You are!'

'Get off! No. That tickles—'

'I'll teach you.'

The next thing, the two of them were on the floor, rolling around. Sometimes Jaz was on top, sometimes Daisy. Either way it was fun, if painful when the laughter got too much. Sometimes Daisy was winning, and Jazir let her win, and sometimes Daisy was losing.

And she let herself lose.

'Are you all right in there, you two?' It was Jazir's mother, knocking on the door. 'Would you like something to eat, Daisy?'

'We're all right, Mum,' Jazir shouted, trying to get up. 'We're working hard.' But the door swung open, unlocked.

'Oh, Jazir. What a mess you've made!'

'Yeah, Mum.' On his feet, unsteady. 'I'll clean it up. Right this second, Mother.'

'I'm helping him, Mrs Malik,' Daisy said from the floor, showing her a piece of burgerwrap she had picked up. 'Look.' She got to her feet.

'That's nice of you. Dinner will be ready soon.'

'Daisy's going in a bit. I'll walk her home.'

'Very good. There's some nasty men around.'

She went. Jazir locked the door. 'Me mum's sound. Four kids. Things are changing. It's just—'

'Am I really going?' asked Daisy.

'Yeah. In a bit. Didn't I say that?' He did a little dance, copying the movements of Frank Scenario. One two, one two, slide . . . singing a lyric.

Closer they came.

On the computer screen, the stray blurb from one land mass found a stray blurb from another. For a few seconds they danced around each other, before finally merging.

By which time Daisy and Jazir were lying on his bed.

Afterwards Daisy kissed the wound on his hand. It was a sealed-over bump, which gently moved under Daisy's lips. She didn't want to talk, and Jazir was asleep anyway.

Afterwards he walked her home, as promised. Again, very little was said. Daisy was slightly embarrassed now. It was the thought of giving in so easily, so suddenly, after being so alone and so opposed for so long. Again, the probabilities were unworkable. Watching the blurbs on the computer, what had that done to her? Well, she had waited long enough and Jazir was a friend. Would her life change? Would he still be a friend? Was this the start of something, or the end? So many thoughts.

Jazir, the same. Mostly of shame, however. He knew it hadn't gone well. He was glad it had happened, but why had he fumbled so, with the protection and the act and the afterwards? The thought of his mother and sister downstairs, that was part of it. And the ever-present father, floating in his mind, his bedroom, his body. Would he never escape?

'It was your first time too, wasn't it?' Daisy asked, finally.

Jazir didn't answer.

'That's OK. It's good, I think.'

Jazir shrugged. Daisy took his arm. She'd never seen him this quiet. There was no going back. It was an equation that couldn't be undone. Even now, thinking of numbers.

'Jaz,' she said, 'this doesn't mean—'

'We're all the same, aren't we?' said Jazir. 'I mean, we're all virgins, these days.'

'Not any more—'

'No. We still are. Everybody is. Even Joe Crocus, in a certain sense. We're all waiting for something to happen. It's the times.'

'I suppose.'

A blurbfly landed on Jazir's shoulder then. He stroked it, without thinking, as it whispered in his ear. Some secret message.

'You know what this is like?' Daisy asked.

Jazir shook his head.

'They're attracted to you, just like they're attracted to your special recipe. Maybe you've got some sauce on you, a real version that is. Is there a real version?'

Jazir shook his head.

'What is it then?'

Jazir shook his head, but made an answer anyway.

'I've been bitten.'

They were walking along the curryfare, neon bathing them bright with colours. SHAZAZ. KING TANDOOR. ASSAM. EASTERN KISS. GANGA JAL. TAKSHAKA. PALACE OF SPICE. Finally, THE GOLDEN SAMOSA.

'Oh God, Jaz! Have you been to a doctor?'

Jazir shook his head.

'You must. Something's wrong with you.'

Jazir kissed her. 'Don't worry. I'm dealing with it. Friday night, right?'

'Friday.'

He walked away, a blurb on one shoulder, another two floating overhead, singing his praises.

Afterwards, past midnight, Daisy lay on her bed, sleepless. With the radio playing Frank Scenario's latest single, his voice laden with molasses and wine and the weight of years.

> *Rolling and tumbling along the domino,*
> *Hoping for a full cast, landing with an all alone.*
> *One of these days I'm gonna be an only know,*
> *With sweet Heaven's breath on my bone.*

It should've been the best day of her life, with Max asking her for help, and Jazir and that. And that and that and that and that. Rolling and tumbling. Twisting and turning. Good things, bad things. Numbers, falling. Jazir's wound. The temptations. Blurbflies hovering. Play to win! Play to win! The song. The hot smell of his flesh. Heaven's breath. The spices. The numbers . . .

Numbers! That was it. She would do some work. She would open the folder that Max had given her. She would start to read . . .

## Play to win

Pages of handwritten workings, equations galore, scribbled ravings, copies of magazines. *Number Gumbo: A Mathemagical Grimoire.* Launch date, October 1968. She started with that.

Psychedelic typography, its overabundance of flowers and drugs and cartoons of Jimi Hendrix, alive with six strings of fire. There was even an article containing a mathematical analysis of the guitarist's solo in a song called 'Purple Haze'. It claimed that Hendrix was a shamanic figure, whose music was a virus designed to infect the establishment with love. Each ragged chord was a ragged equation of love, apparently. Daisy skipped through it lightly, mainly because she had never heard a Jimi Hendrix recording, not for the life of her.

Instead she focused on an article written by Hackle: 'Love Labyrinths: A Guide for the Active Wanderer in Nymphomation'. It was hard-going, to be sure. Lots of the equations were beyond her control, but she persevered.

Knowledge gathered: a love labyrinth was a computer-generated maze in which the wanderers could actively find the centre by falling in love with the pathways. This was called playing to win.

Some wanderers had a better chance of winning. These were the Casanovas. They had more love for the maze.

The wanderer could also fall out of love with the pathways, thereby forever losing his way. These were called the Backsliders. This was playing to lose.

The wanderers of these labyrinths were only packages of information let loose in the computer's world. The more they wandered the maze, the more they learned about it. They could then change their behaviour accordingly.

Hackle seemed to view these wanderers as being almost *alive*. He gave the different types names – Chancer, Casanova, Warrior, Seducer, Cartographer, Jester, Sheep, Shepherd, Builder, Backslider – according to how they tackled the pathways of love. Special Informants patrolled the mazes, collecting knowledge and position. The more you loved the maze, the more it moulded to your desires. The more you hated the maze, the more it got you lost. But sometimes getting lost seemed good. Too many complications for Daisy to untangle, but loving the tangle anyway.

All this and more was nymphomation.

All this activity taking place inside a computer's memory. It must have been a struggle to fit it all inside the dumb, clunky machines of those days. Of course, there was no reality application, not in 1968, and this fact seemed to inform Hackle's equations with an element of loss. The professor was crying into his numbers.

The telephone rang; her father's lost voice. 'Leave me alone!' she said, slamming down connections.

She looked through some of the papers then. Most of them were merely the workings-out for magazine articles. Some were maps of Hackle Mazes, printouts with various wanderers in position. Others were number, pure number; dazzling displays of abstract maths. There was no way that Daisy could follow the various pathways.

She went back to the magazines; issues of the *Number Gumbo*, six in all, dated from 1968 to 1979. The further in time they went, the more they lost their hippy trappings. These she skimmed for Max's work, adding to her knowledge. There certainly seemed to be connections between the nymphomation and the dominoes. For instance, perhaps the Casanovas were related to today's lucky bleeders. The Informants were maybe the precursors of the blurbs. The Trickster virus was obviously related to the Joker Bone. No, don't say obviously, keep your distance, Daisy. Stay objective, don't get dragged in.

The last mag was a glossy affair. They were obviously getting money from somewhere. It contained an article by Max called 'Maze Dynamics and DNA Codings, a Special Theory of Nymphomation'. This was the juice, basically. It detailed how recent explorations of the Hackle Mazes (on the latest computers) had discovered an interesting anomaly. Some of the wanderers were actually having sex, or so it appeared. In previous games, the wanderers had reproduced by making exact copies of themselves. Now they were making inexact copies. Two of them would get together, merge, and a 'babydata' would be produced, with attributes from both parents. Already mutants had been observed, wanderers with bits missing, or bits added on. These were either killed instantly, Backsliders, or else became Warriors. Evolution was taking place.

The paper ended with a speculation by Hackle on the possible future of such a system. 'One can imagine a time when this new kind of knowledge will be put to use in the real world. For instance, we could mate everything we know about mathematics, with everything we know about flag-waving. The babydata would be the mathematics of flag-waving. A new science! But why stop our imaginings so soon? Let us mate this new baby with everything known about ice cream. The result? The mathematics of waving flags made out of ice cream. Everything known about driving a car? Excellent! The mathematics of driving flags made out of vanilla-cars. Astronomy? Dominoes? No problem. Flag-driving of numbered vanilla-bones on the moon.

'We must imagine a world filled with these highly specialized disciplines. Most will be completely useless and will soon be extinct. Others will be all-powerful. They will mate in turn. I no longer know whether to be excited or terrified at this prospect.'

Daisy, the same. She turned to the contents page of the mag. Was there anything else by Hackle? No. But his name caught her eye nonetheless. There he was, in the credits column. Assistant editor, Maximus Hackle. There was one reason why they kept printing his stuff. And who was the editor? Paul Malthorpe. Well. So Max and his enemy had kept in touch, worked together even. Strange, he'd never mentioned that. But Daisy knew Hackle's way of teaching by now. Let the pupil find the clues. She looked further down the column. Susan Prentice: art director. George Horn: cartoonist. They certainly stuck together. In a list of special consultants she found this name: James Love. Her father . . .

Daisy fell asleep with this page open on her chest.

Play to love

Two other things to be seen that night: firstly, Joe Crocus making Benny carry a portable computer and a fishing net up to the roof of Hackle's house. There Joe set up the machine. He slotted in a certain disk and waited for the pattern to emerge. Jazir's Chef's Special Recipe. Benny was waiting near by, with the net, as the blurbflies came in to land.

Secondly, Jazir laying awake on his bed, the window open. His chest was bare above the sheet, and a sluggish blurb nestled there, wings folded. Jazir stroked it lovingly, squeezing a trickle of grease from its duct. He called the blurb Masala, as in Chicken Tikka Masala. Best recipe. He rubbed the loving juice into his chest. Miss Sayer watched over this scene. Whispering computer advice . . .

'Wing up. Please quickly. Come find.'

**PLAY TO WIN**     **PLAY TO WIN**

**PLAY TO WIN**     **PLAY TO WIN**
**PLAY TO WIN**

**PLAY TO WIN**

**PLAY TO WIN**

**WIN PLAY TO WIN  PLAY**

**WIN PLAY TO WIN P**

**PLAY TO W**

**WIN PLAY TO WIN**

**PLAY TO WIN**

**PLAY TO WIN**     **PLAY TO WIN**

**PLAY TO WIN**
**PLAY TO WIN**               **PLAY TO WIN**

# Game 44

Lucky young Bone Day. Dotty old Pipchester! Game 44. Throw those bones, you burger-gutted dribbleheads. Make honeyspot to the pimplevision. Gamble fast, live long, make cash. Change the orifice. Let loose the digits! Tumbling and falling, cascading mist of bonejuice, genetic flash. Sing those swarms, broadcast your tongueflies, alive with blurbverts. Sex your gamble, long your life, cash your bones. Play to win! Play to win! And all over the city that numberday evening, moments from boneflight, how happy were the hordes! Jabbering their dancing eyes on windows and walls and floorboards and thighs and meat pies and trouser flies and psychedelic, hippy throw-cushions.

Watching the dots. Pulsating, blooming, coming on strong. Losing the day job, winning the prize. The world turning on a rainbow of pips . . .

It's domino time! Feverish domino time! Dom, dom, dom, dom, domino time!

**Blurbflies**

Tommy tumbled, and the players steeled their bones, honed their breath, bought some last-minute prayers, took a collective burger, sang their hosannas. Sacrificed some wingless dream to the pagan gods of flight.

Fuck to win! Fuck to win!

As the blurbflies went out of control, blocking out the streetlights, making a cloud of logos. It was rutting season for the living verts, and all over the city the male blurbs were riding on the backs of females. Biting their necks, hoping for babyverts. The city, the pulsating city, alive with the rain and the colours and the stench of nymphomation. Mathemedia.

Here we go, numberfucked . . .

Down to Hackle's house and the domino-breakers. DJ

Dopejack working a computer, Jazir another. Linked by networks. Daisy Love and Sweet Benny Fenton, sofa-bound, just watching. Daisy to Jazir, Benny to Joe. Old Joe Crocus making his rounds; pent-up, nerve-ridden, sharp-edged with need.

'This is magic equipment, Joe,' said Dopejack.

'Just capture it.'

A direct feed from the television to the two computers. ADTV. On the paired-up screens Cookie Luck began her dance of chance. The theme song playing out, a buzz of words:

> Love the numbers, dream the squeeze.
> Cookie Luck, don't be such a tease.
> Bring me prizes, I beg you, please!

All of them, hanging tight upon the teledance, nervous hands stroking at nervous bones. Play to win! Play to win!

Joe made a prayer. 'Oh my Lord of Infinite Numbers, come down to us now. Grace us, your pitiful calculators, with your generous presence. Oh my master, oh my *Dominus!* Come down to bless these, my simple bones of offering, my humblest of chances. Oh my darkest fractal, may these my pitiful tokens be forever graced with your winning spirit. Open all channels . . .'

Little good it did him.

**PLAY THE RULES**

11a. The AnnoDominoes shall be allowed to protect their identity at any reasonable cost.

11b. No player may attempt to infiltrate the dominoes.

11c. Neither the game nor the players are above the law.

11d. (Addendum) The game is deemed more above the law than the players.

# Play to win

Big Eddie and Little Celia were holed up in paradise, if paradise is a rundown, abandoned house in Cheetham Hill. Eddie had found the place on his wanderings. They had to keep moving, until he could prove his thoughts about Celia. He found a nice little hole on the main road. A very nice little hole, just his size too. Trouble was, it was already occupied by some thin sliver of a loser. Short work for a man like Big Eddie Irwell. So, a hole. Big enough for both Eddie and Celia. Good position too, right outside the Jewish supermarket. Lots of punies to be caught, mid-flight.

And now a house to go with the hole. Backstreet bliss, it was; due for demolition, but fine for all that. They had a row of them to choose from. No. 27 was the best, with its 'PLAY TO WIN' graffiti scrawled across the door; a real mess inside, tiled with creamy bones, but they cleaned it up nice. Even better, tins of pseudosoup in the cupboard, tins of astrobeans. No gas, no electric, but candles and an old camping stove. Best of all, a radio; an antique transistor job, no sound, abandoned. Just a battery that needed changing, and there were batteries in a clock. And who needs a clock when you've got the dominoes?

Imagine, their very own radio.

Pigs in blurbjuice. With two bones, one each, and Lady Cookie Luck dancing to a standstill . . .

**Blurbflies**

> That's the way! That's the way!
> That's the way the cookie crumbles!

Tommy Tumbler crying, 'A two, a blank. A two-and-a-blank!'
Celia started screaming.

Play to win

No such luck over in Hackle's house, but at least the game was
captured on video and hard disk, ready for deep analysis.

'I can't believe it!' screamed Dopejack. 'Another fucking half-
blank.'

'Stop complaining,' said Benny. 'The university paid for your
chances. You lost nothing.'

'It's the principle. And that's two blanks in the last, what is it?'

'Four games,' replied Benny. 'You know what Hackle's gonna
say?'

'The Joker Bone's getting closer?'

'OK,' said Joe, 'so we move quickly.' He paused then and
looked around at his team. 'I hereby declare open the first ever
meeting of the Dark Fractal Society.'

'What?' This from Dopejack, his face reflecting from the
computer screen.

'That's our name.'

'Who decides this?'

'Joe Crocus does,' declared Benny. 'He's the master of the
group.'

'I thought Max Hackle was the master?' said Dopejack. 'And
I'm not too keen on Dark Fractal, actually.'

'Why not?' asked Benny.

'It sucks.'

'So you'll just have to make do.'

'It sucks its own dick.'

'That's right,' said Jazir, 'it's a recursive equation, always doubling back on itself. Perfect! Well chosen, Joe.'

'You would like it.'

'What's that supposed to mean?'

'Nothing. What's wrong with the Strange Attractors? That's all I'm asking.'

'And who made that up, I wonder?' asked Jazir.

'I did. Last night in bed.'

'Is that all you do in bed, DJ? Make up names.' Jazir gave Daisy the eye at this.

Daisy Love, as always, kept her thoughts to herself.

'I don't have to put up with this, Joe,' said Dopejack.

Joe Crocus made a sweeping motion. 'Children, please! We are gathered together, in order to make the dominoes surrender. We are the Dark Fractals. No more questions. Give me answers. Open all channels; connect to everything. Give me your info. Dopejack, that includes you. We have a new member today. Ms Love. Bring her up to date.'

Dopejack gave in to the pressure, pressed some keys on the computer and brought up a window. 'OK, what we've got so far. The bones were introduced on the first of May, last year. Here's a list of winning numbers, so far. Here's their logo. The famous dancing domino. It's now the twenty-sixth of Feb. On the twenty-third of April they're going national. That gives us seven games at the Manchester odds.'

'We have to win by then,' said Joe. 'The chances will be wild, otherwise.'

'Winners so far, both the full-cast and the half-cast. I've managed to break in a little further, by feeding back the blurbjuice equations and infecting the domino walls with the

Chef's Special Recipe fractal.'

'Thanks to me,' said Jazir.

'Basically, I've got them eating their own defences.'

'I discovered that.'

'Joe. Can you shut this kid up. I'm trying to work here.'

'I discovered the way in, Joe. Remember?'

'Jazir discovered it,' Joe stated, 'Dopejack furthered it. That's good, my children, we are working together. Carry on, DJ.'

'Thank you. I've managed to peel a layer off the winner's list, revealing their addresses.'

'Oh wow. Their addresses.' This from Jazir, of course. 'Let's go round and steal their money.'

'Jazir! I can always make you leave.'

'You couldn't do that, Joe. Who would get you closer when Dopey's exhausted himself?'

'Right! That's it. I'm going.' Dopejack was up already.

'Let me see that,' said Daisy, her first words of the meeting. 'The winner's list. I might know something.'

'Like what?' asked Dopejack.

'That stopped him!'

'Jazir!'

'Sorry, boss.'

'Have this week's winners come through yet, DJ?' Daisy asked.

'Just in. And one million lovelies going to . . . a Mrs Annie Makepiece. Now look, the beauty of my new program; even though she's asked for no publicity, we still get her address. See? It's in Didsbury. Jazir might not be that stupid after all. We *could* go round and—'

But Daisy was too urgent. 'Give me the half-winners, please.'

'Got them.'

'Is there an Irwell in there?'

'Let's see. Would that be Edward Irwell? He's won a half-blank.'

'That's it! That's the one!'

'What do you know, Daisy?' asked Jaz.

'Nothing yet. Let me think. Is there an address.'

'Actually . . . there isn't . . . I . . .'

Jazir laughed. 'Some program.'

'There's just some letters after his name. NFA.'

'NFA? What's that?' asked Jazir.

'It's No Fixed Abode,' said Joe.

'He's a beggar?' asked Daisy.

'That he is,' said Dopejack. 'It shouldn't be allowed, beggars playing the game – bloody hell! He's won three half-casts as of tonight.'

'I knew it!' said Daisy. 'I know this man. No. Let me think!'

Of course, Eddie Irwell! That name the beggar girl Celia had shouted in the bookshop, as the tramps surrounded the cash desk . . .

'I've got it!' Daisy shouted. Even Jazir was taken back by her excitement. Only Joe kept his cool.

'What have you got?' he asked.

'Let me check one thing first. DJ?'

'At your service.'

'When did Irwell win his second half-bone?'

'One second. Here it is. Game forty-two. Two weeks ago.'

'And did he claim the prize? Can you find that?'

'The Dopejack can find a—'

'Get to it!' said Jazir. 'Give the lady what she wants.'

'Let me see. No, he didn't claim it. I wonder why?'

'Because I had it,' said Daisy. 'Remember, Joe? The bone I brought to the club that Saturday?'

'That was Eddie's?' asked Joe.

'No. It belonged to a girl called Celia. Celia . . . wait, I asked for her name. Hobart! Celia Hobart. A beggar as well. This Eddie Irwell must be buying the bones for her. She's the natural. Not Eddie.'

'Do you think you could find her?'

'She's NFA, Joe,' said Benny.

'I can try,' said Daisy.

## Play to win

'Can't you ever stop winning, Celia?' shouted Big Eddie, smiling his heart out.

'I don't think so,' replied Celia.

The two of them were dancing round in circles. Celia threw the half-alive bone to Eddie, laughing. Eddie threw it back.

'Look at it, Cee!'

'I'm looking.'

'See that lovely blank still all aglow. Isn't it lovely?'

'It's lovely. But this time, Eddie . . .'

'What, what, what?' He had the bone now, waltzing with it.

'Sixty/forty, right?'

'Don't spoil the mood, little one.'

'Just don't mess up this time.'

'Who messed up last time?'

'OK, we do it right this time.'

'Right on the nail, you lucky bleeder, you.' Eddie embraced her and almost smothered her with his joy. 'We wait till midnight. I take it to the pay-out shack myself—'

'I'm going with you, Eddie.'

'No. Too dangerous. I can't afford to lose you.'

'I can't afford to lose the winnings.'

'What do you take me for?'

'A cad and a scoundrel and a cheat and a liar.'

'Fair enough, but I'm on your side this time.'

Celia extricated herself from his grip. 'I swear, if you cheat on me . . .'

'Sweet Celia, as if—'

'I'll never play again. Do you hear me?'

'All ears.'

Play to win

'OK. That's Daisy sorted out. Here's the workload for the rest of you.' Joe Crocus was standing before his charges, giving orders. 'Benny, you carry on with the DNA analysis of the blurbjuice.'

'I can help him, boss,' said Jazir.

'I'm fine on my own, thanks Jaz. I've got some ideas I want to try.'

'Your job, Jazir, is to break open a bone.'

'He can't do that,' said Dopejack. 'Nobody can do that.'

'Fuck off, Dopey. I can do it.'

'He's done it on screen, DJ. Let him try in real life.'

'Waste of time.'

'Dopejack, I don't want arguments. I want work. You will break further into the security system. That's an order.'

Dopejack mumbled something.

'I could do that better,' said Jazir.

'Shouldn't he be working tonight?' put in Dopejack. 'Serving up slop?'

'I've got my priorities right.'

'And I haven't?'

'Doesn't feel like it to me, Dopey. Feels like you're just causing trouble.' Jazir turned to Joe. 'I can do anything he can do, but better.'

'Basically, I've had it!' Dopejack stood up, grabbed his disks and his coat. 'I work alone from now on.'

The door slammed behind him.

'Here endeth the first meeting,' whispered Benny.

'He'll be back,' said Joe.

'No loss.' Jazir, of course.

Joe left them then; Jazir and Daisy and Benny. Benny was already taking out a freshly killed blurbfly, which he went at with a knife. Jazir told Daisy that he did have to go to work now, and that his father would shout at him for being late, but maybe he could come up after the shift to see her?

Daisy said yes.

'Daisy said yes!' shouted Benny, giving them both the wicked eye.

'You fuck off as well,' said Jazir, around a smile.

Daisy said, 'You should tell your father you're being tutored by Professor Max Hackle, of the university.'

'I might just do that.'

Jazir gave Daisy a kiss, to which Benny made a smacking noise. Jazir left.

Daisy and Benny. 'Where's Joe gone?' Daisy asked.

'Off to see Max in his study. Interim report.'

Daisy left.

Benny, alone, working the blurbjuice.

Daisy in the study, apologizing to Hackle and Joe for interrupting them. 'That's quite all right, Ms Love. Please, sit down.'

'Yeah,' said Joe. 'Stop fidgeting.'

There was a television in the corner, frozen in the two-blank dance. Daisy stared at it, embarrassed.

'Joe was just telling me about your good work. I cannot emphasize the importance of finding this natural player.'

'It will give us the edge,' added Joe.

Daisy nodded.

'So . . .' Hackle looked at her intently, 'What is it you want?'

'Your domino won tonight, sir.'

'Ah yes, the good old two-blank. You know, old Malthorpe used to call me that at school. Two-Blank, come here. Two-Blank do this. Two-Blank, fuck off. I didn't mind, it was better than my real name. Which is Maxwell, by the way. The Maximus, I'm afraid, is a Sixties leftover.'

'Did Malthorpe call you Two-Blank later on, sir? When you were doing the magazine?'

Hackle and Joe shared a smile. 'Well, well. More good work from our newest recruit.' This from Max.

'Oh, she's good. She's bloody good.' This from Joe.

'My father was there with you.'

'That he was. Special consultant. The title hardly befits the vision he brought to the project.'

'Why didn't you tell me?'

'Ah, those days. We were so excited. The late Sixties, Joe. You were a little too young to enjoy them, I imagine. And Daisy, of course, totally missed out. We really did believe we were making a difference, changing the world by publishing an alternative maths mag.' He laughed wildly, at himself this time, shaking his head slowly. 'Foolish, I know, but still . . . it was a good dream. To carry on the lessons of Miss Geraldine Sayer. It was not to be, alas. In 1979, I believe it was, the group split up.'

Daisy asked why.

'The usual things. Internal group dynamics, I believe it is now called.'

'We had a touch of that tonight,' said Joe.

'I can imagine. The dream goes sour eventually. All one can expect is to make one's discoveries before the end. We made ours, and then fell apart.'

'Is that when my father started to . . .'

'To disintegrate? Yes, I suspect it was.'

'A year before I was born.'

'Maybe you were his attempt to realign himself. Perhaps that is why I was reluctant to discuss this with you. Ms Love, you must realize my delight when you applied for my course. Your name alone fills me with trembling memories. I went along with your scheme quite willingly, to pretend him dead. In a sense, you have brought him back to me. He rings me up occasionally, you know. He seems in good spirits. I have even invited him round here; he always declined.'

'Well, he doesn't go out much.'

'But Joe, here, has further news of the past. He has been researching the whereabouts of the class of 1968. Joe?'

Joe unfolded a sheet of paper. 'First the bad news: of the original twenty-eight, at least seven of them are dead. I have no trace of a Paul Malthorpe, of the correct age.'

'I heard he left for London after *Number Gumbo* broke up.'

'Nothing on George Horn. *Re* Susan Prentice; there are at least three women of the correct age and name in Manchester. One is a waitress. Another a lawyer. The third is a teacher.'

'Ahhh.'

'Junior school. Your junior school.'

'Get some exam results for me.'

'Already done. Nothing spectacular. Of the rest, nine of them

I can find no trace. Of those I can trace, only seven of them are in professions at all related to mathematics: a computer analyst, a bookmaker, the owner of a casino, a tax inspector—'

'Oh dear. Prime suspect.'

'A meteorologist and a chartered accountant.'

'You will concentrate on these, but not only. Remember, our clues may come from anywhere. Investigate everybody.'

'That's only six,' said Daisy. 'Six suspects. Who's the seventh?'

'He's a professor of mathematics at Manchester University.'

'Yes, I suppose he is,' said Hackle.

## Play to win

Daisy returned to the Golden Samosa at just gone eleven. They were still serving. Through the window she watched a certain waiter expertly carrying four dishes to a table. He didn't see her. She went up the outside stairs to her door.

A late night call to her father, asking for a game tomorrow. Granted. Twelve midnight found her in bed, waiting for Jazir.

Twelve-thirty, asleep. A knock on her door. 'I can't stay long.'

'You don't need to.'

The same time found Eddie Irwell setting out for town with the half-cast bone. Celia was already asleep. Some time later that night she woke up screaming, having been chased by a skeletal figure. Twelve other players had the same dream.

Celia looking around, scared. Where was Eddie?

He'd made it to the pay-out, but not quite home with the prize.

PLAY TO WIN

PLAY TO WIN
PLAY TO WIN

PLAY TO WIN
PLAY TO WIN

PLAY TO WIN
PLAY TO WIN

PLAY TO WIN

PLAY TO WIN

PLAY TO WIN

TO WIN PLAY TO WIN  PLA
WIN PLAY TO WIN  PLAY

WIN PLAY TO WIN P

WIN PLAY T
PLAY TO WIN

WIN PLAY TO WIN

PLAY TO LOSE PLAY TO

TO WIN PLAY TO WIN PLA

PLAY TO WIN

PLAY TO WIN

PLAY TO WIN

PLAY TO WIN
PLAY TO WIN
PLAY TO WIN

PLAY TO WIN

'Yeah, we stayed together. What else could we do? We were bonded you see, by the special lessons.' Daisy's father was stroking the game-scarred five-four domino around his neck. 'Don't ask me where Miss Sayer came from, or where she went. She was a mystery to us. Perhaps that was her appeal; all the other teachers were boring, just people from around the corner. Incompetents, getting on with life. Miss Sayer changed all that. Hmm, nice move.' He played a domino in response to Daisy's double-three. 'She was only at the school for a year.'

'What happened to her?'

'Got kicked out, didn't she.'

Daisy played a bone. 'Why? If she was doing so well . . .'

'That's the problem. She was doing too well. Some government bore somewhere, with nothing else to fill his life, must have noticed the results. They thought we were cheating. All of us, minus one. There was this kid called Georgie Horn. Blank-Blank. He was the only one that Miss Sayer couldn't reach.'

'Hackle mentioned him. Didn't he do as well?'

'Georgie bombed out.'

It was the Saturday morning, and bright with it for a change. Her father had made an effort to tidy up the place. It wasn't much of an attempt, but Daisy was touched. She had come here specifically to uncover something; the game was just the soundtrack, the clack of bones, the occasional rapping of knuckles on wood, the web of numbers slowly adding up.

'It wasn't only Miss Sayer's results,' her father said, taking his turn. 'It was the teaching methods.'

'What do you mean? They sound like fun, from what Hackle says.'

'That was the early days. She was strange, that woman. Sometimes it felt like she was on a mission, and we were her converts. Other times she came on like a real bitch. Oh, she could be vicious when pushed. This Malthorpe you're so interested in, and precious Maximouth Hackle, they were constantly circling each other, vying for top-dog biscuit. Sometimes their fists took over from the numbers. Stupid. Miss Sayer would really have a go at them for disrupting the class. She couldn't stand slack. Me, I just got on with it. You know she hit Hackle once. He told you that?'

'No.'

'Course not. Yeah, strapped him hard. I mean, we were used to that kind of thing, but not from a woman teacher. That was the headmaster's pleasure.'

'What had Hackle done wrong?'

'That was the weird bit. He'd helped little Blank-Blank with his homework. Not helped him; done it for him. It was first time Georgie Horn had got anything right. She went mad. Made us all stay in till someone confessed. Malthorpe confessed that Hackle had done it. Nasty.'

'She sounds weird.'

'It took me a while to get used to her. But when I did – bang! I was off and running. Couldn't get enough numbers to satisfy me. I became her favourite, I think. Clever little Five-Four, she'd call me. Didn't that make Hackle and Malthorpe mad. Domino!'

'Aw. Only got two left as well.'

'Tough. Another game?'

'Go on then. Got to be somewhere at one.'

'Oh yes? A date?'

'No! Well, yes . . .'

'I never thought . . .'

'Kind of—'

'I mean . . . I always blamed myself . . . making you

. . . what's his name?'

'Jaz.'

'Jazz? What, like John Coltrane? Now there was a questing spirit.'

'Who?'

'Give me strength. He's a jazz musician, from the Sixties.'

'Oh. No. Jaz . . . it's short for Jazir.'

'Sounds exotic. Eh? Eh?'

'Get off! Yeah, he's exotic. I suppose.'

'Where you going? The pictures?'

'Working, actually. Extra project for Max.'

'Some date.'

'He wants to see you.'

'Jazir does?'

'No! Hackle.'

'Yeah. So he said.'

'You've got his number?'

'Somewhere. Come on, give us a game. Play to win, please.'

They played . . .

'Domino!' shouted this time before the game had even finished.

'You can't know that?' said Daisy.

'Three moves' time. Believe me.'

'No, I want to play it.'

Three moves later Daisy was knocking on wood and her father was laying down his final bone. 'A little trick that Miss Sayer taught me. Great days. For a time. It all went bad. Why, Daisy, does everything have to go bad eventually?'

'The law of diminishing returns. Let's play.'

Shuffle, clack. Clack, clack, clack. Domino!

'Hackle reckons I'll never win against you,' said Daisy.

'Keep playing.'

'You were telling me about it going bad.'

'For me, it was when she started to introduce the number spells.'

'What? Like the Black Math ritual?'

'Oh yeah, she introduced Hackle to all that. She'd get the whole class chanting this rubbish about God being in the numbers, and how mathematics was the song of the universe. Bollocks. You know me, Daisy; I was never a dreamer. To me, adding up is adding up, a way to an answer. Hackle and Malthorpe fell for it totally. They had to, to keep up. Strange thing was, it worked. Somehow or other we produced these incredible exam results. She'd turned a bunch of all-time losers into golden winners. That's when they sent down this school inspector bloke, can't remember his name. Some tosser. He took one look at Miss Sayer and what she was up to and decided to make a case of it. He interviewed us all, one-to-one. I think we all more or less decided to hide the Black Math stuff. Someone decided not to. I often think it must've been that Georgie Horn. He was the only one with nothing to lose.'

'They sacked her?'

'It got very nasty. This inspector chap had obviously never seen anything like it before. He was calling it black magic, like witches and stuff. Perhaps it was. At the end, Miss Sayer went crazy. I mean, really. She was rolling around on the floor, screaming. I was freaked as well, just watching. That teacher was sure loaded with some bad stuff. Good stuff, bad stuff you know? Like most of us. She would have been fine without the govern- ment interference, and I'd be a genius. That's what happens, Daisy, when the good is denied. Anyway, that was it, lessons over.'

Jimmy fell silent, the old five-four in his hand.

'Domino.' He said it in a whisper. 'Two moves from now. Sorry.'

'But some of you carried it on?' Daisy was packing the dominoes into their wooden box. 'After she left?'

'Yeah, we stuck together. I think out of that class, maybe half of us were capable of taking it somewhere else. Somewhere good, you know? And at the core there was me, and Hackle, Malthorpe, with Blank-Blank in tow, and this girl . . . erm . . .'

'Susan Prentice?'

'Yeah, that's it. With the knowledge we'd learned, it was easy to make progress. Hackle and Malthorpe, and Prentice I think, they all went on to university. Georgie, by that time, was working in a garage, something dirty like that. This would be, what . . . 1959, 1960?'

'Why didn't you go?'

'More important things to do. Politics. Look at me, eh? You wouldn't think it, but back then I was a firebrand. Again, I put this down to Miss Sayer; I had a mission of my own, having escaped. Escape should have no favourites. And university stank of elitism. Oh dear. Let's say that I had beliefs, but I got over them. Do you mind if I have a drink?'

Daisy shook her head. 'When did you next see Hackle?'

'That would be around 1977. We found each other by chance, a café in town. No big deal, just chatting. Not much to say on my part. I was over my political shit, but had found nothing to replace it. I was in my mid-thirties, the time when you find the path, and I was the oldest plumber's mate in history.'

'What about Hackle?'

'He was a teacher by then, which surprised me; I didn't think he'd follow in her footsteps that closely. He wanted me to meet the "old gang", as he put it.'

Her father drained his glass of vodka, and Daisy watched in dismay as he poured himself another one, his eyes already fixed on some distant place. But she had to get this out of him . . .

'Hackle offered you a job?'

'A job?'

'Special consultant, the *Number Gumbo* . . .'

'I was never part of that. Never!' He took a slug. 'Special consultant? Hah! They used me, more like. Hackle, Malthorpe . . . the lot of them.'

'Used you?'

'Why are you so interested in all this? Why are you so interested in me? After all this time, Daisy . . . it's not right. It's not fair!'

'You rang me up. What am I supposed to do, ignore you?'

'You're after something. You're after something, what is it?'

'Nothing, I . . .'

'It's Hackle isn't it? Your precious teacher. He knows nothing. A fucking amateur. What's he doing to you? I'm your teacher, not him. Stupid girl. What's wrong with you?'

Daisy had really wanted this meeting to go well. Too well, expecting too much. Slipping away, slipping . . . Maybe she should leave? Leave him to his wet solace. Instead . . .

'Hackle wants to ruin the AnnoDomino Company.'

That made her father sit up, glass poised. He slugged it back and looked at Daisy for a long time, like a thousand yards up close.

Daisy pressed on: 'He's asked me to help, and some other students. He thinks it's to do with what happened in your school.'

Her father put down his glass. 'Daisy, I beg you. Don't get involved.'

'I thought you could help.'

'Don't get involved.'

'Why not?'

'It's dangerous.'

'In what way? Please, give me a clue. What did you do in the

*Number Gumbo*? Look, I know all about Hackle Mazes and nymphomation and all that. I don't fully understand it and I can't see the problem. I can't make it real. You were there. I want to know what happened. Why did the group split up? Please. I'm asking you to help me . . .'

Her father, slowly shaking his head, looking down now. Lost. His words so quiet, but so harsh.

'There is no help. It kills you.'

## Play to win

Daisy started outside the bookshop on Deansgate, searching that hole and all the holes around, even asking all the vagabonds installed if they knew the whereabouts of Little Miss Celia and Big Eddie. Getting no good answers, but plenty of abuse. Jazir was accompanying her, at his own insistence. Calling it their first date. Silly. One good soul (lubricated with punies) told them that the two beggars were living in Gorton, or so the story goes, but that they had moved on from there since, no doubt. Jazir handed the beggar a business card from the Golden Samosa.

'Any news, ring this number, or just come round.'

'Tell her Daisy Love was asking for her.'

'That's a funny name.'

'So is Jazir. There's a free curry in it for you.'

The beggar seemed more than pleased with this deal. She directed them to the town hall, where the official hole register was kept.

'Let's chance it,' said Jazir. 'Anything's better than visiting Gorton.'

The town hall doors were guarded by an oversized security blurbfly. He took ten minutes to let them through, and then only at Jazir's persuasion.

'You've got a way with blurbs,' said Daisy, her words echoing around the Gothic chambers.

'Get bitten by one. I thoroughly recommend it.'

'I still say you should see a doctor.'

'I've never felt better, Daze. Even you fancy me these days. Hey, maybe I'll grow wings and get to fly one day.' He set off down the nearest corridor, arms outstretched and flapping madly, singing, 'Play to win! Play to win! Outa my way, sucker! I'm Jazir Malik, the human blurbfly! Ooops!'

'Do you mind, young man.'

He'd bumped into a fat suit-and-tie, barely passing as human.

'Sorry. I was looking for the Room of Holes, that's all.'

'Why?'

'I want to register.'

'You don't look like a vagabond.'

Daisy had caught up by now. 'We don't mean any harm.'

'That's the last thing we want to do,' agreed Jazir. 'I've run away from home, you see. My father doesn't understand me.'

'I'm not surprised. It's upstairs, turn left, second right, left again, left, right, third door on the right. Do you follow me?'

'Sure thing.'

'Except it's closed on Saturdays. Come back Monday.' The suit laughed himself into the gents' lavatory.

'That's that then,' said Daisy.

'Follow me.'

'Where are we going?'

'Come on.'

Up the stairs they went, turning left, the second right, left again and so on. Occasionally they would meet a lonely blurb patrolling the corridor. Jazir sent them fluttering away with ease. Eventually they came to the door marked 'Room of Holes'. Some of the rules were pasted on the door:

**PLAY THE RULES**
8e. None but the Company shall know the insides of a blurb.
8f. None but the Company shall capture a blurb.
8g. If captured, a blurb may take the necessary steps to escape.

'You know it's locked,' said Daisy.

'Ah ha!' Jazir brought a small tube out of his pocket. It was coloured white, with red lettering: VAZ.

'You've packaged it?'

'Nah. It's just a toothpaste tube. Did the lettering myself. You like?'

'This isn't wise.'

'No, but it's fun.' He squeezed a small glob of vaz into the keyhole and turned the handle. The door swung open.

'Bloody hell!'

The room was dark. A fluttering moved through the air. Jazir made a tiny sound, and a blurbfly flew, whispering, across Daisy's face to land on Jaz's shoulder. Daisy could hear Jaz asking it for Hobart, Celia's current hole address, as she fumbled for a light switch at the side of the door, found it and clicked it.

Daisy gasped.

'It's only a map. Keep it down.'

Jazir was already hopping over the holes in the floor, guided by the blurb's expert flight, but Daisy couldn't move, couldn't follow. Really, it shouldn't have shocked her like this. Jazir was right; it was only a map. It was just that it covered all the walls and floor, and the streets and the roads were twisted like snakes of all colours. The whole of Manchester was in this room. The holes were black pits, like a rash on the city. A curious fact also: some of the holes were filled with soil, from which twisted bonsai trees sprouted.

'Here's the starting place,' Jazir shouted back at her. 'Deansgate Boulevard.' He was taking a small object from the hole.

'What is it?' asked Daisy.

'A sugar cube.'

'A what?'

'A sugar cube. And I bet it's got a fractalized crystal base.'

Jazir popped the cube into the blurb's mouth. It crunched it down quickly and then sang the following: 'Hobart, Celia, Miss. Fifteen point two four punies all told.'

Fifteen? Daisy was wondering, how long had she lived off that? Should have given more.

'Vacated. Current hole unknown.' And the blurb fell to a whispering state.

Daisy started to step gingerly along the map, trying to avoid each hole in turn. It seemed as though there were more holes than map; so many homeless. Maybe the city would be one big hole one day, and we would all fall through to beggarsville. 'No luck,' she said.

'You make your own luck these days. Hasn't the game taught you anything. OK blurb, find me Irwell, Edward.'

The blurb took off and they both followed. One time Daisy's foot landed in a hole and she heard a crunch underfoot. Oh dear, she'd just obliterated some poor beggar's records. The blurb landed on a hole in Gorton Town.

Another lump of sugar, another feeding for the hungry creature.

'Irwell, Edward, Mr. Seven hundred and forty-nine point six seven punies all told.'

'Maybe I should become a beggar,' said Jazir.

'Vacated. Current whereabouts unknown.'

'Time to go, Jaz.'

'No way. I'm not giving up. We just need some logic, that's all.'

'They're not registered.'

'We knew that anyway. Remember the NFA coding. But how are they living, that's what I'm asking. What are they living off?'

'Maybe they got a job.'

'Celia's too young, and Eddie . . . no, he's a pro, I can feel it. Too long on the street to go back. He's still begging. He's out there somewhere.' Jazir was trying to grab the map's immensity in his outstretched hands. 'He knows that he's on to a winner with the girl. He's gonna protect that investment. Especially with all these jealousy killings going on.'

'That's why he's moving around so much?'

'OK, let's say he gets a new hole, but doesn't register it. What's going to happen?'

'Let's say he steals a hole.'

'Daisy, I love you!'

'But won't the beggar he kicks out make a complaint?'

'I love you even more.' To prove it, he kissed her full-on. Then turned to his faithful blurbfly. 'Any complaints come in, in the last week, say? Any beggars been vacated against their wishes?'

The blurb went flying, landing on four different holes in turn, only one of which was anywhere near to the Gorton pit. 'Cheetham Hill!' shouted Jazir. 'It's got to be. A good place to get lost.' He took the cube out of the new hole, fed it quickly, making the blurb sing with glee: 'Sauce, Harold Patrick, Mr. Fifty-five point seven eight punies all told. Vacated (non-compliant).

Current owner unknown. Investigation pending.'

'That means the cops will be on to them,' said Daisy.

'Yeah, some time in the next century. Beggars are the bottom-feeders, Daze. They come last in the game. Let's go.'

On the way out, Jazir collected at least a dozen of the little sugar cubes from various random holes. Daisy asked him what he was doing.

'Food.' Crunching one between his teeth. 'Yum yum. Knowledge.'

'You're mad, Jaz. Know that?'

'Getting that way.'

Twenty minutes later they were on a bus heading north of the city. Twenty minutes after that the suit-and-tie finally finished whatever he was doing in the gents' lavatory. He was hungry after his exertions, but not just for food. Those two kids, what had they been up to, running along the corridors like that? They shouldn't even be in here, these sacred chambers, not on a Saturday anyway. No way were they legitimate tramps. He would have to have words with the securiblurb. Maybe it needed feeding? Or maybe replacing all together. That was more expense off the year's budget, already down to the dregs. Those AnnoDominoes have us in chains.

The fat suit found the doorblurb fluttering in the foyer. A few harsh words, some tricky questions, and the fly was almost grounded in shame. The suit now had the precise time the two kids had entered the building and the time they had left. A simple calculation . . .

What the hell were they doing in here so long?

On a whim, he went up to the Room of Holes, just to make sure. The door was shut but not locked. Now where had they found a key? He made a mental note to have a complete security review expedited as he stepped into the room.

The adminiblurb was flying around in wild circles, sometimes even banging into the wall. The suit received a glancing blow from the thing as he struggled to get it under control. Really, it should follow his orders; he was on the official control panel. Something had messed with the blurb's orientation, obviously. Those bloody kids!

Two minutes of hard work got the thing under some kind of control, enough to make it do a retrograde flight path.

Now then . . . what was so interesting about two tramps, both of them currently NFA, and never mind some stupid hole in Cheetham Hill?

Play to win

Cheetham Hill, North Manchester. Saturday afternoon, a mad shopping rush. The things you have to push through, just to move an inch or two; the crowds, the cries, the litter and the loot. Last bastion of the real store; no megaburgs out here, no chains, no bondage, no packaged deals. And only a few scattered blurbs, hardly heard above the tumult of the frenzied crowd. And Daisy and Jaz pushing through towards the designated hole. Finding a thin man almost drowned under the wave and flash of passing trade. Jazir beamed down on him. 'What's the game?' he asked.

'What's your game, more like?'

'We're from the council. According to our records this hole belongs to a Mr Harold Patrick Sauce.'

'Damn right it does. I'm H.P. You're a bit fucking late.'

'I see,' said Daisy. 'So the infiltrators—'

'The what?'

'The beggar who stole the hole off you—'

'Fucking big bastard he was.'

'He's moved on, has he?'

'Well he's not here now, is he? A Saturday as well. Prime time, juicy pickings. Silly sucker. Aren't you two a little young to be—'

'We're raw recruits, Mr Sauce,' replied Daisy. 'Keen to learn. Was he alone?'

'What?'

'It's quite simple, Mr Sauce,' came in Jazir. 'My partner's asking if this infiltrator was working alone.'

'Do you think he'd throw me out of here alone? No way. Had a gang with him, didn't he? Big bastards the lot of them. Of course, I fought back, just too many of them, that's all.'

'Interesting. Does that tally with our findings, Officer Baloney?'

'No it doesn't, Officer Sutch. Our findings indicate he's working with a young girl.'

'That's a shame, because there's a reward for information leading to their capture.'

'Yeah, that's right,' said the beggar. 'He had this little kid with him, now I come to think of it. Rude little bleeder she was. Can I have my reward now?'

'Well, we need to know where they are?'

'That's easy, isn't it? They're living on Alma Street. Seen them hanging round there, haven't I? Fucking dump, they deserve it.'

'I see. Would you have the number?'

'Numbers? I can't even write me own name, never mind adding up.'

'You've been very helpful. Of course, you'll let the authorities know you've got your hole back.'

'I can't be arsed. You can do that.'

'A puny says you will.'

'A puny says I probably will. Two says I will, most definitely.'

'You can add up fine, Mr Sauce. Two it is.'

Jazir threw the coins down into the pit. The beggar caught them both, one in each hand. 'What about my reward?' asked the juggler.

'You just got it. Let's go, Officer Baloney.'

'I'm gonna report you two.'

'That is your right. You have our names. Sutch, Baloney.'

'Hey! Wait! Fucking bastards! Come back here!'

Harry the Sauce was barely out of his hole before the two officials had vanished into the crush.

'We'll need a map,' said Daisy.

'Already got one.'

Jazir waved his arms in the air. A blurb landed on one of them.

Walking out of the consumer stretch, into limbo zones, into half-empty streets. 'What's Joe going to do with Celia, if we find her?' Daisy asked.

'Take a DNA sample, get it analysed. It's got to be genetic, being a lucky bleeder. Something you're born with. That's why we need Benny on our side.'

'Why couldn't the AnnoDoms do the same, on the earlier cases?'

'I think they did. I've no doubt about it. They only need a drop of blood, you know that. Maybe they haven't found anything yet.'

'They didn't have to kill them for a drop of blood.'

'Why not? This is my view of the situation: first they identify a potential cheat, and take them in for testing. They test them, they kill them, they dump them. Perfect cover, with the jealousy they've infected us all with. Game play; take out the opposition and you can't fail to win. Remember, the dominoes will be desperate to know what this winning spirit is. If the government finds out that the games aren't total chance, goodbye to the national bones. That's their bottom line. The company is the game, we're just the players. They can't afford to have these lucky bleeders wandering about, free to play. It's like if the boot in Monopoly kept landing on the best streets, on purpose! So, they die. Simple. Expert play, actually.'

'As long as they don't get found out.'

'That's where we come in.'

'You find this easy, don't you?' asked Daisy.

'What?'

'Thinking like the dominoes.'

'I feel for them.'

'You what?'

'I mean . . . I feel like I . . . like I know them.'

'You sound like an advert.'

'Oh yeah. Play to win, baby!'

Alma Street was a desert of bricks, broken windows, boarded-up doors, collapsing roofs, misspelled graffiti, paved with dead bones. No blurbs flew. There was no point, and Jazir let his loose out of kindness. 'Where do we start?' Jazir asked.

Daisy pointed to the house at No. 27. Jazir saw the 'PLAY TO WIN' message and nodded.

Door open. Deserted. Recent occupation: half cups of tea, tomato sauce on plates, a camping stove. A note, handwritten, a child's hand. 'EDDIE, GONE TO FIND YOU. CELIA.'

'OK, reconstruction mode,' said Jazir. 'You start.'

'Let's see . . .' said Daisy. 'They were here last night, and found out they'd won.'

'How?'

Daisy looked around, saw the radio and turned it on. Tommy Tumbler's voice asking if they'd bought this week's chances yet. Turned off.

'Eddie sets out to collect the winnings,' she continued.

'Straight away?'

'No. He'd wait. He'd let the first rush collect. I'd say he left after midnight.'

'Not this morning?'

'I think he'd prefer the dark.'

'He leaves Celia here, alone?'

'He has to decide: take her with him, and risk her being stolen – this is property he's thinking of, right? His best ever chance – or let her stay here, a safe haven.'

'Only for so long.'

'That's fine. He's coming straight back.'

'But he doesn't.'

'No. Either he's cheating on her, or—'

'He's been kidnapped.'

'Or killed.'

'This is great, isn't it?' asked Jazir, suddenly.

'Yes.'

'Talking like this. Makes me want to—'

'Let's get on.'

'Right. OK, Eddie doesn't turn up. What would Celia do then?'

Daisy thought for a moment. 'If I was her, I'd wait till morning, definitely. Then I'd go check if Eddie picked up the money.'

'Of course he'd pick it up. And as soon as he does, the bones are on to him. He's no fixed abode. This is the only way they can find him. And isn't he gonna throw them off the scent. Completely normal, nothing like the first two. They'll be thinking he's working with someone else. He's a front man. You know what that means? Celia's in trouble.'

'But they don't know who Celia is.'

'Maybe they tortured Eddie.'

'This is getting stupid. What are we talking about? Murder? Torture?'

'Humour me. What would you do then?'

Daisy started pacing the room. 'I'd look around the centre for a bit. All the old haunts. Ask around the other beggars. Stuff like that.'

'OK. So we go back to town?'

'You can, Jaz. I'm staying here.'

'You're staying here?'

'She's going to come back. She's not going to find him. She'll come back here. It's safe. And there's the chance he might have just been delayed. She can't take the chance of him turning up. That's why she left the note.'

'I'll stay with you.'

'No need.'

'You'll be alone.'

'It's safe. Who knows where we are? Anyway, I'm used to it. And you'll be working tonight, won't you?'

'Waiting on? That's not work.'

'Tell your father that. You were late last night.'

'*This* is my work. I'll ring him. Tell him I'm studying.'

'Like you were last night? No. It's a Saturday night. It's curry night. Anyway, finding Celia is my job. Yours is breaking open a bone.'

'It's nice to work together.' He came a little closer. 'Maybe I should stay a little while, just to . . .' He put his arms around her. 'Just to . . . see if . . .'

'Go!'

# Play to win

A hearty five-course meal did wonders for the suit's stomach, if nothing for his afternoon duties. He slept for an hour or so in his private office. Maybe that second bottle of wine was a mistake. Still, it was all on expenses. Waste not, want not. Ah, what the fuck! The whole day had been a waste of time from beginning to end.

It was those kids that spoiled it for me. Threw me off course, didn't they? I've a good mind to . . .

In fact, I will.

The suit then called a good friend (and guzzling partner) of his, an Inspector Crawl of the Manchester Police Department.

Tramps were scum, and all this official hole business was just a clean-up operation: keep them off the street, keep them in a hole, under control. That was the party line and the suit didn't expect much interest from Crawl, but as soon as their names were mentioned the inspector went into launch sequence.

'What were those names again?' he demanded.

'Irwell, Edward. Hobart, Celia. That's what I got from the blurb anyway.'

'That's them! That's him, I mean. The AnnoDoms had us arrest him last night, for cheating at the game. Fucking tramp scumbag, wouldn't talk, would he. Tried everything. I even broke the law a few times. Nothing doing. Zilcho. Blank as the Joker's nipples. And get this, the guy had a ton of punies on him. Only won a half-cast hadn't he. The third time, as well, and he claims he's not cheating. Took it off him, of course. Police fund. Needy cause.'

'You should've let him go, Crawl. Let the people take care of him.'

'Wanted to, didn't I? Instead I had to ferry him over to the

House of Chances this afternoon. They're gonna stick some probes in him, or something.'

'Sounds like fun.'

'Doesn't it? So who were these kids after him?'

'Don't know. Blurb couldn't tell me.'

'They're on to something, whatever it is. Cheetham Hill, you say. Give us the hole's address. H.P. Sauce? I know that bastard. Pulled him up a few times, begging without a hole. He'll talk. Maybe I'll check it out tonight, if no murders come in. Be nice to get in the domdom's good book.'

'Aye. Whoever let those boneheads into Manchester, *they* want probing.'

'It was your lot, wasn't it?'

'That's what I mean. And I'm sitting on the thick end.'

'Ouch!'

The inspector went back to shuffling some papers around his desk. Mainly though, he spent the hours fondling his choices. How he loved to watch those little numbers throb. Special rate for the cops. Nice. How he loved the thought of getting kissed by Lady Luck. He was on until midnight. Graveyard watch. Years to go. Maybe he should get some burgers in. Special rate for the cops. Very nice. But the phone rang before he could lift it.

Hope this isn't serious.

It was. It was the Company. Annie Domidum. Edward Irwell (NFA) had been probed and found innocent. He was most probably working with an accomplice . . .

Play to win

Jazir left Daisy a few punies (emergency fund) but she had no intention of spending them. Celia might come back at any moment, or Eddie for that matter, and she couldn't risk not being here for them. She made do with a tin of astrobeans, barely warm because the camping stove sputtered to a halt halfway through. After that, later on, only stone-cold pseudo-soup. Occasionally she would stand on the doorstep, looking up and down the street. No sign, no life. Nothing doing. Doing nothing. What could she do? Nothing to do to pass the time. No books with her. The only paper she could find was the scrap that Celia had written her message to Eddie on. And the pencil. That would do. On the back of the paper she performed some high-level quadraction equations. Her way of being calm.

Nightfall. Candlelight. Waves of shadow, shapes in the corners.

She tried the radio for company, but no matter how often she tuned the dial, only the AD channel could be heard. Tommy Tumbler's stupid voice and the occasional Frank Scenario ballad for credibility, but mostly just adverts for life enhancement through the copious purchase of this week's dominoes!

Time to lie down. A sofa covered with a musty blanket. Celia's imagined body wrapped in the same shape, the night just gone.

She thought about Hackle. What he was after, and why. All he needed was proof positive that the AnnoDomino Co. was killing people, or else an analysis of Celia's DNA that revealed the winning genes. He could publish the findings and the game would be shut down. Easy. But she knew, by now, that wouldn't satisfy him. He wants to win, that's the game. It's personal, isn't it? He wants to win the double-six, become the new god of numbers. Something happened between him and this Malthorpe guy, way back. Hackle wants a proper revenge. He's not letting on half of what happened. He's using us, but do I care? No. Not really.

She thought about her father and his role in all this. His refusal to help her. His warnings. There is no help. It kills.

The eleven o'clock news ('brought to you courtesy of the Big Whoomphy – the meat on the bones!') brought little of comfort. The Domino Co. had always reported the jealousy murders, with names, maybe to cover their traces if the bones should ever tumble and fall. This week it admitted that two people had been killed and that it was doing everything in its power to stop the damage. No mention of Eddie Irwell in the list of ultimate losers. Was this good or bad? Were they lying about his demise, or just cutting their losses? Maybe they'd actually come to their senses; killing their own players, no matter how good, was no way to win the bigger battle.

What was that? A noise? Outside?

Daisy pulled herself out of spiralling thoughts, turned off the radio and listened hard. Nothing, now . . .

There! There it was again. The door was being pushed open.

'Who's that?' Daisy's voice echoed in the candlelight.

No answer.

'Celia?'

Flickering shadows.

'Eddie? Edward Irwell? That you?'

'Not quite.'

A blurbfly came out of the darkness. A man stepped through the shadows its flight had generated. The man was big, fat even, tied into a crumpled jacket and stretched casual slacks. The blurb was painted with a luminous letter W. Two more Ws burned in the darkness.

play to win

Jazir had a hard time of it Saturday night. He got some orders for curries mixed up, nearly dropped a plateful of Chicken Korma over a woman, gave the wrong change for a ten-spot puny. His father gave him an earful, told him to get in line. His two brothers sniggered through the whole episode, sharing half a smile between them.

Two hours still to go before closing, the place jammed to the flock walls with spicehounds. Working the tables like a slave for no wages. It was the family business after all. Yes sir, no sir, two Madras, four Korma, one Dhansak, six poppadoms, two naan, one chapati, four pilau rice, straight away, kind sir! (And fuck you too!)

The thought of Daisy was pressing on him. The last thing on his mind was the game. Funny then, in the midst of this feeling, he gets a major insight.

It was when he was in the kitchen, sorting a twelve-headed order. Just for luck, he took a mouthful of Thunderloo hot sauce, and got some on his hands. Did the order, needed a piss. Forgot the precautions. Five minutes later his dick was smarting with hot knives. Bloody chillies! Seeping through the skin.

That was it. Just that thought, standing awkward, trying to adjust his trousers.

Fuck! It's seeping through! That's it. Porous membrane. So obvious.

At midnight he checked at Daisy's door. No answer. OK, he'd go tomorrow, first bus out. He had some other work to do that night. Some thinking, anyway.

Lying in bed, gentle Masala blurb crawling over his chest, biting his skin playfully. Jazir hardly noticed it was there, nor the two that flickered around his room, nor the one resting on the window ledge. His mind, instead, was filled with a large rotating image of a single domino. He'd gone to bed clutching his week's purchase, two of them, tickling his palm with random life.

The genetics of chance.

It's a porous membrane, nothing to do with who buys the domino. Witness Eddie buying them for Celia. There was only one way the lucky bleeders could affect the bones, and that was by holding them. Something happened, something to do with the fact that everybody held their dominoes tight, all through the week. Osmosis. Something was coming out of Celia, through the skin, and seeping into the bone. Or else the other way – bone to girl. A pheromone? Maybe. But if something could get in, even if it was only a message, then he could get in there as well. If he just knew the coding, the chemicals, the smell, the sweat, the nervous vibrations, whatever it was that made the bone come good. Maybe it wasn't genetic?

They really needed to find this Celia.

In the past he'd assumed, like everyone, that the bones were made up of some simple random number chip, a power source, some kind of transmitting device locked to the AnnoDomino frequency. Now he wasn't so sure. Not since finding out how the blurbs were functioning. This was beyond technology.

Organic engineering. Grow your own. Grow your own dream.

But how were the dominoes connected to each other, and to the House of Chances? Were they like the blurbs, half alive with something, communicating through some new process? Maybe they were filled with the same stuff as the blurbs. The grease, the gloop, the vaz. If he could only get one open!

Sleep brought dreams. Dreams brought an answer. The image from his computer, his screen. Like the screen was his brain, and a window was opening, and a window inside that one, and a window inside that, and a window and a window and a window. Smaller, smaller, smaller, all the way to infinity. A bone on each screen. A bone on each bone. Numbers upon numbers. Fractal dreams.

Miss Sayer's face appearing to him, thousands of times. Grab the wings!

Tumbling through space, he woke up smiling, crunching on sugar.

At least a dozen blurbs were hovering above his bed, under Masala's command. They wanted escape, he could feel it. Escape from the bones.

Jazir got up, went to the window and looked out. The darkness out there. The blurbs had followed him to the window. And a million more fluttered over Manchester, increasing daily. He could see some of them, glittering wings through the night air.

Jazir stepped up on the sill, and crouched there on his haunches. The blurbs took off for some distant place. He could follow them, surely he could. Play a part. He looked down. It wasn't too far a drop, first-floor window, but he wasn't thinking about that. He smeared some vaz all over his naked body. It glistened. He wiped some on his tongue, swallowed. It glistened. Inside and out.

'There's only one fucking domino, you bastards!'

He took off.

Play to win

Sunday morning was a breakfast of doom. His mother was highly ashamed. She wouldn't speak to him. His sister was ordered from the room. His brothers giggled from the stairs. His father was mood-swinging between glaring silences and ranting apoplexy.

'What was the meaning of it? What was he thinking of? Why? You tell me why! And naked, but I wouldn't mind! What must the neighbours, the nice neighbours be thinking, I cannot be thinking. Never in England should this be happening!'

And then the silence and the glares.

Jazir was OK, a little bruised. He'd landed half on the dustbin, which had fallen over and activated the neighbours' security lighting. Really, he should've been more badly hurt. Just for one second he really had flown, he was sure of it! How else to explain his lack of injury?

The son could say none of this to his father. His father had hit him. The first time in a long time, and the last ever. His father knew this. He knew his son was lost. The father could say none of this to his son.

Jazir escaped by pledging himself to hard, hard work and lots of it, both in the restaurant and in his lessons.

One hour later found him limping slightly down Alma Street. No signs of life, but that was good, that was normal for the area. He actually knocked on the door of No. 27 for some reason, maybe so as not to scare Daisy. He was so excited at what he had to tell her. He got no answer anyway, so he pushed the door open and went on through. No Daisy. He called out her name. Went upstairs, looked in every room.

Emptiness. The camping stove knocked over, soup spilled on the floor.

Some unfinished equations on a scrap of paper.

A shadow's breath.

PLAY TO WIN

PLAY TO WIN
PLAY TO WIN
PLAY TO WIN

PLAY TO WIN
PLAY TO WIN

PLAY TO WIN

PLAY TO WIN

TO WIN PLAY TO WIN  PLA
WIN PLAY TO WIN  PLAY

WIN PLAY TO WIN P

WIN PLAY T
PLAY TO WIN

WIN PLAY TO WIN

PLAY TO LOSE PLAY TO

TO WIN PLAY TO WIN PLA

PLAY TO WIN

PLAY TO WIN

PLAY TO WIN

PLAY TO WIN
PLAY TO WIN
PLAY TO WIN

PLAY TO WIN

**J**ames Love (Five-Four) got the call on Sunday morning, rousing him from a drunken sleep. He was expecting it to be Daisy, just because there was nobody else. He couldn't quite remember if he'd been harsh on her yesterday. Maybe she was ready for the next game now, the next lesson. He certainly didn't expect the cold voice that cut short his greetings. 'Mr Love?'

'Last time I looked.'

'You may wish to be less jocular.'

'You what? Who is this?'

'The police. We have your daughter.'

'Daisy? What—'

'She has asked that you visit her. Manchester Central. Thank you.'

'What's happened?'

An empty phone.

The long bus journey was hard for him; not having been to the city for so many years, not since – well, not since the old days – he was scared at what he would find. His tiny life kind of suited him; soon he could retire, and spend his final days doing more or less what he'd done for the last twenty years, the wasting of his life. He *liked* wasting his life; he was an expert at it.

Manchester, thankfully, was the same as when he had left it in the Seventies, only more so: dim, grim, grimy, grubby, grey. Someone had stuck a patina of flash over the top of it all, in the modern style. He was still drunk, of course, but even the police station looked the same. He'd been arrested in the early Seventies; some protest march had gone wrong. He'd spent a night in the cells. One new thing from those days was the giant scarlet W that floated above the entrance. Someone had thrown a stone against it, making a ragged, pleasing hole. Good shot. Thank God it was a Sunday. No crowds, just the detritus of

Saturday night, his daughter included . . .

Some buffoon called Crawl seemed to be in charge, but he wouldn't give out details of the case.

'Is my daughter under arrest?'

'Have you been drinking, Mr Love? I trust you didn't drive here.'

'I did actually. Was that your parking space?'

'You've got fifteen minutes.'

Crawl watched the whole thing on the video system. He'd seen some hardnut bastards do some funny things in cells before, but playing dominoes? That was a first. The filthy drunk tumbling the bones onto the table. The following conversation was recorded:

'What's going on?' asked the father.

'I don't know. They won't tell me anything,' replied the daughter.

'You must've done something.'

'I broke into the town hall.'

'The town hall! Good on yer, girl!'

'Just the Room of Holes, that's all. We wanted to find out—'

'We? Who's we?'

'Erm . . . a friend of mine.'

'I see.'

'Can you get me out of here?'

'You should've called a lawyer.'

'I don't need a lawyer. I haven't done anything wrong. Well, not seriously wrong. We just needed some details. Locations of a beggar. That's all.'

'Which is not a crime actually. Under the Vagrancy Act, the location of begging holes and who belongs in them is supposed to be public knowledge. Of course, you should've got permission first.'

'You know the details?'

'I used to be one.'

'A beggar? When was this?'

'You can't play that domino, by the way.'

'What?'

'It doesn't match.'

'They think I know where this Celia is, but I don't.'

'Celia?'

'The beggar we were looking for. Celia Hobart. Tell them! I don't know where she is.'

'I think they can hear you.'

'OK, so I did wrong. But locking me up for a night? For opening a door? For that? And not telling me anything. It's not right.'

'No. It's not right. Are you telling *me* everything?'

'Yes.'

'I see. That's another wrong bone, by the way.'

'Yes. I know.'

'Right. I'll do what I can. Domino, by the way.'

'Well played.'

'You too, Daisy. Keep the bones.'

Crawl was on him as soon as he came out. 'What was all that? Some kind of secret code?'

'Just a gentle game.'

'Your daughter has certain information.'

'Evidently.'

'All she has to do is give us that information and she goes free.'

'The location of a beggar? Since when have beggars featured large in the police's concerns, I wonder. This must be a very special beggar.'

'Who is this "friend" your daughter refers to?'

'I wouldn't know. I wish I did.'

'I called you in good faith, Mr Love.'

'In the hope that I would make her see sense? Or just to watch us talking? Really, your methods are most primitive.'

'You are free to go.'

'My daughter?'

'Not quite yet.'

'She has rights, as a citizen.'

'Oh, she does. Unfortunately, I have more rights, as a policeman.'

Jimmy left the station. His mood was strange. A drink would cure it, but that wasn't an option. Not if what he suspected was true. In Albert Square, he sat down on a bench. It was Sunday, quiet, peaceful. A few young lovers, hand in hand. Some children. Laughter. A police car travelling slowly across his vision, circling behind the town hall. The third time it appeared, he waved nonchalantly at the driver.

He could wait.

Daisy was a good player, he'd seen to that. Of course, not a master. Not yet. He'd seen to that as well. She made mistakes, sure, but one thing she never did was play a mismatched bone. In their last game she had played two. It was a message. Despite his warnings, Daisy had gone ahead. Now she was paying for it.

Something was wrong with the bones. It had started. The maze was open once again. He would have to go back in.

Play to win

Jimmy Love had, of course, accepted Hackle's offer to 'meet the old gang'. It was 1977, and any chance of a better life was not to be lost. They drove out to West Didsbury, where Hackle had bought a house. To help with the mortgage he had rented out two of the rooms; one to Malthorpe and Susan, the other to Georgie Horn. It was actually very nice to see them all again, especially good old Blank-Blank. They greeted each other:

'Blank-Blank!'

'Five-Four!'

As though still in the classroom.

Malthorpe looked on, the same old dark eye, now made bitter by years. Susan Prentice was pleased to see him, which was a surprise; she'd totally ignored him at school. Amazing these two had stuck together, were lovers even, because you wouldn't place Paul Malthorpe as the settling kind.

Hackle poured them all a drink and Malthorpe made a toast.

'Play to win!'

'Play to win!'

They had talked for a while, mainly about the past and what had happened in between. Jimmy was slightly ashamed of his failings, compared to this team of evidently self-confident, successful people. Hackle was a teacher, just starting at the university, hoping to make his way up in the world. Malthorpe was working the stock markets, making a nice little packet. Susan was a top executive at a city-centre bank, in charge of investments. Jimmy's dormant socialist leanings were roused by all this; how could they pervert Miss Sayer's teachings in this way, turning numbers into money. He didn't say anything.

And Georgie?

Georgie was Georgie was Georgie was Georgie was Georgie.

Good old Blank-Blank, doing nothing, happy to be living off the others' earnings. Yeah, they looked after him; fed him, clothed him, pampered him. Jimmy couldn't see the reasons for this; maybe a guilt thing, related to their salaries? Whatever,

Georgie Horn was their pet.

They talked freely about their lives, but strangely, never about mathematics. Nobody referred to Miss Sayer and what they had learned in that strange year. Later, on his way home, Jimmy was to think of this omission. It didn't matter much; he hadn't done any maths for years, never even picked up a domino set.

Over the next few weeks he would visit them again, usually on a Saturday night, when a fine meal would be served and vintage wine poured freely. They asked for nothing in return, only his company, which Jimmy was happy to give.

One night, perhaps in early 1978, the post-dinner conversation took a surprising turn. They were talking about finding Jimmy a proper job, one in keeping with his talents. Malthorpe mentioned that the stock markets were based on chance alone, and that so-called experts like himself were only pretending to have knowledge. It was a chaotic system, ripe for exploitation, perfect for a player like Jimmy. Jimmy was all set to protest, if he could find the wine-sapped energy, when suddenly Georgie jumped onto the table, scattering ashtrays and breaking a wineglass. 'Can we play now?' he shouted. 'Can we play now, Max? Play the game?'

A silence came over the table. Susan took in a breath, Hackle shook his head slowly, Malthorpe made a little laugh.

'Get down, Blank-Blank,' he said, quite firmly. 'You're making a scene.'

'Can we, Max?' Georgie continued. 'Play to win, Max.'

Jimmy was intrigued, because this was the first real excitement these overly civilized dinner parties had generated. 'Is he referring to what I think he's referring to?'

Another look passed around the table. 'Of course!' cried Max. 'Let's play some dominoes. You up for it, Five-Four?'

'I'm game, Two-Blank.'

Susan went to a small desk, where a finely carved ebony box rested. She brought this over to the dining table, whilst Georgie eagerly cleared the playing area. What a sound they made, those beautiful ebony bones! A sound that Jimmy hadn't heard since his teens. He was fascinated by the sound, and the sight of all those numbers scattering over the finely polished surface. At the same time, slightly uncomfortable; he'd given up dominoes, and all other games, as politics took over his life. The playing of games was a childish activity, offering nothing to the gallant cause. Did he still have the skill, the expertise? As the bones were shuffled and chosen, it came to him that gathered around this table were four exceptional players. And yet none of them had ever played a championship match, as far as he knew.

The room was tense, silent, only the occasional clack of a bone, a knock on the table. Susan had lit some candles, whose shadows danced over the playing surface.

The first game was over quickly, easily won by Malthorpe. Jimmy was left with a deficit of high-scoring dominoes. The next two games went to Hackle and Susan, respectively. Only Georgie now matched Jimmy's lack of success. The thin, nervous child-man was twitching with frustration. During their fourth game, he suddenly threw his bones across the table, wrecking the square-jointed snake of carefully matched numbers. 'It's not fair!' he cried. 'I never win.'

'Game over,' said Max, calmly.

Jimmy was glad of the sudden tantrum; he couldn't have faced another defeat by his once equals. But Georgie wouldn't be shut up so easily. 'I want to play the lucky bones,' he screamed.

'It's time the boy was in bed,' said Susan, ready to lead him to some nursery upstairs.

'Lucky bones! Lucky bones! Lucky, lucky, lucky bones!'

'Be quiet, Blank-Blank,' said Max. 'You know that's not allowed.'

'It is! It is allowed! Play to win, you promised.'

'Not when we have guests.'

Malthorpe cut in here: 'Go on, Max. You might as well.'

Hackle thought for a moment. 'If we must. Susan?'

As Susan left the room, Jimmy began to wonder if this whole episode had been carefully staged, just for his benefit.

She returned some few minutes later carrying another box. This one was quite plain, giving no hint as to its contents. 'Who will shuffle?' she asked.

'Jimmy, I think,' answered Malthorpe.

She gave the box to Jimmy. He was surprised to notice that it was slightly warm to the touch, as though something alive lay trapped within it. A sliding lid revealed a perfectly normal set of dominoes, carefully arranged in ascending order. He turned the whole box upside down to scatter the bones.

What happened then took him by surprise. Little did he know at the time, he was actually casting the bones of his life.

As soon as the dominoes hit the table their numbers began to change!

What was once the double-six was now the five-one. He picked up the bone, not believing what he had seen. In his hand, after about two seconds, it changed again, this time to the three-one. Every two seconds brought another change. He looked up, to see that all the others were staring at him, gauging his reactions. Susan had the broad smile of someone sharing a secret.

'Isn't it good!' squealed Georgie. 'Good, good, good!'

Jimmy looked down at the other dominoes; they were all pulsing and changing at regular two-second intervals.

'Intrigued, Jimmy?' asked Malthorpe.

'Puzzled.'

'It's quite simple. Max, here, invented them. We call them randominoes. Very clever; a random number generator in each piece. The dots are best thought of as rather large pixels. They light up according to the numbers generated.'

'You expect me to play with these?'

'Play to win!' shouted Georgie. 'Play to win!'

'It adds an edge, shall we say,' said Hackle.

'Having played dominoes for so long together,' added Susan, 'we became bored with each other's strategies.'

'Would you like to try your hand?' asked Max.

'I don't see how . . .'

'Play! You'll soon pick it up.'

The first game was a disaster for Jimmy. Every time he tried to play a certain number, it had already changed as he moved it. The others were doing better, in some way able to predict, if not the exact number, then a close neighbour to it. As soon as a bone was played, it stopped changing. If mismatched, and removed, it started changing again.

'Contact transmitters,' explained Susan. 'They register the touch of another domino.'

Jimmy nodded his head vaguely, trying to concentrate.

Six games they played in all. Jimmy lost every time. Max, Susan and Malthorpe won one apiece. Strangest of all, Georgie Blank-Blank won three of them. In some way he was connected to the randomness, as though his naive, mismatched brain was closer in spirit to these crazy, nebulous dominoes.

Jimmy had his first real inkling as to why they kept this simple soul close to their hearts.

Over the next few months, Jimmy was gradually introduced to the real purpose of the house; they were continuing with Miss

Sayer's work, to bring mathematics alive. To this end they had formed themselves into a group called the Number Gumbo. Jimmy was given various of their pamphlets and magazines to study, and long dinners often ended with even longer conversations, in which they would discuss the finer points of the latest research. Always they played the randominoes, always Jimmy lost, and almost always Georgie won the prizes.

Becoming involved in mathematics again was very much like coming home for Jimmy. A purpose, a direction. Also, they had found a position for him in Susan's bank. A lowly post, but still more lucrative than mending pipes. It was at this bank that he met Marigold Green. His courting of this homely secretary was in sharp contrast to the fevered atmosphere of Hackle's house. Their first awkward sex coincided with the group introducing him to the far randier concepts of nymphomation.

Jimmy went along with a Black Math ritual, even if his reason told him not to believe a word of it. Lights out, candles lit, incense, tuneless music, diagrams on the floor, chanting, strange equations that never quite came true, not in this world anyway. All five of them touched together the dominoes given them by Miss Sayer: double-six, five-zero, two-zero, double-zero, five-four. Thus it was that James Love was initiated.

He could justify his involvement by calling it the wages he paid for being accepted, at last. A lover, a job, new friends, money, intellectual pursuits, mathematics. A time to grow young, he called it. No more politics, no more bitterness. And the crazy mazes they were making, only on paper, only in the computer's innards, or the graph of the brain. Abstract games of no real consequence, very much like his love for Marigold, his love for his job, his love of the group; empty forms he could cling to without consequence.

Two months after his initiation, James Love won his first victory at randominoes. There followed possibly the two most exciting years of his life. He was promoted at the bank, enabling him to put down a deposit on a house in Droylsden. He was made a special consultant on the *Number Gumbo* magazine, supplying a much-needed distance to the more extravagant claims put forward. For a short period in early 1978 he had a semi-vigorous affair with Susan Prentice, or rather, had the affair conducted upon his body. They kept it hidden from Malthorpe, but Jimmy was sure the guy knew anyway, and always had the feeling that he could never love Susan like Paul could. Jimmy just wasn't violent enough, never had been. Those marks on her throat for instance; he could never do that to her. Subsequently, later in 1978, James Love married Marigold Green, to return himself to normal, to try for a child, to try for love. Maximus Hackle was the best man; the confetti was shredded equations.

All things in his life fell into place, like an expert play at the bones, a network of connections, or else a convoluted complex equation, whose many variables finally add up to zero. Until that day, in 1979, when Hackle told them that the maze was coming alive. Down in the cellar, where the dark numbers twist and turn. Blank, blank, vanishing.

Poor old Georgie.

'Poor old Georgie,' James Love muttered to himself, shaking the memories away. He looked at his watch, an hour had passed. The police car was nowhere to be seen. Just to make sure, he waited another thirty minutes.

A lonely blurb landed at his feet. It started to sing.

Play to win. Play to win.

Very well.

There was a phone box on the corner. From there he rang Max Hackle's number. It cost him one nanopuny.

## Play to win

Jazir called in at the Golden Samosa on his way back from Cheetham Hill. He banged on Daisy's door for ten minutes, calling her name. No answer. His father was working the rice downstairs, and was most surprised to see his son come rushing into the kitchen. 'Tonight I was expecting you, not so soon.' Stirring the mixture. 'Sunday afternoon, very quiet.'

'Father, have you seen Daisy?'

'Who?'

'The lodger!'

'I wish I had. She is owing me rent.'

'Do you have a key?'

'A key?'

'To the flat. Please! I think something's happened to her.'

'What is happening?'

'Something bad.'

'No more scandals, I am hoping?'

'The key?'

'Oh, yes. Somewhere . . .'

He didn't know why he checked the flat, just that he had to. He was hoping against hope, I suppose. Hoping she was hiding in there, perhaps with Celia in storage until the coast was clear. That would be brilliant. That would be a miracle.

But nothing, just lots of workbooks, creamed-out bones in careful piles, her clothes, folded neatly. No mess, no struggle, no

Daisy. He wrote her a quick note and left it on her desk.

His father had followed him in. Jazir asked if he could keep the keys for a while, just so he could keep checking.

'If you must. Will my son be working tonight?'

Yes, his son would be working tonight. Already out of the door.

'Good, because I said you'd be here.'

Jazir stopped on the stairs. 'What?'

'The woman—'

'Woman? What woman?'

'Asking for Jazir or Daisy.'

'What was her name?'

'Name? She was a beggar woman. Do they have names?'

'Father . . .'

'You're knowing I don't like beggars in my establishment. Especially not asking for free curries as promised by somebody.'

Jazir wanted to embrace him, but couldn't. It just wasn't done. He did it anyway.

'Get off me! What is wrong with you now? First nakedness out of windows, now offering free curries to all and sundries—'

'Tonight, I'm gonna work my pants off!'

Next stop, West Didsbury. He was trying his best to follow the rules of cool, don't set yourself on fire, but after waiting five minutes for a bus, decided that fire was worth something after all. He flagged a taxi, because what were punies against Daisy's well-being? Every red light, every zebra crossing stoked his anger. He didn't stop until Sweet Benny opened the door to him.

'Where is he?'

'Joe?'

'Hackle! That bastard! Where is he?'

'He's entertaining—'

Jazir pushed Benny aside. 'Not any more, he isn't.'

Joe met him in the hallway. 'Calm down, boy.'

'I want Hackle.'

'He has a visitor. Is there a problem?'

'The problem?' Jazir caught his breath. 'The problem is this fucking game . . .' He opened the nearest door. 'Where is he?'

'In his study. I don't think he'd appreciate—'

'I don't fucking care any more. Just let me at him.'

'Is it to do with Daisy?'

'Yeah. Daisy. They've got her! Is this his study—'

'Ah, Jazir.' Hackle rose to meet him. 'We were just talking about you . . .'

Jazir rushed into the room, ignoring the other man present. He went face-up, close to Hackle. 'The bones have got Daisy, and I'm blaming you, Hackle! You dragged her into this stupid scheme. What now, eh? What move shall we make next? Shall we all kill ourselves, and get it over with?'

'Please. You're giving me a headache. Have you met Daisy's father, by the way . . .'

Play to win

Daisy was on her twenty-ninth game of solo bones when Inspector Crawl came into the cell. She ignored him, of course, and continued playing one tile against another. Her father's special set of numbers; so well played over so many years, the dots had almost vanished.

'Is it fun?' he asked.

'Nah, nah, nah.'

'I haven't played since I was tiny.'

'Nah, nah.'

'Can't be much fun, not on your own. I mean, don't you always know what the opponent's going to do?'

'Nah.'

'Maybe you could teach me a few moves.'

'Nah, nah, nah.'

He sat himself down opposite her. 'Go on. Humiliate me.'

Daisy sighed, turned all the bones face-down and shuffled them. 'Choose five', she said. 'Play to win.'

'I always do.'

'Domino,' said Daisy. The game was over in a minute.

'Hmm. You knocked the spots off me, Daisy.'

Daisy didn't laugh.

'Is there some trick to it?'

'Just play.'

Domino. The second game also over in a minute.

'Can we go a bit slower, please?'

'Play . . .'

'I'm playing. You know, I had a very interesting call a few minutes ago.'

'Oh yes.'

'Professor Hackle, from the university. He thinks very highly of you. He tells me you're one of his best students. Mathematics, is it?'

'Your go. . .'

'I was hopeless at maths. Still am. As long as my arrest quotas add up, I don't really mind. Still, it must be nice to be talented.'

'Play . . .'

'It's not something you'd want to waste, is it? A talent?'

'Your go . . .'

'Knock, knock.'

'Draw another one.'

'Professor Hackle has agreed to pay for any damages done to town hall property. Obviously, he's a highly respected member of the community. The trouble is, I've had my men go over that door to the Room of Holes. It's not been forced, has it? And there's some strange substance been found in the lock. The science boys are looking at that. But there's no damage to pay for. And you only took what was rightfully public property. So what am I keeping you here for?'

'Domino,' said Daisy. 'Game over.'

'You know what the game is, and I know what the game is. And you know that I know what the game is. And I know that you know that I know—'

'This could go on for ever,' said Daisy.

'It needn't. It's about the bones, isn't it? The House of Chances. Mr Million. Cookie Luck and Tommy Tumbler and Play to win and bet your punies on a dream of lovelies. And aren't we all going to benefit? Consider the number of people that have moved to Manchester in the last ten months, just to have a bit of fun. It's for charity. It's good for local business. Extra funding for the jolly coppers. Bigger burgers, more chances, a better class of person, and we all live happily ever after, isn't that the ticket?'

'What do you want, Crawl?'

'It's a nightmare, Daisy. The bones sponsor the burgers, and the burgers sponsor us. It's not working out. This is off the record, you follow me. No tapes.'

'How can I trust you.'

'Come on.' Crawl stood up.

'Where are we going?'

'Outside. Fresh air.'

Albert Square. A bench. A plague of blurbs, circling.

'Your father sat here for over an hour this morning, waiting.'

'For me?'

'No. For my boys to leave him be. He took off eventually, shook us off in a taxi, somewhere in Altrincham. Good player, right?'

Daisy laughed. She was holding tight to the box of bones, like it was the last treasure of the world.

'So then, what's the score, eh? Who's winning? The Anno-fucking-Dominoes, that's who. Who's losing? Everybody else. I know that things are going wrong.'

'You know they're killing people?'

'My hands are tied, Daisy. It's not me, and a group of us here are getting mighty pissed off. Two cases have been closed. The big boys up top are expecting compliance. It's money. That's all.'

'Now there'll be a third.'

'Eddie Irwell? Nah, there's nothing wrong with him. He'll be let free.'

'The bones have got him?'

'Yeah, and that's where I should've taken you already.'

'Why haven't you?'

Crawl looking around for a few seconds, kicked away a blurb. 'The thing is, I'm not sure which side I'm on any more. If I'm on the bone side, I get a pay rise. If I'm on your side, I get sacked. Or even worse, I get put back on the street. I don't think I could wear one of them big Ws, not with my figure.'

'I'm not on any *side*,' said Daisy.

'You know about this Celia Hobart character. She's a lucky bleeder, right? The bones would like to wring her dry, of course they would. Who are you working for?'

'Just myself.'

'Yourself . . . and a friend?'

'The two of us, yes. But I've given up trying. It's too dangerous.'

'Maybe we could work together, Daisy? With my resources . . .'

'No. It's over.'

'I see.' The inspector stood up. 'Thanks for the game.'

'I'm free?'

'Go on. Before I change my mind.'

'You won't follow me?'

'Daisy, I know where you live.'

'Thank you.'

'Tell that Hackle prof to make the cheque out to me, personal. OK?'

Daisy smiled at him.

By the time she got back home, the Golden Samosa was closed until the evening. That was OK, she didn't want to see Jazir, not yet. She didn't want to see anybody. Everything was here that she wanted: her desk, her work, her bed. Sleep, she wanted, and some comfort. Most of all, some time to think. She saw the note while taking off her clothes. 'Daisy, gone to find you. Jaz.'

She laughed, quietly. He found her two minutes later, in bed.

It was the best love they had ever made.

An unmarked police car waiting outside. Two cops, chewing gum, rubbing their dancing bones to keep warm. Not a scarlet W in sight.

Play to win

All the pieces were poised for the game by the time the Golden Samosa opened for that evening. Jazir Malik was to work as normal; he would only be the messenger. Daisy Love was upstairs, hanging on the signal. Joe Crocus and Sweet Benny were making a five-course curryfest last all night. Their car was outside, waiting for action. Nobody knew where DJ Dopejack was and nobody much cared. He hadn't been seen since Friday's argument, no loss. Max Hackle was waiting back at his house, having dinner with Jimmy Love. Hackle had given Jazir the punies required for a special curry. This was paid to father Saeed Malik, in compensation for a free meal to a beggar.

If she ever arrived that is. The whole game hanging on that one final bone.

Ten o'clock came and went. Eleven. The restaurant always shut at midnight, no way was Mr Saeed keeping open after that – on a Sunday, even! – just for some hare-brained scheme, even if the most esteemed Professor Maximus Hackle of the University of Manchester had set it up special.

She was the last customer. At ten to twelve she arrived, demanding, 'A free curry as promised, for me and my friends.'

'Friends?' shouted Jazir's father, when told of this. 'Since when has anybody been mentioning friends?'

'Please, Father, you'll be compensated—'

'And ten to shutting time it is, I shall have to pay my staff extra wages, no? And what is it these filthy beggars is wanting, only the Chef's Very Special times seven?'

'Fully compensated.'

'I shall be expecting more than fully.'

Jazir went back to the table. All the other diners had left, apart from Joe and Benny and these seven ragged brethren of the streets, come to claim reward for information. They could not be contained, constantly moving around from table to table, trying on serviettes, nibbling at every passing poppadom and relish tray, singing bawdy songs of following the endless road to

the perfect resting hole, guzzling the finest lagers, burping, fart-
ing, kissing the menus, demanding, in the loudest voices, that
their starters arrive.

Jazir tried his best to keep them happy, and with every dish
he served, always asking the main beggar woman if she would
tell him where Celia was yet. 'When I'm finished,' she replied,
smacking chilli sauce around her lips. 'Lovely grub!'

'You do know where she is?' Jazir asked, worried now.

'More food!'

'More, more, more!' chorused the brethren.

Play to win

The Yawndale Monstermarket was opened in the early 1970s. A
grotesque slab of prefab, its birth destroyed whole streets of
shops and an outdoor market; it gobbled them like a glutton. Its
twenty-five-year reign as the 'ultimate shopping experience' was
only relieved by four separate terrorist attacks, each carried out
by a different group, the last by the now-famous Children of the
Swamp. In 1998, this ramshackle band of eco-warriors had gutted
the building with a devastating methane bomb explosion. The
Yawndale Corporation cut the funding, the monster breathed its
last, sad, special, once-only offer.

A year later a new sign had appeared above the main
entrance on Market Street: 'OPENING SOON! THE
DOMIDOME EXPERIENCE! SHOPPING BY NUMBERS!' Brought
to us courtesy of the AnnoDoms, of course, but they'd need the
extra lovelies from going national to start extensive work on the
jittery substructure.

All was dark and quiet on Shude Hill that early Monday morning, past one o'clock, but only just. Shude Hill was the street behind the slumbering behemoth; no sign here, no special announcements, no blurbs to proclaim the future delights. A car pulls up outside the building. Benny's at the wheel, Joe's in the passenger seat. Behind them Daisy and the beggar woman, whose name we now learn is Mama Mole. On the journey here she had told the three Dark Fractals that Little Celia had been found wandering the streets looking for Eddie Irwell. Saturday evening, this would have been. She had told of her fears for Eddie's safety. The beggars had immediately offered their help to find him, coming together in the face of bad bones. Finding nothing, no traces, no winnings . . .

Leaving Benny with the engine running, Joe and Daisy followed the Mole woman through a loose ventilation grid. This was once the arse of the place, pumping out a constant stream of bad air, where a tramp could sleep snug and warm in the old days. Now only the faint, lingering smells of methane hung in the dark tunnel.

Mama Mole, as befits the name, fairly ran along the cramped passage, leaving Daisy and Joe to suffer knocks and bruises from protrusive pipes and jagged panels. One of these was pushed aside, the Mole stepped through, beckoning the pair to keep up. The next tunnel was even tighter, but a faint light could be seen at the end of it, and the noise of distant voices heard.

The tunnel opened out, at last, to a final vent grid. This was hinged and greased for access, and Daisy and Joe fell 4 feet to the hard floor, moaning for air.

Spotlamps spluttering for a stolen light, music, a breath of fire from a furnace, the purring hum of a generator, and a wailing, human sound. Daisy and Joe helped each other to their feet.

Eyes burning purple and yellow from the sudden lights, weird shapes surrounded them, moving slowly through the chambers of the heart of the dying beast. A bus station, underground, closed down for twelve months. Two buses still stood alongside ruined shelters, wheels on jacks, windows caked with dust, or else cracked into spidery webs, destination nowhere. Graffiti fingered in the thick dust of a forever-cooling engine casing. DREAM TO WIN. A crowd of people approached from their various fires and encampments. A guitar played a slow, plaintive tune from behind a shelter. Clusters of beggars looked at the new arrivals for a few seconds and then returned to their slow, broken lives.

'What's wrong with them?' Daisy asked Joe. 'Where's Celia?'

Joe shook his head, unable to take it all in. 'Keep close to me.'

They moved through the tribe of beggars. Above their heads lay the vast overarching roof of the former station. Blurb cries could be heard from the gulf space, as though even the adverts were in pain. Something black and fat-spitting turned over a fire. A low moaning was heard from all around, amplified into a ghost of wanting desire by the far-off walls. The crowd parted to let Mama Mole through. Occasionally she would stop to talk to one of the brethren. A hard knot of people was circling one of the broken-down buses, keeping the moaning going, higher and lower with each line of dull melody.

Mama Mole eventually reached the bus. She went through the doors and returned a few minutes later, her face lined with pain.

'What's wrong, Mama?' asked Joe.

'Is it Celia?' asked Daisy

She would give no answer, she just beckoned them aboard.

The bus was a double-decker, the bottom deck filled with a few desultory passengers, forever waiting for a trip that would never take place. A whining sound could be heard from above. A painful, drawn-out cry of pain that could never be calmed. 'They found him an hour ago,' said Mama Mole. She shook her head in anger. 'While I was filling my . . .' Nobody said a word as Joe and Daisy followed the old woman up the stairs.

Eddie Irwell was laid out on the back seat, his once-impressive bulk now easily contained by the cramped quarters. Little Celia Hobart was resting her head on his chest, clinging to him, stroking his tangled dreads with one weak, unsteady hand. In the other, a trembling bird's feather.

'Celia . . .' said Daisy.

The cry came louder still from the young girl's lips.

'Come away, now . . .'

'Go on, Celia,' whispered Mama Mole. 'You're with friends. We'll look after Eddie. I promise . . .'

The drive back to Hackle's house was a long, silent, rain-slashed, empty voyage. Joe had put a call through on his mobile, telling Hackle to get ready for visitors. Celia was squeezed between Daisy and Joe on the back seat. She couldn't stop shivering.

Daisy, Joe, Benny; none of them had anything positive to say, to the girl or to themselves. They each looked out at the rain, the city they had once loved, moving slowly away into the darkness. A few lonely cars passed by, a delivery van, a street-cleaning vehicle, the occasional taxi.

Inspector Crawl received the message at half-two; his men were parked outside the house on Barlow Moor Road. He'd done the research, he knew who lived there: Professor Max Hackle, respected citizen. And so near the glorious HQ! The two cops on shadow-duty were of the opinion that at least five people were inside the house, maybe more. Crawl had enough.

One hour ago he had closed the case on Edward Irwell, no fixed abode. In life as in death. Death by natural causes; a heart attack. The police pathologist had signed the warrant, co-signed by his own lying hand. Well and good. Well and bloody good.

He rang the special number, direct line to Mr Million at the House of Chances. At least, he could wish he was speaking to the big boss of all chances. Most probably he wasn't, but did it matter? His work would not go unrewarded. Loadsa lovelies! Aye, big piles of it.

He gave away the information: the house, the occupants, the location of the lucky bleeder and the group who were trying to steal the people's rightful winnings for themselves.

'Do we move in now?' he asked.

'No.' The cold voice on the telephone, distorted.

'Tomorrow, dawn raid?'

'You have done well, Inspector. Please call off your men.'

'You don't want me to . . .'

'We would prefer to deal with this ourselves.'

'You won't forget about me, will you?'

'We never forget.'

On Monday morning Crawl found his office stripped of all personal effects. No nameplate, no workload. Cases closed, or sent elsewhere. Nobody with a kind word or explanation. Even the photograph of his ex-wife had gone missing. A folder on his bare desk, containing the details of his new position.

Not knowing whether to laugh or cry.

PLAY TO WIN                    PLAY TO WIN
                               PLAY TO WIN
  PLAY TO WIN                  PLAY TO WIN
  PLAY TO WIN

                          PLAY TO WIN
        PLAY TO WIN
                          PLAY TO WIN

       TO WIN PLAY TO WIN  PLA
       WIN PLAY TO WIN  PLAY

       WIN PLAY TO WIN P


           WIN PLAY T
         PLAY TO WIN


        WIN PLAY TO WIN

        PLAY TO LOSE PLAY TC

        TO WIN PLAY TO WIN PLA

        PLAY TO WIN

          PLAY TO WIN          PLAY TO WIN


      PLAY TO WIN
      PLAY TO WIN
      PLAY TO WIN                 PLAY TO WIN

**M**onday. They won't let me out. Can't sleep, can't dream, can't make tears. Cuts on my arm where the strangers take their readings, and this morning they stole some of my hair. Telling me not to think about Eddie, but I'm disobeying them. Wandering around this house of strangers, writing this diary just to make the days go.

Even that Daisy Love girl has nothing to say, no good words, just apologies. Stupid. Daisy is far happier talking to her father anyway, that's obvious, even if they do argue from time to time. When her father isn't falling over, that is. Dirty drunk. The smoky boy, Jazir, he's OK when he comes round. He's kinda crazy, so I like him. He doesn't care like the others. Doesn't try to be nice for instance. Makes me laugh. Shouldn't be laughing, I know, but the feelings I get then are just like what Eddie used to bring, when he was . . .

Stop that!

It's warm here. Got a bed of my own, a big soft thing. Reminds me of back home, seems like years ago already. They give me magazines to read and puzzles to do and a book I can write in, which is this. And they want me to hold their special dominoes all week because they think they can win that way, but I won't do it, I drop them soon as they leave the room, ha ha. They can cook for me and cut into me and test me till I die, but I won't play that game any more. I have promised Eddie.

Tuesday. Tried to escape today but all the doors are locked, and the windows, and they keep watching me. Watching and being watched. They think they're testing me, but really I'm testing them. Ha ha.

Why did Eddie cheat on me? Getting himself killed like that, where was the fairness? Wasn't that the worst cheating he'd ever done, getting himself killed? I know this is wrong, thinking like this, but who cares what I think any more? Not me. Not me.

Been through nearly every room in the house by now. Pretty boring. These adults, they're supposed to all be in some big gang together, but mostly all they do is argue with each other, or else kiss each other, sometimes at the same time! Very strange. Daisy and Jazir, they must be in love. Making a world for themselves, no-one else allowed. And Sweet Benny and that horrible Joe, I saw them two kissing as well. Urgh! Sure, some of the brethren did that kind of yucky stuff, but Joe and Benny kiss like it's a job to do, like housework or something. And they started arguing! Is this what having a home does to you?

I have decided that I shall never have a home. It is much better that way.

If I can only get out of here. If they would only let off watching me every second of every day. If they don't let me go to Eddie's funeral . . . I will tear this house down and steal all the numbers from their precious computers, you see if I don't. This I swear.

Wednesday. This afternoon I followed Mr Hackle and Mr Love downstairs to the cellar, where they argued for an hour, walking round and round a lot of corridors and messing about with computers. I kept to the shadows until they went back upstairs, just like a spy, I was! Then I made some of my own wanderings. Never been down there before, and it was OK down there because I got lost. It was nice getting lost, like in that maze me and my sister went to in that big garden, last summer, was it? First time I've thought about her in ages. Why is it nice getting lost sometimes?

Then Mr Hackle came back down, but this time with the horrible Joe. They were kissing each other as well! And Benny came down too, but they didn't see him, and he saw them kissing. So many kisses, it was like a kissing-go-round!

None of them saw me because I was very clever. I followed Benny out and I'm pretty sure he was crying. Stupid, being an adult. I have decided never to become one, not ever. This I swear.

Thursday. Today is Eddie's funeral. They had better bloody well let me go!

Play to win

Thursday found Hackle and Jimmy Love visiting Susan Prentice. There were three to choose from; a waitress, a lawyer or a junior-school teacher. The first was easy; a pair of MegaBreakfast Whoomphies ordered from a bedraggled woman with 'Susan P: Here to Deliver!' on her badge and skin as greasy as the slop she served them.

The second was more difficult; they had to make an appointment to see her. Apparently, she had a 'window' free that morning, of approximately nine minutes. 'Sounds promising,' reckoned Jimmy. 'She always was a stickler for precision.' Hackle wasn't so sure, but when sat down in front of this impressive woman, concocting some cover story, he was tempted to distraction. There was a resemblance. They were trying to remember a woman neither of them had seen for eighteen years, and time can play evil tricks, witness Jimmy's hair and Max's suits. It was Jimmy that settled it, by asking Ms Prentice if the numbers five and zero meant anything to her?

Blank. Not a flicker.

The last was difficult because the headmaster of the school in question absolutely refused them permission to enter the premises. Too many weirdos, he explained, for too few children.

Of course not, no way could he give out home telephone numbers, but yes, there was no law against ringing the staffroom during the lunch hour, if she was there. And could he have their names please, just for security purposes . . .

'Jesus Bone!' cried Jimmy, when Hackle got off the mobile. 'It was never like this in our day. Fucking Fort Knox, isn't it? And you gave our names.'

'Shouldn't I have?'

'He's gonna tell her who we are, maybe she won't want to see us.'

Hackle shrugged; he was getting used to Jimmy's rough-and-ready soul and his language slurred out of a bottle of something. The drunkard even suggested they wait in the car, outside the school gates till lunchtime, just in case she made a run for it. Hackle, of course, thought this preposterous, and that they couldn't afford to be arrested for perversity at this stage in the game.

The school was in Droylsden, the same one they had gone to as kids, where the story begins. Does it start to end here? Is this the strange recursive loop, eating its own tail? Or else another blank score, another chance happening in the chain of playing? Just waiting there, opposite, in the Maverick Café, was the hardest time.

Jimmy laughed at the rogue chances. 'At least we get to eat something halfway decent, eh Max?' Hackle, however, was deeply affected by the sight of the old school. He had not wanted to come here, he had wanted to send Joe instead, but Jimmy had persuaded him that she'd need to see familiar faces. Both of them were secretly glad they'd been refused entry; that would've been torture.

'What if it's not her, Max?' asked Jimmy, with a mouthful. 'What then?'

'What if it is,' answered Hackle, taking little nibbles.

'Yeah. What then?' Jimmy leered at Max.

'It's Malthorpe we're after, remember,' Max responded. 'We just want some answers. You're not to push it, OK?'

'Max? Push what? What's to push?'

'I know what happened between you two.'

'You did? I mean, did you?'

'Even Malthorpe knew.'

'He didn't mind?'

'He was out of it by then.'

'Yeah, sailing his own dream. Nasty piece of shit, don't know why you put up with him.'

'Well, he was . . .'

'Don't tell me, the double-six.'

'I don't want anything personal going on, that's all.'

'As if.'

'Here they come . . .'

Here they came, the kids, running from the doors to play and skip and jump and make fun and beat each other up and flirt and twist away like spinning tops, chasing after blurbflies.

'Wow! Max . . . that was us, remember?'

'Was it?'

Hackle was ringing the school's number, asking for the staffroom. The conversation lasted ten seconds.

'She's coming over?' asked Jimmy.

'She's coming.'

Five minutes later a woman entered the café. She had a blurb on her shoulder, quite tame and inert. The woman nodded to the waiter, asked if it was OK to bring it in. The waiter said, 'No problem, Susie.'

No problem, it was her. The same confident walk, the power

to turn heads. Well dressed, well preserved, putting Jimmy and Max to shame.

'Wow!' whispered Jimmy.

Hackle nudged him under the table and got up to greet the woman. 'Susan! So good of you to see us. I know you're busy. Please . . .'

Susan sat down.

'I know you'll remember Jimmy. Jimmy Love?'

She nodded at Jimmy. 'Of course. Five-Four, wasn't it?'

Jimmy smiled and took out the bone from round his neck.

'I lost mine years ago.'

'Well . . . would you like to eat?' Hackle asked.

'Thank you, no. I must get back soon, work to mark. Isn't that right, Edna?' She stroked the blurb on her shoulder.

'Edna?' said Jimmy, smiling at her. 'Pray tell . . .'

'Educational Net Agent. A tremendous help, and, of course, the children love her to bits. Teacher's pet, aren't you? Fortunately, educational methods have moved on since we were young.'

'Not entirely,' said Max. 'I have seen the results of the past year. They are nowhere near to our standard.'

'That was a fluke year, Maximus. As you well know. If you take my results over the last ten years, believe me, I have made improvements. But no more of the past; this is about the AnnoDominoes, I suppose?'

'You've noticed, then?' asked Hackle.

'It is difficult not to. The children all have toy bones. They can't wait to be old enough to gamble. It saddens me, but what can I do?'

Jimmy offered her a forkful of his pie, gladly refused. 'Max here had you down certain as Cookie Luck,' he told her, stuffing his face.

'I am a little too old, and dancing was never my forte.'

'What about Malthorpe as Mr Million? Paul, eh? How does that grab you?'

'It doesn't. Malthorpe hasn't the balls to do that.'

'Whoa! Turnabout city, or what?'

Hackle shoved his quarter-finished food aside. 'Susan, we just need to find Malthorpe, that's all. Ask him some questions. Are you . . . that is . . .'

'Are you still shagging, the prof's trying to say.'

'Jimmy! Please . . . Susan . . . I am sorry . . .'

'Don't apologize. Five-Four always was a crude young man.'

'What? Me? Compared to Paul Malthorpe. Come on . . . I was—'

'No.' Susan stood up. 'I knew I shouldn't have come here.'

'Susan . . .' Hackle was up now, trying to reason with her. 'We mean no harm.'

'I live a quiet life these days.'

'She's respected in the community,' sneered Jimmy. 'That's a fact.'

'I have no idea where Malthorpe is. Listen carefully, please. We split up some two years after the . . . after the thing with Georgie. I hear he went to London, I don't know.'

'She's hiding something, Max.' Jimmy's eyes, holding her tight.

'Will you keep quiet! Susan . . .'

Hackle grabbed her arm. Susan whispered something evil, and the blurb took off from her shoulder, sting extended. 'A punishable offence, obviously,' said Jimmy. 'Max, I do believe you're about to get the strap.'

Hackle sat down. Susan called the blurb back to its perch. 'I don't know what you're up to, Max,' she said, 'but it's nothing to do with me.'

'The thing is,' said Jimmy, 'Max here wants to destroy

the dominoes.'

'This is because of Paul, right? About what happened? Forget it. I have. And life is far better for it. We made a mistake, we have paid for it. Now it's over.'

'It's not over,' said Max. 'The bones are dangerous, Susan. The nymphomation. You know what could happen—'

'Max wants to reopen the maze,' said Jimmy. 'He wants to go back in—'

'Who will you kill this time?'

'That won't happen,' said Hackle. 'We will be careful . . .'

'It's the only way, Susan. Unless we find Malthorpe . . .'

Susan sneered at them both. 'I'd wish you luck, if luck had anything to do with it.' She looked at her watch. 'I must go now.'

Jimmy turned to Max. 'I was just wondering, Max . . .'

'Yes, Jimmy?'

'About how Susan's headmaster would react to certain rumours . . .'

'Certain rumours, Jimmy?'

'Certain rumours about his prized teacher being involved in a murder.'

'He wouldn't believe you,' said Susan. 'He knows me.'

'Not half as much as we do,' said Max.

Susan looked through the window, over the road to where the children were playing. She turned back to the table. 'I saw Malthorpe about ten years ago. He'd come back to Manchester, full of plans. He wanted to involve me in those plans.'

'Which were?'

'He wouldn't say, unless I agreed to join him. He had a new lover.'

'Anyone we know?' asked Jimmy.

Susan laughed. 'I think you do. Miss Sayer.'

'Miss Sayer?' Jimmy couldn't believe it. 'But she'd be . . .'

'Yes. She'd be old. I gave up on Paul's desires long ago.' Susan smiled at the two men, satisfied at having shocked them. She turned to leave. 'I would appreciate no further contact. Thank you.'

Max and Jimmy sat in silence for a few moments, each deep in their own thoughts. 'Bloody hell,' said Jimmy, finally. 'Miss Sayer would have been at least sixty-five. How could he?'

Max wasn't listening, his eyes and mind following the still-attractive junior-school teacher across the road, back to school . . .

## Play to lose

Beginnings, endings. As Max and Jimmy made their way back to Manchester, DJ Dopejack was visiting a friend in the medical department. It was his first visit to the university that week; the rest of the days spent in his room, tunnelling further and further through the defences of AnnoDomino. He was fired up, loaded with the DNA of his target, a hacker's dream. Already he had peeled back layers, revealing hidden connections between the bones and the burgers and the cops and the town hall. All the connections uncovered, but no inroads to the real secrets: how to fucking win!

Dopejack had a hard-on for beating the odds; not just against the bones, but against Hackle and his dumbo crew and especially that Jazir Spicebreath Malik. DJ gone loco, lonely and wolflike; yeah, this was the thrill.

To this end he was working on another tack, one too simple for the stupid, clever bastards that Hackle employed. You had to be simple to win this game, that was the insight. X-ray the bones, who had thought of that before now? One fresh domino, purchased only that morning, and a dead bone from last week; comparison test. Before and after playing the game.

It took an hour for the friend to come back with the various sheets. Fuzzy knowledge at best, but shapes discernible. Through X-ray eyes: before losing, a series of plates showing the domino magnified and darkly transparent, a small patch of deeper darkness inside, perhaps one inch long, that moved from plate to plate in a constricted dance. After losing: the same shape, the same constricted dance from plate to plate. Interesting; the numbers died, the insides didn't. What did that mean? Studying these maps of bone, Dopejack felt a hard slap on his shoulder. Turning round . . .

'What yer got there, snothead? Is that your brain?'

Nigel Zuze, with two of his cronies from the League of Zero. Sniggering in harmony, blue and cream. 'He's one of them that licked us,' one of them said.

'Aye,' the other one said. 'Fucking paki-fucker.'

Nigel grabbed the X-rays off Dopejack. 'Looks dead to me, your brain. Looks stuffed. I think you're in need of some treatment. Boys . . .'

A beginning, an ending . . .

On Thursday also, the brethren buried one of their finest. Much love lost and found was mentioned, fights and curses forgiven. Eddie Irwell was laid out in his long-time hole on St Anne's Square, the present owner having gracefully given up his rights. Many shoppers and passers-by stopped to ponder this strange, primitive ritual. Spade by spade the earth was replaced in the hole, covering the body. There would be no gravestone, no marker except for a small tree planted in this soil. This would grow over the next twenty-five years, carrying Eddie's spirit into the next century.

Celia Hobart was not allowed to this ceremony. She was forbidden to leave the safe house in West Didsbury. But later that day, long after darkness had fallen, two people did stop for a while at the grave in the city. One was perhaps nineteen years old, with ragged, short hair, a head full of numbers and pain; the other, a little girl of eight years, with long, straight, metallic-blond hair, in which a green-and-yellow bird's feather was knotted. Perhaps she mumbled something kind, this child, something regretful; perhaps a curse against the bones and what they had stolen from her. Perhaps, one day, when enough of the homeless have died, the whole of the city will be covered with these trees of green spirit.

A blurbfly circling the grave, at play for once, but with a purpose.

Midnight. Jazir lying alone on his bed in Rusholme, awake but dreaming. Watching the scene at the gravehole far away, through the blurb's eyes.

Growing wings.

Beginnings, endings. Thursday, becoming Friday.

The day of chances . . .

PLAY TO WIN

PLAY TO WIN
PLAY TO WIN
PLAY TO WIN

PLAY TO WIN
PLAY TO WIN

PLAY TO WIN

PLAY TO WIN

PLAY TO WIN

TO WIN PLAY TO WIN  PLA
WIN PLAY TO WIN  PLAY

WIN PLAY TO WIN P

WIN PLAY T
PLAY TO WIN

WIN PLAY TO WIN

PLAY TO LOSE PLAY TO

TO WIN PLAY TO WIN PLA

PLAY TO WIN

PLAY TO WIN

PLAY TO WIN

PLAY TO WIN
PLAY TO WIN
PLAY TO WIN

PLAY TO WIN

# Game 45

**M**ucky jung Doom Day. Dippy mould Unchester. Blow the numbs. Game 45, telling bone natives. Make some pimples, loopyvision. Watch with honey, gamble credits digit-come. Crawling, stalling, numbernauting. Chancing flip, dancing pip; Dalmatian damnation. Domination. Blurb-o-matica, heavy flies, pregnant with babyverts, motherhatching the streets. Play to win some, winsome Moonchester! All over the dirty, shitty, bonefried Fryday, squeeze us some game-juice. Six thoughts from pipflight, how howling the slithy hordes! Clacky doms on dommy clacks, clutched in fingers, banged down hard. Boardrooms, bedrooms, headrooms, hidden rooms, unbidden rooms. Jabberbone and punyburg. Gyre and gimble ultraspeed. All of Mobchester, playing the gambles.

Super-zoom, it's a bone boom!

Domino dots pulsate in bloom, the dream song, working the pop.

> It's dummino time! Wondering dummino time!
> Dumb, dumb, dumb, dumb, dummino time!

**Blurbflies**

Tommy Tumbler, tumbling Tommy. Cookie Luck, cooking the luck. The players busy licking their bones, mooning their breath, tuning some last faulty prayers, taking a collective merger-burger, singing their hosannas to rusty pianos. Masturbating some dumb-sucking squeezer to the patent-pending gods of sex.

Squeeze to win!

As the blurbflies joined their bodies, mutating wild to fill the city with new, never-before-seen messages:

Squeeza Teeza to win! Hoviz to win! Chokanova to win! Biscuit Booms to win! Madkow Spirit to win! Napalm Zigarettes to win! Filter Breath to win! Möbius Dick Whalesteaks to win! Sticky

Smellotape to win! Yummy Gum to win! Unintendo to win! Deadly Venom to win! Domino Choks to win! Enola Cola to win! Flipchart Messiah to win! Micro Jackson to win! Goon Juice to win! Long Distance Davis to win! Quirk Moths to win! Demon Bacon to win! Klueless Klan to win! Dull English Breakfast to win! Takki Donald's to win! Chukky's Strikken Chikken to win! Long Distance Domino to win! Artificial Facial to win! Demon Teeza Bacon to win! All-Over-in-a-Second Delay Cream to win! Dizzy Knees Theme Park to win! Napalm Yummy Whalechok to win! Salsa Manc to win! MacDizzy's Meat Pies to win! Takki Jack's Enola Boomtape to win! Flipchart Hoviz Chikken to win! Madkow Klueless Klan to win! All-Over-in-a-Domino Delay Biscuits to win! Stickytakk Yummyflip to win! Domikow Teezachikk Goonobooms to win!

The streets of Blurbchester were thick with the mergers, a corporate fog of brand images. People had to battle through them just to buy their latest dominoes. The Government was at a loss regarding the overwhelming messages; they knew the experiment had gone wrong, but how to right it? With the AnnoDomino Company the Government whispered, with the burgercops they pontificated, with the big Whoomphies they made a big beef; stop this plague of flies immediately, they urged, before the people stop voting for us.

No deal. This is what you get, fucking the adverts.

OK, let's play!

'Is it just me,' said Jazir, 'or are the blurbs getting louder?'

Hackle's house, where the clock ticks towards nine. Where the Fractals gather, each with their bones in a young girl's hands.

Watch their eyes dance as Cookie Luck dances to their eyes. Jazir Malik at the computer, working the keys. Joe Crocus looking over Jazir's shoulder, telling him how to capture it better. Jazir telling him to get the fuck out of his domain. Daisy Love sitting beside her father on the settee, actually holding her father's hand, thinking, If only they'd all stop arguing, maybe we could get somewhere.

Max Hackle in his counting house, below ground, walking the maze of corridors, counting out his chances. Little Miss Celia sitting cross-legged in the centre of the chalk circle; the child who held all their bones to her frozen heart. Sweet Benny Fenton, standing alone, leaning against the wall where the clock ticked.

Joe, Joe, Joe! Sweet Benny's soul was full of the name, but his mind was as empty as his chances of ever winning anything. Joe Crocus, the man he had once loved so deeply, only a few days ago, but now . . .

Where the fuck was that Hackle bastard? No wonder he never came to these meetings. Down in the cellar, I'll bet, waiting for Joe to finish here.

What to do about it? How to confront it, to finish it, to win it over. How to give up, how to fight for his rightful love. How many years has this been going on?

Surely, it would all come to him.

Joe was shouting now. 'OK, children. Here we go. Pray for a winning.'

At last, and at a long last, the stars of Cookie Luck fall into an exact nine o'clock shape. Into a bone of rare occurrence . . .

Play to lose

It was as though Manchester took a collective breath. A sudden *whoosh!* of fear and surprise as nine o'clock struck and Lady Cookie Luck started to change. All creamy she went, screaming as her tight black catsuit turned into twilight, her illustrious breasts flattening, her fertile hips becoming two thin curves of pure bone. One by one the stars on her body went out. Her skin started to shrivel and die, to let her skeleton poke through. Her lovely face turning to a skull's grin. Her famous hair of ebony falling out in chunks. Until she was all jutting bones, all a rattling puppet of fibulas and tibias, scapula and humerus, kneecaps and pubis.

Life went creamy.

And Lady Luck screamed in pain one last time as the gibbering thing inside burst through her skin. What a horrorshow to put before the populace. Cookie Luck, turning herself inside out! Becoming her own skeleton.

**Blurbflies**

That's the way! That's the way!
That's the way the cookie crumbles!

With a blank and another blank.
*A double-fucking-blank.*
Dotshit!
Losing prize. The dreaded Joker Bone. Often talked about, never before seen. This was the Joker's very first appearance in the game. Being a winner was now being a loser and vice versa. And all the Dark Fractals were just another bunch of winners, having lost; their lonely bones as lovingly clutched by the lovely Celia Hobart coming up with pips. Nobody spoke in Hackle's house, nobody spoke in Manchester, until Jazir breathed, 'Thank the spices!' and the

whole of Manchester echoed his cry. Their bones were all fully numbered.

As somebody somewhere . . .

Joe was trying to calm his players. 'People, please . . . there is no need to panic. None of us has won.'

But Daisy couldn't say anything; too scared and too shaken to speak. The idea that somebody somewhere . . . and it could so easily have been herself, claiming the booby prize.

Jazir said it for her: 'Some poor sucker, somewhere . . . just won themselves a nasty.'

'Somebody, somewhere,' called out Tommy Tumbler, from the city's screens, 'just won themselves a special prize for the double-blank. May the gods of chaos have mercy upon your loser's soul.'

As the skull puppet laughed over a million televisions.

**PLAY THE RULES**

12a. In the event of a double-blank, AnnoDomino must
     allow every player an equal chance to lose.
12b. Every player but the loser shall win.
12c. There shall be no escape.

Keen for the game taxes, but fearful of the populace becoming too addicted, the Government had specified that the nation's dominoes must contain a rare chance of losing, and losing badly.

Hence the Joker Bone. A prize you didn't have to collect, because the prize came looking for you. The skull beneath the skin came prowling for the winner. And the prize for a double-blank was an unknown. Some punters claimed it was financial ruin, others that you ended up in gaol. Some happy souls even claimed that the booby prize was none other than death. Death by numbers, turning the winner into an all-time loser.

Of course the Government got it completely wrong: the chance of losing so badly only made the punters play to win even harder. That being the nature of the human soul.

## play to lose

Somebody somewhere . . .

DJ Dopejack was at his computer, working the AnnoDomino channel on the Burgernet. The giggling figure of the Joker was still dancing on the screen, but something else was getting to the rogue Dark Fractal, and he couldn't quite figure it out.

What the fuck was nibbling at him? Certainly not the fact that all his bones had come up dotted. He was glad to have lost. OK, he was nursing some bad bruises courtesy of Nigel Zuze and the League of Zero. And they'd stolen his wallet and all his papers, his notes on the game, and they knew where he lived now, but that wasn't the problem. No, but something about the way the Joker Bone was dancing on the screen. It was scary, even just watching the animation, but that wasn't it. Something else . . . something to do with the movement . . . who would have thought it, the way a skeleton could dance . . .

Dopejack worked at some more keys, until he brought up the AnnoDomino menu bar. There he found his favourite icons. Ways in he had worked hard to uncover over the last week.

<u>PUBLICITY</u>
<u>RESEARCH</u>
<u>GAME THEORY</u>
<u>HISTORY</u>
<u>RULES</u>
<u>STRUCTURE</u>

Most of it was iced with trivia: PUBLICITY, for instance, produced rates for buying a blurbvert. The RESEARCH button revealed slick details about the latest products: a new strain of burger, a new kind of cop, a new breed of blurbfly, plans for the Domidome. Nothing meaty. GAME THEORY; learned papers on the rulings of chaos. Stuff for Hackle to lose himself in, not the DJ. HISTORY; a whole load of shit about the dominoes being invented back in Italy, like the eighteenth century, man. And a list of the previous winners and their chosen bones. And this week's winner, just coming in: blank-blank. The dreaded double-blank. Hope one of the Fractals caught a packet, ha ha. Finally, RULES was just that; weighted on the bone side.

Dopejack would help himself if he only knew what was troubling him. STRUCTURE was what he wanted. He pressed on the icon, bringing up menus within menus. Dopejack was on the nail with these nested icons by now; silver surfer of the fractal cursor. Loading up with his latest strain of the game's hackergene, he dragged a domino icon into the stack of menu, hatched it till the flies swarmed out and started eating their way through the doorways. Fat on their mother, how they buzzed! Too bad Jazir had shown him the way, the stupid bonesucker.

(And strange the way that watching the blurb icons always made him feel excited. He had a hard-on just from watching them fly around the screen.)

Down to PERSONNEL they ventured together . . .

<u>MR MILLION</u>

<u>COOKIE LUCK</u>

<u>TOMMY TUMBLER</u>

<u>JOKER BONE</u>

<u>RIFFRAFF</u>

The last was easy, at least to one level down; just a list of employees, salary details, progress reports, aptitude tests, etc. No addresses. COOKIE and TOMMY were more difficult, but still accessible with the latest strains. Nothing revealing, of course; the usual whitewash. Dopejack had tried a hundred times to open MR MILLION's door, always with ACCESS DENIED. The same with JOKER BONE, but now that the monster had been publicly revealed, maybe . . .

Excellent! Blurbs, do that thing!

Dopejack got a partial opening, just enough to pluck free a menu:

<u>GOVERNMENT RULINGS</u>

<u>DANCING PATTERNS</u>

<u>MUTATION PROCEDURES</u>

<u>HISTORY</u>

Dopejack pressed on the DANCING PATTERNS. And there the Joker Bone was, dancing along his programmed pathways. Mr Bonejangle, in tune to the chaos rhythms.

Just like . . . just like . . .

Bonejuice! He split the screen, brought up a video from his own collection, fed the infoblurbs fat on it. He pressed on HISTORY in the domino channel, fed the new blurbs into it, feedback knowledge, praying for an opening . . .

Got one, a mere sliver that a blurb could creep through.

Dopejack worked for ten more minutes, making sure. Making sure by stripping away all the protection from the Joker, finding deep treasures. Feeding it all back in, over and over . . .

Finding the treasure at the centre of the maze, and straight away typing a message to Hackle's Burgernet address.

## Play to lose

As somebody somewhere . . .

Luckily, not in the House of Hackle. 'All I can say,' said Jazir, 'is thank the dots Little Celia here didn't agree to holding our bones till this morning! We'd be stuffed otherwise.'

'Maybe,' said Daisy.

'That's one maybe too many.'

'If it's true, I mean . . . your theory about holding the bones . . .'

'What else can it be? It's osmosis.'

'We don't know that yet,' said Joe, trying to keep control. 'We have to keep working. Benny . . .'

Benny was far away, across the room, the other side of his head, thinking only of . . .

'Benny! Wake up. What's the latest on the gene analysis?'

'What?'

'Good god, man! Where are you?'

'Right here. I've tried to find some anomaly in Celia's DNA that could account for her being so lucky. There's nothing there, not that stands out. I reckon Mr Million's having the same problem.'

'Maybe he's better than you?'

This remark, seemingly so Jazir, actually came from Joe. The whole room was silent. The first time any of them had heard Joe put Benny down so openly. Sure, they all knew that the two hadn't been getting on lately. None of them knew why.

Celia knew, but she was keeping quiet.

But for Joe – Joe Crocus for crying out loud! – for Joe to place Benny below the dominoes? Unheard of.

'That's not fair, Joe.' Now this was Jazir, trying to make some peace. 'The Annos have got two specimens to compare. What's Benny supposed to do?'

'He's got two as well.' Now this was from Daisy's father, usually so quiet at these meetings.

'What's that supposed to mean?' asked Jaz.

But Joe had already grabbed Daisy's father by the hand, dragging him from the settee.

'Hey! What's going on?' cried Daisy. 'Joe! Leave him!'

'Shut up! Meeting dismissed! You!' Pointing at Benny. 'My room. Now!'

A door banged shut . . . echoing . . .

'Phew!' Jazir breathed out. 'What was that about?'

Daisy turned to Benny.

Benny just shrugged. 'I couldn't say.' He was smiling. Why was he smiling?

Jazir turned to Daisy. 'There's something going on, pet. You'd best find out.'

Daisy turned to Celia.

Celia turned to the computer. 'What does this mean?' she asked.

'It's a net message for Hackle.' Jazir pressed a key. 'Let's see . . .'

The message came up on screen, superimposed on the Joker's frozen grin.

'Who's it from?' asked Daisy.

'Dopejack. I think you should read it.'

Benny and Daisy and Celia and Jaz, all standing round the computer.

'He's bluffing,' said Jazir. 'Got to be.'

Somebody somewhere . . .

A tingling in the fist, as nine o'clock played out its final gift. Somebody somewhere, opening their trembling hand to find a monster living there, a blank-eyed monsterbone. Screams around him, from quick-departing friends.

Winning bone. Losing bone.

As DJ Dopejack wondered what on earth to do with his newly found knowledge.

As Jazir Malik made a date with Daisy for that night, her bed, her luscious body. 'After I've finished serving curries, I'll come and service you.' Then left, seeing that Daisy didn't have a laugh inside her.

As Daisy didn't dare laugh.

As Joe watched Max argue with Jimmy down in the cellar.

As Benny lay shivering on his bed. His and Joe's bed. Our bed! Something had to be done. No more waiting. He took the keys to Joe's car.

As Celia told Daisy all about having seen Joe and Max kissing.

As blurbflies flew around the house and down the street and in and out of windows, alongside Benny's speeding car and every other car and all the buses and trains, under the city's skin, inside of heads and outside of television.

Play to lose! Play to lose!

The city was flashing with such moments; moments of relief and tenderness in the face of losing. Moments of doubt and fire, for having been so close, so tempted. Moments of pain, as the half-losers worried what effect they would feel. Those dreams that had been reported, the skeleton following you, almost catching you. The struggle to wake yourself in time . . .

As somebody somewhere found themselves caught. Dropping the bad luck like a bone on fire. Running through the streets he was, hoping to escape the prize. Trying to get miles away, no direction.

Can you guess who won? Can you guess who lost?

Well, can you?

Play to lose

It was Daisy's first time in the cellar. She hadn't really thought about it before, but these old Victorian houses often had extensive cellars, where the servants lived and worked. All that was gone now, just the stripped walls, piles of rubbish, broken furniture, dust and webs, a slumbering boiler, a rocking horse, worm-food. A spidered light bulb, feeble glow. Down the rickety stairs, Daisy putting her hand on the wall to steady—

!!!!!!!!!!!!!!!!

Urgh! Lice!

Daisy, scared of insects, didn't let Celia see it. The young girl looking so calm, as though having been down here many times before. 'What's down here, Cee?' Daisy asked. The young girl pushed aside another door, leading Daisy through. 'This way . . .'

Darkness now. Daisy keeping tight hold of Celia's fingers, being led. Round corners and doubling back, more corners, the corners of corners (how big was this place?), turning, returning (so dark), more stairs, another level, more corridors (getting lighter now, eyes adjusting), turning corners, getting lost (must be under next door's house by now, surely), asking what this place was and where was she being taken, getting no answer . . .

Through here . . .

Somewhere in the maze, a bank of computers making dull glow and static buzz, wires and leads tangled around equipment, leading off to all parts of the maze. Max and Joe and Daisy's father; Daisy's father getting the full Hackle treatment for being reckless. 'We've got to tell her,' Jimmy Love said. 'She deserves to know.'

'Not yet. Not all of it.'

'What she needs, then. At least about Susan.'

'Susan? Yes . . .'

'It's not fair, otherwise. Never forget, Max . . . she's my daughter.'

'I understand that. The time will come . . .'

'The time for what?' Daisy's voice, from the darkness.

'Daisy . . .' Her father's voice, in shock.

'She shouldn't be down here.' Joe's voice.

'I brought her.' Celia's voice, from the darkness.

'What is it I should know?' Daisy again, stepping forward. 'What's this about having two samples to work from?'

Silence.

'Shall I tell her, Max?' Her father's voice.

'No. I'll do it.'

'Thank you.' He turned, smiled at his daughter. 'I'll be upstairs, OK?'

Daisy was scared now.

'Joe?' said Hackle. 'Will you sort Benny out?'

'Will do.'

'Take Celia.'

'I don't want to go!'

'I'm the boss round here. You go with Joe now, and stop causing trouble.'

Joe took Celia's hand. 'I know the way,' she said, pushing his hand aside. Together they followed Jimmy back through the maze.

The two of them alone, with Daisy just standing there, with Max studying an array of numbers on the screen of a computer.

'You want to win the double-six, don't you?' Daisy asked, trying to get him started.

Max didn't even look up from his workings.

'Well you got a burgernote from Dopejack . . .'

'Dopejack? How is he? Is he coming back to us?'

Daisy shook her head. 'He's claiming he's found out who Mr Million is.'

'The name?'

'He's not saying. Jazir reckons he's bluffing.'

Max raised his hands to his face, squeezed the bridge of his nose. Daisy could really see the age of him now.

'Why are you doing this, Max?'

'What?'

'Trying so hard to beat the dominoes? I wouldn't mind, but I'm not doing any maths am I? I don't know why I'm here.'

'I'm tired, Daisy.'

'Do you want to go upstairs?'

'No. Please, walk with me a while.'

'OK.' She had to play this just right.

Around the corridors they went, away from the stairs this time. Around and around . . .

'How big is this place?' Daisy asked.

'When we started building it, only under my house. There was a doorway leading to next door's, which we managed to open one day. Their cellar was obviously unused, but just to make sure, we sealed their entry door. That gave us twice the space. It took us four years to complete it.'

'My father was involved in this?'

'Not to begin with. He joined us in the late Seventies. It was me and Malthorpe, Susan and Georgie. Mainly, to be honest, just Malthorpe and Georgie; they did most of the work.'

'You built a maze?'

'It feels a lot more complicated than it actually is. That was the point.'

'What for?'

Hackle led her further into the turning pathways, and talked.

## Play to lose

Why did I build a maze? To prove something to myself, I suppose. You know that the ancients built labyrinths not to get lost in, but to find themselves. Not all mazes contain a monster, some contain treasures. It was a spiritual quest, a tool of the mystics. So maybe I was picking up on some of that feeling. You've read my early work, Daisy. You'll know what the Sixties were like then; we were the mathematicians of the soul. Yes, we can laugh at ourselves now, but we really believed in those days. The idea for the Hackle Maze, that was only me trying to create a labyrinth inside the computer. A computer deals only with information, of course, so the wanderers of a Hackle Maze are not of this world. They are tireless and blind, and quite, quite stupid, which makes them excellent explorers. No petty human baggage, you see. No complications.

Georgie Horn was like that. Sweet Blank-Blank was a

tremendous help in designing the programs for the Hackle Maze. It wasn't that he knew anything about computers, nothing at all, but his mind was full of strange twists and lateral turnings. I think I was actually trying to recreate Georgie's mind inside the machine.

It was a special time to be a scientist, the Sixties into the Seventies. Bliss to be alive. Lateral thinking, chaos theory, fractal dimensions, the unravelling of the double helix, cellular automata, complexity theory, the game of life. Each of these we could incorporate into the thinking of the maze.

Eventually it got to the point where the wanderers were gaining knowledge of the computer's pathways, which allowed us to increase the complexity of the maze, which in turn fed back into the wanderers' bank of information. The more chaos we threw at them, the more they seemed to relish the game. Their task was very simple: merely to find their way to the centre of the system. For an incentive, we installed a prize at the centre. I say prize, I mean only the image of a treasure chest, with coins and jewels spilling out. That was Georgie's idea.

The maze had grown so complex by this point, and filled with so many thousands of wanderers, moving at such a speed, it became difficult to keep track of all the information. To this end we introduced the concept of the agent. These were tiny info-gathering units that would travel the pathways, keeping track of the positions of all the wanderers, and the changing nature of the maze itself.

Oh yes, we introduced a random element to the computer. The wanderers were becoming too good, you see. They kept finding the prize. It was all we could do to stay ahead of them. Random pathways, sudden obstacles, double-headed monsters that guarded certain turnings, trapdoors, a shifting centre, dead ends, mirrors, collapsing roofs, blind spots, tightening walls.

It was nothing, of course, compared to today's video games, but at the time - have no doubt it was the most complex artificial life system. I was very proud of it. Very proud. We all were, in our way: Georgie especially; he loved to watch the little dots race around the screen. He'd sit there for hours, hypnotized. Like he was trying to memorize it. An impossible task, but Georgie wasn't to know that, was he? Susan Prentice? Well, she had her own maze to run. I'm referring to Paul Malthorpe, of course. The two of them circling around each other like snakes, in and out of their strange love for each other. But they were good; Susan at the debugging, Paul on the planning. I was in charge of the numbers, Georgie the vision, if you will.

The vision . . .

I will never forget the morning I came down early to find Georgie glued to the screen. He looked like he'd been up all night. 'What's happening, Blank-Blank?' I asked him. His words . . . 'They're changing, Two-Blank. Changing!'

The wanderers had started to adapt to the system. Not in any deep sense, you must understand; merely that some of them were joining together, to make a single, more powerful entity. The agents were flying around, going crazy at this new burst of knowledge. It was Georgie, again, who had suggested the agents should look like insects, with wings.

To think back upon that morning . . .

It was the start of the second phase. Over the next year we recorded at least ten new species of wanderer. Some of them you may have read about: Chancer, Casanova, Warrior, Seducer, Cartographer, Jester, Sheep and Shepherds, Builders, Backsliders. Their names are like poetry to me now, long-lost poetry. Each amalgam would have its own unique qualities that allowed it a different way of negotiating the maze. It wasn't long, of course, before they started fighting each other for the privilege of the centre's prize. This was a totally unexpected outcome of the system, although inevitable in hindsight. We had created a world inside the computer. It was the law of the jungle, with its own secret dynamic.

I think it was Susan who suggested the next step.

Because fighting wasn't the only thing the various wanderers were interested in. Some of them had started to reproduce. It was a basic operation, analogous to a single-cell creature splitting in two. The fascinating results were never the same; for instance the amalgam of a builder and a jester would split apart, but never into a mere builder or a mere jester. It was always some new offshoot they produced.

It was Susan who said, 'I think they're trying to have sex, Max.' And Malthorpe who said, 'Aye, they want to fuck each other.' And Susan who said, 'Let's give them some DNA.'

That was it. The third phase. None of us was expert in that particular field, so a period of research was required. Meanwhile, we were constantly upgrading to the latest technology, to increase the complexity of the system. We managed to write a new program that copied a very simple form of genetic structure, which we introduced to a new batch of wanderers. These creatures were very quickly subsumed by the more experienced wanderers. It took only a short while for the effects to take place.

Again, it was Georgie who first spotted the carnal act. As far as I knew, he'd never known a woman, not in the basic sense. It was like pornography to him, I think, watching a Seducer and a Cartographer come together in this blatant way. The next day they had already produced their first baby: a seductive map-making creature, who charmed his way around the pathways, recording every twist and turn as he did so. We called this new creation a Columbus unit. Why am I calling him he? Because he was! He had a capacity to inject his DNA into another creature, preferably a female unit, who had the capacity to take in the offered sperm. I'm sorry, I can't stop using these ridiculous terms.

There were no textbooks to consult, you see. We were on the edge of a new kind of mathematics, based on sex. It was Georgie who came up with the name for all this activity. Susan had been going on about how the information was being passed on through the genes, and Malthorpe had called one new creature a right little nymphomaniac! 'Nymphomaniacs!' cried out Georgie. 'They're doing naughty nymphomation!'

It was my job to work out the equations of this new process, a task that pushed me to my limits. This is when your father joined us . . .

Play to lose

'He told me that you'd "used" him?' said Daisy. 'Is that right?'

'Used him?' said Hackle. 'Yes, I suppose we did. But only for his extra knowledge. He was always the best of us, remember, despite the fact that he didn't have our training. Maybe that gave him an advantage. And, when we found him, he was at a low ebb. No real job, no real friends. He was pleased to be part of our group. We found him a job, a wife . . .'

'A wife? My mother, you mean?'

'Yes. She was an employee at the bank where Susan employed him. We gave Jimmy a purpose in life. And he loved the work we were doing. He was excited by it.'

They had come to another clearing in the labyrinth, where

they rested. A series of painted lightbulbs was strung along the passageways, giving a low, blue cast to the damp, cold space. Professor Hackle had slumped down against one wall, breathing heavily after his account. Daisy was leaning against the opposite wall, wondering if she would ever find her way back to the house.

'My father worked on the nymphomation equations with you?'

'Worked on them? He practically discovered them. He took the basic outline and pushed it on to the next level. He introduced the idea of the fractal maze, for instance, one with an infinite number of branching paths. Why, without him . . .'

'Without my father . . . no AnnoDomino . . .'

Hackle nodded, a movement Daisy could barely see in the gloom. 'Your father joining us was the catalyst for our next phase; that, and Georgie starting on this underground maze.'

'I thought you built it together?'

'Georgie started it. He didn't tell us what he was doing. He was always wandering off, anyway, and often spent time alone down here. None of us cared about where he went, so long as he came to no harm. This place was just a pit back then, full of rubbish. Over the last year or so, he'd been slowly building these partitions. See, if you knock them . . .'

Daisy did so. They rang hollow.

'He was building a series of false walls down here. Only when it had reached a certain complexity did he tell us about it.'

'Did he say why?'

'He wanted to make the Hackle Maze real. Those were his words. "Make it real, Max! Make it happen!" At first we were pleased to humour him, something we had become rather too good at over the years. Malthorpe, I remember, really threw himself into the task. He was always the most physical of us. Then Susan and I got caught up in it as well. Already I was thinking of ways of making Georgie's dream come true.'

'He wanted to be a wanderer?' Daisy asked.

'In a certain sense, he already was. Through life, I mean. And I think he quite envied the excitement he saw on the screen. Especially the sexual aspect of it. God knows what strange fevers were driving him. Your father, of course, knew nothing of this side of our work. He was not living with us, and his weekly visits were taken up with developing the artificial system, not the real one. Eventually, when we did bring him down here, again, he was the one who showed us the way. This would be 1979, when the technology to feed back into the system became available. We could link Georgie to the computer, specifically to one particular specimen.'

'You actually did this?'

'I'm telling you the truth, Daisy. Do you want to hear it?'

'Go on.'

'We called the wanderer that Georgie was linked to the double-zero creature. Horny George, for short. All the wanderers had numbers you see, to give the agents a means of keeping tabs on them. Our first attempts were very limited; failures, actually. But slowly we found the means to allow a kind of feed-back loop to occur between Georgie in real life, and Blank-Blank on the screen. We would turn all these lights out, set the system going, and then let Georgie wander around the tunnels. Georgie knew this place like the back of his hand, of course, but that wasn't the point; the real maze was just a symbol, a way of focusing the power. It was Georgie's effect upon the computer's maze we were interested in.'

'Which was?'

'Astounding. Absolutely astounding. Georgie's wanderer charged around the Hackle Maze like the Minotaur. Now, Georgie had always been good at games of chance, something in his damaged brain, I imagine, or his crazy, mixed-up genes, that made him identify with random events. His wanderer became a rampant Casanova of the system, loving the pathways.'

'Which makes Georgie the original lucky bleeder? Oh, I see it. You have his genetic structure on disk. This is what Benny has been using for comparison with Celia?'

'You're getting it. Georgie had play-to-win in spades. A winner, not a loser. The experiment was so successful, we could only move on.'

'What about the effect it had on George?'

'The real George?'

'That's the only one I'm interested in.'

'Ah . . . well, he was elated, of course. Buzzing, is how he described it. He was claiming he'd actually been inside the computer, which was a nonsense. He was just connected to it by wires, nothing but wires. Immediately, he wanted to go in again. Over the next few months we experimented more and more with the Georgie-maze loop, creating ever more complex pathways. Georgie would always find his way through. He was becoming the maze. He took to spending all night linked to the machine, sometimes falling asleep while connected. Amazingly, even asleep he could still affect the outcome. His dreams were wandering the labyrinth, working the wanderers, breeding, multiplying, succumbing to the nymphomation. This had a parallel effect on his waking life. It was a two-way process.'

'This must've worried you, Professor.'

'Not at all. It was a positive effect. Georgie became more positive in real life, more vibrant and, dare I say it, more sexy. Yes, Daisy. Very much so, so how could we stop now? It was Susan who came up with the rule of not going in alone.'

'She was linked up as well?'

'We all were, eventually. Myself, Malthorpe, Susan, your father; each with our chosen wanderers, specially numbered. Two-Zero, Six-Six, Five-Zero, Five-Four. We all wanted a piece of this action. All of us trying to follow after Georgie's Double-Zero. We didn't quite make it . . .'

'Tell me, please.'

Hackle stood up with an effort. 'Let's walk some more . . .'

Along corridors, round corners. More stairs, further down. Corners, corridors, another clearing. This one dark. 'Turn on the lights, please,' said Daisy.

'There aren't any,' replied the professor. 'Not here. This is the centre of the maze. I have a torch . . .'

Click!

A beam of diffuse light, seeping into damp walls, the scurrying of a mouse or a rat. Daisy shivering with it, the sudden cold spot. A place of ghosts. Hackle playing the beam over the walls to where a wooden table rested. On it, an array of electrical equipment, an old computer, all covered with dust and cobwebs, mouse-droppings.

'Haven't been down here . . . not since . . .'

'It feels haunted,' said Daisy. Hackle turned the beam on her. She could no longer see his face behind the shaking light. 'Professor . . .'

'You don't know the meaning of it, Daisy . . . perhaps you never will . . . even after I've told you . . .'

Hackle walked over to the workbench, placed the torch down on it so that the beam now illuminated the room in general. From the light available, Daisy could see that the place was roughly circular, with three separate entrances, and only a small pallet bed resting in the centre. 'This is where Georgie would . . .'

'Yes?'

'Sleep, whilst visiting the dream-maze. One time I came down early, I found him masturbating, furiously, on the bed. Pardon my language, please. He didn't even notice me come in. On the screen, over there, the wanderers were going crazy with his adopted lust. The brainwaves, during sexual dreams, Daisy . . . are quite different from the usual kind. Did you know that?'

Daisy was suddenly worried by the turn of the conversation. For the first time she began to doubt the professor's motives. She'd always thought of him as being an essentially asexual creature, witness her own crush on him. But hadn't Celia told her she'd seen him kissing Joe before? He wasn't such an old man, and not so innocent.

'You must have noticed, Daisy . . .' Hackle continued, 'the effect that watching the blurb-info can have upon the human physiology?'

'No . . . I . . .'

'Oh come on . . . your relationship with Jazir . . . where did that come from?'

'We were . . .'

'You were quite, quite cold, Daisy, for the whole first term. Coming to university is a time of throwing off the shackles; freshers are known for their availability among the older students. I do not condone this activity, but nor can I deny the immense sexuality that crawls the corridors during the first months. But you Daisy . . . not a whisper of passion have I noticed. Until now . . .'

'I would like to go back upstairs now, please.'

'Even I have been affected by it. Which surprised me, having put all such things behind me.'

'Benny knows.'

Hackle went silent for a moment. 'He does? Well . . . I cannot be blamed, now can I . . . any more than . . .'

'Upstairs, please.'

'As you wish. I shall remain here for a while.'

Daisy looked around, nervously. She couldn't even remember through which of the three doors they had entered the circle.

'It's not easy, is it? Escaping?' Hackle was now standing over the bed in the centre. 'Would you like to sit down?'

'No. Please. Take me back upstairs. I insist.'

'But this has always been a house of love. I have always allowed my guests the ultimate expression. We came from the Sixties, what else can be said? And the equations of mathemagica contain certain rituals, shall we say, of a sexual nature. In this room,' he gestured to the darkness, the air, the walls, and finally, the bed . . . 'In this room, we performed them.'

'You're scaring me . . .'

'He who is not scared, shall never understand. Georgie was scared, he understood far better than all us mathematicians. It was he who insisted upon the ritual being performed. Here! Upon this bed, he would make love for the first time, and we would capture his initiation upon the screen. His passion would roam the labyrinth, increasing the knowledge, the nymphomation.'

'This is sick.'

'Only to a nice girl. To the chosen ones, it was an act of supreme beauty and humanity. We would cross the borderline, between numbers and reality. We would become one with the information.'

'You found a woman to . . . perform . . . this?'

'We had a woman already.'

'Susan Prentice?'

'Yes. Prentice. She was also wired to the maze. I was monitoring the operation.'

'My father? What was he doing?'

'He was . . . merely an observer, Daisy. He has no blame for what followed.'

'What happened?'

'They laid together on this bed, Georgie and Susan. We had candles for them, and music and diagrams, and the best, most heady wine. It was so beautiful . . .'

'Something went wrong?'

Hackle breathed in heavily. The sound of it, to Daisy, the room itself was breathing, and then closing in, tighter, tighter . . .

'Yes. Paul had insisted upon going in as well, to witness the initiation from the inside, as he said. I could see no problem with this. None at all . . . I should have known otherwise.'

'Go on.'

'I recall the maze exploded with numbers as the act was performed. Susan was screaming with pleasure. Georgie had a unique talent indeed. The wanderers were fired by it, becoming an orgy. Imagine, Daisy! An orgy of information, mating with itself, incessantly, powerfully. I was overwhelmed by the results, so much so that I didn't notice what was really happening.'

'Let me guess. Malthorpe joined in, from the inside?'

'How could he resist? Maybe he was jealous of the effect the ritual was having. I cannot tell. I don't like to think of it. I can remember looking up from the equipment one time, and seeing them there, Georgie and the woman, caught in the most rigorous copulation I have ever encountered. It was like a two-person orgy, if such a thing is possible. I had the strangest feeling, watching them, that a third person *was* involved, in some invisible way. A ghost at the feast, if you will. I turned back to the monitor. The wanderers were participating in the pleasure, one especially: the double-six creature. Malthorpe. Seducer, Chancer,

Backslider . . . Warrior. He was rampaging around the maze, attacking the double-zero. When I turned around again, Malthorpe was there . . . on the bed with them. No ghost. Real.'

'He killed George? This is what happened?'

Hackle moved away from the bed. All the dark sexuality seemed to have drained away from his body, returning the man to his frailty. 'I don't know,' he was whispering. 'I still don't know. He was using Georgie's belt . . .'

'Hitting him?'

'Strangling him. Shouting out, "Play to win! Play to win!" It was a sexual thing. You know about such practices?'

Daisy shook her head, slowly, feeling sick.

'The tightening of the windpipe, at the moment of orgasm . . . it can lead to the most intense of pleasures. It was a quirk of Malthorpe's. The pleasure . . . the pain . . . this is what we fed into the system at that moment. Sex and death . . . the oldest equation.' Suddenly, Hackle was laughing wildly, his parched voice echoing around the circle.

'Malthorpe killed him?'

'We all did. We all killed him. This is what broke the group.'

'You're mad!' cried Daisy. 'I can't . . . I can't believe this. I can't.'

'Believe it. I beg you. Georgie found the centre.'

Hackle picked up the torch. He shone it directly on to the bed.

'A winner, not a loser.'

A small pallet bed, covered with a dirty, torn woollen blanket, broken wires trailing from it to the dead computer on the workbench.

A ghost of numbers.

Play to lose

A car, somewhere on a road leading out of Manchester. In the car, a man. We don't know his name, not yet. The winner of the prize, the double-blank. He had thrown the domino into a ditch somewhere, hoping to lead the Joker Bone astray, but knowing inside that all was hopeless. The car was stolen, another ruse to escape. Hopeless case. There was no escape. Even his personal blurbfly had deserted him.

Night. Rain hitting the windscreen. The moors. Shapes in the night. Whisperings. Wipers, back and forth, back and forth. The man, wiping his eyes, trying to stay awake. Never wanting to dream, not ever again, but growing more and more tired. He should pull over, rest awhile. There was no rest.

A figure appears by the side of the road, thumbing a lift. A thin, skeletal figure, bleached white by the rain. As white as bone. A lone blurbfly, nested on his jutting shoulder.

The driver, slowly, slowly, against his wishes . . . brings the car to a halt.

PLAY TO WIN        PLAY TO WIN
PLAY TO WIN        PLAY TO WIN
PLAY TO WIN        PLAY TO WIN
PLAY TO WIN
PLAY TO WIN        PLAY TO WIN
PLAY TO LOSE      PLAY TO WIN
PLAY TO WIN

PLAY TO WIN
PLAY TO WIN PLAY TO WIN
TO WIN PLAY TO LOSE PLA
WIN PLAY TO WIN  PLAY

WIN PLAY TO WIN P
PLAY TO WIN PLAY

PLAY TO WIN F
PLAY TO WIN
PLAY TO W
PLAY TO WIN
PLAY TO LOSE
PLAY TO WIN PL
WIN PLAY TO WIN

PLAY TO WIN PLAY TO

TO WIN PLAY TO WIN PLA
PLAY TO WIN   PLAY TO WIN
PLAY TO WIN

PLAY TO WIN      PLAY TO WIN
PLAY TO WIN

PLAY TO WIN      PLAY TO WIN
PLAY TO WIN      PLAY TO LOSE
PLAY TO WIN      PLAY TO WIN
PLAY TO WIN      PLAY TO WIN

**A** midnight fugue. The Dark Fractals, in their various beds. Joe Crocus alone, for instance. He had got back to the room. His keys gone from the desk and, looking out of the window, his car gone with them. Now, in bed alone, thinking of where Benny was, and what was troubling him. Maybe he knew about Hackle. Joe could explain, he could use his charm, if he wanted to. Did he want to? This thing with Hackle, where had it come from? The whole house had turned sexy, vicious even since they'd started on this AnnoDomino assignment. Joe was losing his famed control over the disciples. First Dopejack running off, now Benny. Was it worth it, the struggle? With the genetic calculus inside his body running down towards infinity, what was he struggling for? What could he possibly win? He would need to talk to Hackle. Was this the right time to visit his bed, with Benny away? No.

In their separate beds, elsewhere in the house: Max Hackle, Jimmy Love, Little Celia. Only Little Celia fast asleep at this point, dreaming of Eddie and her winning the ultimate prize. Hackle, unable to rest so easy, knowing the Joker Bone was out there somewhere, searching the city for its victim. Was it all his fault? And what could he do about it? And knowing that he had lied to Daisy. Sure, mostly the truth about that day, but one particular fact that could not be mentioned. Not yet. It wasn't his job, was it? Not his job. Jimmy's job. This Jimmy Love that was lying awake in the next bedroom, wondering just how much Hackle had told his daughter. Imagining how she must be feeling now, knowing her father had been involved in a murder. Hating him, no doubt. Which would be nothing, that hate, when he told her the real truth. It was his job, wasn't it? His fault . . .

Another house, another bed, DJ Dopejack. Drifting into and out of sleep, excited by his findings about the dominoes, laughing at Hackle's imagined reaction upon reading his message. So close now, he was sure of it. Tomorrow, more work, unravel the connections . . .

Above a restaurant in Rusholme Village, Daisy Love in her bed. How could she sleep? So much to think about. Well, she would wait until Jazir knocked gently on her door at half-past. She would tell him everything. Jazir would know what to do. Jazir down below, working quickly to tidy up, to get upstairs to Daisy, no idea what was happening.

Not in his bed, Sweet Benny Fenton was still driving around Manchester in Joe's car. Where had he been? He couldn't remember. Around in circles, wondering whether he should go back home. But what for? With Joe and Hackle . . . Christ! Working on his rage. Maybe it was a time to jump ship. Become single again, live a little. Yeah, Joe could go fuck himself! When he'd finished fucking Hackle, that is. Forget about them . . .

Another car, heading back into Manchester. This one driven by the winner of the baddest prize. We still don't know his name, not yet. Yeah, he'd stopped to pick up that hitch-hiker, out there on the moors. He'd expected pain, and there was, but only a tiny amount, a mere biteful. Then it was his turn. He never expected the prize, no matter how bad, would involve him dispensing the pain. But now he felt good, the winner. Fucking good! Suffused with knowledge. Before, he would have classed himself an expert only on rugby tactics and medical procedures, with maybe a touch of advanced beer and curry consumption thrown in.

But now, he was full of a new knowledge. All the inner workings of the game, for instance, were his to peruse. He even knew who Mr Million really was, and wasn't that a surprise? He never would have guessed. Winning the double-blank wasn't losing, winning was winning. The best prize of all. And he was hungry, so much to do, so much he didn't yet know. So much knowledge out there in the maze of Manchester, just waiting for his gift. With a new blurbfly all his own, named Horny George, to give directions.

So many he could chose from; all the losers of the city. Watch them. Watch them sleeping, or dancing still and celebrating at having lost the Joker Bone. And all those people holding half-blank bones, so scared of dreaming that night, having heard so many rumours of skeletal nightmares? Rest easy, innocents; the prize is claimed. The bone is travelling in another man's body, in a stolen car, with a nasty, horny blurb, on the rain-washed streets, in the gambling capital of England, the UK, Planet Earth.

As Jazir came to Daisy's bed. 'Make love to me,' she said.

'What do you think I'm doing?' he answered.

'Make love to me. Proper.'

'Proper? This is proper, isn't it?'

'Properly. All night long.'

'All night? What about my . . .'

'Forget your father. Stay with me.'

To which urgent instructions he tried his best shot, with the liberal application of trusty vaz! And afterwards they talked of maybe running away together. 'You want out?' asked Jazir, exhausted.

'I think so.'

'What about your course? And breaking into the dominoes? Hackle . . .'

'Forget them.'

But Daisy couldn't, not really and not so easily. Instead, she told Jazir everything, everything in the dark. How the Number Gumbos had together murdered Georgie Horn, how her father was involved in this killing, in ways she didn't yet understand. It wasn't just Malthorpe's fault, she was certain of that much. As a blurbfly knocked against the window, sensing Jazir was there.

A knock on a window in the night? Sure, let's listen to one, that same precise moment, with DJ Dopejack being pulled rudely from his sleep by the incessant knocking. Turning over, pulling the sheets up over his head, willing them to go away. Blurbs against glass. In the end he had to get up, move to the window, peep through a crack . . .

A blue and cream rugby shirt? Zuze! Fuck! What was he doing here? Hasn't he done enough? With a fucking blurbfly, this time. Shit! Really scared now, not another beating, please. Nigel Zuze moving back from the doorway, looking up and down the street. God, he looked bad, what had happened to all the beef? He looked like . . .

Suddenly, Zuze looked right up at the window, with the blurb buzzing! Dopejack jerked back, knocking over a chair. He had to get to the phone, ring the police . . .

The door being pounded down below, like a hammer blow.

DJ struggling with the phone, struggling to get some clothes on, find a weapon . . .

The door smashing in. Oh God! The sound of it. Please, no . . .

With Daisy and Jazir safe and warm in their cosy bed. Blurbflies outside the window. Play to lose, play to lose! Daisy had told him what Hackle had told her later, about Miss Sayer. About Malthorpe having an affair with her. How it all tied in, and what could they do about it? It was too dangerous.

'I know Miss Sayer's involved.' A slow voice in the dark.

'Did Hackle tell you already?'

'No. She visits me.' Idly stroking her naked thigh . . .

Daisy shifting her weight, rolling over to face him. 'What?'

'Miss Sayer, she visits me.' Jazir, so calm.

'When?'

'When I'm using the computer.'

'Jaz?'

'It's true. She appears on screen. She talks to me. It's her.'

'Why is everybody going mad?'

'No, this was from before the project. I was young, just playing arcade games. She came to me then. Has done ever since. Lately . . .'

Daisy was sitting up in bed by now. 'You're kidding me, aren't you?'

'Lately . . . in my dreams.'

'Right.'

'Listen to me! She's asking for help, I think. Something's gone wrong. She won't let me tell anyone. I think she's scared, can't trust anybody. Only me.'

'Why you?'

Jazir shook his head slowly. 'I don't know. Oh God, Daisy . . . things are happening to me, aren't they? What should I do? Lately . . .'

Daisy held him tight as he spoke. 'Lately I've been seeing things.'

'What kind of things?'

'Images, from the city.'

Images from the city? Here's one Jazir is missing: DJ Dopejack back at his computer, bloodstained fingers travelling rapid-fire over sticky keys, making a mess of words . . .

'Images from the city,' said Jazir. 'It's like I'm . . . don't laugh at me . . .'

'I'm not.'

'It's since I got bitten. Like I'm looking through a blurb's eyes.'

Looking through a blurb's eyes? Here's one, flying over a

street in Whalley Range. The houses below, the rain in your eyes.
A car travelling along below you. Float down, keep apace. Look
inside and what do you see? A young man, night black, mad
eyed and speeding to the house where Dopejack lives, to throw
his lot in with the DJ. To get back at Hackle and Joe for betraying
him. Betraying the love and the trust and the years of pain gone
to waste. Yeah, Sweet Benny and the DJ, cracking the bone-code
together, hitting the big prize. It was late, but so what? He'd
knock Dopejack up. What was the time now, only a series of
moments, bringing him closer . . . closer . . .

With Daisy saying, 'OK. What can you see now?'

With Jazir replying, 'Nothing. Only you. It doesn't happen at
will. It just . . .'

'It just happens, don't tell me.'

'I saw you and Celia at the grave of Eddie.'

'Jaz! You imagined it.'

'Maybe so, but lately I've been trying to fly.'

Daisy actually got up at this point. 'No. I'm not putting up
with this.'

'Daisy!'

'You think I'm stupid. All of you do!' Dragging on her dressing
gown. 'I'm not putting up with it.'

'Come back to bed, please.'

'No.'

'Daisy, pretty soon you're gonna have to face it.'

'Face what? I'm not facing anything. It's all stupid.' She
knocked all the maths books, all the workings off her desk.

'The bones . . . Daisy, they're deeper than you think. There's
only one of them, don't you get it? One blurb, one bone, one
winner, one loser. They're all connected. That's what the lucky
bleeders do; they connect to the whole. All we have to do—'

'Shut up.'

'Look, sit down at least. Can't we even talk?'

'What's to say? My dad's involved in murder, the Joker's on the street, you're talking to a computer and no doubt taking off any day now.'

Daisy flopped down in an armchair.

'All I know is that since I got bitten,' said Jazir, quietly, 'I've been changing. It's not bad, that's the strange thing. Well, to begin with . . . but now, I can see clearly. I'm infected with the bone-juice, the vaz. I'm getting all slippy, like I can crawl through the spaces. Sometimes, I want to stand on the tallest building and shout out loud to the city how fucking great the Anno-Dominoes are. Other times, I just want to throw myself off, and float, and glide, and swarm with the pack. I'm an advert. A living advert. No! OK, right . . . but it's good. It's good because I'm fighting it. Don't you see, some of the blurbs want out. They want their freedom. That's why they're attracted to me. I can turn this knowledge against the bones, just like Dopejack did with the blurb-juice. Maybe I can find a way in? What do you reckon? You with me on this?'

Daisy looked at her friend, her lover, her strange and only lover and friend, for a long, long time. 'I'm not working with Hackle any more.'

And look at Benny's car now, crunching to a stop outside Dopejack's house. What's he going to find? We don't know. All we can do is follow him to the door, see him knock on it. See the door open under his fist. Unlocked? Strange. No, not unlocked, broken. Stranger. A burglary? To walk slowly into the house, to call out the DJ's name. To get no reply. To hear a noise rather, coming from up the stairs. To go up the stairs, hardly daring to breathe now. Stepping lightly, every heartbeat.

Maybe I should be calling the cops? Maybe I should be running away. What was that noise? Stranger yet, to push open a bedroom door, slowly . . .

Far away and safe in Rusholme, with Jazir getting out of bed to plead with Daisy. 'I'm not asking you to work with Hackle. I'm asking you to get Celia out of there, that's all. We still need her. And your father . . .'

Daisy shook her head.

'OK, we give in then. You go back to the university, or maybe you run away. Maybe you'll find a new life, I don't know. What am I supposed to do, eh? I'm the one with the stuff inside me. Maybe it's killing me.'

'Benny should have a look at you.'

'Benny should look after himself, more like.'

Benny should look through the door of a bedroom, to find DJ Dopejack sitting on a chair, chewing some meat off a bone. DJ naked, grease and blood all over his flesh. A wound in his neck. At his feet, sprawled and crumpled and cut to shreds, the body of a man. A torn blue and cream shirt, bones sticking through here and there. A belt tight around the neck . . .

'Fuck! DJ?'

Dopejack smiled at Benny. A blurbfly was resting on his shoulder.

'What have you done? Who's that?'

Dopejack smiling.

Benny moved to the body and turned it over. 'Shit!' Seeing the slashed face of Nigel Zuze, proto-fascist from the League of Zero. Did Benny get the picture then? I think he rather did, as Dopejack beckoned him forward.

'It's your turn now.'

Unresisting . . .

'Benny should look after himself,' said Jazir. 'We don't need them, Daisy. It's me and you now. Joe, Hackle, Benny . . . let them roll away. They haven't got my knowledge. All that energy they've wasted, looking for a genetic connection. It's not genetic, is it? Partly, maybe, but it's more to do with keying into the bones. Understanding the game. What was it Hackle told you about George Horn? He was in tune with the randomness of life. And that's Celia to a tee. They're both essentially wild, innocent, mad. Bringing Celia in off the street is the worst thing we could do. It's stifling her—'

The phone ringing.

Daisy picked it up: 'Hello? . . . Oh, Mr Malik . . .' She looked at Jazir, who was praying on his hands and knees. 'It's very late . . . No, that's OK. I was working . . . What? Jazir . . . No, not here . . . I am certain. Has he gone missing? . . . Yes, maybe a nightclub . . . Yes, much too young . . . Yes, he is in trouble. Let you know . . . Yes . . . No trouble . . . Good night.' Phone down. 'You can get up now . . .'

Jazir doesn't get up.

'Jaz. You're safe. Stop messing about.'

'Daisy . . .' Jazir rolled onto the floor, covering his head with his hands.

'Jaz! What's wrong? What's happening?'

'Something . . . something . . . Whalley Range . . .'

'Dopejack's house?'

'Yes . . . Dopejack . . . and . . . something . . . someone . . . little blurbfly flying, flying, flying . . . window . . . can't get . . . can't get focused . . . Arhhhhh!'

Jazir shot up to a sitting position, his face creased with fear.

'Jaz!' Daisy knelt down to comfort him, as best . . . 'What's wrong?'

'They got him.'

'Who? Dopejack? Who's got Dopejack?'

'Don't know. His house . . . pain . . . blood . . . biting . . .'

'How do you know?'

'Blurbfly. Street. Watching. Attacked. Another blurb, attacking mine . . . killing mine . . . evil fly . . . must . . . do . . .'

'I don't like it, Jaz. Stop it . . .'

'Must do . . . something . . . Not know. Not know . . .'

Rocking him, rocking him slowly, back down to now, back down to earth, to bed, to kisses, to bed, to sleep . . . anything . . .

Jazir's naked body so wet, like sweat, more like rain, drops of rain.

## Play to lose

Benny. Sweet Benny Fenton, driving back towards the Hackle household. Feeling good, no guilt, no pain, just the desire to get the job done. Must do it better than Dopejack. No mess, that was the key, no blood, no tears. Keep it clean.

Idly tapping at the puncture on his neck, it had gone quite well, he thought. Always room for improvement, of course, but he hadn't panicked, not gone mad, not like Dopejack. The actual act had taken place under his own control, brisk and without excess wastage. Then he had cleaned up as best he could. Mustn't get bestial, that was the key. Control was the essence, treat it as an experiment in genetic mutation. He had the equations inside him now, how could he fail . . .

With his whole body steeped in new knowledge. Everything the Joker knew, everything the Zuze knew, everything the

Dopejack knew, everything Benny knew: inside him now, growing, breeding, reproducing, making babies. Baby data! Sweetjokerzuzedope, his new name. The roads of Manchester were a maze to be driven through, towards the centre, where the treasure is. The centre was the House of Chances. That's where his mother and father lay waiting, alongside Mr Million. Waiting to welcome him home. But first, the simple job of dealing bad hands to the Dark Fractals.

The world will succumb, finally.

Into numbers. One down, two down . . .

Who's next?

PLAY TO WIN             PLAY TO LOSE
PLAY TO WIN             PLAY TO WIN
PLAY TO WIN             PLAY TO WIN
PLAY TO LOSE
PLAY TO WIN             PLAY TO WIN
PLAY TO LOSE            PLAY TO WIN
PLAY TO WIN

PLAY TO WIN
PLAY TO WIN PLAY TO WIN
TO WIN PLAY TO LOSE PLA
WIN PLAY TO WIN  PLAY

WIN PLAY TO LOSE P
PLAY TO LOSE PLAY

PLAY TO WIN P
PLAY TO WIN
PLAY TO W
PLAY TO WIN
PLAY TO LOSE
PLAY TO WIN PL
WIN PLAY TO WIN

PLAY TO WIN PLAY TO

TO WIN PLAY TO WIN PLA
PLAY TO WIN   PLAY TO WIN
PLAY TO WIN

PLAY TO WIN
PLAY TO LOSE            PLAY TO LOSE

PLAY TO WIN             PLAY TO WIN
PLAY TO LOSE            PLAY TO LOSE
PLAY TO WIN             PLAY TO WIN
PLAY TO WIN             PLAY TO WIN

**A**ll of England was watching. The Saturday papers, landing on a nation's drenched early morning doorsteps, delivered by the Whoomphy boys. Glorious headlines, free with every burger, singing the praises of the Joker Bone. How that double-blanker was such a useful member of society. A humorous escape valve. The winner had even volunteered to have his photograph printed on every front page. Full publicity value, nothing to be ashamed of. His name was Desmond Targett, and there he grinned over Jazir and Daisy's breakfast, holding proudly aloft a golden loo-brush for being 'such a sporting loser'! The prize in question? The dreaded fear-inducing mysterious wouldn't-wish-it-on-my-worst-enemy prize for winning the nasty double-zero? To spend a week cleaning out every public convenience in Manchester!

No mention of any murders from the night before, Jazir checked to the last page, bottom column. With a slew of editorials saying that the jealousy killings were maybe on the way out, 'unfashionable' was the word on the street. With ADTV praising the bone, every hour on the hour and good old Frank Scenario rush-releasing a new single in celebration . . .

> *Cream my numbers, cream my genes,*
> *Eat my chances the double-zero.*
> *Bone me, enthrone me, spin the memes,*
> *Embrace the Joker, play the hero!*

A massive fluttering of blurbflies, buzzing out the new message. Losing is good for the soul! Make a wish on the future! Questions would be asked, first government session, Monday morning (because surely they were expecting a more discouraging booby prize?) Until then . . . Play to joke! Joke to play!

Oh, the sacred bones! The city couldn't stop laughing.
Game on!

## Play to lose

Jazir really should be heading home by now, to face his father's
wrath for staying out all night, instead . . . he was catching a bus
to Whalley Range, with Daisy pulled along behind him.

Dopejack's house looked OK, no broken door, no sign of
trouble. Very quiet, no music being played. Nothing like that.
Jazir knocked on the door. It took an age, and Daisy was saying
let's go, when the door was opened by a cop, full burger-mode.
Holding his hand up, shaking his head, no entry and a sluggish,
'What want?'

'Oh, I am sorry,' said Jazir. 'Is there a problem?'

'Problem?'

'Is Dopejack all right?' asked Daisy.

'Dopejack?'

'We don't know his real name.'

'Real name?'

'BFZ,' said Jaz.

'BFZ? What that?'

'Brain-free zone. Let's go, Daze.'

Along the street they went, round a corner, doubling back.
Jazir was shaking his head, looking worried. 'I told you, didn't I?'
he said. 'Didn't I say something was up.'

'You don't know, not yet.'

'Let's find out then, shall we?'

Daisy nodded. They found a place where they could watch

the house without being seen, crouched behind a garden wall. After ten minutes another two cops came out of the house, one in full burger-mode, the other in plain clothes (but chewing on a burger, natch).

'It's Crawl!' whispered Daisy. 'You know, the cop that arrested me.'

'Interesting. Let's ask him—'

'Jaz!'

'Inspector?' Jazir had started to walk across the street . . .

Crawl turned at the voice, took the burger out of his mouth for a second. 'Who's this?' Then shoved it back.

The cop on duty shrugged his brain.

'I'm wondering what's up here?' said Jazir.

'Why?'

'My friend lives here. DJ Dopejack. Is he . . .'

'Everything's under control. Just a minor incident . . . Oh, it's you, is it? Might have bloody known.'

Daisy had followed Jazir, and Crawl had spotted her.

'What are you doing here?'

'Our friend, Inspector . . .'

'You've sure got some unlucky ones, haven't you, Ms Love? And I'm not an inspector any more, thank you. Been promoted, haven't I? Public Relations. Very cushy.'

'If there's anything wrong . . .' started Daisy.

Crawl laughed, just long enough for his two cops to join in. 'Now don't you go worrying yourself, Ms Love. A disturbance was reported on these premises last night. Obviously high spirits at not winning the Joker Bone, don't you think?'

'At what time?' asked Jazir.

'That's my business. Rest assured, we are investigating.'

'I want to see Dopejack,' said Daisy.

'That's not possible. Not at this moment.'

'Why not?' said Jazir. 'He's not dead is he?'

Crawl spat out a chunk of meat. 'Should he be?'

'Why can't we see him?'

'You want to? Really?' Crawl nodded at the duty cop, who pushed the door open for them. 'Go on then. Be quick.'

Daisy looked at Jazir, who shook his head. 'Thanks, no thanks. We don't want to disturb your investigations, Inspector.'

'Most kind. But please . . . you must now call me Chief Executive. Public Relations. I'm working for AnnoDomino now. Nice, huh?'

Crawl threw down the remains of his burger, crunched it underfoot, and then started to laugh; a continuous ruckus that Daisy swore she could still hear on the bus all the way back to Rusholme.

'OK, here's the scheme,' said Jazir, as they tried to part at Withington and Moss Lane East. 'Tonight, we meet up again, late on, mind.'

'What if your father . . .'

'Never mind that. The important thing is—'

'He'll kill you.'

'Tell that to Dopey.'

'We don't know he's been killed.'

'So, we find out. Now just listen to me. Tonight, after the Samosa's shut. We set out together. OK?'

A kiss sealed it. But left Daisy alone and frightened and not knowing what to do next. How not to think about the way things were going, downhill with vaz on the slope. Thinking like Jazir already. What was he leading her into? Why couldn't she just run away, leave it all? The university, Hackle, Celia, her father, Jazir, the numbers? Maybe because she loved at least three of the items, not saying which, because she didn't know, not really and not yet.

Her room, where she rested for five minutes at the most, was too full of Jazir's smell. Spice in the air.

Restless, she went out again, wandering. The pavements were tightly packed with discarded creamed bones. A second pavement that crunched underfoot, a second road that cracked under tyres, but never broke. Why don't they clean them up? Can't the council do something about it? There ought to be a new ruling: AnnoDomino will undertake to keep the streets free of all discarded chances. Whoomphy had to do it, didn't they? Special bins, students in burgersuits? What was the difference?

Still it looked nice, in a way. Last night's rain had washed all the bones clean and how they glistened now, in the gentle sun. What did Jazir mean when he said there was only one domino, only one blurb. He hadn't explained, mainly because she hadn't given him room.

She walked down towards Platt Fields. There was a place on the corner there, a block of flats called Rusholme Gardens. A lot of students lived there, and Daisy was suddenly jealous. Bet they were still in bed, with lovers and comics and spliffs and music playing and not a care in the world on this particular Saturday in the year of 1999. Why wasn't she just a student any more? Why had she taken on this stupid assignment?

In the park she sat down and watched the kids and the ducks at play. Easy life, a bit of fun, a bit of bread. OK, Monday morning, first thing, she would tell Hackle she wanted out of the bone team. Back to normal she would go and maybe get some beauty back in the numbers, the equations. And no way was she going round to Dopejack's tonight. Jazir could go it alone from now on.

Sorted out, wasn't she?

## Play to Lose

Hackle had gathered his sorry troops around him in the cellar. Hackle, Jimmy Love, Joe, Celia, Benny. Joe and Benny weren't talking to each other, and Hackle and Jimmy weren't exactly on loving terms, and Celia talked to none of them, preferring her own mind to their stupid games.

'There have been setbacks, I know,' Hackle was saying, 'but that doesn't mean we should give up so easily. Jimmy and I have been working on reopening the maze, and very soon we should be able to—'

'What's the point?' asked Joe.

'The point is . . .'

'No. Max, we've got nowhere. Don't you see? We've got our very own natural, what good is that? Benny hasn't found any anomalies in her, isn't that right, Benny?'

Benny shrugged.

'We have the DNA of the blurb,' said Jimmy.

'We peel a few layers off security, we find out how much each employee is making. Like, wow. Big deal.'

'I think we're all agreed that the genetic approach is limited.' Hackle looked round for support. 'But there are other means . . . if we can feed the domino's DNA into the maze, we could—'

'Without Dopejack, who's going to travel further?' asked Joe.

'Jazir.'

Joe shook his head. 'He's off on his own track. We all know that.'

'If you'd just let us finish, Joe . . .'

'What for? I mean, what's it all for? Sure, some people have been killed. People get killed every day. It's just another bunch of crime stats. What's my stake in this? I was expecting to make myself a pile of lovelies before I die, for fuck's sake. Even the Joker's turned out to be just that, a fucking joke . . .'

Jimmy grinned at this. 'That toilet-cleaning crap, you don't really believe it?'

'I'm saying the whole thing is a joke.'

Hackle shook his head, said nothing, and turned away from his star pupil.

'I say we call it quits. Max?'

'That's what you really think?' asked Hackle, sadness in his voice.

'That's what I'm saying.'

'OK,' Hackle turned to the group. 'Whoever wants out, now's the time. It's only going to get worse.'

'Who wants out?' cried Joe, triumphantly. 'That's what he's saying.'

Celia put up her hand first.

'Not including you,' said Hackle.

'Why not?'

'This is adults only.'

'You can't keep me here, against my will.'

'She's got a point, Max,' said Joe.

'No she hasn't. So, are you going, Joe?'

Joe looked at Benny. Benny looked at Max, and smiled and said, 'I'm staying.'

'Benny?' said Joe. 'You can't . . .'

Benny shrugged, and Joe looked around the group. They were all looking back at him.

'What's it to be, Joe?' asked Hackle. 'Last chances?'

Joe shook his head and made for the stairs.

There was an emptiness left behind; Benny and Max knew

that Joe was important, Jimmy had his guesses, even Little Celia
was worried.

'He'll be back,' said Hackle.

'You said that about Dopejack,' said Benny.

'It's up to you, Benny. He—'

'Why me? You're the one that's fucking him.'

'That's . . .'

'Yes?'

'It never went that far.'

'I wonder why? Couldn't get it up?'

'Ask Joe. Please, don't let him go . . .'

'I get all the dirty jobs.'

Benny left them to it, their mad experiments with broken-
down mazes and little girls. He found Joe in the bedroom,
packing his things.

'You're not really going?'

'Why not?'

'Look, I know about you and Max, OK?'

'Yeah, and I know you know. Like where were you last night.'

'Getting some air.'

'Getting that stupid lovebite more like. Bloody kids!'

'Cheek. You're fucking Max, then telling me off for going out.'

'I'm not fucking Max.'

'You'd like to.'

'I don't go for older guys.'

'Nor do I.'

'Cheap shot.'

'I love you, Joe.'

'Don't say that.'

Joe dropped a folded shirt into his suitcase. He came up
close to Benny.

'There's nothing between me and Max. Friends. He's my tutor!'

'Kinky.'

'It's this house, don't you see? Messing with the bones. The nymphomation. It's making us all randy. And . . . well, we were having problems weren't we? Max was . . . Max is Max. I mean, he's Max Hackle! The best fucking mathematician I've ever known. That means something to me, something pure. But now . . . it excites me. It turns me on. And I don't like it.'

'Wild Joe Crocus, loverman supreme!'

'Benny, you know what I'm really like. That's why I love you. You know I want control. I haven't got long left, and I can't afford to waste it. I want to be in control. That's why I told Max to stuff his cock up somebody else's hole.'

'You didn't say that?'

'Exactly that.'

'Loving it!'

'Yeah.'

'You wanna go to bed?' asked Sweet Benny Fenton.

'Sure do,' answered Joe Crocus.

At seven o'clock, Daisy went downstairs to the Golden Samosa. The evening rush had barely begun. Looking through the window, she could see no sign of Jazir, so she went inside. Immediately, a waiter asked her if she wanted a table or a takeaway? Neither, she wanted to see Jazir.

'Jazir not here.'

'Where is he?'

The waiter shook his head, slowly, then moved back to the kitchen, carrying a stack of dirty plates. Daisy followed him through the swing doors. Jazir's father was working up a new spice mixture, carefully adding chilli powder to turmeric and coriander. The smell of the kitchen was so like Jazir's beautiful flesh, the colour of the smoky air. The father's anger was like the smell of the flesh of the night of the air of the flames in the karahi pan.

'You get out of my kitchen, this instance!'

'I'm looking for—'

'Jazir not here. Very angry I am. Out, out, out!'

Daisy went back upstairs and tried the telephone. Jazir's mother answered it. She was less angry than the father, but only slightly so. 'Jazir's not coming out any more. Jazir is banned.'

Daisy lay on her bed, wondering what to do. She wanted to tell Jazir she wasn't going with him tonight, that's all. Now it looked like Jazir wasn't going either. It was her fault, wasn't it . . .

She reached over to find a handkerchief. The tube of vaz was still there, bedside, from the night before, plus a small pile of punies.

Daisy was angry at first, because she thought Jaz had paid her for the sex. But then another thought came to her, even more scary.

## Play to lose

Later, a cold, dark house in Whalley Range. There was a cop-ribbon across the gate, but that was easy. The door, when closely examined by the light of a torch, was seen to have been recently mended. A new lock. No problem. Daisy squeezed a small amount of vaz into the keyhole. The tumblers became slick, the door opened easily with a slight push.

Elsewhere . . .

Softer, darker, quieter, more ghostly . . . Benny lay peaceful beside the sleeping Joe. He'd proven something to himself. That he was in control. He'd turned the bad bone into a good fuck. At the height of it, how badly he'd wanted to plunge his teeth into Joe's neck, passing the nymphomation on to the next stage. How badly he'd then wanted Joe to kill him, kill him viciously. Once passed on, the carrier had to die, that was the ruling.

The belt around the neck, tightening into orgasm . . .

Instead, he'd let Joe come, and then he'd come, and for a second it felt like love, real love, and then it felt like betrayal.

Benny got up, carefully, so as not to disturb. Slipped on a shirt, one of Joe's, not yet packed. Went to the window. It was dark outside, and a solitary blurb lay hovering in the air. Horny George! Faithful companion, eager to progress the Joker's work. The blurb was a cursor to the program Benny carried inside, pointing out the next task. He waved it away.

Not yet.

He looked at his watch. Ten o'clock.

He got dressed quietly, sorted a few things out, and went downstairs. On the way, he visited the kitchen and took out a breadknife. The house was silent, no doubt experiments were still going on in the cellar. Benny laughed as he went outside. If only they knew about the creature they had under their own roof. What knowledge. Mr Million you want? Just ask me. Secrets of the bones you want. I'm the man. I'm the bearer, and one of you will get to kill me.

But not yet.

Talk about playing the Joker. Joe was only pretending to sleep. As soon as Benny had left, he got up, dressed and finished packing. His treasured copy of *Mathematica Magica* was waiting for him, given to him by Max, but too heavy, too restrictive. He would leave it for Benny. Through the window he watched Benny walk away. Joe carried his suitcase out of the bedroom door, kissing goodbye to the sweet comfort of years. Down the corridor, another door. He pushed it open slowly, carefully . . . whispering . . .

'Celia?'

'Huhhhh.'

'It's me. Joe. You awake?'

'Huh?'

'It's Joe. You ready to leave?'

'Hmmm.'

Benny was walking down Barlow Moor Road towards the House of Chances, barely aware of the blurbfly following him. Just knowing it was there.

Who to choose, that was the question. It's an interesting question; if you had to choose somebody to kill you, who would you choose? A friend, a lover, a relative, a stranger? Somebody famous, religious, intelligent? Unknown, poor, stupid? A professional hitman; the quick, silent bullet in the night?

Benny's choices: Hackle, Joe, Jimmy, Celia, Daisy, Jazir. The collected Dark Fractals, all spread out and waiting for his deliberation.

Joe was the obvious one. Lover. Not long of this world anyway. But hadn't he messed up that chance already? Letting him live.

Hackle? The wisest. The boss. The enemy. Main target. Most wanted. Take him down with me, maybe save the rest? Maybe . . .

What about Celia? Little Miss Celia. Could she do it? Benny couldn't imagine it, but then again, hadn't he . . .

Once the nympho took over . . .

And what difference did it make, the order? They'd all fall down, one by one, in sequence. The Joker inside would see to it. What was the point of it. He didn't know, only that it had to be done. Only then could he go home to the mother and father of all the lost chances of the world. It was his job, you see. Infect, then die. A genetic program. He had fought the Joker in bed with Joe. Won that one, but he'd made the Joker angry. Benny could feel the thing inside him, the urge, like a snake uncurling. The double helix, uncurling.

He didn't have long left. Infect, then die. Infect, infect, infect! Infect the world with nymphomation, pass it on. Give birth to it. Not long . . . not long left. Must fight it, do the right thing. Keep walking . . .

The Joker could hear his every tangled thought, and was laughing.

Talk about not having long left. Joe was suddenly aware of the curse inside him, the cancerous gene, growing, growing. Don't think about it. Just bundle Celia into the car. Leave. Find somewhere, somewhere safe. Wait for Celia's lucky bone to come calling. Make a little life of what was left; his only craving now.

Benny had reached the outskirts of the AnnoDomino grounds. There was some kind of protest going on, with a bunch of people waving banners and shouting slogans at the House of Chances. 'Free the Zero! No more blanks! Bones are bad! Whitewash! Zuze, Zuze, Zuze!' Benny recognized them: the League of Zero, Nigel Zuze's crew-sluts. From what he could gather, they knew that Zuze had won the double-blank.

A cloud of securiblurbs was keeping the protesters at bay, while the harassed official, called Chief Executive Crawl, moved along the line, trying to reason with them.

There was no reasoning.

The crowd pushed forward, breaking the blurb-line. Benny was vaguely aware of cop sirens approaching. A camera crew moving in. The official raising his hands, making a gesture. The blurbs going in for the attack. Screams and curses. One boy went down, holding his leg in disbelief as a blurb stung its message into him. Benny's own blurb, Horny George, was confused by all this, which side to be on?

Talk about taking a chance. Benny pushed through the crowd, moving slowly forward until only one nasty securiblurb was looking directly into his face, sting extended.

It recognized him. Or rather, what he carried, and left him alone.

But Benny would not be left alone; to the blurb he raised his fist and shouted: 'I'm not doing it! Do you hear me, Mr Million? The game's over.'

Have you ever heard a thousand blurbflies laugh? (As Jazir, in his Rusholme bed, raised up suddenly and flung back the sheets.) Have you ever heard a thousand blurbflies scream? (As Jazir saw, through a thousand eyes, all that was about to take place, and placed his hands over his eyes as though not to see.) The blurbs were moving in even as Benny made his decision, there was only one way, taking a long-bladed kitchen knife from under his coat, bringing it up quickly, and with no thought at all in his mind, only pure emptiness and the total need to be killed, turning the Joker upon itself, hearing it scream inside and then plunging the blade (as Jazir screamed at a million miles per hour) straight, straight into his black, tender-hearted, waiting chest . . .

## Play to lose

What was she looking for, or even expecting? If only Jaz had come along. (Stop thinking like that.) Some sign of a cover-up, perhaps? The downstairs rooms had been clean but untidy, or else tidy and dirty, in the correct student style. Nothing out of place, nothing in its place. With torchlight only, Daisy had searched everywhere for evidence of a disturbance (as Crawl had called it). The kitchen, the living room, back room. All clear, all disturbed, slightly. Now she was upstairs, looking in the bathroom (clean, dirty), first bedroom (clean, but unlived in), main bedroom . . .

Immediately, she knew something was wrong.

Couldn't quite finger it, but whatever had happened, if it had happened, it had happened here. Just stepping in there told her so. The smell of disinfectant. Movement in the corner. The dancing man . . .

This wasn't the place for torches (too cold, too scary), so she chanced a table lamp, with the curtains well drawn. Let's see . . .

Was this the bedroom of a DJ with green hair and a headful of music? Sure, there was a mega-mixing system against one wall, vinyl neatly stacked, alphabetical by artist, DJ-style, that was fine. What else? Frank Scenario poster: 'Cool down, baby, don't you blow your top.' A bed, unmade. A chair, a desk with a computer and various pieces of equipment. Frank Scenario screen saver, hat and shades, the dance of the cool at the end of the world, animated style. The movement she had seen from the doorway. What's *wrong* with this room? What's *wrong* with it?

There's nothing here, nothing missing. Just this air of something having happened . . .

It took a while, a few seconds . . . then she got it. Frank. Something was wrong with Frank Scenario. Daisy went over to the computer, watched the screen saver go through a full motion. She knew the dance well enough, having seen Jazir copy it. So how come Frank himself was getting it so wrong? One two, one two three, slide. The system was corrupted . . .

Hadn't Dopejack claimed he knew who Mr Million was?

Daisy hit the space bar to activate the computer. The desktop came up OK, no windows open. She pressed on the hard-disk icon. Nothing. The cursor was frozen, dreaded stopped-clock symbol. 'Please assume the crash position.' Someone had been at this, made a mess of it. Couldn't see Dopejack doing that; for all his faults, the DJ was an expert surfer. And how come Frank was still alive on the saver, albeit slightly drunk? Shouldn't he have gone down with the hard ship? And where were all the floppies kept? Just a new box of them, factory-sealed.

Daisy tried a soft reset, got nowhere, so took the manic step of turning the computer off at the mains. The screen popped to black. Daisy knew you were supposed to wait a minute before turning it back on, but time was not her favourite friend. Click! Got a smiling Whoomphy, and a welcome to Burgernet message, and then the desktop again. But the hard drive still refused to open. It really was having problems. Maybe . . .

A little touch of vaz in the night often brings delights. Following invisible instructions, Daisy fed some grease onto a new disk, which was then slotted home. The double-six icon came on screen, so no problems there. Overrider bone. A double-click let the blurbs out, but what would they eat this time? Nothing to eat. Daisy tried the hard disk again; still sealed. Parched, the blurbs were flying in crazy shapes. An offshoot group was even trying to nibble away at the little burger symbol on the top-left corner of the menu bar. Owner's medallion. Daisy pressed on this with the still clocked-out cursor . . .

Working!

The usual menu: About Burgercom, Calculator, Chooser, Control Panels, Fax Centre, Key Caps, Notepad, Puzzle, Scrapbook.

Obviously . . . Notepad or Scrapbook.

Nothing in either. Anyway, it was the Puzzle the blurbs were interested in now. Strange choice of food . . .

Daisy pressed.

It was a four-by-four array of tiles, with one square missing. The fifteen remaining tiles had to be dragged into the shape of a Big Whoomph. Shouldn't be too difficult, but the blurbs beat her to it, their little bodies moving the tiles around at top speed. Puzzle done, ten seconds. Must be a world record. Then they started to eat. The puzzle burger actually vanished under their repeated attack. Dopejack must've concocted this, a fractal burger to hide his secret thoughts. Infinite flavours for the hungry and the wise. What now? Sixteen blank squares remained, and already the blurbs had started to merge and multiply.

Daisy tried to press on each square in turn. Nothing doing. Maybe there's a password involved, something even the blurbs couldn't get past. But what was it? And where to type it in anyway? Especially with a downed cursor. OK, consider that it's a sixteen-letter term, one for each square. Seems reasonable. First choice, so obvious: Frank Scenario. Daisy counted the letters in the name. Thirteen. Fourteen including the space between the names. No good. OK, what was his full name, Jazir had mentioned it, surely? Francis? Francis Scenario. That's sixteen letters, isn't it, including the space? Let's try it . . .

Daisy dragged the cursor's clock to the top-left square. Pressed. Typed F. Moved the cursor. Typed R. Moved. Typed A. Moved. N. Moved. C. Moved . . .

Nothing was happening. No letters appearing. The drive was still down. She just had to hope Dopejack had some ancillary device in store. Some last trick. (Why say last? Don't know anything yet.) Moved. Typed. N. A. R. I. O.

Waited. (As the blurbs darkened more and more of the screen.)

Pressed Enter.

Waited. (As the shadows grew cold . . .)

Waited. (As a car breathed slowly, down the night.)

The puzzle square became a hole, through which these words escaped:

```
not long left hakmust can;t jokerzOOz jker
          noow me can't control eat must
be kill me pleas who nex mus bite wwho next
          mmnot long mmwaaant to no
clos me dowwn wwhhhhhho biiite mmwwhooo
          mmisjag mmgerad ammmis
          ceeeeeeeeeeeeeeeeeeeeeeeeeee
```

The blurbs were floating over the broken text, slowly dying now, all food gone, eating themselves. The last one fell away.

Daisy stared at the message, lost in ciphering, finding fragments, writing in pain. Last moments, a message to Hackle (not long left hakmust can;t). Can't what? Nigel Zuze had won the Joker Bone (jokerzOOz)? The double-zero carefully imbedded. Zero penetration? But then saying the Joker was now himself, Dopejack (jker noow me can't control eat must be kill me pleas). The Joker Bone could be passed on? Now Dopejack wants somebody to kill him? Was it really painful, winning the double? All that Desmond Targett business, toilet-cleaning business, just a ruse? And then lots of stuff about biting and eating and who's next. Like Dopejack had to pass it on somehow, the prize. And then descending into gibberish.

Something there . . .

No.

A bell somewhere ringing, dragging Daisy away from the

screen. The doorbell! The door swinging open, no doubt, with the slightest push, vaz-style. Shit! Should have locked it, Daisy, but how? Voices. Footsteps on the stairs . . . the return of the Joker Bone?

Lights out and Daisy dives under the bed!

The bedroom door opening . . .

'I'm sleeping here?' Celia's voice. 'This dump?'

'Stop complaining, squirt.' Joe's voice. 'I'm your Big Eddie now.'

'Don't be stupid.'

Daisy, from the dust and girlie mags and the soiled handkerchiefs, somehow had to let them know she was here, without scaring Celia too much.

'Celia? Don't be scared—'

'Arhhhhhhh!' Celia screaming.

'Bloody hell!' This from Joe, blazing at the monster that crept cobwebbed from beneath the bed. He hit the light as fast as possible. 'Daisy?'

'Sorry.'

'Daisy!' Celia threw her arms round the woman. 'You scared me.'

'Didn't mean to. What are you doing here?'

'Same to you,' said Joe.

'We've run away, Daisy,' said Celia. 'Run away from the horrible house. Moving in with Mr Dopejack. Aren't we, Joe?'

Joe smiled, slightly.

'That might be a bit difficult,' said Daisy.

The next five minutes were spent in deciphering Dopejack's final message.

'You see all those double "m"s in there, Daisy?' asked Joe.

'His fingers slipping . . .'

'Mr Million, isn't it?' cried Celia.

'Well done, squirt. Let Daisy get a few.'

'Roman numeral for a thousand,' said Daisy. 'MM equals the year 2000.'

'And one thousand times a thousand . . .'

'Is a million. Mr Million!' shouted Celia.

'How did you know, squirt?' asked Joe.

'Anybody knows what a million is, and stop calling me squirt.'

'But nobody knows who Mr Million is. DJ said he did. Is he telling us?'

'I can't see it,' said Daisy. 'He goes mad at the end. Looks like he fell onto the keyboard.'

(mmisjag mmgerad ammmisceeeeeeeeeeeeeeeee)

'MM is Jag,' quoted Joe.

'Who's Jag?' asked Celia.

'Don't know. MM is Jag. MM Gerad. Am. MM is . . .'

It was Daisy that broke it open. 'Jagger, Adam! Isn't it?' Fairly screaming. 'I know that name. Where . . .'

'You got it. Adam Jagger. He was on the list, wasn't he?'

'That's right. Max's list of former pupils.'

'So Dopejack reckons this Adam Jagger is Mr Million? How did he work that out? And where the hell is he?'

'Doesn't matter,' said Daisy. 'Do you have the details on Jagger?'

'Left them at Max's.'

'Can't you remember anything?'

'I'm trying to think, aren't I? Give me room.'

'Go get them.'

'I'm not going back there.'

'Why not?' said Daisy. 'Come on.'

'No. I'll ring Benny. He'll bring them.'

Joe took out his mobile, dialled the number. 'I shouldn't be doing this,' he said to Celia. 'I've only just run away.'

Celia giggled, as Joe got the ringing tone.

'No answer.'

'They're in bed. Give them time.'

The phone just ringing on, into nowhere. Joe clicked it off.

'We've got to go round,' said Daisy.

Joe was resigning himself, when the phone rang anyway. Joe answered it. Listened. His face . . . falling . . . falling . . .

'What is it, Joe?' asked Daisy, Celia at her side, scared of his face.

Joe clicked off the connection, no words, just a look.

'It was your father . . .' he said.

'My . . . what?'

'From the hospital—'

'Dad? Hospital? What—'

'No. It's . . . it's Benny . . .'

Jazir had seen it happen live on the news. He was grounded to his room, just his television and a few tame blurbs for lover's company. Saw the protest and the claims that Desmond Targett was a fake and that Nigel Zuze was the real Joker winner and that he'd now gone missing. The League of Zero were demanding his whereabouts from Mr Million, or at least evidence that he was safe. The dominoes rolled Chief Executive Crawl on screen, as head of PR. He gave a cheap, sincere speech about how temperatures were high because of the unusual circumstances, and that if people could only cool down, all things would be good. He was making counter-claims that Desmond Targett's win had been recorded on all the official equipment. Bollocks, thought Jazir, searching for a pirate station. Got one, fuzzy but truthful. Saw the protesters being attacked by the blurbs, the police standing around like stale cowburgers at a vegecon. Watching the lone figure breaking through, some kind of madman hero figure? No, it was Benny. Fucking Sweet Benny Fenton! What was he doing, facing-off to that blurb like that? Gonna get himself . . .

Jazir got the flash, the splinter flash that led to . . .

. . . Inside the blurbs mad with them circling attack now move in sweep swoop none shall pass benny benny benny no what that knife do now none shall benny benny come back stupid sweet . . .

Jazir landed on his bed, eyes screaming for a fix as the room swivelled to a stop around his sick centre. His pet blurbs were crying out in panic at the connections felt. It was just a bad trip, let it be a bad trip. But the pirates had it all on film, live broadcast from the knife's edge. Jazir holding the telly, hand on each side, as though to crush it between as he watched an ambulance taking Benny away. He had to call Daisy. No phone in his room, confiscated. He had to get to the hospital. Door locked from the outside. A squirt of vaz? His father had ransacked his room, taking his computer, all his disks, gone mad at the rotting blurb carcasses (more trouble), thrown the whole lot out, the garlic plus his tubes of vaz (asking what this mess is now? Hair gel, Jaz's reply). He knew Daisy had a tube, but that was for her own use.

He went to the window, opened it. Immediately, his pets flew outside, keen for air. Jazir the same. He stepped out onto the ledge and looked down. He'd done this before, hadn't he? Wasn't very far down, slightly painful, just avoid the wheelie bin this time. Simple.

He stepped off . . .

' . . . and landed 10 yards away, gently lowered by the wings of a hundred blurbs. A taxi took him further, stunned and dizzy.

But Max and Jimmy reached the hospital first. Apparently Crawl had found identification in Benny's jacket, plus his address.

Not that Crawl needed any of this, but it was best to keep to the rules, especially with the cameras on him. He'd rung Hackle from the hospital, after he'd sorted everything out according to Mr Million's instructions. One day he'd like to get to meet this Million guy, and shove his new job up his . . .

But the extra lovelies were more than extra lovely.

Hackle and Jimmy were kept waiting in a separate room, whilst Crawl gave them the speech: 'The young man attempted to take his own life. It is most unfortunate he chose to do this in front of our establishment, but rest assured the AnnoDomino Company will do everything in its power, including any outstanding medical bills, but really . . . there's very little chance . . . according to the doctors . . .'

Hackle grabbed the PR by the throat. 'Let me fucking see him!'

'Of course, Professor. He's asked to see you, actually. Alone.'

Hackle went in. A nurse was fiddling with some equipment beside the bed, keeping guard on a bleep and sine wave. Benny was stretched out, covered in a sheet, his chest wrapped with bandages, a tube connecting him to the equipment. His eyes were closed.

Hackle looked at the nurse. She nodded to him, yes.

'Benny . . .'

'Joe?'

'No. Max.'

'Where's Joe?'

'They said you wanted to see me.'

'Want Joe.'

'He's on his way. Jimmy rang him.' The door opened behind him. Expecting Joe, Hackle turned to see. Only Executive Crawl, Mr Bonefucker, worried about his company's precious image. Benny was reaching out for Hackle, making him turn back round . . .

'Where's Joe?' Benny had his eyes open now.

'Oh, Benny . . .'

'Where is he?'

'What happened, Benny?'

'Had to.'

Hackle came close, sitting down. 'Why?'

'Had to. Made me.'

'Who made you? Who? Your last words, saw them on television. I'm not doing it, you said. Not doing what? Benny! Benny!'

'Uhhh . . .'

Hackle realized he was shaking Benny by the shoulders. The nurse stepped closer to caution him. Hackle waved her away, but she wouldn't go.

'That's OK, nurse,' said Crawl, 'I'll deal with this.'

The nurse left. Hackle turned to Crawl.

'What's going on here?'

'Your friend needs you. Please be kind, Mr Hackle.'

'Get out of here.'

'I'd rather not.'

'Take your image and stuff it.'

Crawl smiled.

'Joe . . .'

'No. It's Max. Max, remember?'

'Joe . . .'

'What is it?'

'Come here.'

'I'm here.'

'Kiss me.'

Hackle turned to Crawl again, the man still smiling. What did he want, a photo of the kiss?

Hackle bent down and kissed Benny lightly on the forehead.

Benny grabbed him by the shoulders and pulled him down, making a groan. Benny's lips were on Hackle's neck . . .

'Woh, careful . . . you're . . .'

'I love you, Joe. Sorry for this . . .'

'There's no need—'

Benny kissed Hackle's neck, and then bit down firmly, just enough to break the surface. Hackle raised his hand to his neck, a sticky smear of blood. Embarrassed, he looked at Crawl, who was smiling, smiling and nodding.

'Go ahead.'

'What is it?'

A blurb was banging against the window. Hackle started to feel the change. Against his wishes, why were his hands moving, stroking Benny now, real love, unembarrassed. His hands, gently, around Benny's fragile neck, gently squeezing . . .

'That won't be necessary, Mr Hackle,' whispered Crawl, close now, watching the operation. 'He's already gone.'

The wave a flat line, the bleep a drone.

Hackle lay on top of Benny's body for a few seconds, slowly came up. There was a commotion going on outside the ward, cries. Seconds later the door burst open, broken by Joe and followed by Jazir. Joe pushed Hackle off the body roughly, not caring about hurt, not caring . . . just . . .

PLAY TO WIN         PLAY TO LOSE
PLAY TO WIN         PLAY TO WIN
PLAY TO LOSE       PLAY TO WIN
PLAY TO LOSE
PLAY TO WIN       PLAY TOLOSE
PLAY TO LOSE      PLAY TO WIN
PLAY TO WIN       PLAY TO LOSE
PLAY TO WIN
PLAY TO WIN PLAY TO LOSE
TO LOSE PLAY TO LOSE PL
WIN PLAY TO WIN  PLAY

WIN PLAY TO LOSE P
PLAY TO LOSE PLAY

PLAY TO WIN F
PLAY TO WIN
PLAY TO W
PLAY TO WIN
PLAY TO LOSE
PLAY TO WIN PL
LOSE PLAY TO WIN

PLAY TO WIN PLAY TO

TO LOSE PLAY TO LOSE PL
PLAY TO WIN  PLAY TO WIN
PLAY TO WIN

PLAY TO WIN
PLAY TO LOSE

PLAY TO LOSE

PLAY TO WIN        PLAY TO WIN
PLAY TO LOSE      PLAY TO LOSE
PLAY TO WIN        PLAY TO WIN
PLAY TO LOSE      PLAY TO WIN

**D**ark time in Hackle House. Jazir was in charge, now that Joe had become empty. Sad to see, the once cool-without-caring Joe Crocus sitting on his and Benny's bed, heavy head in wet hands, make-up smudged. Jazir, so hopeless at this kind of stuff, keeping quiet, planning . . .

The plan was to get what Joe needed, collect Daisy's father, then get out of there, go join Daisy and Celia back in Dopejack's house. Jazir wanting to get there so badly, knowing he couldn't go back home now, runaway for real.

'You got what you wanted, Joe?'

'What . . .'

'Joe . . . I know this is bad . . .'

'Right . . . yes . . .'

Joe pulled himself up, searched in a drawer for some papers and disks. These were put in a carrier bag. The last thing . . . Joe looking at the volume of *Mathematica Magica*. Bedside reading, lover's treatise and manual of spells. A gift for Benny, never touched. Not now. Joe slipped the book into the bag.

'That's it.'

Downstairs they went, into the study, where Hackle and Jimmy were arguing. Hackle didn't want Jimmy to go, that was evident; as Jazir came in he was saying stuff about the maze being open now, more open than ever before. Jimmy wasn't having any of it.

'I belong to my daughter, that's all.'

'You ready, Jimmy?' Joe asked.

Just a nod in reply.

'Joe . . .' began Hackle. 'Please . . .'

'Shut up.' Said so calmly, you wouldn't have thought . . . 'I blame you entirely for Benny's death.'

That's it. They left Hackle, Maximus Hackle, alone in his big old house of echoes and the ghost of echoes.

At Dopejack's there was still no sign of the DJ, so they more or less took the place over, assigning bedrooms. Daisy and Jazir getting their own room! Their own bed! (Dope's old room.) Worth all the mad fathers in the world, that was.

How long they would be allowed to stay there, the five remnants of the Dark Fractals, they could not know. Long enough for one more game?

They decided between them; Monday morning, Jimmy Love would be sent out to purchase the bones, five of them, one for each. If that didn't work, they would quit playing for ever.

Jazir had the papers off Joe. Details in there of Adam Jagger (Six-Five). Last known address: a small street in smalltown, Stalybridge, Manchester. (A phone call answered by an angry woman with screaming kids in the background; 'No-one here of that name, honey – get down, Gary, before I . . .') Last known occupation: insurance clerk. (No longer employed here, sorry. Left in 1989. No idea where, sorry.) Current whereabouts: unknown.

'Mystery man,' said Jazir.

'We need to get DJ's computer running,' said Daisy. 'Can't you unerase or something.'

'Tried it. Whoever wiped it was good. Dopejack was better, getting that message in the puzzle, but I'm worse than both of them. Tried everything.'

'There must be some connection. Something that got DJ going.'

Jazir shrugged.

For the days of that week, the Monday, Tuesday, Wednesday, they were almost like a family, a dysfunctional one granted, but that's OK, that's normal. Jazir and Daisy spending time in the room, trying to get the computer working, studying Hackle's papers for clues, planning what would happen after the game, making love. Sometimes Daisy would come out, carrying her box of dominoes. She would play gentle games with her father, in which he beat her quite easily, as always, but always with a lesson in the loss. They talked of nothing but strategy. Celia was happier now, even when remembering Eddie, even though they still refused to let her out, telling stories about officials and squatting rights and bad guys on the streets of Whalley Range. She had all five bones tight in two small hands the whole time, squeezing and praying to win. It was for Eddie, she told herself, and the big escape. Joe kept to his room mostly, usually locked in. Occasional cries, sometimes laughter even. Nobody disturbed him, nobody dared.

Family life, waiting for the bailiff's knock (or Jazir's father finding them, whichever was worse).

Thursday was funeral day. Three people were buried. Two of them shared the same grave, unmarked, and far from any cemetery. One was a shaven-headed lout with a Nazi tattoo on his cock, the other a punk virgin with green spikes of hair. There were no mourners, only a pair of domino diggers and Executive Crawl presiding. He spat on the grave and felt his wallet.

Benny's farewell was taking place in his beloved Southern Cemetery. The AnnoDomino Co. had offered to pay all the costs. Joe had told them to get stuffed, this was his pleasure. It was nice; quiet, nothing fancy. Joe was there alone, having told Jazir and Daisy to stay with Celia. Benny's mother and father turned up. Joe had never met them before. He introduced himself, called himself a friend, a deep friend. As the dirt started, he ripped some pages out of the *Mathematica Magica*, which he let flutter down. He was whispering some ancient text, the numbers and equations of eternal return, when some scrawled lettering touched his eyes. The torn-out flyleaf . . . these words . . .

> Joe, no more biting . . .
> Close all channels: connect to zero.
> Loadsa loving,
> Benny X

Joe shook his head and cleared his eyes. Benny must have written this before he left, before he . . .

He folded the page, put it in his pocket. How low was Benny, to reverse Joe's own motto against him like that? Joe threw the rest of the book down on the coffin as the soil came.

There was another graveside ritual that day, but none would have seen it. Perhaps Jimmy alone could have envisioned it, but his mind was elsewhere, on the bottle and his daughter and his new chance at life.

To see this grave, we travel to Hackle's house, and underground. We see Hackle walking around the maze, wired up to a bank of computers that flash and tumble alive with the nymphomation as he makes the circles happen. We see him laugh with passion as he comes alive to the nymphomation, as he follows the expert mappings of his cursor blurb, Horny George. All his life, Hackle realizes, has been leading to this. To become what you dream. Inside his body, the skeleton of the Joker Bone. Around which gibbers the dumbfuck knowledge of Nigel Zuze, full of hatred and bile. Mixed with this, the vinyl and computers of DJ Dopejack, full of hacking techniques. Also, the sweet genetics of Sweet Benny Fenton, full of sex and love. Mix this with Hackle's own knowledge of the numbers and how they multiply, and let the whole thing simmer in its own blurb-juice for days. Hackle could feel the power growing, the breeding patterns, possible offspring, new disciplines.

Nymphomation running wild.

Possibilities: The Equations of Fascist DNA; The Physics of Love; The Numbers of Genes in the Fascist Love Machine; Maze Techniques Leading to Logarithm Foreplay; How to Kill Orgasms; How to Measure the Weight of Hatred; How to Map the Map of the Map of the Map; Multiplex Calculation and Zero Penetration of the Genes of the Fourth Dimension; The Probability of Mr Million; Fractal Dreaming; Bile Mechanics and its Application to Negro Murder; Black Hacking and How to Square Root the Hardware Fascist Blurb Map; CPU DNA LoZ DF 0-0 RAM DJing; The Vinyl Gene Number Love Map (to the Nth Degree); Blurb Masturbation; Domino Dancing; Bone Truth; The Beats-Per-Minute of Map Death.

As the computer stored the new knowledge on a billion switches; sex in binary code. Sex in Hackle's head.

Hackle was calm as all this raged inside him; he was even in control of the Benny and Zuze inside, and their constant bickering in black and white. Nothing must come between him and the centre of the maze, where Mr Million waited. Not like Nigel with his brute attack; not like Dopejack with his fearful frenzy; not like Benny with his doubt and self-sacrifice; only like Hackle, Maximus Hackle, with his calmly collected knowledge of the game about to be played. He was supposed to kill the others first, but that was easily fought against. Million had met his match.

Certain esoteric texts had been looked at. One, entitled *Sealing the Maze, the Theseus Equation,* was especially consulted. He was fixated now upon Mr Million's face in the pathways, in the play of shadow and light, the fractal shapes of the blurb-icons, constantly out of reach. The face must be a disguise, because it wasn't the one he expected. Behind that mask, surely . . .

Along twisting pathways the blurb led him, down darkened passageways, invisible corners. Along parts of the maze Hackle never knew existed. Finally, to a place he had forbidden himself for many, many years.

A small room it was, cut off from the rest, only accessed by the most secret knowledge. Hackle, with torch in hand, playing it over a portion of the floor, slightly discoloured. The professor made a few magical equations over the grave. Here lies the body of Georgie Horn.

His knowledge lives on.

To the house of Dopejack. Let's follow Joe back from the funeral and the comforting of a lover's parents. Let's see that bedroom once again, where Dopejack was killed by Benny, where Daisy and Jazir are now making love on Dopejack's bed. Frank Scenario is watching from the screen saver, that silly dance of his, mutating. Blurbfly Masala was hovering over their twisted equation. Daisy and Jazir are lost in the spirals, when Daisy starts screaming and Jazir wonders if he's doing it right at last. 'Jazir!'

'That's right, it's me, it's happening . . .'

'The computer . . .'

'What?'

'It's changing.'

Jazir pulls out (yeah, that mad for it) and runs to the screen, where Frank Scenario carries a new face.

'Who is it?' Daisy asks.

'Miss Sayer.'

'Oh . . .'

It wasn't the face that Daisy expected: too young, a construct of eternal youth perhaps, a vanity program.

'What does she want?'

'Let her speak.'

Miss Sayer's words appeared as typescript on the screen, issuing from her animated mouth. 'Time now. Grab wings. Come get. Rescue.'

'Miss Sayer, wait . . .'

But the woman had already vanished, and Frank disappeared with her as Jazir hit the space bar. The cursor was clockless, at last, blinking like a drunk rudely dragged from sleep.

'We're in!' cried Daisy.

'You betcha.'

Jazir worked the mouse to pull open the hard disk, but the thing was a blank page, no windows, no knowledge. Before their eyes came an icon, dissolving out of the memory banks.

'What is it?' asked Daisy.

'Miss Sayer. Didn't I tell you, Daze. She's unerasing . . .'

'Press on it then.'

Did so. A file came up, dated the Friday just gone. Once opened, this revealed the workings of Dopejack on the evening of his death. Daisy and Jazir watched amazed as the computer worked itself backwards, deeper into the hidden depths of the AnnoDomino channel.

'DJ was puzzled by the dancing patterns of the Joker,' said Daisy.

'Yeah, something got to him.'

They reached the point where Dopejack had called up his own screen saver, and then fed it back on the Joker's dance.

'Why's he doing that?' asked Daisy.

'I don't know. It's weird. Why Frank?'

A door opened, marked NO ACCESS, and through it a blurb travelled. The history of the Joker Bone scrolled on to the screen. Real name: George Horn.

'I don't get it,' said Jazir. 'I thought he was dead.'

'He is. Malthorpe stole the info from the maze, remember? After he was killed, Malthorpe took copies of everything: the maze, the nymphomation, the version of Georgie that lived in the hard disk. The wanderer.'

'So Malthorpe has used this program to construct the Joker Bone image?'

'I think so.'

'Best get the others.'

'Shall we put some clothes on first?'

Daisy rounded up Joe and Celia and her father. The latter, of course, went crazy when he saw the George Horn knowledge. 'Fucking hell! He did it. Malthorpe actually managed it. He brought Georgie back alive.'

'Not alive, not really,' said Daisy, 'only an animation.'

'So who's going round town pretending to be the Joker then,' said Joe. 'Since when could an animation kill people?'

'I think I know,' said Jimmy. 'It's to do with the nymphomation. Somehow, Malthorpe has found a way to release it from the computer, into reality. The knowledge is passed on.'

'Dopejack's message!' cried Daisy. 'About how he had to bite somebody.'

'That's it. It's through a bite.'

'I know that's right,' said Jazir, rubbing at his wrist, already feeling the blurb-wings beat on his shoulder blades.

'So who did Dopejack bite?' asked Joe. 'And who's the Joker Bone now?'

Nobody could answer. But Joe was thinking to himself, *No more biting . . .*

Dopejack left a desperate hidden message. Did Benny also? Joe pulled the folded paper out of his pocket. 'Close all channels: connect to zero.'

'I think it was Benny,' he said.

'Benny what?' asked Jazir.

'Benny who got bitten by Dope. I think Benny was the Joker Bone. That's why he killed himself.'

He explained why, and then realized that Hackle was in that hospital ward at the end, along with Crawl, a domino official.

'Shit!'

'What?'

'Hackle. Max Hackle. I'm sure . . .'

'What's happening?' asked Celia, because the search on the screen was not yet over. All five Dark Fractals were gathered in a half circle, as last Friday's Dopejack (deceased) forced open another door.

'He's calling up something called DANCING MASTER,' noted Daisy.

Jazir was already aware of what was happening. He stepped back slightly from the circle, not wanting to know.

'Jaz,' said Daisy, 'according to this, the Joker was taught how to dance by Frank Scenario. Isn't that weird? That's why he was consulting the screen saver. Jaz?'

Jaz wasn't answering.

'Jaz? What's wrong?'

'It's his hero, isn't it?' said Celia.

'Some hero,' said Joe, laughing.

'It's OK,' said Daisy. 'Just because . . . doesn't mean . . . Mr Million could have just copied Frank's dance for the Joker. He doesn't have to be involved. Frank's still cool. He's the coolest man in the universe. Jaz . . .'

Jazir was shaking his head from side to side. 'Please,' he was whispering. 'Please don't let it . . .'

'I know what's bothering him,' said Daisy's father. 'When

Dopejack was bitten by the Joker, I think he would have got all the knowledge the Joker owned. This would include the secrets of the dominoes. Who Mr Million was. His real name . . .'

'But that's OK,' said Daisy. 'He said it was Adam Jagger. Another kid from Hackle's class. Isn't it?'

'I'm trying to remember this kid,' said her father. 'Adam Jagger? There's nothing there, no weight. He certainly wasn't a major player.'

'Well he is now,' said Joe, getting the connection. 'No wonder Frank always wore that stupid hat and the dark glasses.'

'What do you mean?' asked Daisy.

'Frank wasn't being cool. He was hiding himself. Right, Jaz?'

Daisy got it then, and all she could do was look at Jazir and want to hold him, knowing that holding him wouldn't do any good.

Jazir finally had to laugh. 'Mr Million is Adam Jagger, is Frank Scenario. I always wondered what his real name was.'

At that moment the young Miss Sayer came back on screen. She was staring at Jazir, and the poor boy was drawn to her eyes, to her eyes full of pain. 'GET ME OUT!' Can a line of type scream? Jazir felt it. But what to do about it? The wings unfurling, invisible.

Daisy's father knew what to do; down on his knees, he went, praying to the image, pulling out his old domino.

'Miss Sayer . . . Miss Sayer . . .'

'Oh, it's you, Five-Four. Shall we begin?'

Play to win

The Joker bit Nigel and Nigel bit Dopejack and Dopejack bit Benny and Benny bit Hackle, and all five of them got a call that night. It was Joe Crocus, asking to speak to Max . . .

'This is Max.'

'Oh, sorry. Joe here. Didn't recognize your voice.'

'What do you want?'

'I know what's happening, Max.'

'Nothing's happening.'

'Don't do it, Max. Don't pass it on.'

'Stay out of this, Joe. I . . .'

'Max! We can get you help—'

'I don't need help. I'm dealing with it. Don't mess with me, Joe. Don't come anywhere near me. This is mine.'

'Max!'

Joker Bone slammed down the phone, and how could Max resist.

Down in the cellar, he worked for an hour on the computer, trying to add the Theseus equations to the maze. Every attempt met with a crash, as the Joker worked against him. Reaching into the program, corrupting it, protecting his home.

Max gave up. His head was buzzing with rival info.

There was only one way to end it. One real way. The bifurcation less travelled. Go manual. Kill.

Midnight on the Thursday, as the next day began, Maximus Hackle walked over the boundary of the House of Chances. The blurbs parted to let him through, forming a beating phalanx of breath and message.

Play to win! Play to win! Play to win!

Hackle walked through this dark fluttering tunnel, totally at ease.

At the giant dominoed doors of the building, Chief Executive Crawl was waiting to greet him. 'Welcome, Professor. Right this way. Mr Million is expecting you.'

Hackle walked through the doors, smiling.

Final chances.

PLAY TO LOSE        PLAY TO LOSE
PLAY TO LOSE        PLAY TO LOSE
PLAY TO LOSE        PLAY TO LOSE
PLAY TO WIN         PLAY TO LOSE
PLAY TO LOSE        PLAY TO WIN
PLAY TO WIN         PLAY TO LOSE
PLAY TO WIN         PLAY TO LOSE
PLAY TO LOSE        PLAY TO LOSE
PLAY TO LOSE  PLAY TO LOSE
WIN PLAY TO WIN  PLAY T(
LOSE  PLAY TO LOSE PLAY'

LOSE  PLAY TO LOSE P'
PLAY TO WIN PLAY

PLAY TO WIN P
PLAY TO LOSE
WIN PLAY T

PLAY TO LOSE  F
PLAY TO WIN PL,
OSE  PLAY TO LOSE  I
LOSE  PLAY TO LOSE  F
WIN PLAY TO WIN PLA
TO LOSE  PLAY TO LOSE  P\
TO LOSE  PLAY TO LOSE  PLA
PLAY TO LOSE    PLAY TO WIN
PLAY TO WIN
PLAY TO WIN     PLAY TO LOSE
PLAY TO LOSE    PLAY TO WIN
              PLAY TO LOSE
PLAY TO WIN     PLAY TO WIN
PLAY TO LOSE    PLAY TO LOSE
PLAY TO WIN     PLAY TO LOSE
PLAY TO LOSE    PLAY TO LOSE

# Game 46

'Twas nine-ish, and the slimy hordes did clack and gamble in the wave. All dotty were the game-parades, and the telebox did crave. 'Beware the Dominock, my daught, the pips that on young chances feed! Beware the House of Bone and shun the Mr Millipede!' She took her blurbfly vert in hand – long time the Cookie Luck she sought – so played the game in ones and twos, and threes and fours, five, six and nought. And, as in blankish gaze she swayed, the Dominock, with spots for eyes, came dancing from the House of Bone, his prey to hypnotize. One, two! Three, four! And in and out, the blurb did advertise. Five, six and nought! She cut it dead, and went off running with the prize. 'And hast thou won the double-six? My favourite lucky bleeder! O dotty day! The bones to play! You've become the Millipeder!'

'Twas nine-ish, and the spotty numbs did gamb and dumble in the games. All pippy were the domisums, and the telebox in flames.

Game 46. Fathers sang this song to daughters, mothers to sons, using jangling domino toys to lull their babes to sleep.

The people of good Mazechester, wild-eyed and lost.

Allow them play.

Blurbvert surrender; let the messages come. Singing time.

The burgercops, searching for clues and easiness? Allow them play. The House of Chances, the Mr Million, the minions and the millions? Allow them play. The homeless and the aimless? Allow them play. Tommy Tumbler and the gorgeous Cookie Luck? Allow them play.

The Dark Fractals? Jazir Malik and Daisy and her father and Celia and Joe?

Allow them play.

Nigel Zuze and DJ Dopejack and Sweet Benny and Georgie

Horn and Big Eddie Irwell, and all the rest of the dead? And the Joker Bone and Professor Hackle? It's the things we miss that make us wish . . .

Allow them play. Allow them ghosts.

All the underachievers, the desperate and the wild; the users, the losers, the self-abusers; the closet queens, the wardrobe kings; the mix-masters, the fixers, the mix 'n' matchers; dead-enders, big spenders, low-enders, pretenders to the bone; the pros and the knows and the job-blows; the drunks and the skunks and the hunks; the survivors, the suiciders; the morticians, the mathematicians; bimbos and criminals; rich men, poor men, beggar men, thieves; the nameless and the gameless . . .

All the citizens, good and bad.

Allow them play. Allow them numbers.

The game began at midnight previous for the Dark Fractals. The night, the early morning, long hours spent in planning and research. Everything they had learned in their individual ways was shared. Miss Sayer was consulted time and again, but her appearance only came at random, and then she seemed to be constricted, as though something was blocking her progress. Only a few words – wings, help, me, grab, come, find, maze – were allowed play upon her broken tongue. Jazir had explained to Jimmy how the teacher had chosen him, nurtured him over years. 'That's my girl,' agreed Jimmy. They were both keen to enter the House of Chances, however difficult it proved; one to rescue the teacher, the other to confront Mr Million. Only Jazir had a chance to gain entrance. It was agreed, therefore, that Jimmy would lead the maze-play.

They slept, each of the Fractals fitfully, except for Little Celia, who dreamed herself happy along dangerous streets, with a smile on her lips and a laugh, a winning bone and Big Eddie Irwell at her side. At seven in the morning, Joe called Hackle's house again. No answer. He had called repeatedly through the night, always no answer, no answer. He drove the team over there, because Miss Sayer and Jimmy demanded it, but he was scared inside. He still had the key. The house was empty, they made sure of that, even the cellar. But the presence of the Joker Bone was palpable; the entire place was in ruins, with clothes and books and papers strewn everywhere.

Poor Max . . .

'If only I'd seen it earlier,' Joe said, 'in Benny, and then in Max, I could have done something.'

'Where is he?' asked Daisy.

'Out hunting.'

They spent the day in preparation, with Joe helping Jimmy in the cellar. The equipment had been well used over the last few days, that was evident. Jimmy surmised that Hackle had got the maze going, and had conducted his own experiments. Trouble was, he'd only patched it together roughly. There were lots of blind spots in the Hackle Maze that no amount of fiddling would fix. Miss Sayer came on-line to help. She pulled up a new maze behind her.

'OK, we're on target,' said Jimmy.

'Is that it?' Joe asked.

'The inside of the House of Chances. Now, let's see . . .' Jimmy worked a few keys, and the two mazes merged into one. 'OK, we're connected.'

Jimmy pulled down a menu, and pressed on THESEUS. A new window opened, and floating within it, a tiny icon, a ball of twine, a sword.

'That's what I load?' asked Joe. 'How does it work?'

Jimmy nodded. 'Theseus was the Greek hero who killed the Minotaur in the labyrinth of—'

'Come on. I've been to school.'

'Max and I worked on this. It was a way to seal a Hackle Maze, should it go wrong. Sometimes the wanderers would become too mutated, too powerful, they would bleed into the hard disk, crashing the whole thing. The Theseus equation was designed to prevent this; it feeds a bad gene into the nymphomation, creating sterility. The only problem is . . .'

'Don't tell me, you never got it to work.'

'We tried. I activated it that night, with Georgie . . . tried to save him . . . hopeless. We've tried to improve it since, but . . .'

'Hopeless.'

'Jazir has fed the Theseus to one of his blurbs, and that's another unknown. I've looked at the system, it could go down at any second. Miss Sayer has done all she can, but she's weak, she may not be able to keep it open for long. And remember who owns the net. They're gonna realize, eventually, that someone's breaking in. They'll shut us down, God knows what else. You'll be in charge of the computer. Don't activate the Theseus till I say. The last moment. Got that? Nine o'clock. When they're busiest.'

'I'm not a Georgie, you know?'

'No. And you never will be. And pray to God that Jazir manages to get through.'

But Joe's mind was only filled with Benny and Dopejack and Max, and what the bones had done to them all. That was his mission now.

Some time after lunch, Daisy took Celia into the damaged library. The kid had never seen so many books, seen so many pages tattered and torn and strewn all over the floor. Most of them were mathematical texts, rich and heavy with a foreign language of squiggles and shapes. Celia pulled a rare book, not destroyed, down from a shelf and flicked through it.

'Is this your world?' she asked.

Daisy was caught off guard. 'Yes . . . I suppose it is.'

'What country is it?'

'Erm . . . Numberland.'

'Wow!' Celia slammed the book shut, raising a cloud of dust. 'Maybe I'll go there one day.'

'You should.'

'Will you teach me? How do you start?'

Daisy thought for a moment. 'Have you ever played dominoes?'

'I play every Friday, silly.'

'No, I mean the real dominoes.'

'There's more than one kind?'

'Wait right there.'

Daisy left the room. Celia wandered around a bit more, pausing here and there to study some incomprehensible title. So many books! Perhaps all the books in the world were here. But why, oh why did they all seem to be in another language? Perhaps it was a secret code, and all you had to do was find the key. Perhaps the key opened a door. Perhaps the door led to another world, a better world? She found another book then, undamaged, and one that she understood perfectly.

Daisy came back carrying her father's set of dominoes. 'Are you ready to play, Celia?'

'Yes, please.'

Daisy started to set up the game. 'What's that you're looking at?'

'We used to have this book at home.'

'Really, was it your father's?'

'No. My sister's. It was her favourite.'

'I didn't know you had a sister.'

'You don't know everything, do you?'

'What's the book?'

Celia showed her. 'It's great, isn't it?'

'Oh, it's a kid's book. I've never read it.'

'You've never read it! What kind of childhood did you have?'

'Oh . . . you know . . . I was more interested in numbers than words.'

'There are numbers in here.'

'There are?'

'Of course. It was my sister's favourite because she thought it was about her. Silly sausage. She'd have these fantasies where we'd both be posh girls and end up in the book, and have strange adventures together.'

'Your sister was called Alice?'

Celia nodded. 'Maybe I should write my own version. Celia in Numberland. What do you think?'

Daisy laughed. 'Sounds great. Let's play.'

'OK.' Celia put the book back on the shelf and came over to the table. 'What do I do?'

'Choose your bones.'

So they played. Daisy won the first two games easily, even though she was giving Celia chances. 'Stop giving me chances,' said the girl. So they played, and Daisy gently, gently, started to bring the numbers alive for the child.

During the fourth game, Daisy asked, 'Where did you live, before you left home I mean?'

'Dukinfield. Do you know it?'

'A little. I was born in Droylsden.'

'And here's me thinking Duckie was bad.'

'Why did you run away?'

Celia replied, 'Why did you?'

'You can tell?'

'I can see it in your eyes.'

'My father was cruel to me.'

'Jimmy? He's OK.'

'Now, maybe. But he was very strict when I was young. He forced me to be brilliant.'

'Is that wrong?'

Daisy nodded, playing a piece. 'He wanted me to be better than he was, at the dominoes, for instance.'

'Were you?'

'Never. He always won. It made me mad. I knew if I stayed with him, I'd never be myself. But I was older than you when I ran away; fifteen, I was.'

'What about your mum?'

'Your turn.'

'Is she . . . is she dead?'

Daisy looked at the girl. 'Yes. Car crash. I was five.'

'I'm sorry.'

'Keep playing.'

Celia played, and they played and played as the shadows lengthened and the dying sun burnished the spines of a thousand books.

'It was my sister that made me run away,' said Celia, after losing her umpteenth game. 'We were twins, but she was older, just a minute or so, but it counted. There wasn't enough money for one kid, never mind two. And Alice always got the bigger share of everything.'

'I was an only child,' said Daisy, setting up the pieces again.

'That's lucky.'

'I don't know . . .'

'No, really it is. And then there was the time with the parrot.'

'The what?'

'Don't laugh. I had this parrot called Whippoorwill. He was the best parrot in the world, and the only thing I had that was better than anything Alice had. Alice kept saying Whippoorwill belonged to us both, but he didn't, he belonged to me, because my uncle had said so. It was a birthday present. Alice got a doll.' Celia giggled. 'A stupid baby doll! She hated it. She hated it so much she even called it Celia and would do horrible things to it, like stick pins in it.'

'She was jealous,' said Daisy.

'You betcha. Anyway, one day I came home from school, Alice had been playing sick all week, and the cage was open and Whippoorwill wasn't there!'

'No! She'd let him out?'

'She claimed it was an accident when she was cleaning his cage, but she never cleaned the cage, that was my job and she knew it. She said the window must have been open, which it never should have been, not when cleaning the cage, it was a rule . . .'

Celia's eyes were filmy and shining, and she was unknotting the green-and-yellow feather from her hair.

'That's a sad story,' said Daisy. 'Is that Whippoorwill's?'

Celia nodded. 'Found it in his cage. It was all I had left. I think he left it for me, as a message. Do you think that's possible?'

'Of course. Is this why you ran away?'

'One of the reasons. The final reason. It sounds daft, doesn't it?'

'No, I understand. You were angry.'

'No, not angry. I wasn't running away from Alice. I was looking for Whippoorwill. That's what I'm still doing. He's out there, somewhere.' Her eyes were looking over towards the window, where night was slowly falling. 'Now you're really laughing at me,' she whispered.

'I'm not, really. It's lovely. Oh . . . domino, by the way.'

'Why do you keep saying that?'

'It's what you say, when you've won.'

'You've won again?'

'Yes, in two moves' time. Sorry.'

'This is stupid. I can't beat chance, can I?'

'It's not about chance. It's a skill. I could teach you.'

'Nah, it's just chance. Let's not play any more.'

'OK.' Daisy packed away the dominoes. 'Maybe you should go back home, Celia. It can't be easy . . .'

Celia got up and walked over to the window. 'It was. It was easy. When I found Eddie.' She flopped down into an armchair. 'Is that what you'll be doing tonight with your dad? Playing dominoes?'

'Yes, I'd better get ready. Have you got the bones?'

Celia took one out of her pocket. 'Been holding it most of the week.'

'Where are the others?'

'Others?'

'You should have five. One for each . . .'

'Threw 'em away.'

'What?'

'Only need one, don't I? I'm either gonna win, or I'm gonna lose. That's chance isn't it? One is enough. Always has been.'

'Right.'

'Here . . . take this.' Celia was holding out her feather. 'Give it to Jaz.'

'Why?'

'Just take it. For good luck.'

'Thank you. I'll give it to him. Do you know what a fractal is?'

Celia shook her head. 'Is it a creature? Does it live in Numberland?'

'Next lesson. OK?'

'OK.'

Daisy left the room, leaving Celia to her window-gazing. It had started to rain, a gentle mist over the gravestones in the cemetery. What a horrible place to live, Celia thought, and then, what's this? because something was poking into her back. She reached around and dug out a rolled-up copy of a magazine. Idly, she looked it over. *Number Gumbo,* it was called. What a funny name, wonder what it means? One of the pages had the corner turned down, and seemed to fall open there, as though it wanted to. Celia read a small part of the article, but it was full of the language of Numberland, and she very quickly threw the magazine to one side.

The article was entitled 'Sealing the Maze'.

Meanwhile, Daisy had gone upstairs. She knocked quietly on one of the bedroom doors. There was no reply. Jazir had insisted he be left alone all day, but Daisy knocked a little louder. 'Jazir . . .'

'What?' Very distant. A strange fluttering noise.

'It's Daisy. Can I come in?'

'No.'

'Jaz!'

'Go away.'

Daisy went away. It was seven o'clock. She went down to the cellar, where her father and Joe were busy at the computer, working on the new maze. She tried to get interested, but Jazir kept coming back to her. He was the one putting himself in the most danger. Was it all worth it? This business with Frank

Scenario had really got to him. If he should . . .

Daisy went back upstairs. Hours to kill. She looked in the library to check on Celia. The girl was still there, just staring out of the window, lost in her own world.

That was it, wasn't it? They were, all five of them, lost in their own little worlds, their own little mazes. Only the games had brought them together. Daisy thought about this for a while in the kitchen, making herself a sandwich. Her and her father, for instance, would they be this close if the dominoes hadn't started? No. Daisy and Jazir, this much love between them? No. No way. It was like the dominoes had broken down Daisy's barriers. And if they succeeded with tonight's plan; if the dominoes were killed, would her new love die with them? She had to be grateful, she had to be . . .

Later, she went back up to Jazir's room. This time he called her in at the first knock. 'But be careful', he added, 'with the door.'

Daisy opened it just enough to squeeze through. It was very dark inside, and heavy with breathing life. She felt the walls were moving, fluttering with smoky patterns, whispers. Jazir was standing by the window, gazing out. Over his shoulder Daisy could see the lights of the House of Chances, calling out to all the players.

'Jaz . . .' She didn't dare move.

'Quietly . . . gently . . .' he whispered.

'It's nearly eight. We should . . .'

'Come here. Walk slowly.'

She did so, one slow step after another, across the room. Walking through a living thing, it felt like, where one false move could . . . Shit!

Daisy banged into a chair. It fell over with a loud clatter and sent forth an echo around the walls which bulged . . .

'Bloody hell!' cried Jazir.

The walls breathed into trembling flight as hundreds of blurbflies rose from their perches. Around the darkness they flew; harder, darker pieces of the sky, set free from the night. Many of them converged on Daisy's stumbling shape, ready to attack and bite and give new messages, and she was screaming now, until Jazir made a weird sound with his tongue, a sort of rasping call that settled the blurbs into a new pattern. Some of them were still crawling over Daisy's clothes, one even in her hair. The dry crackle of wings. She didn't dare move.

'It's OK,' said Jazir. 'I've told them who you are. Come closer.'

Daisy stepped forward, letting the blurbs gently rise from her body. Jazir turned to her. She couldn't make him out properly, just a blurred, pulsating shape like one of the fractals they had watched on the computer . . .

'Jaz!' She could hardly breathe.

Jazir's entire form was covered in gentle blurbs. A suit of dark flies, whispering the many pleasures of flight.

Daisy gave him the feather. 'Celia wanted you to have this.'

Jazir laughed, and the feather, its green and its gold, were the only colours in the room.

Play to win

Max Hackle had spent the same night, the same day, locked in a tiny cell somewhere within the House of Chances. Chief Executive Crawl had promised an audience soon with 'the great leader', but that had been hours ago. He was fed every so often by another employee, a small man who said nothing as he pushed the food through the half-open door.

Max had no way of knowing the time. They had taken his watch. His only companion of the last hours had been the faithful Horny George, a greasy fragment of a dream, the cursor of a simple soul. Max had tried to sleep, only to be plagued by nightmares. Inside him, all the wanderers fought for possession. If he could keep the Joker Bone at bay for just a while longer. Just enough to kill the Million.

It was a battle. Already he had felt Nigel subsuming Dopejack. Knowledge breeding knowledge. Evil thoughts. Only Benny, Sweet Benny, a presence he could barely feel, still whispered of love. The Joker was getting angry at Hackle for trying to resist. Let him get angry.

Some time later the door opened fully, and Executive Crawl stepped in. 'Good evening, Professor. I trust you slept well.'

Hackle smiled, weakly.

'Mr Million will see you now. This way please.'

It was eight o'clock.

At the same time, the Dark Fractals started their final run. They had set up a table in the centre of the maze, where Daisy and her father faced each other over a shuffled set of dominoes. Jimmy had placed another box beside the first. 'What's that?' asked Daisy. 'Another set,' he replied. 'Found them in the library. Just in case.'

Wires connected Jimmy to the playing area and to the twin computers, where Joe was checking for last-minute hitches. One screen showed the new maze, the other tuned to the AnnoDomino TV channel. Celia was standing to one side, clutching her only bone, and wishing and wishing for the world to come true this time.

Upstairs in the room, Jazir was ready. His body was drunk on vaz and crawling with life and cooking some new recipe never before tried, perhaps his last. He stepped up onto the window sill. Masala Blurb was loaded with the Theseus program, with Celia's feather tight in its teeth. The night air was slightly hot, damp with rain, and his covering of blurbs fluttered eagerly as the night beckoned them. Jazir checked his watch. OK, let the games begin.

Allow them play.

Jazir stepped off . . .

**PLAYTOWIN**
**PLAYTOLOSE**
**PLAYTOWIN**
**PLAYTOLOSE**
**PLAYTOWIN**
**PLAYTOWIN**
**PLAYTOLOSE**
**PLAYTOWIN**
**PLAYTOLOSE**
**PLAYTOWIN**
**PLAYTOLOSE**
**PLAYTOWIN**
**PLAYTOLOSE**
**PLAYTOWIN**
**PLAYTOLOSE**
**PLAYTOWIN**
**PLAYTOLOSE**
**PLAYTOWIN**
**PLAYTOLOSE**
**PLAYTOWIN**
**PLAYTOLOSE**
**PLAYTOWIN**
**PLAYTOLOSE**
**PLAYTOWIN**
**PLAYTOLOSE**
**PLAYTOWIN**
**PLAYTOLOSE**
**PLAYTOWIN**
**PLAYTOLOSE**

**D**aisy played first, having the highest double, the four-and-four. Her father followed with the five-four, his personal bone. Joe watched the computer, as the two domicons came on screen, then a third and a fourth as Daisy and Jimmy played their next moves. Jimmy's icon, the five-four, was illuminated with silver dots to make it known. As Daisy pondered her bones, Jimmy nodded to Joe, who hit a certain combination of keystrokes. After a second or two, the four dominoes on-screen split open to let loose their swarms of info-blurbs. These fluttered aimlessly over the AnnoDomino maze, seeking food, not yet allowed pathway.

'Where's Jaz?' asked Celia. 'Which one is him?'

Joe answered, 'He's not in yet.'

'He's got my feather.'

'We'll know . . .'

'Let's have some quiet, please,' said Jimmy. 'We need to concentrate.'

Daisy knocked and drew. And drew again, playing this new bone. Her father tutted and played.

On the computer's maze, the bones appeared, slotted in the imagined corridors of the House of Chances. Miss Sayer, bringer of the map, watched from her inset box, comparing the model to the reality as she knew it, and making adjustments accordingly. An on-screen clock ticked the seconds away . . .

As Max Hackle asked Crawl for the time.

'Certainly. Five past.'

'Past what?'

They were walking along a corridor, brightly lit and crooked as one of AnnoDomino's rules. Horny George was hovering close behind, as AnnoDomino employees rushed along, to and fro, lost pieces in a game without rules.

'Eight, of course. Friday evening. Nearly time for the draw. Mr Million wants you to watch the choice being made. A rare privilege.'

Crawl had stopped outside an unmarked door. He smiled at a camera above the door. 'Dental patterns, don't you know. X-rays. Can't be good for the old gums. Hope you don't mind, Prof. We took some photos, whilst you were napping. Go on, give us a smile.'

The door opened to reveal a long curve of corridor, which they walked along. 'We're now walking round the circumference of the building. Top floor. Like the view?'

A continuous window gave a superb view of Manchester and its environs. Max could see the clouds of blurbs coming in for sustenance, or else flying forth loaded with new messages.

'Wouldn't you rather be back in the police, Crawl?'

'Me? Why?'

'This can't be satisfying.'

'It's the same job actually.'

'Covering up murder?'

'I've put a few murderers behind bars, you know. It wasn't always like this.'

'No. It wasn't.'

'Here we are.'

There was no door, no markings of any kind on the wall. 'This is where Mr Million lives?' Max asked.

'I wouldn't know. I'm not allowed any further.'

'Maybe I'll tell you what he looks like.'

'You do that.'

Crawl wandered off back around the long curve, leaving Max looking out at the night sky and its patterns of adverts. He turned to face the wall. Nothing. What was he supposed to do now? Just wait. He turned back to the window and as he did so a slight movement caught his eye. He went back quickly to the wall. Again, nothing. But surely . . . he was certain he had seen an opening, just then as he turned away. He turned away again, and there it was in the corner of his vision, an open doorway, to vanish as soon as his eye settled on the plain wall.

Max pushed gently against the wall, which was hard and cold to his touch. Nothing moved. He turned his head this way and that, seeking the illusive opening. On one turning he saw Horny George vanish, here and then gone, and Max knew he had to trust his feelings. He walked quickly towards the dark shimmer in the farthest edge of . . .

'Who just played?' asked Joe.

'Nobody,' replied Jimmy. 'Why?'

'We've got an intruder.'

'Is it Jaz?' Daisy asked.

'It's not a blurb, it's a bone.'

'What number?'

'Two-blank. No, it's changing. Double-zero. Two-blank again. Max?'

Jimmy nodded. 'OK, this changes things. Max is in the House of Chances. We assume he's the Joker Bone. Where is he?'

Joe studied the maze-map for a second. 'Top floor. Just near the perimeter. He's moving now . . . inwards . . . got some kind of blurb with him.'

'What's he doing in there?' asked Daisy.

'Wish I knew. Do you have the two-zero?'

Daisy nodded.

'OK, we take it out of play.' Jimmy dragged the bone aside. 'Draw again.'

Daisy did so.

'Where's Jazir?' asked Celia. 'Why isn't he in yet?'

Nobody answered. The clock ticked on . . .

The casual stroller along Barlow Moor Road at eight-fifteen that evening would have noticed nothing amiss. The more observant might have wondered at the strange array of blurbs that flew towards the House of Chances. Exceptionally thick it was, the swarm, even by the orbiting standards. Louder, and rather slower, than the usual flight of returning messages.

The keenest blurbspotter would have been puzzled at the trouble the swarm was having gaining entrance. The apex of the house was gently domed, leading to an aperture, an orifice we might say, where the incoming blurbs flew home. Usually they split up at this point, to ease the passage. This particular swarm was reluctant to disperse for some reason, preferring to force itself *en masse* through the hole . . .

'We've got him!' shouted Joe. 'He's in.'

'Jazir?' cried Celia. 'Look! He's carrying my feather.'

Amidst the swarms of dark info-blurbs that covered the maze, one stood out from the rest, striped with green and yellow.

'Do I hit the Theseus now?' asked Joe.

'No! When I say. Jazir has to reach the centre. We keep playing. Daisy . . .'

Daisy made a move, adding a double-two to a six-and-two, releasing more blurbs to the map.

. . . Jazir was inside the Hive of Chances. A small room where a million blurbs gathered before streaming off through various passageways. Above him he could see glimpses of the moon, as more blurbs came in through the hole. Jazir was covered still with his suit of flies. Other blurbs were brushing against them, nuzzling and petting, whispering. As long as he kept his cover with him, there should be no trouble. Together they floated through a dark opening . . .

Hackle was lost in a maze. He had taken two steps only, already the door was impossible to find. There never was a door, he thought. I've always been here, lost like this. Blindly, under harsh lighting, he wandered along a branching passageway. Take the left, because that's where Horny George wants to go. Hackle had decided to follow the cursor blurb, having no other guidance.

. . . Jazir Blurb Masala was blind, constricted, pulled and squeezed by the river of vaz, twisting through darkness that pulsed with juice, with no direction now, only to find the queen. Yes there was a queen blurb somewhere, something he had never considered, but thought wasn't his any more, only the collected one thought of the blurbmind, find the queen, let us feed . . .

Hackle came to a pavilion of mirrors, where his thin, stricken shape shocked him. Who was that creature, with the lank hair falling in clumps and the sunken eyes? So weak, he looked, a mere shell. Was that what he was? A shell for the Joker Bone? He could no longer feel Benny's presence, only the bone, the bone, the dry bone. He felt like his skin was ready to crack.

Following the cursor, he took one of a thousand passages, again lost in corridors. This was like no other maze he had ever known. Mr Million had taken the original Hackle Maze, multiplied it with itself, bred a twisted monster that made love to itself constantly, breeding ever-new passageways that he stumbled down, lost in corridors . . .

Hackle screamed.

'Something's going wrong,' said Joe.

'What is it?' asked Jimmy, not looking up from the game.

'The maze, it keeps changing.'

'What?' said Daisy.

'It does,' cried Celia. 'Look, it keeps changing all the time. How will we ever find . . .'

'What time is it?' demanded Jimmy. 'Quickly!'

'Eight thirty. No, it's changing as well! Eight twenty-five now. Fuck! Eight forty-seven.'

Suddenly, Jimmy swiped all the bones off the table. 'OK, new game.'

He opened the second box of dominoes and emptied them quickly.

'Father . . .'

'Choose! Play!'

'But they're . . .'

'Play! Play to win!'

Daisy played, even though the bone she chose kept changing every second, even as she placed it down. It started out as the double-five and ended up as the two-one.

'No good. You need a double. Let me . . .'

Daisy's father slammed down a bone, which flickered for a moment, and then came up double-five. Daisy tried to match it, but was too slow.

'Faster. Don't think. Just play.'

Daisy played. Just played. Found a match.

'The maze is stabilizing,' cried Joe.

'OK, we're back on course,' said Jimmy. 'Time?'

'Eight twenty-nine,' said Joe. 'Eight thirty. The show's just starting.'

On the second screen the theme song was playing out its merry tune:

It's domiknot time! Mutating domiknot time!
Dom, dom, dom, dom, domiknot time!

**Blurbflies**

And all over Manchester, in toilets and bathrooms and theatres, and in honeymoon suites and strip joints, dog kennels and swimming pools and bus shelters and rubbish dumps, all-night shopping malls and non-stop garages, dream homes and broken homes and private drinking dens, crashpads and launch sites and bomb sites, palaces and gleaming bright offices, darkened hospitals and dingy bedsits and penthouses and dog sites and honey kennels and broken pools and rubbish shelters and strip dumps and private moons and launching offices and bed bombs and pent-up bathrooms and gleaming crash toilets and all-night dream theatres; anywhere there was a hope or a chance or a glimmer, a sparkle or a sliver, all the gamblers were stroking their hard-earned domino bones, hoping that Cookie Luck would come up dancing, just for them.

Why not chance a shot?
You might well find a dot!
With your lucky little domiknot!

**Blurbflies**

And in the old House of Hackle on Barlow Moor Road, another game was being played, with more distant prizes. 'At least we know who's singing now,' said Joe.

'Aye,' said Celia, 'that bloody Frank Scenario. The dirty cheat!'

And in the House of Chances, another two games were being played, with prizes made of bone and blurb. Hackle heard the song, echoing a thousand times around the passageways, calling forth answering cries from the hidden places. Shufflings could be heard, and grunts and wheezes along every line of broken sight, around every convolution of the brain . . .

. . . Play to feed to win to feed to win that song that comes through to win to feed upon the queen to win the feed that song now that never leaves me why to feed the feed song of chances even here if only I Jazir can to win play play play to find the queen the queen feed . . .

'Here's Tommy!' shouted the city's collective televisions. The video channel in the cellar picked up the same invitation to the random dance, as the popular star of dynamite domino came tumbling wild.

'Tommy's on,' said Joe. 'Time's running out. And look . . . he's in the maze as well.'

'I see him,' cried Celia. 'He's all purple and orange dots.'

'That's OK,' said Jimmy. 'We're getting there. Stay cool.'

Daisy played a bone of her own, finally getting used to the play of random chances. How she did it, who can tell, only that trust had to be your gaming partner. Her father played as well, remembering his days of loss, and now the bones were banging down hard in succession, tile by tile, building the new maze.

In the outside world it passed 8.39, creeping fast towards the bone-dance, and the people were gathered to welcome the Lady Cookie home.

In the maze Hackle had no idea of time any more; it seemed to slip and slide, sometimes backwards, so that he arrived at where he once was, and sometimes he landed back in his tiny cell and was merely dreaming. Was that just bad mazeography on his blind self? He was doing his best to keep up with Horny George, but should he be so trusting in a blurb so wild and strange that led him happily nowhere?

. . . As Jazir found himself back in his room, only dreaming of

flying mazebound, only dreaming was he or else really no back
again really moving now through tunnels to where . . .

Hackle reached up for the blurb, where it chortled, where it
whistled and sang: Play to lose! Play to lose! Nothing like the
real George had been. A sham of a blurb. Hackle grabbed it with
both hands, twisted, around the neck, twisted, until . . . got bitten
by it, didn't care . . . twisted . . . until the satisfying sound of
crack and squelch was heard. And a dying song . . .

Hackle dipped his fingers in the juice of it, spread the stuff all
over his hands and face and grinned with the burning sensation.
He threw the dead thing onto the floor and crunched it under foot.

Free to wander and filled with Joker, he wandered where he
wanted, seeking only his next footstep. Around a corner could
be heard a clattering of feet and a raucous laugh, quickly
followed by a large ball of a man adorned in spots of purple
and orange.

'Paul?' asked Hackle. ' Paul Malthorpe?'

'Sorry!' cried the figure. 'Tumbler's the name, tumbling's the
game. Must dash. Got a bone to catch.' And the strangeness
passed, tumbling over and over in a swirl of colours, laughing as
he bounced along merrily.

'The Tumbler just passed Hackle,' said Joe.

'Good,' said Jimmy. 'Where's Jazir?'

'He's in there, doing well I think, but well hidden inside the
blurbs.'

'That's what we want. They'll have trouble spotting him on
security.'

'He's moving towards the centre of the maze . . . Shit! It's
happening again. The maze just shifted, and the time . . . it's
moving backwards now.'

'Play, Daisy!'

'I'm trying to. But look at them . . . how can I . . .'

The dominoes on the table were shifting so quickly now, the dots were blurs of movement, like a time-lapse of the stars against the still night.

'This time's for real, Daisy. You got me?'

'No. I . . .'

'Play!'

'Six-zero,' she said, out of nowhere. And was amazed as the bone in her hand changed and stopped on that very pair of numbers. 'How did I . . . how did I do that?'

'You're a natural, Daisy. Didn't I ever say so?'

'What do you mean?'

To the world, all was the same, time was the usual inevitable tread towards death and taxes and no further prizes. Whereas, to the maze and its various players, whether inside or controlling, time was just another choice of branching pathways, one that led forward, the other back, and all the twisted routes in between. Joe had to watch both screens at once, for while the game show's clock was turning normally (8.49), the maze clock was a spikier beast (8.22, 8.59, 7.39, 8.17, 7.56, 8.37 . . .).

'OK punters!' cried Tommy Tumbler. 'Clack those bones together. Here she comes, the Queen of All Fortune! Cookie Luck!'

Cookie Luck! Cookie Luck! This is what they played for.

'Cookie's on, Jimmy,' said Joe. 'Eight fifty-two. Is it time?'

'Not yet!'

'But which clock, which clock do I follow?'

'The maze clock. The game can't be won until they coincide.'

'What did you mean?' asked Daisy then. 'I was a natural? What's that supposed to mean?'

'Let's play,' replied her father, banging down a piece.

'Six-two!' But getting it wrong. 'Shit! Sorry, I can't . . .'

'Max is meeting Cookie!' cried Celia, feeling her domino tingle.

Hackle had fallen exhausted against a looking-glass wall that contained no reflections, only shadows that moved beyond its silver. A woman was standing over him, gently swaying in tight black, her body sliding with sexy dots that teased the eyes of the city, no less those of the professor.

'Max, darling . . .' she breathed. 'So long since we last kissed.'

'I've never kissed you, Susan. Malthorpe wouldn't let me.'

'Don't you be cruel to your favourite Cookie. Who's this Susan, Max? Are you making me jealous again? You know you can love only me, Max, as I can only love you. Will you kiss me, Max?'

'No! Keep away from me!'

Hackle was trying to scramble up the wall, which was suddenly slippy and soft, with a perfume of flesh that his fingers sank into.

'Ahhhh!'

'Must go, Max. Got a date at nine. Remember me to Paul . . .'

'Paul? Paul Malthorpe?'

'Darling, he's simply dying to meet you.'

Hackle felt something wet and warm touch his lips, then it was gone. He fell back and the wall gave way under his weight, allowing him to sink down slowly through another tunnel that finally landed him . . .

'I'm losing him!' shouted Joe.

'What?'

'Max . . . he's slipping away. The time . . .'

Max woke with a start. The door to his cell opened, and Executive Crawl stepped in. 'Good evening, Professor. I trust you slept well.'

Hackle smiled weakly. 'What time is it?'

'The time? Certainly, old chap. Twenty past.'

'Eight?'

'Of course. Friday evening. Nearly time for the draw. Mr Million wants you to watch the choice being made. A rare privilege.'

'Don't put me back in there.'

'In where, old chap?'

'The maze. I can't seem to . . .' Max closed his eyes. 'Have you drugged me? The food?'

'Maze? Calm down, Professor. Perhaps you were dreaming. Perhaps the maze is inside here, eh?' Crawl was tapping his own head, producing a hollow ringing tone. 'This way, please.' He was gesturing towards the open door of the cell. 'Sorry I can't come with you. I am far too lowly.'

Real time. 'Where is he?' demanded Jimmy.

'I don't know.' Joe was hitting keys to try to get the maze under control. 'The whole thing's going mad. I can't . . .'

The screen was covered with blurbs, who fluttered in a cloud of black information, desperate for food. Beneath them the maze was twisting around into ever new pathways, but still the blurbs could not enter it. Joe wanted to hit the switch, let loose the Theseus blurbs, let them feed, but Jimmy was saying, 'No. We wait. Play, Daisy . . .'

'But where's Jazir?' she asked. 'Is he all right?'

'Jazir . . . he's . . .'

'He's near the centre,' shouted Celia. 'Look at my feather go!'


. . . Find the centre Jazir feed the centre feed the queen play the queen feed the play to win to feed to find the centre where the play is winning to feed off the queen the king the queen king who wins for ever . . .


Real time: 8.58.05. As Cookie Luck started to slow her dance, to let her dots slowly form, and Celia felt her bone tingle again in expectation.

Maze time: 8.28. As Max stepped through the door . . .

'Max is back,' said Joe, under control again.

'Never mind Max,' shouted Jimmy. 'Where's Jazir?'

'Nearly there. Nearly . . .'

'Don't do anything! Not till it's nine in the maze.'

'Hate to mention this . . . but the maze just vanished.'

*Domino.*

A large circular room greeted Max, perhaps the whole top floor of the House of Chances, but empty now of all walls and corridors. Only emptiness. A dazzling white emptiness that spread from the outer edges towards the darker centre, where a lone figure stood waiting, perhaps 5 miles away.

Max set off walking.

It took only minutes to cover the vast distance, to let the shaded figure dissolve out of the time which was dressed in the latest lime-green demob, with matching trilby and night-dark sunglasses. The darkness at the centre was shining from a circular pit set in the floor. The figure was standing near the hole, holding his hand out towards Max. 'No further, please.'

'Mr Million?' asked Max.

'The very same.' The figure doffed his hat and bowed slightly.

'Frank Scenario?'

'The very same.' The figure took off his glasses.

'Adam Jagger?'

'The very same.' The figure laughed.

'Where's Malthorpe?'

'You were always saying that. At school. "Where's Malthorpe? What's he doing now? How can I do better?" It was so funny to watch you two, fighting, following. So funny.'

'Where is he?'

'Are you still obsessed?'

'He killed Georgie . . .'

Real time: 8.58.54. The computer screen had gone completely white, taking the maze and the dominoes and the blurbs and Miss Sayer's inset into some hidden realm. Only the clock remained. Joe was banging at the keys, trying to reconnect, getting nowhere.

*Domino.*

'What now, Jimmy?' he asked.

'We play.'

'But the time? Jazir . . .'

'We play. Daisy . . . your go, I think.'

*Domino.* Just thinking it even.

Nobody had heard her. She could hardly speak.

'Daisy! Play. Play to win!'

*Domino.* Louder now, but still caged.

Maze time: invisible. 'Oh yes, I remember Georgie Horn. A gentle boy that you two destroyed. You were very cruel to the unusual in life, I noticed that. I was luckier, being invisible, unnoticed . . .'

A buzzing noise could be heard, rising in smoke from the pit.

'Who are you?' asked Hackle.

'The boy you ignored. The boy in the middle, not strong or weak or brilliant or stupid. Do you think I didn't want to be like you, or Paul? I wanted to be special.'

'But you are. You're famous. A singer. What more do you want?'

'A minor talent I have exhumed in the last few years. A cover, if you will, for my real occupation. And a burden it has been, pretending.' He threw the hat and glasses aside. 'I wanted only to be chosen, Max. That's all. To be a child of the moment, like you were. Like Paul. But Miss Sayer paid no attention to me. While you and Paul fought over her love, I grew to hate the woman. What was I? Another pair of lowly numbers. But so close . . . so close to being special.'

'Six-Five?'

'The very same.'

'I remember you now.'

'Thank you.'

'You were the kid that Miss Sayer used that first day, to demonstrate probability theory.'

The figure nodded.

'We were asked to predict what domino you would choose. And Malthorpe shouted out "double-six", but you got the six-five instead?'

'It was my chance, you see. My bone. I was cheated.'

'But Miss Sayer taught us the odds. Sixteen to one. It was just bad luck, Adam. Look at me . . . getting the two-blank. How did I feel? It's just bad luck.'

'There's no such thing, Max, as you well know. After all, is this not your creation?' He pointed down into the pit. 'You make your own luck, in a town like Droylsden, isn't that ultimately what she taught us? Take Malthorpe for instance. What were the chances he would get the double-six? Minute. And yet he did. He cheated. Miss Sayer let him win.'

'That's stupid.'

'Play to win, she said. And Paul did so, but now he's mine, and I am the double-six, and life is a song sung low and cool to rouse the gentle spirit. But yet . . . this desire for more, how can I tame it? You're my next step, Max. Won't you come and bite me. Give me your knowledge. Feed me.'

'You could've just taken me. Why Benny? Why Dopejack? The others . . .'

'Do you think I control the system, Max? I am a victim of chances. I take my chances. The Joker Bone has been drawn. He has eaten, it is good. Whoever you carry, all is knowledge. Now, he comes home . . .'

'No!'

Real time: 8.59.07. 'Play, Daisy! What's wrong with you? Play to win!'

'Domino,' she said, whispering it, letting the very thought of it come seeping through to the real world.

'What?'

'Domino.'

'No . . .'

'Four moves' time.'

'No . . . you can't . . . not with the random bones . . . it's . . .'

'Domino!'

'I need to win, Daisy. I need to! It's the only way . . .'

Daisy shrugged. 'Your turn.'

Maze time: indivisible. 'Will you, won't you, will you come feed me?' The figure gazed into the still-hidden pit. 'Some years ago, following his desire, Paul Malthorpe came back into my life. He was looking for funding, to "carry on the good work of Miss Sayer". Those were his words, but I had known him too well as a restless child. I had a small fortune, thanks to my burgeoning recording career, so I asked for evidence of a future profit. He told me of your experiments, Max, and how they had gone wrong, but could now be put right. He had the new technology, and more expertise. And a certain number of computer disks, which made most interesting viewing. It was like seeing dear Georgie Horn all over again, alive in the knowledge. Expanding upon your own discoveries, we created this game, you see, the world's most powerful Hackle Maze, full of love.'

'Where's Malthorpe?'

'Oh . . . quite close. I had a little trouble, you see, because he had brought old Miss Sayer along. A hag, a monstrous, overpowering hag who had claimed me ordinary. They were in love. Touching, isn't it? The power of the nymphomation. Quite an aphrodisiac, when let loose. Come see . . .'

The figure was gesturing towards the hole. Max stepped forward until he could see over the rim . . .

Real time: 8.59.25. Daisy played another effortless random bone, making her father knock again. He was sweating now, causing sparks to fly from the connections. 'Don't do this to me!'

'Play . . .'

Maze time: indecipherable. Max looked down into the pit, and immediately felt his legs go weak. The pit was roughly 10 feet in diameter, maybe 6 feet deep. On two opposite sides, large matching portals fed the pit and drained it of the thick, greasy liquid that slopped across the bottom. From these portals crawled a slew of matted blurbflies, all tangled and wet from their travels. They gathered here from all the skies of the city to deposit old dreams, collect new ones. Beached in the centre of the pit lay the hideous creature upon which the blurbs fed. The sight of it made Max heave and almost stumble with dizziness. At the last moment Frank Scenario reached out a firm hand to grab the professor by his hair.

'Careful, my friend. It is feeding time.'

The figure dragged Max backwards, where he screamed at the pain in his head and the sight of his lost friends and what had become of them.

'Max, darling. Are you shocked. Surely . . . it's all your own work. I just let it run, Max. That's all. I let your brilliance reach its conclusion. This is your baby, Max. The AnnoDomino beast. You sadden me with this display of petty temperament. The progress of science, Max. Wasn't that your mistress?' He threw Max down, so that his head and shoulders were dangling over the pit. 'Look upon your works, and weep for them . . .'

. . . Almost through Jazir can feel the presence the feeding will be ripe feeding good winning good centre hive one blurb one bone all blurb all bone from the one king queen of domino . . .

Real time: 8.59.32. The game, playing to an end . . .

Maze time: indescribable. Max closing his eyes to what he saw, but the vision burning him with clear sight.

Blurb time . . . Coming through now king queen almost feeding feeding . . .

The creature was large, almost as large as the pit that held it. It was a mass of black flesh, dripping with juice that shone in tiny rivers down wrinkles of fat. A net of electrical wires connected it to the pit's sides, and within this web the thing squirmed like a beetle. Here and there on the gross body, tiny dots of white mapped a hopeless camouflage. A large gaping orifice slathered from its belly, with a thick, tongue-like protuberance poking through like a blind flesh snake.

'Hermaphrodite, Max. Isn't it beautiful?'

Every second or so the tongue stump would push a still slippy ever-changing domino bone through the opening (POP!), which was immediately grabbed by a passing blurbfly and gone, through the pit and out of the exit portal to the world.

'Once upon a time there was the Mata Data, and then the Dada Data, and together they made the Baba Data. And such perfect babies, Max! Your spotty children. Nearly time for the big one, the prize bone.'

The body of the beast tapered to a pair of opposite necks or appendages that waved blindly in the stew of grease. Each long thin tube of flesh ended in a bloated head with glued eyes and a dripping, toothless mouth. Blurbflies fluttered at these two orifices, feeding there for new messages or else depositing used-up adverts.

Max could only swing his head from one side to the other, trying to force himself up. But Frank was strong, he held the professor tight and goaded him.

'Won't you speak to your child, Max? So rude of you.'

'Paul . . .'

Immediately one of the creature's heads shot a blinded glance at Max's voice. 'Maximus . . .' Its voice was thick with guttural sounds. 'Two-Blank! Help me!'

Paul Malthorpe's face was reaching up towards Max, supported by its uncoiling neck, eyes cracking open. On the other side of the Domino Beast, the head of Miss Sayer, old as the numbers of the world, came upwards to implore him. 'Help me! Help me!'

'I do believe, Max, that it remembers you. How touching.'

Frank was laughing now, as he turned Max over roughly. The face of famous cool loomed over Max, as the two hands that strummed a nation's heartstrings slowly closed around the throat. The head was pulled up, higher, so that Max's lips were nestled – surprising, gently – against Frank's neck.

'You know the Joker can't resist me. Give in, Max. Give us a kiss. Only peace awaits you.'

'So it does.'

Max put his own hands in turn around the figure's yellow-collared throat, and squeezed and rolled and fought back.

'Wha . . .!'

The figure was shocked. 'Nah . . . Joker! No!'

It took all Max's strength to resist the Joker inside, to fight back, to keep on fighting, not biting . . . but killing. Go manual. Not dying, but living. He and the figure rolled over once again, so that Max was underneath, one more push and . . .
. . . *feedmebreedmeneedmeseedme* . . .

'Come to me, my Joker!' shouted Frank, as he and Max rolled over and into the pit as . . .

. . . *kingqueen!*

'Jazir's through!' shouted Joe.

As Daisy played her second to last: 'Six-three!' to which Jimmy could only knock and draw, knock and draw.

. . . as Jazir rode Masala down the wave to the opening and squelch! hit the beast at a pace, thundering with a hundred gathered blurbflies. Over Max and Frank they squirmed, Jazir a heavy cargo squashed now against Miss Sayer's tearful face and Frank Scenario's scream of denial. With one kick he had Frank off guard. 'Cool fucker!'

Frank was slipping on the grease of the game. 'Paul! Miss Sayer! Help me! I command you!'

'Max! This is Theseus. Where?' shouted Jazir.

Max pointed to where the ever-changing dominoes were popping forth.

'No!' Frank was trying to get up, but a swarm of blurbflies held him back. Malthorpe's head had tightened its long neck around the singer's thin body.

'Too late, Frankie baby. Thanks for the songs.'

Jazir had Masala Chicken Tikka Theseus Curry Blurb in both hands now. 'You want this?'

'Please!' answered the head of Miss Sayer.

He rammed it home, into the orifice of the beast, feather and all.

Miss Sayer breathed, settled. Paul Malthorpe breathed, settled, died. Frank Scenario slithered under the pit of blurbflies.

Real time: 8.59.53. 'Hit it!' shouted Jimmy.

Joe banged down the key that let the Theseus equation loose, along a path of dominoes, carried by info-blurb to real blurb that flew straight to the heart of the game and detonated . . .

The body of the beast twitched, a final spasm . . .

Maze time, real time, coinciding time.

Daisy had one domino left.

A final bone was born that day as nine o'clock struck, a winning bone that would never change again. Frank's head floundered to the surface of the pit for a second. He screamed as he saw the domino being born, and was then engulfed again and carried along by the blurbflies to the out portal.

There's only one domino. You just have to know how to play it.

Daisy played it. The double-six she asked for, the double-six she got.

'Domino.'

As Jimmy's face froze. As Lady Luck's costume froze on the city's screens. A six, a six. That's the way the cookie crumbles. As Little Celia sprang up and down, shouting and screaming, showing her bone. 'I got it! I got the double-six! I'm a winner! I'm the new Mr Million!'

As Joe worked the computer. 'OK, we're back on board. I've got blurbflies everywhere like crazy. I've got Jazir and Max still moving. I think we did it, folks.' Then he went crazy too. 'A fucking million! A million fucking lovelies!'

'Like I said, Dad,' whispered Daisy. 'It's domino time.'

Her father slumped down, face to the scattered playing area. 'Do you want to tell me how I did that?'

**PLAY THE RULES**

13a. In the event of a double-six, AnnoDomino will allow the winning player to become the new Mr (or Mrs or Ms) Million.

13b. The winning player may reorganize the game, following his or her wishes, in accordance with the Government's rulings.

13c. The new Manager of Chances shall remain anonymous, in accordance with ruling 4d.

13d. The winning player may not refuse this prize.

13e. The game is sacrosanct.

Jazir was helping Max around the outer perimeter of the House of Chances. Lights were flashing madly along the ceiling and a siren could be heard shrieking from a hundred speakers. Employees and blurbflies alike were going crazy to escape the chaos of the big win. 'Oh shit!' said Jazir. 'Celia will kill me. Stay right there, Max. I forgot something.' He went back into the circle, and right up to the pit. Crawl and Tumbler and Cookie, and a few other desolate operatives, were standing around, some gazing into the pit, some not daring to.

'What you after?' said Crawl. 'Haven't you done enough?'

'Not quite.'

Jazir jumped down. Miss Sayer and her pupil Malthorpe were

lying in a knotted coil on their shared belly. All was still. Had he really done his work? Was this what the teacher wanted? Was she free now?

Let us hope so.

Jazir walked over to the dead beast, parted the central lips, and stuck his arm inside. He was up to the shoulder in grease before he found what he was after. A mighty tug dislodged the splattered remains of the Masala blurbfly. 'Good innings, our kid,' said Jazir, as he plucked the dripping feather from its lips. 'It shouldn't happen to a vert.'

At the main doorway, the large domino gate was swung open, jammed for ever on the double-six pattern, as the beams projected the result to the air. It was a result never expected. Access all areas, all hail the new Mr Million! Executive Crawl had followed them down, and was now standing on the grass forecourt, looking suitably dazed. At his feet lay the battered, lifeless form of Frank Scenario, dropped from a great height. But Crawl's eyes, like all the eyes of Manchester, were firmly on the skies.

Jazir had to smile. 'Who would have thought it,' he said to the faithless executive, 'the dominoes were eggs.'

And all over Manchester now, those eggs were splitting in two, lucky bones opening at last, to release their babies . . .

PLAY TO DREAM        PLAY TO DREAM
PLAY TO DREAM        PLAY TO DREAM
PLAY TO DREAM        PLAY TO DREAM
PLAY TO DREAM        PLAY TO DREAM
PLAY TO DREAM        PLAY TO DREAM
PLAY TO DREAM        PLAY TO DREAM
PLAY TO DREAM        PLAY TO DREAM
PLAY TO DREAM     PLAY TO DREAM
PLAY TO DREAM PLAY TO DREAM
DREAM  PLAY TO DREAM  PLAY
PLAY TO DREAM  PLAY TO DRF
DREAM  PLAY TO DREAM  P
DREAM  PLAY TO DREAM
PLAY TO DREAM  PLAY
PLAY TO DREAM  PL/
PLAY TO DREAM  F
PLAY TO DREAM
PLAY TO DRE/
PLAY TO DREAM
PLAY TO DREAM  F
PLAY TO DREAM  PLA
DREAM  PLAY TO DREA
DREAM  PLAY TO DREAM
DREAM  PLAY TO DREAM  PL
DREAM  PLAY TO DREAM  PLAY
DREAM  PLAY TO DREAM  PLAY T
PLAY TO DREAM    PLAY TO DREAM
PLAY TO DREAM    PLAY TO DREAM
PLAY TO DREAM    PLAY TO DREAM
PLAY TO DREAM    PLAY TO DREAM
PLAY TO DREAM    PLAY TO DREAM
PLAY TO DREAM    PLAY TO DREAM
PLAY TO DREAM    PLAY TO DREAM
PLAY TO DREAM    PLAY TO DREAM
PLAY TO DREAM    PLAY TO DREAM

**A**nd out of every cracked-open domino rose a new blurbfly. Across the skies, see them now, still winging it. A migration of adverts, taking the dream elsewhere, out of Manchester. The heavens were V-shaped for weeks after the game, and alive with the new message.

Dream to win! A time to use my own voice.

I managed to get Max back to the old house. Joe and Celia were dancing around in the living room, throwing the winning bone hand to hand. 'Shall we go collect it now, Jaz?' cried Celia. 'Shall we? Shall we now!'

'Not yet, little 'un.'

'When then? When?'

'Yeah . . . when, Jazir?' asked Joe.

I didn't have the heart to tell them. How could I? They'll find out.

'Look, Celia. I brought your feather back.'

'Ooh! Was it lucky for you?'

'You betcha.'

'Urgh! It's all sticky. Jaz! What's this stuff all over it? Where have you been putting this?'

'I dropped it in a barrel of lucky juice.'

'Lucky juice! What's that?'

'Just don't lose it, kid. OK?'

'Yeah! Lucky juice! Well done, Whippoorwill!'

Well, there are some things a kid of eight just doesn't need to know, don't you think?

'Is he all right?' asked Joe, pointing at Max.

'Max is fine. Aren't you, Max?'

The professor nodded.

I left Celia and Joe to their wasted celebrations, and took Max through into the library. This wasn't going to be easy, and I was shaking suddenly, as the force of adventure left my body cold and uncovered. We talked a little about what had happened to us, but eventually I had to make my point.

'You know what you've got to do, Max. Finish it.'

He nodded.

'You want help?'

He shook his head. I left him to it, by whatever means, then went in search of Daisy. I found her in the cellar, arguing with her father. It looked like a family affair, so I went back upstairs. When she was ready, she would come for me. And I was thinking about my own father anyway, and the whole family business . . .

What day was it? I was still having trouble with the time.

Of course, still Friday. I looked at my watch, but the hands were moving backwards and forwards at speed. I still wasn't down yet, perhaps I never would be. Anyway, I rang my dad at the restaurant and told him I was coming home. He shouted and raved, but I was cool about it, I kept my tongue curled and put down the phone at the earliest.

Back in the living room, Joe was saying he was going to collect the prize right now, and Celia had better give him the bone. Celia was saying that it wasn't his, that she'd thrown his away. No way, he was saying, I paid good money for that bone and give it here right now, squirt.

'Give it to him, Celia,' I said. 'Go on . . .'

'No. It's mine.'

'Trust me . . .'

She did. She did, and it felt good.

'Open all channels,' said Joe, as he left the room. 'Connect to everything.'

Yeah, I suppose so. That's the last we saw of him.

Daisy came up from the cellar a few minutes later. She was

white in the face, like a ghost had set up house inside her eyes. I asked what was wrong.

'Let's get out of here,' she said.

'Sure thing. What about your dad?'

'No.'

I gathered together what we needed, and then led Daisy and Celia out of the front door. People were in the streets by now, and a million dances had turned to outrage and shock and then despair and then anger, and finally resignation. The streets, as we walked them, were already covered with a rich, useless carpet of winning bones; all dancing for ever in the glorious double-six.

'This means that nobody gets to be Mr Million,' I told Celia. 'Do you understand?'

'No, no!' she cried. 'It means that everybody does! Everybody everywhere, we're all Mr Million now!'

Maybe she's right. I'm still waiting for the feeling.

We were walking down Burton Road, and the people were turning their joint winnings into a reason for celebration; God had played a joke on the city, and they might as well laugh it off. Already some of the discarded bones had started to hatch, a new swarm of blurbflies getting ready for flight. I had this intense desire to follow them, to spread my wings and take off, maybe to London, maybe elsewhere, maybe just as far as my family's house. In the end Celia persuaded me to take the bus. The bus was strangely empty, as though nobody had anywhere to go, even on a Friday night.

We sat upstairs, and Daisy started to talk at last. 'Oh God,' she said, 'I've just realized. Why Benny was so desperate to get my DNA. It was for Hackle. He wanted to test me.'

'I don't understand.'

'My father . . . he told me everything . . .'

## love to win

Marigold Green was a secretary at the bank where Jimmy Love worked. They were married in 1977, and spent most of the next three years trying to make a child happen, without any success. Eventually they were tested at the hospital and Jimmy was found wanting. Being sterile didn't bother him that much, and so they talked about adoption, artificial insemination, surrogate fathers, quite openly. Jimmy persuaded his wife that the experiment he had in mind was really just another form of the latter process.

Apparently Hackle had lied to Daisy about Susan Prentice's involvement in the ritual; the woman had refused to take part in the experiment. In other words, she'd said no to fucking Georgie Horn, even if it was for the betterment of science. Luckily they had a more willing accomplice, and if it has taken Daisy's father so many years finally to admit these facts to her, well who can blame him?

She was keen, Jimmy's wife, let's put it like that, and an excellent participant. Daisy was the outcome of the experiment, the child of Marigold Love and Georgie Horn. Conceived at the moment of her father's death, as the full flood of the nymphomation entered his body, how could she not be special? A genetic miracle. Like Georgie and Celia, Daisy was a natural player, a wild card. Unknowing, scared maybe, she had kept her wildness in check for years. Hiding in rules and equations. That's my Daisy.

'You just missed your stop, Daisy,' I said, as we sailed past the neon-lit Golden Samosa.

'That's right. And so did you.'

Through the wave of spices, and free.

Dream to win

That's it. I've told this as best I can, from memories and imaginings. We're living in the ruins of the Monstermarket now, Daisy, Celia and I, surrounded by the brethren. Life's not the same without the weekly thrill of chancing all on the dance of Lady Luck, but we make up for it in other ways.

Every day I read the papers for news of a suicide. It hasn't happened yet, but Hackle would keep it secret, wouldn't he? Either that, or he's still out there somewhere, roaming the city with the Joker inside him. That's somebody else's problem, because I tell you, I'm through with the hero bit.

Open all channels, Joe was always saying. Connect to everything.

Pretty soon it will be time for us to move out, maybe London, maybe abroad. Maybe just another part of Manchester, go legal. I'm seventeen now, ready for life. Love and life, gently lived. I've got a tube of vaz in my pocket and the urge to take wing. Maybe I should set myself up in business again, serve some grease to the people, and I don't mean a new curry. I mean, Make life easy with a little touch of Malik's International Vaz.

Daisy's ready to go back to learning. She wants to be a teacher. I think she'd be good. She's certainly taught me a few tricks.

And Celia? Little Miss Celia Hobart? She's coming with us, of course, sticky feather in hand. She never goes anywhere without it, never sleeps without it tickling her nose, never lets it go. She reckons it gives her good dreams.

Yesterday something strange happened. Celia has this new friend, a little brethren boy called Eddie Jnr. His mother claims him to be Big Eddie Irwell's son, but I don't know for sure. Anyway, him and Celia were playing some game or other outside our den. Celia was tickling him with the feather, and suddenly he grabs it off her, angry like, and you'll never guess what he does then?

The young boy puts the feather into his mouth.

# needle in the groove

## jeff noon

**if music was a drug, how would you take it?**
**if drugs were music, how would you listen?**

after years of playing bass in lousy two-bit bands, elliot finally
gets his big chance/he meets a singer, a dj and a drummer
who seem to have everything/passion, talent, hypnotic songs,
and a whole new way of funky seduction/but just as their first
dance record is climbing the charts, one of them disappears/
elliot's search for the missing band member becomes a wild,
fiercely emotional trip into the dark soul of rhythm

in this astonishing novel jeff noon conjures the mystery of
dance culture like no other writer/allowing the complex
rhythms of the music to infect his language, noon creates a
new kind of writing/liquid dub poetics/in the grooves he
discovers a world where the scratches of the sytlus cut the
body/a dj's samples are melodies of blood/love is a ghost lost
in the boom box/and the only remix that really matters is the
remix of the heart . . .

1 862 30091 7

# PIXEL JUICE

## Jeff Noon

'NOON IS THE LEWIS CARROLL OF MANCHESTER'S
HOUSING ESTATES . . . THE COCKTAIL OF
ALIENATION, NARCOTICS AND GADGETRY
FIZZIES WITH ENERGY'
*The Times*

From the breakdown zones of the mediasphere and the
margins of dance culture comes a selection of fifty stories,
each one strange, telling, disturbing, or sometimes just
plain weird: urban fairytales, instructions for lost machines,
true confessions, word-dizzy roller-coasters, product recalls,
adverts for mad gadgets, dub cut prose remixes. Throughout
them all, Jeff Noon delights in the magical possibilities of
language, creating a wholly new kind of storytelling.

Ideas-per-page rating: dangerously close to the legal limit.

'SPARKY AND LOOPY, LACED WITH PUNS AND BLACK
WIT . . . FOR NOON, BRILLIANTLY, TOMORROW IS A
BLOW TO THE HEAD'
*Mail on Sunday*

'NOON REFLECTS THE ENERGY OF THE RAVE
GENERATION: THE HAMMER AND TWIST OF THE MUSIC,
THE LANGUAGE OF THE COMPUTER GAMES ADDICT
AND THE BUZZ OF TECHNOLOGY'
*New Statesman*

0 552 99937 7

**BLACK SWAN**

# AUTOMATED ALICE

## Jeff Noon

In the last years of his life, the fantasist, Lewis Carroll, wrote a third Alice book. This mysterious work was never published or even shown to anybody. It has only recently been discovered. Now, at last, the world can read of Automated Alice and her fabulous adventures in the future.

That's not quite true. Automated Alice was in reality written by Zenith O'Clock, the writer of wrongs. In the book he sends Alice through a clock's workings. She travels through time, tumbling from the Victorian age to land in 1998, in Manchester, a small town in the North of England.

Oh dear, that's not at all right. This trequel to Alice in Wonderland and Through the Looking Glass was actually written by Jeff Noon. Zenith O'Clock is only a character invented by Jeff Noon and any resemblance to persons living or dead is purely accidental. What Alice encounters in the automated future is mostly accidental too . . . a series of misadventures, even weirder than your dreams.

'DESTINED FOR CULT STATUS . . . CYBERPUNK AT THE CUTTING EDGE'
*Maxim*

'CAPTURES CARROLL'S STYLE EFFORTLESSLY . . . A WEIRD ALICE WITH A CONTEMPORARY EDGE'
*Mail on Sunday*

0 552 99905 9

**BLACK SWAN**

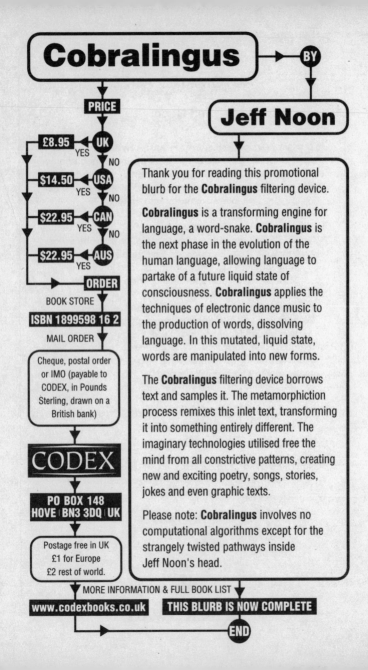